VIRAL EXECUTION

BOOK THREE IN THE CANTRAL CHRONICLES

Book One - Precisely Terminated
Book Two - Noble Imposter
Book Three - Viral Execution

AMANDA L. DAVIS

Viral Execution

Volume 3 in the Cantral Chronicles

Copyright © 2011 by Amanda L. Davis

Published by Scrub Jay Journeys

P. O. Box 512

Middleton, TN 38052

www.scrubjayjourneys.com

email: info@scrubjayjourneys.com

This is a work of fiction. Names, characters, places, and incidents either are the product of the author's imagination or are used fictitiously. Any resemblance to actual persons, either living or dead, events, or locales is entirely coincidental.

Print Edition: ISBN: 978-1-946253-10-1
Mobi Edition: ISBN: 978-1-946253-11-8

Second Edition - First Printing November 2020
Printed in the USA
Library of Congress Control Number: 2020920700

Facebook facebook.com/AmandaLDavis

CHAPTER ONE

"Felicia Sharon, you're accused of one thousand counts of enslavement and mistreatment of fellow persons as well as ..." Simon stood at the front of the crowded courtroom, looking at a stack of papers in one hand. "... ten million counts of mismanagement of authority." He wrinkled his bushy white eyebrows. "Ten million? Can that be correct?"

Monica crouched on the marble tiles just outside the room, peering through the crack in the barely open double doors that allowed her a glimpse of what once housed the Council of Eight's meetings.

Someone inside the court answered Simon's question too softly to hear over the buzzing of the wall slaves and Seen who watched from rows of cushioned benches lined up in the room.

"Ten million it is, then." Simon shook a bony finger at Felicia. "What do you have to say for yourself?"

She stood behind one of eight mahogany desks, wearing the simple black dress of a Seen, her hands resting on the desk's top. "I did what I could, Simon. You must know that. I helped Monica in the end." She raised her hands, jingling a metal chain that bound her wrists together. "Without me, she would have failed."

Monica nodded, though no one in the courtroom could see her. Felicia shouldn't have to stand trial. Fox would have won if she hadn't helped stop him.

1

"You had my brother transferred!" someone in the crowd shouted.

More cries of protest rang out.

"My daughter lived in the southwest wing and got transported to the fields!"

"Your husband terminated my child!"

The shouts blurred together in a chaotic cacophony.

Simon banged an old boot against a desktop. "Order! Order! This is not how trials are supposed to go. We've been over this. Must I remind you with every Noble who comes to trial?"

Some of the shouts diminished, but one man called out, "How can we know what she says about the computers is true? She just wants us to release her!"

Monica clenched a fist. If only Simon would let her speak. She could tell them the truth.

"Aaron Markus, my brother"—Felicia choked on the words—"tried to kill me for what I did. Why would I risk death, then turn around and lie about my deeds?"

"That's probably a lie, too!" the same man yelled. The crowd erupted into more shouts.

Shaking her head, Monica let out a long sigh. At this rate it would take weeks to put all eight Council members on trial.

Simon banged on the desk again, and everyone slowly quieted.

A hand touched Monica's shoulder. She whirled around and jumped to her feet.

A dark-haired woman in black Seen dress stood beside her, a frown marring her pale features. "You're not supposed to be here."

"Tresa!" Monica pulled the courtroom door closed, muffling the buzzing voices. "You startled me. I thought you were watching the trial."

"I was, but I slipped out during a break." Tresa's frown deepened. "You'd better disappear. The fewer Nobles who know your identity, the better."

Monica shrugged. She had avoided Nobles her entire life, so it wouldn't be difficult to continue doing so. She needed to be in that courtroom standing in support of Felicia, the woman who had saved her.

Heavy footfalls sounded down a nearby corridor. Trig, a large Seen man, led Aaron Markus toward them.

Suppressing a shudder, Monica edged away from the double doors. Aaron—the man who once ruled the world and had tried to kill her. He shot her an angry glare, but with his hands bound in chains and Trig standing by, Aaron wouldn't do anything violent.

Tresa rested a hand on Monica's shoulder. "Trig, Felicia's trial isn't over. Why are you here?"

"I was told to come. You can see here." Trig dug in the pocket of his Seen uniform and pulled out a scrap of paper. "A boy brought me this. He said it was from Simon."

"Alfred?" Monica took the note. Tresa's son often ran errands for Simon now.

"No, some other boy. I don't know his name."

She turned the note over, revealing the words *Bring Aaron to the courtroom. His time has come.* written in a neat script that didn't look like Simon's normal scrawl. Maybe he was trying to write more neatly now that he held an official office.

"That doesn't look like Simon's writing, Trig," Tresa whispered. She looked over her shoulder toward the closed doors. "They'll be breaking any moment. They've been stalled for half an hour now."

"You brought me up here for nothing, then?" Aaron scowled and shook his chains. "These trials are a farce. You won't accomplish anything with them. Wall slaves aren't intelligent enough to understand a court system."

"Dismissed!" Simon's shout echoed from behind the closed double doors. "Get out of here, all of you, and don't come back until you can behave!"

Tresa grabbed Monica by the shoulders. "Come on. If Simon sees you here ..."

The doors burst open. Men and women marched out, all chattering loudly. Most wore scowls or frowns, but others seemed excited, like this was a game.

Trig steered Aaron to the edge of the crowd and stood beside Monica and Tresa near a paneled wall.

Aaron shrugged off Trig's grip. "I can take care of myself, Seen. I don't need a bodyguard."

As the crowd filtered into side halls, a few people glanced at Aaron. The grumbling conversations took on an angry tone.

Monica backed against the wall and watched the crowd closely. No one would dare hurt Aaron out in the open, would they?

Simon's gray head appeared in the midst of the people, and he elbowed his way to Trig's side. "Trig, confound you, what are you doing here? It's not safe for Aaron to be out of his cell!"

A shattering noise sounded nearby. A woman screamed. Tresa's grip on Monica's shoulders tightened, sending pain down her arms. She tugged away from Tresa. "Is Felicia safe?"

"Garth is with her." Simon squinted at the crowd flowing by. "He'll make sure she stays out of harm's way."

"Put that down!" A man's voice echoed up the hall. "Stop!"

The crowd parted in a rippling motion as people scooted to the sides. A man in Seen uniform charged Trig.

"He has a knife!" a woman screamed.

Tresa gasped and pushed Monica behind her.

Aaron dodged to the side. Simon threw himself in front of Aaron as a burly Seen man, even bigger than Trig, ran toward them with a shard of glass clutched in one hand. Blood dripped down his wrist, but he didn't slow.

"Fisher, don't!" a woman called. "They'll kill you!"

Trig darted forward, but Fisher slashed at him with his makeshift knife, slicing Trig's arm. Trig punched Fisher in the face, but Fisher shoved Trig to the side and dove at Aaron.

4

Aaron raised his chained hands in a defensive position. Fisher hit the side of Simon's head with a clenched fist.

"No!" The sharp scream escaped Monica's throat. "Simon!" Trig grabbed at Fisher again, but he lurched out of the way.

Fisher raised the glass dagger and plunged it into Aaron's neck. "Aaron!" Monica and Tresa cried his name in unison.

Blood splattered across the floor and dripped down Aaron's chest. Gasping, he pushed feebly at Fisher with bound hands. "Why?"

Fisher released the dagger, still embedded in Aaron's neck, and stepped away. "You had my daughter terminated."

Trig grabbed Fisher from behind. Fisher relaxed his shoulders. "I won't fight you, Trig. I've had my revenge."

Aaron gasped again and fell against Simon, knocking him down and pinning him to the floor.

The crowd pressed in around Trig and Fisher. "Got what he deserved," someone muttered.

Simon crawled out from under the Noble's body. "That was unexpected." He clambered to his feet. Blood covered his shirt and hands, and he shook a finger at Fisher. "What were you thinking, man? If he dies …"

Trig unfastened Aaron's chains and bound them around Fisher's wrists. Fisher stared silently straight ahead.

Aaron's eyelids fluttered, and he reached for the glass shard. Monica knelt beside him. "No, don't touch it." She looked up at Tresa who stood there gaping. "You have to help him. I know he's a Noble, but—"

Aaron yanked the glass from his throat. Blood gushed from the wound, pulsing with every beat of his heart.

"Aaron!" Monica clamped her hands to his neck, but the blood oozed between her fingers and onto the floor.

"Keep up the pressure." Tresa knelt beside her and laid her hands over Monica's. "Simon, get Aric!"

"Let 'im die," someone growled.

Simon edged toward an opening in the group of people, but two men shifted to block his way, their arms crossed and expressions sour.

One man spoke, "Don't do it, Simon. We'd have sentenced him to death anyway. He knew that."

A small boy pushed his way to the front. "Simon?"

Monica locked gazes with the boy. "Alfred! Get Aric, quick!" Warm blood still pulsed against her fingers.

Alfred nodded and darted away. A man grabbed at him, but he slipped by with ease and disappeared in an instant.

The man stepped forward. "Get away from Aaron, you two." He pushed past Trig who held Fisher against the wall.

Monica gulped. There was nothing she and Tresa could do to stop the man if he decided to finish killing Aaron. She pressed harder on Aaron's neck, but the blood wouldn't stop flowing.

Trig glanced between Fisher and the man. "Trey, leave them alone."

Trey stared at Trig for a moment, as if sizing him up. After a few seconds, Trey stepped back into the crowd, muttering, "He'll die anyway. They can't fix a neck wound like that."

The crowd started to disperse, talking among themselves as if nothing had happened.

Aaron's gasps grew ragged. As he gulped, his Adam's apple moved beneath Monica's hands.

"Hold on, Aaron," Monica whispered. His skin now cold, his gaze darted from Tresa back to Monica.

"We're coming!" Alfred's shrill cry carried over the noise of the milling people.

"Get out of my way!" Aric's shout sounded close by, but the Seen grew louder. They blocked the hallways.

Monica fought the urge to rise to her feet. She had to keep the pressure on Aaron's wound, but the Seen! How could they do this? They had to let Aric through!

6

"Let them by, you miscreants!" Simon charged forward waving his blood-covered arms. He pushed two men to the side and pulled Alfred through the crowd. Aric followed close behind, a black bag clutched in one hand. He ran toward them, but Simon stayed behind and whispered something to Alfred.

With a quick nod, Alfred ran back into the crowd and disappeared once more.

Trey grabbed Aric's arm, but Aric shook him off with a snarl. "Don't touch me, Seen!" Aric opened his bag and dropped to his knees at Monica's side. "Hold on, Uncle."

"We should just kill them all," Trey muttered. "Save us the trouble of these stupid trials."

Aric fumbled with some gauze. "Got to stop the bleeding." Aaron's eyes closed.

Her heart thumping, Monica watched Trey inch closer. If he decided to cause more trouble, could Trig stop him? Trig hadn't been able to stop Fisher, and Trey looked bigger than Fisher.

Aric slipped a thick wad of gauze beneath Monica's fingers and over the wound. "You're doing a good job. Hold that in place."

She nodded. "Should someone tell Melody?" Aaron's wife would want to know.

"No, there's enough chaos here." Aric pulled a curved needle and black thread from his bag. "There isn't time to take him to the infirmary." He poured a clear, potent-smelling liquid over the needle and thread. "And we have no supplies left there anyway, thanks to Simon's dispersal of the medications." Shaking his head, he moved the needle and thread closer to Aaron's neck. "This probably isn't going to work. He's lost too much blood, and I don't have the right tools, but I'll do what I can."

"Is there anything else I can do?" Monica bit her lip. Aaron had tried to kill her, but no one deserved to die like this.

"Not really." Aric gave Tresa a clean cloth, then eased Monica's hands from the wound. "You did a great job." He opened the wound farther with his fingers, drawing forth more blood.

Gulping, Monica looked away.

"I have to close the artery before I can stitch up the skin," Aric murmured. "Tresa, please wipe blood away from the site and monitor his vital signs."

"Yes sir."

"What's going on?" Felicia stalked out of the Council room. Garth followed close at her heels, his large shoulders hunched.

"Madam," Garth said, "you must stay in the Council room. Simon ordered it."

"Felicia," Monica called. If Felicia saw her brother like this … "Please, it's safer for you in the Council room."

Simon jogged over and stood between Felicia and her brother. "Felicia, I must insist you return to the courtroom at once."

"Not until you tell me what's happening!" Felicia shook off Garth's attempts to guide her away. "I've been completely cooperative with all of your demands thus far, and enough is enough. I heard people calling Aaron's name."

Trig whispered something to Simon, then walked through the crowd and down a hall with Fisher at his side.

A few people clapped Fisher on the back as he passed, and murmurs of "We'll vote in your favor" and "Good job" floated through the corridor.

"Simon, stop stalling." Felicia set her hands on her hips and craned her neck. "Whose blood is that on your shirt? Is Aaron all right?"

"*All right* is not the phrase I'd use." Simon looked down at his clothing. "I'd best get cleaned up. We need to leave soon."

"Aric, his heart rate is dropping too quickly!" Tresa's words sounded strained.

"I know! I know!"

Monica finally risked a look. Blood pooled around Aric's knees and covered his and Tresa's arms up to their elbows. She gulped. How could Aaron survive so much blood loss?

Aric pressed a needle into Aaron's neck and pulled a suture tight. "There's nothing I can do; our blood supply is drained. We're out of everything but antiseptic!"

Felicia pushed past Simon. "Aaron!" The name escaped in a short shriek. "Who did this?"

"Don't worry, Felicia, the perpetrator is in custody." Simon started to pat her on the shoulder but stopped and drew his blood-covered hand back to his side.

"Don't worry? My brother is dying!"

"It's what he deserved!" someone shouted.

Felicia whirled and faced the crowd. "You Seen and wall slaves think you're better than us? You murder as soon as you're given the chance. People are burning the city just because they can—because they want to do something to express their anger, but they're destroying themselves." She shook a fist. "Killing us won't help, but I'm sure that won't make any difference to you. I would be willing to do any work a fair court assigns me, but how can I listen to murderers and their hypocritical accomplices?"

The crowd stirred and murmured amongst themselves. Some took a few steps forward and then back again, as if trying to decide what to do.

Monica edged away. Felicia was just going to make them angrier.

"Madam, calm down." Garth stood beside her, his hands behind his back.

Simon nodded. "There aren't many here who will side with you, no matter what you say. They've been beaten down for too many years. The brutal termination of friends and family has a way of deafening the ability to listen to reason."

"Aric." Tresa's whisper barely sounded above the mutterings.

"I know." Aric heaved a deep sigh.

Monica crouched beside them. Aric poured some clear liquid over his hands and scrubbed them clean, allowing the disinfectant to spill to the floor and mix with Aaron's blood. A needle still protruded from Aaron's neck, and the thread lay slack in places.

Tresa wiped her hands on a towel.

"You're not finished, are you?" Monica shook her head. If they were, it must mean …

"He's dead." Tresa finished wiping her hands, then laid the towel over Aaron's face. "We'll have to inform Melody."

"Dead?" Felicia covered her face with her hands.

A loud cheer echoed around the hall. Someone even threw a hat in the air.

"No, no, no!" Simon waved his arms. "This is not how civilized people should behave! A man has died. You should not react this way!"

The cheer grew louder, drowning out Simon's protests.

Tresa spoke to Aric, but her words were overpowered as well. After a moment, she turned and ran down a side hall, sidling through the crowd with little trouble.

Monica edged close to Aric and spoke into his ear. "Where is she going?"

He shook his head. "Can't hear you!"

"Death to the Nobles!" Trey punched the air with a fist. The crowd took up the cry. "Death to the Nobles!"

CHAPTER TWO

"It's time to go. Now!" Simon's words were almost lost in the jeers from the Seen and wall slaves.

Still crouching where Aaron lay dead, Monica stared at the crowd. Trey stood at their front, waving his arms and yelling, stirring the people into a frenzy.

Grabbing his bag, Aric nodded toward the wall.

Monica returned the gesture. The wall passages. That could be the way out. She had to help Felicia and Aric escape.

"We'll have to leave the body." Aric leaned close to Monica. "Can you lead us through the passages?"

"Yes." Monica scanned the walls with a quick glance and located an access panel. She crept toward the door.

A woman grabbed at her. "You're not going anywhere!"

Aric pushed the woman aside and yanked open the door. "Come on!" He shoved Monica into the slave passage.

"Where do you think you're going?" Trey's yell sounded through the wall.

As Monica scampered down the passage a few feet, scuffling noises breached the wall where she entered.

Felicia stumbled into the passage, quickly followed by Simon.

"Let go!" A thump and a loud crack echoed outside, and Aric stumbled into the passage, slamming the door behind him.

Darkness enveloped the hall. A latch clicked. Someone pounded against the panel.

Someone's breath tickled Monica's ear. "We're meeting Tresa at evacuation site A," Simon whispered.

Thumps sounded outside, and more cries filtered into the crowded passage, muffled by the stone and plaster wall.

A hand pushed Monica forward, ushering her down the hallway. "Garth's holding Trey for now," Aric said.

The wall shuddered, and a sickening crunch followed. "Maybe not anymore," Felicia whispered.

"Death to the Nobles and their supporters!" Trey's cry assaulted their ears.

"We'd best run." Simon shoved Monica down the hall. "Lead the way!"

She stumbled, then regained her footing and darted forward. She turned down a side passage, her bare feet smacking wood planks. Garth couldn't be helped. He'd given his life to save them. As the shouts diminished, tears pricked her eyes. What had she done by setting these people free?

Her foot caught on something metal. She tumbled forward and smacked her hands on the ground.

"Watch out for pipes!" Simon grabbed her by the collar and hoisted her back to her feet. "No time for tumbling!"

Monica rubbed her aching neck and continued running. Lights flickered on overhead, triggered by her movement. She squeezed into a narrower passage, and footsteps sounded close behind.

Hopefully Aric would be able to keep up, As the largest of their group he might have trouble in the tighter hallways.

Monica motioned to Simon to stop and knelt by a wall-slave access panel. They were probably far enough away from the mob to go back into the Nobles' halls. She pushed the door open and crawled into a carpeted parlor.

After climbing to her feet, she scanned the room for any sign of life. "It's empty."

Simon exited the passage, followed by Aric.

Felicia emerged last, her gaze darting back and forth across the room. "Which way to the transport?"

"Here, I think." Monica opened a door, revealing a dark staircase. Would there ever be an end to this running? Would there be even more danger outside the palace walls? Would others hear of the court riots and start their own?

Simon tapped her on the back. "Get a move on! They'll have guessed where we're going. With Seen guards at the palace entrances, it isn't safe to leave that way, and those murderers will know it."

When she stepped onto the first stair, a twinge ran through the scar on her right leg, but as she continued into the dimness, the old wound didn't complain again. "I thought the transports wouldn't run anymore. We're just meeting Tresa at the station, right?"

"No." Simon's hand pressed against her shoulder, urging her on. "Why would we meet there if not to use the transports? They run on their own systems. They work despite your meddling with the main computers."

She pulled away from Simon's touch and trotted on. Whispers floated down the stairs behind her, likely from Aric and Felicia. More noises came from below, and a glimmering green light flickered into view.

Monica increased her pace and entered a cavernous room that echoed each footstep. Tresa stood holding a green light in one hand, two children huddled by her. A Nobles' transport waited nearby, silver lights pulsing across its sides. Twin beams at the front illuminated three metal rails leading into a dark tunnel.

A second transport thrummed behind the first, its nose almost touching the leader. Metal bars forming ladders led up the back of the transports, bars Monica had put to use when escaping to Cillineese just weeks ago.

Tresa raised the green light above her head, shining its sickly glow across the platform. "The lights aren't functional here anymore."

Monica rushed to Tresa's side. "You made it."

"Yes, just fine." Tresa rested her free hand on the head of the little boy clutching her skirts. An older dark-haired girl stood nearby, her arms crossed. Tresa smiled at her, but the girl's face remained somber. "Emerson and Elaine are worried ab—"

"Always rushing ahead aren't you, Monica?" Simon emerged from the dim stairway. "It's rather dangerous to be doing that at times like these."

Aric and Felicia exited the stairs a moment later.

"Mother!" The girl ran to Felicia and wrapped her arms around her mother's waist.

"Elaine!" Felicia knelt and hugged her daughter. "What's going on?" Elaine asked as she pulled away.

"We're going to New Kale. Aunt Veronica is waiting for us. Everything will be all right."

As Monica watched the two embrace, a lump formed in her throat. Would her own mother be as happy to see her?

Shouts sounded. Footsteps clattered in the stairway.

Tresa scooped Emerson into her arms. "They're coming!"

Aric ran across the platform to the first transport's side and laid a hand on the door. "Hurry! Get Felicia and the children to safety." A chime sounded from the transport, and a portion of its side rose and rested on the transport's top, revealing a sitting room. Tresa ducked inside with Emerson.

Felicia gripped Elaine's hand and followed. Aric helped them inside and started to lay a hand on the door, but Tresa shook her head. "Don't! Alfred and Jonas aren't here yet!"

A second later, two young boys burst from the dim stairway, each holding a large bundle.

The yells of the mob grew, and the boys broke into a run. "Alfred!" Tresa handed Emerson to Felicia and ran from the transport. "Jonas, hurry!"

Alfred passed his bundle to Simon but kept a small cage in one hand. "We got everything you needed!"

Simon took the package and shoved it at Monica. "Get in the transport."

Alfred nodded and held out the cage to Monica. A brown rat stared at her through the bars. "I'm keeping Vinnie, right?"

"Right." Monica nodded. "Hurry! They're getting closer."

A frown etched Jonas's pale features as he handed his bundle to Simon. "I think Trig's dead. And … they're coming."

Tresa put a hand to her mouth. "Trig!"

"Let's go." Jonas helped Alfred into the transport and followed him in but skirted away from Felicia and her children.

Simon tucked his bundle under an arm and nodded at the second transport. "Aric, open the door."

Aric jogged over and palmed the transport's door. "Can you drive one of these, Simon?"

"Of course I can." Simon grinned his crooked-toothed smile and headed to their transport. "Aric, Monica, let's go!"

Tresa hugged Monica. "Stay safe."

"What?" Aric turned from the second transport door and headed back to Simon's side. "I'm not going with you to Eursia. I was just opening the door for you. I need to go to New Kale to make sure my family is safe."

Tresa stepped into the first transport with Felicia and the children. "Felicia, close the door."

Felicia shook her head. "Aric needs to come with us. Veronica and Regina are waiting—"

"There's no time for this, woman!" Simon grabbed Aric's hand and pressed it to Felicia's transport door.

"Hey!" Aric jerked free, but the door started to rumble closed.

"No!" Felicia tried to reach for the wall, but Tresa pulled her back. The door fell closed, hiding them from view inside their transport.

New sounds of people running echoed through the cavern.

Monica edged toward the second transport. "Simon …"

"I'm not going with you," Aric said as he reached for Felicia's transport.

Trey appeared in the stairway flanked by a crowd of Seen men. Felicia's transport chimed once and started to pull away from the station.

Trey stepped forward, as if driven by the sound. "Stay where you are, *Nobles*."

Simon puffed out his chest and waved for Monica to get behind him. "Noble? I am not a Noble!"

The first transport chimed again and disappeared into the tunnel.

Monica backed up to the transport and dropped her bundle inside. "Aric," she whispered. "Get in."

"Noble lovers die just the same." Trey gestured behind him, and the two men dragging Trig pulled him forward. "Fisher had the right idea, and now I'm helping him finish it. All Nobles must die."

"I think it's time to go." Simon tightened his grip on his bundle and pushed Aric to the transport. Aric nodded, his face grim.

"Don't let them get away!" Trey charged forward, grabbed at Simon, and caught hold of Simon's bundle.

The other Seen swarmed around them, jumping down in front and behind the transport.

Monica gasped. "Simon!"

Simon dropped his bundle and whirled away from Trey, but the younger Seen's fist connected with Simon's chest. Simon's glasses fell from his face, and he bent over double.

Aric grabbed Monica and pulled her through an open doorway into the transport's control room. He punched a few buttons on a brightly lit display panel. The door closed. As he typed in commands on the touch screen, the transport hummed and vibrated.

Monica jerked away from his grasp. "We can't leave Simon!"

"Stay here." Aric opened the door again and slipped out, shutting the door behind him. A second later, something banged against the metal.

"Aric!" Monica tugged on the doorknob, but it wouldn't turn. She dashed to the front of the transport, almost tripping over a tool box. A glass panel revealed the tracks and people below. She climbed onto a high-backed seat near the controls and craned her neck to the side. If only she could see what was going on. Would Simon be all right? What was Aric thinking? He couldn't fight off Trey by himself.

The transport swayed, and she steadied herself against the control panel. Shouts echoed all around. Aric? Simon? She strained to see but caught glimpses of only two Seen men.

A chime sounded. Her heart leaped. No! Another chime sounded, and the transport started forward.

She jumped from the chair and tugged at the door. "Aric! Simon!" The metal knob wouldn't budge. Something crunched beneath the transport, sending shudders through the metal. A series of thumps hit the rear wall.

Releasing the knob, she stepped back from the door, dread rising in her throat. The transport lumbered forward, uncaring of the men it left behind. She crawled onto the chair and stared at the controls. Metal tracks and concrete floor whipped by in her peripheral vision.

Red, blue, and green lights blinked on the computer display, but how did they work? She was no tunnel-bug driver.

She splayed her fingers over the controls. Turning the bug back would put her in danger as well, and if the Seen killed her, who would take down the Eursian computers?

Tears filled her eyes as she drew her hands back. She had to stay the course. She had to continue on her own.

CHAPTER THREE

The transport hummed across the metal tracks, turning corners and traveling through dark tunnels. After a few minutes the tunnel rose above ground level, and the transport skimmed through a field of tall green plants.

Monica tapped the control screen. A map appeared showing grids of city houses and fields sectioned into lots. She couldn't return, that was obvious, but guilt pricked her with every passing second. Tears welled in her eyes. Could she have helped Aric and Simon more? What about Trig and Garth? Had all four men died?

She tucked her feet onto the chair and rested her chin on her knees. How could things have turned out so badly? She was on her way to Eursia. That much had worked out. Wasn't freeing people the right thing to do? Then why did it end in bloodshed?

A series of poundings jerked her from her thoughts. She peered over the control panel at the grassy fields whipping past. Had the transport run over something? The pounding came again—three knocks from the back of the transport.

She tugged on the door leading into the main room, but it still wouldn't budge. How was she supposed to get out? She looked around. Aric hadn't had time to consider that when he locked her in. He probably thought he would return.

The pounding came again and this time continued. She scrambled to the control panel. There had to be a way to stop the transport. The thumps could mean something was going terribly wrong. Had the mob damaged the transport during the struggle?

A large blue button on the wall read Emergency Stop. She slapped it. A whining noise issued from below. The transport lurched, throwing her to the floor. Her elbow slammed into the tool box by the chair. Jarring pain shot through her arm, and she struggled to her feet.

The pounding stopped.

Letting out a long sigh, she bent over and flung open the box lid. Tools! Maybe if she escaped from the room she could see what had been making that noise. She selected a screwdriver and knelt in front of the door. Two screws at the base of the knob held it in place.

She inserted the driver in one and started turning. At least she had seen this done before. The wall slave repairmen were kept busy with small jobs around the Cantral palace, and one of her borrowed chips had been assigned to assist a repairman.

As soon as she removed the two screws, the knob dropped into her lap, revealing the latch mechanism and the knob on the other side. A push with her finger sent the opposite knob falling. It thumped against the door before clattering to the floor and rolling out of sight.

She pressed her face to the hole the knob left behind and looked past the small latch mechanism. A chair stood against the door, one winged arm underneath that had kept the knob from turning. Other than that, the sitting room looked the same—a leather couch, a second armchair, and a coffee table. What had caused the thumping?

A new thump sounded, this time from the side of the transport. Monica stiffened and regripped the screwdriver. A field worker knocking? She hadn't seen anyone through the front window.

The transport rumbled, and light shone into the main room. Someone groaned, and a blood-covered hand clasped the edge of the transport, barely visible from her viewpoint.

Viral Execution

Monica gasped and pushed against the door. The latch held despite the doorknob's absence. The groan came again. Whoever was out there was in pain and needed help.

She stuck a finger in the knob mechanism and tried to turn it by hand. The metal latch rubbed against her fingertips, threatening to rip off the tender new skin that had recently grown over old wounds.

"Could use some help here." Aric's voice sounded strained.

"Aric!" Monica threw her shoulder into the door. The metal shuddered, and the latch seemed to bend, but it didn't open. "Are you all right?"

"No!"

She pounded against the door again, but it still didn't budge. "It won't open!"

"Just a second." A scraping noise sounded on the other side of the door, and it swung open slowly.

Aric lay on the floor, his face covered with blood, one hand clutching the leg of the chair. Panting, he hauled himself to his feet. "Help me get Simon inside."

She scrambled to the edge of the transport and peered over. Simon rested in the tall grass beside the tracks. Bruises covered his face and neck.

"Oh, Simon!" She jumped down and knelt beside him. The grass smelled sweet, but the scent of blood on Simon's clothes almost overpowered it. More blood stained the metal train wheels and the gray undercarriage.

She gulped. Whose blood was that?

Simon's eyes moved beneath his closed lids, and he groaned softly. "Ungrateful wretches."

"Is it safe to move him?" She looked up to the open transport door three feet above her head.

Aric appeared at the opening. "Well, it isn't safe to leave him there." He wiped his sleeve across his split lip, catching some drops of blood before they fell.

She slipped her arms under Simon's and hoisted him to a sitting position.

Crouching in the transport door, Aric reached down and grabbed Simon under the arms. "I've got him."

She moved her hands to Simon's back to protect his spine from hitting the metal edge of the transport floor.

Aric grunted and drew Simon inside.

Monica stayed motionless until Simon rested safely on the transport floor. Aric offered her a hand, and she accepted it, hooking her thumb with his. He hoisted her inside and palmed the transport wall.

The transport shuddered, and the wall descended back into place, cutting out the sun and the smell of the fields.

Aric stumbled back and fell onto the couch. Folding his arms over his head, he groaned. "Can you start the transport again?"

"I don't know." Monica crouched by Simon. "How did you escape? Is he going to be all right? What happened?"

Aric groaned again. "Not so many questions!" He rolled off the couch and rose to his feet before staggering to the control room. "We need to get you and Simon to the port before the riots spread. That captain won't wait long if there are mobs."

Monica followed him and turned the control seat around so he could sit easily. He was right, they had to get going, but did he and Simon need medical help first? "Will you and Simon be all right?"

Aric started typing on the touch-screen control panel, but he held one arm to his chest and grimaced. "I think so. Haven't had time to assess."

The transport lurched forward. Monica steadied herself and stepped back. The fields visible through the front window whipped by at an increasing rate, faster and faster until the green stalks became one long blur.

Sighing, Aric leaned back and closed his eyes. "That's as fast as we can go. We're half an hour from the docks at this speed. That gives Simon time to recover."

"What about you?" Monica followed Aric back into the main room. With the amount of blood on his shirt and face, there must be a hidden wound, something he wasn't mentioning. "Will you be all right?"

He lowered himself onto the couch with a sigh and picked up the bundle she had discarded on the floor in their rush to escape. "I'll be fine." He unwrapped the bundle, revealing some clothes and a satchel. "Most of this blood isn't mine. I got a few swings in. Might have broken a nose or two." Pinching the bridge of his nose, he shook his head. "But someone got me as well."

"I'm glad you're okay." Monica sat on the floor beside Simon. He still hadn't moved. Had the blow to his chest done internal damage?

She clenched a fist. How could Trey and the others turn on fellow Seen? At least hurting Nobles could be justified in some people's minds, but Simon had been just as enslaved as the others. Garth and Trig were Seen as well, but the mob had hurt and probably killed them.

Aric pulled off his shirt, revealing purple bruises across his arms and chest. He selected a red shirt from the pile on the couch and yanked it over his head. "I wonder where Alfred got these." Holding out a blue shirt and gray pants to Monica, he stood. "They're merchant style, kind of threadbare, but they're clean."

She accepted the clothes and looked down at her dress. The black of the Seen uniform hid the stain of Aaron's blood, but the fabric still felt sticky and odd. It would be nice to change. She touched Simon's forehead. His skin felt warm but clammy. "Will he recover?"

"I said I have to examine him." Aric pointed at the control room. "You can change in there." He picked up the last two articles of clothing beside the satchel. "I'll get Simon cleaned up and check him for any hidden wounds."

"Okay." She hurried to the control room and started to close the door but stopped. "Thank you, Aric, for your help. I know you wanted to go to New Kale." Shutting the door before he could answer, she breathed a long sigh. They were alive. Simon and Aric were both alive, and everything was back on track.

She changed quickly and held out her arms. Aric was right. The fabric was kind of threadbare. The loose weave wasn't even as high quality as the Seen uniforms but certainly better than the wall slaves' outfits. The shirt and pants felt foreign after wearing Seen uniforms and Amelia's Noble dresses for so long, but the pants weren't very different from the too-big pants and shirt she had worn in Cillineese when posing as Simon's library assistant.

Settling into the control chair, she closed her eyes. It would probably take a while for Aric to change Simon's clothes and clean up the blood. The bathroom at the back of the transport couldn't be very big, and the transport probably didn't hold much water in its tanks.

She rested an elbow on the chair arm. Everything was about to change. As soon as she and Simon got on that boat, her world would grow. No wall slave had ever experienced sea travel, as far as she knew. It was unheard of to even go above ground outside the palace walls. Just a few weeks ago she had been struggling to survive, starving, begging crumbs from friends, and creeping through ductwork to avoid detection.

As memories of the cramped, filthy wall-slave dorms came to mind, she inhaled sharply. She fingered the two necklaces hanging at her throat—Amelia's chip and Alyssa's medallion. Two people who had died. Two people who helped end the misery in the dorms. There were so many others besides them—her father, Sasha, and brave slave council members who had kept her alive after Fox killed Iain.

She shook her head, trying to rid herself of images of the dead. Yet, the memories shone clearly despite her efforts.

She opened her eyes and watched the fields slip past the transport as it trundled over its tracks. The memory drug, Antrelix, Aric had given her a week ago must still be working. It brought back useful information when she needed it, but pains from the past came along as well.

A knock sounded at the door.

She spun her chair that way. "Come in."

Aric slid a finger through the hole where the knob had been and pushed the door open. "What did you do?" A drop of water fell from his dark hair, his face and hands now clear of blood.

Heat rose to her cheeks. "I had to take the doorknob off. I couldn't get out, and when you were banging on the back of the transport, I ..." She shrugged. "It's the only thing I could think of."

He nudged the open toolbox with a shoe. "I'm glad you heard us. It was so loud out there, I wasn't sure you would be able to." He motioned to the chair. "I'd like to check the controls if you don't mind."

She slid off the chair and stepped back. "How did you get away?"

Leaning over the controls, he shrugged and began scrolling the touch screen with a finger. "Just kind of fought my way through. I've had some self-defense training. And I dragged Simon along. He was unconscious after one blow to the chest." Aric sank into the chair. "When the transport started moving, I grabbed the service bars on the back and held on to Simon." He stopped scrolling, turned around, and faced her. "And when we were clear of the tunnels, I started banging. I couldn't have held Simon up for much longer."

Monica's cheeks grew even warmer. If she hadn't stopped the transport in time, they could have died. It was a good thing she finally realized that the pounding had to be investigated.

Aric knelt in front of the control panel and moved a hand around in the dark recess below. "Simon has some cuts I want to bandage." He frowned, then smiled and drew out a metal box. "Here it is." As he stood, he flipped open two metal tabs keeping the lid in place. "It's a good thing this is here. The transports are the last remaining first-aid stations." He walked into the other room, and his voice faded. "Thanks to someone opening the infirmary to public use."

Monica hurried after him. "Simon said it was necessary to help maintain control."

He crouched by Simon, who now lay on the couch dressed in clothes similar in style to Monica's. All the blood had been cleaned from his face and hands.

"Maintain control?" Aric ripped open a bandage and placed it over a cut on Simon's wrinkled forehead. "It didn't help much, did it?"

Monica bowed her head and claimed the armchair across from them. What could she say? It hadn't worked. But it might have staved off the panic for a little while.

As Aric applied a bandage to Simon's arm, Monica leaned over and tugged her pant leg up, revealing the long, puckered scar that extended from her ankle, around her calf, and reached to her shin. Red pinpricks dotted the sides of the scar where the stitches had been—stitches Aric had removed only a day ago, though he had advised against it, saying the wound could tear open again if she weren't careful. It hadn't given her much trouble recently, but the twinge on the stairs back in the transport station wasn't a good sign.

Monica rolled her pant leg into place and rested against the seat back. As long as they didn't do any more running, it might be all right.

"There." Aric tucked his supplies back into the first-aid kit. "Simon, you can open your eyes now. I know you're conscious, so stop pretending."

Simon's eyes opened, and he scowled. "Pretending? I wasn't pretending. I was resting while you fussed over me like some nursemaid." He sat up and shooed Aric away from the couch. "I'm quite recovered." Putting a hand to his chest, he coughed. A gray pallor washed over his face.

Monica jerked from her seat. "Simon!"

Aric shook his head. "On second thought, you need to lie down again." He helped Simon recline on the couch. "That blow to the chest must have caused more damage than I first thought."

"I could have told you that." Simon rested his head on the couch's arm. His face returned to its natural color, and his breathing became steady. He closed his eyes and immediately started snoring softly.

Monica hurried over and knelt beside the couch. "Will he be okay?"

"I'm not sure," Aric whispered. "I don't know if the fatigue is from heart trouble or a concussion. I didn't see him get hit in the head, but I was distracted, so I can't say. If it is a concussion, then we need to keep him awake. If it is heart troubles, it would be best to let him sleep, but it could even be both."

"How can we know for sure?" Monica crossed her arms. Poor Simon. He really was too old for this kind of thing, something he claimed regularly.

Aric rummaged in the satchel lying on the floor. "If I could listen to his heart, it would help. But the first-aid kit has no stethoscope." He emptied the contents of the bag onto the floor. Two computer tablets and a hand-held computer tumbled out along with a first-aid kit and a small plastic packet holding an identification chip.

Shaking his head, Aric gathered the items and placed them back in the bag. "Nothing helpful. It's too bad I dropped my medical bag." He shrugged. "I'll have to do this the old-fashioned way." Still kneeling, he leaned over and pressed his ear to Simon's chest. Aric frowned and closed his eyes.

Monica sat back on her heels. What would they do if Simon needed help? There weren't any infirmaries at the dock, were there? There certainly wasn't a palace, and if the riots had spread … She shook her head. It was best not to think of it. They would deal with problems as they presented themselves.

CHAPTER FOUR

"I can hear a slight murmur." Aric drew his ear away from Simon's chest and stood. "Do you …" He shook his head. "Never mind."

Monica looked up at him. "Do I what?"

The transport lurched, throwing her against the table. Simon slid off the couch and awoke with a yelp.

Aric stumbled but caught himself on the armchair. He dashed for the control room. "Wait here!"

Monica scrambled to her feet. "Simon, are you okay?"

"What's going on?" He climbed back to the couch and sat. "What did that boy do now?"

Monica rubbed her arm where it had hit the table. "Nothing."

Simon blinked. "Nothing? Then that's the problem, isn't it?" He started to stand, but his skin paled, and he sat down again. "Well, he'd better be doing something to fix whatever it is his nothing caused."

Aric walked out of the control room, his mouth set in a grim line. "We're back underground again, and we're almost to the station, but the tunnel is collapsed ahead. Fortunately, the auto-pilot sensors kept us from running into the rubble." He palmed the transport wall. The door rose, letting in the tunnel's cold air. "You'll have to walk from here."

Peering around Aric's shoulder, Monica tried to get a glimpse of the tunnel, but darkness covered everything past the transport's door. The lights running along the tunnel ceiling must have lost power.

Simon beckoned to Monica. "Well, help me up. We must get going. Fahltrid won't wait for us forever."

Monica took his arm and helped him to his feet. "Fahltrid?"

"Yes, yes." Simon waved her away and approached the edge of the transport. "Our captain. He's the one sailing us to Eursia."

Aric ducked into the control room again and came back carrying three glowing green orbs. He held one out to Monica and one to Simon. "Emergency lights. They should help you find a service access."

"But." Monica cradled the light in her hands. "Aren't you coming, too? We might need you in Eursia. We still have Fox's chip to decipher."

Shaking his head, Aric picked up the satchel and gave it to her. "I have to go to New Kale and watch out for my family. They might need me, especially if word of the Cantral riots reaches them. Besides, Eursia isn't the safest place for me. Heir of the north wing. They'd probably have me killed."

Monica swung the satchel strap over her head and secured the bag at her side.

Simon dangled his legs over the transport edge. "Ah well, we could have used you, but of course your family matters more." He slid off the ledge and landed with a thump on the tunnel floor. "Not that Monica isn't your family, too, you know. She's your cousin." He started walking out of sight, his light held out in front. "Well, mostly."

Monica tucked the glowing ball into her pocket. She slid from the transport and tumbled forward. When she threw her hands out, her palms smacked the stone.

"Are you okay?" Aric jumped down.

"Yes." She dusted off her pants and hands. "But …" She retrieved the light from her pocket. Aric needed to come with them. His family would be all right. Veronica's brother was in

New Kale—he would take care of them. "What if there are mobs above ground?"

"Are you coming?" Simon's voice echoed through the tunnels, sounding as though it came from all around.

Sighing, Aric touched the transport side, and the door closed. "Fine. I'll walk you two through the city, but then I'm coming back. My mother has trouble handling Regina's stubbornness at the best of times. Neither of them is very patient with the other."

"Thank you." She darted around the transport's front, hopping over two of the rails. "We're coming, Simon!"

"Watch that third rail!" Aric called. "It's got enough charge in it to kill you."

Monica jumped over the buzzing metal bar and stood in the middle of the tunnel. "Do you know where an exit is?"

Simon appeared from behind a large boulder, his face illuminated with the orb's sickly green light. "There should be a repair access somewhere nearby, if we can find it amidst this rubble."

Monica held her own orb high, shining the light across the hill of rocks that spread out before them. The waist-high boulders covered the tunnel's path completely. She shook her head. "I don't know if we can get past these. They're pretty big." She glanced up. A large indentation marred the ceiling where the rocks must have dislodged.

"It doesn't matter." Aric walked up beside her and pointed at a shadowy section behind the hill. "I see stairs; they're not blocked."

"Excellent." Simon started climbing the first boulder.

Monica caught up and snagged hold of his sleeve. "Be careful. If you fall …"

He shook her off. "Nonsense. I'm as limber as a mountain goat." He dropped to the other side of the boulder and headed for the stairs.

Aric smiled. "I thought he was too old for such things."

"When it's convenient." Monica rolled her eyes. What was a mountain goat, anyway? "He shouldn't be doing that. What about his heart and his injuries?"

"Do you want to be the one to tell him?" Aric gestured to the door and held out his other hand. "I'll help you over the rocks. You're pretty short, even for a wall slave. It'll be more difficult for you than for Simon." He smirked. "Seeing as both your parents were tall, it's a wonder."

Monica gripped Aric's hand. Clambering over the boulders proved easier than expected. Her bare feet gripped the smooth surfaces without a problem. "You knew them?"

Aric followed close behind and helped her off the last rock in front of the stairs leading to a door. "Not really. I know your father's name. I was only about seven years old when your family was … terminated. I do remember them some. My mother traveled to Cillineese often. In fact, you and Regina played together quite frequently when you were small."

"Oh?" Monica climbed the first step. "I didn't—"

"Enough chatter!" Simon called from the top of the stairs, his hand on the doorknob. "When we exit this tunnel, we are traders! Merchantmen!" He glanced at Monica. "And we must behave as such!"

"But," Monica said, "I don't know how they behave. And if they're behaving anything like the Seen in the palace are, they won't be acting like merchantmen anymore."

Simon glared at her. "You've been a wall slave, Seen, and Noble. I'm sure you can figure out this new persona." He jerked open the door, revealing a narrow staircase leading upward into darkness.

They trooped up the stairs in silence, Simon maintaining the lead, holding his ball of light high. Monica followed, and Aric brought up the rear.

As they continued their ascent, the passage grew darker. She reached out and touched the wall with a hand. What would it be like up there now that the computers were shut down? She had never really been on a city street, not when people were going about their everyday business. But it probably wasn't like that even now. People could be rioting here just like at the palace. Maybe not, though, since the bay was far from the palace; word of the mobs might not have reached them yet.

Simon held a hand out. "Halt!" His green light cast a shine on a metal door in front of them. "This could be interesting. We'll need to scout out the situation." When he pushed open the door a crack, metal squeaked against metal. A sliver of light appeared in the opening and seemed to diminish the light of their orbs. Monica tucked hers back into her pocket, and Aric dropped his into his satchel.

Shouts and the clamor of people sounded outside. The noise bounced into their stairway and reverberated off the walls.

Simon poked his head out the door, and the smell of smoke wafted in.

"Get back in here." Aric pulled Simon inside and slammed the door. "We can't go that way."

Simon poked Aric in the shoulder with a bony finger. "There's no other option. It's the only way to the ships, and a little riot or burning of the buildings will not keep us from our mission."

Monica nodded. "He's right."

"It sounded like more than a little riot to me." Aric brushed Simon's finger away. "We at least need a plan of action."

"Rioting mobs don't heed plans." Simon reached to his face as if to take off his glasses but stopped when his fingers touched the bridge of his nose. "But they do take old men's glasses." He laid a hand on the door. "The port is on the right about one-tenth of a mile from this door. Fortunately for you, I looked at a map when I was planning this venture."

Aric tapped Simon's arm. "Just let me go first. It's probably dangerous, and I bet you've never even been to the docks before."

Viral Execution

Simon huffed and batted Aric's hand away. "Fine, fine. You can clear the way through all the ruffians. I'd rather you get hurt than me. You're younger and can take it better."

"You're very generous." Aric shoved the door open and stepped outside.

Light shone into the stairway, making Monica blink. She held a hand to her eyes and followed the two men. The noise increased to an almost overpowering level—screams and shouts, things banging and clanking together. Her bare feet struck smooth stones, and cold air swirled, tugging at her clothing and brushing her face.

Smoke formed a haze over tall, narrow houses lining the street. People raced in and out of the buildings. Some structures seemed to tilt to the side, as if a strong push would send them toppling. Others stood straight, though paint peeled on their windowsills.

A fire blazed in the center of the street—food crates, pieces of broken tables and chairs, and soiled fabric piled high. The flames crackled. Birds flew overhead, calling in loud voices, and a constant roar sounded in the distance, adding to the chaos.

A loud boom ricocheted through the streets. The crowds scattered and disappeared into buildings in an instant.

Monica flinched. What in the world?

Aric froze. "Was that a gunshot?"

Simon strode ahead. "Whatever it was, it cleared the streets. Let's get going before they come back. No telling if Captain Fahltrid will wait for us much longer or if he's even waited this long."

"Simon," Aric said, "wait. There's no telling—"

The sound echoed again, followed by a scream.

Simon scurried down the street toward the fire.

Aric raced after him. "Simon, you're going to get yourself killed!"

"Wait!" Monica ran behind Aric, looking down each side street. Broken glass littered the alleys, and worried faces peered out from partially open windows and doors.

The loud noise blasted a third time, but the people didn't disperse. More men and women filtered onto the road, some cradling children and others carrying bundles.

"You'll pay for this!" The cry came from close by.

A crowd gathered past the fire. A man shouted, and three people wrestled on the cobblestones.

Monica caught up to Simon and Aric. "Simon?"

Simon edged toward the crowd, blinking. "If only I had my glasses I could tell what's going on."

Aric grabbed Monica's elbow and Simon's arm. "The docks are the other way. We need to go before they recognize me as a Noble. Fahltrid won't wait, remember?"

Nodding, Simon turned and headed in the direction of the docks.

The scuffle broke up, and two men rose from the street, lifting a third, bloodied man to his knees.

Monica's feet seemed glued in place. This was like the transport station all over again. Would more people die?

One of the men raised a black metal object. A bang reverberated in the air, and fire spouted from one end. People ducked and edged away from the man.

Someone shouted. "Let him be an example!"

The man with the black object put it to the bloodied man's head. "The Nobles' rule is over!" A boom sounded followed by a sickening crunch. The bloodied man's head slumped forward, and more blood streamed from his temple.

Aric's hold on Monica's arm tightened. "That was a security guard. I recognize him."

Monica shook her head. What had just happened?

The man picked up the security guard and tossed his body into the blazing fire. The flames crackled, and the smell of burning flesh seared the air.

Bile rose in Monica's throat. "Was he dead when he threw him?" She choked out the words.

"Yes. He was definitely dead." Aric's fingers dug into Monica's arm. "Let's go. Simon's on his way to the boat already."

Someone bumped into Monica's shoulder, and her satchel slid away. She whirled to grab it, but a dirt-smudged boy clutched it to his chest and ran into the crowd.

"Hey!" Monica darted after him, ducking beneath elbows and weaving between people.

"Monica!" Aric's call sounded distant.

She gritted her teeth. They couldn't lose that bag!

The crowd pressed close, hemming her in at all sides. She pushed past a large man, but the boy was out of sight now.

Clenching a fist, she shook her head. No! They needed the computers in the bag. Without them they couldn't decipher Fox's chip. But how would she find one small boy in this crowd? There were dozens of boys around.

Someone grabbed her arm. She slapped at the hand and jerked free.

"Watch it!" Aric stood beside her, his hands held up in a defensive gesture. "What happened?"

The crowd swept them up against the side of a building. Monica crossed her arms and put her back to a wooden wall. "I lost my bag."

"You what?" Aric growled. "We need that bag!"

"You mean this bag?" A blonde girl appeared at their side, one hand clutching the boy's arm and the other keeping a tight grip on Monica's satchel. "I saw the whole thing." She frowned at Aric. "Your face is …" Her eyebrows rose. "You must be the ones I'm looking for. I'm Wheaten. Captain Fahltrid sent me. He was afraid you would be in trouble."

The boy struggled in Wheaten's grip. "Let go!"

"Thanks for getting our bag back." Monica took it and secured it over her shoulder, keeping one hand on the strap this time. She relaxed her shoulders a bit. "And thanks for coming to get us. I was afraid we wouldn't be able to find the ship in all of this." She nodded at the crowd. People still jostled them occasionally, but the building offered protection from the main swell.

An older boy darted forward and grabbed the younger child's shoulder, snatching him from Wheaten's grip. "Oh, thanks, Miss. You found him." He gave the younger boy a shake. "What were you thinkin', Squeak, running off in this muck?" He turned to Wheaten. "So sorry, Miss. He was just lookin' for his mother. Lost her in the crowd, you know."

"Lost his mother, ha!" Wheaten glared at the two. "Get out of here."

He tipped his soot-covered cap to her, a crooked-toothed grin plastered on his face. His gaze traveled to Aric, and he froze.

Pushing the smaller boy behind him, he pointed a finger at Aric. "You're a Noble! You're that north—"

Wheaten slapped a hand over the boy's mouth. "Shut it!"

Monica backpedaled a step. "We need to go."

Wheaten grabbed Aric's arm, and he grasped Monica's. Wheaten tugged them down the street.

The smaller boy let out a shrill cry. "He's a Noble! He's getting away!"

Wheaten broke into a run, dragging them with her.

"Stop them!" someone shouted.

Monica's heart pounded in her chest. Aric's fingers dug into her wrist as they ran through the street.

"Look out!" Wheaten called.

Monica's head jerked back. Pain ripped through her scalp. Aric's hold slipped from her wrist. She tried to turn around but something held her hair.

Hot metal pressed against her cheek. "Noble, stop or she dies!" a man's gruff voice shouted. The hold on her hair remained tight. Her neck ached, and ringing filled her ears.

Aric turned around and stepped toward her, his hands out in a defensive gesture. "Just calm down now. We can sort this out."

Wheaten disappeared down a street heading toward the docks.

Viral Execution

"Can we?" The man pressed the metal harder into Monica's cheek. "Your life for hers seems like an easy way to sort things. I don't kill Seen unless I have to."

Monica gulped. Wheaten had abandoned them, and Simon was nowhere in sight. Would Aric sacrifice himself for her? After what he did in the tunnel, he just might, but—

"Very well." Aric stepped closer, his hands still held out in front of him. "Just let her go, and we can talk. It's hard to discuss our options when you have a gun pressed to my Seen's head. Those triggers can be finicky. We don't want that thing going off by accident."

CHAPTER FIVE

The man slowly drew the gun away from Monica's cheek. She inhaled deeply. The man still held her hair in a death grip, sending shooting pains through her scalp.

"Good." Aric stepped forward slowly. "Now we can discuss this more civilly. My life for hers. Is that right?"

"Of course. I already said that." The man jerked Monica's head back. Her neck made a sickening popping sound. She gasped and collapsed to her knees on the cold cobblestones.

The man's hand stayed tangled in her hair, and her sudden shift made him lurch forward.

Aric charged and wrenched the gun from the man's hand. It went off, and the bang knifed into Monica's ears, blocking out all other noises.

Blood spewed from the man's chest. The crowd surged forward, crushing them. Someone grabbed Aric's arm. The gun went off again, fire spewing from its mouth. Another person fell.

A hand grabbed Monica's arm, and another took her satchel. Smoke veiled her vision. She tried to fight off the person holding her, but the hand only tightened its grip.

Her hearing began to clear. Shouts echoed off the buildings, and the fire's crackling grew.

Someone slung Monica's satchel back over her head. The hand released her, and she turned around.

Viral Execution

Wheaten appeared beside her and gave her a thumbs-up signal before disappearing into the crowd again.

Monica clutched her satchel tightly. The gun went off once more, the bang adding to the cacophony around them. A woman screamed. Peasants fought each other. A fist connected with her arm. Pain flared down to her elbow. She gasped and ducked away, pressing herself against the side of a building. How could she get to the docks through this crowd? She wasn't even sure exactly where the docks were! And where had Wheaten gone?

"Monica!" A gruff man's voice barely reached her ears over the crowd. "Monica!"

She stood on tiptoes, but every head was higher than her own. Who was that? Should she reply? What other option did she have? "Here!"

A man with suntanned skin emerged from the crowd, Aric's limp body thrown over one shoulder. "Monica, I'm Captain Fahltrid. Come with me to my ship."

Gripping her satchel tighter, Monica followed him down the street through the crowd. She had to trust him. What other choice was there?

As he cleared a path through the people with one muscular arm, she stayed at his heels. The throng closed again behind them. If she lost him, she would never get out of Cantral alive.

They broke free from the crowds a few yards down the street, and Fahltrid ducked into a narrow side road. He adjusted his grip on Aric's limp body before motioning to Monica to take the lead. "They're at our backs now, but they'll notice our absence in a moment." He glanced around the alley. "Wheaten! Where are you?" He motioned to Monica again. "Let's get to the ship. She knows the way."

"What about Simon?" Monica took two steps forward. The mob was still near, but she couldn't leave Simon behind, wherever he had sneaked off to. "I didn't see him in the crowd. He disappeared somewhere."

"He's already at the ship. Wheaten led him there when she came and told me you were in trouble."

Monica blew a relieved sigh, then jogged ahead. There was only one way to go, so she couldn't get lost now. As she and Fahltrid skulked through the deserted alley, the noise of the crowd quieted but was soon replaced by another roar, this one different, moving in a rhythmic pattern.

She looked over her shoulder at Fahltrid, who still carried Aric like a sack of supplies. "What is that?" she asked.

An inhumane screech sounded overhead. She ducked and dodged toward a building. What in the world? The screech came again.

Fahltrid shook his head and kept walking. "Just the sea and the gulls. You're not afraid of a little bird, are you?"

"No, of course not." Monica dashed after him. A bird made that noise?

A white-winged creature swooped over their heads and called with the same sharp cry.

Monica shuddered. So that thing was a bird—a gull. Of course she knew what birds were, but knowing differed from seeing. Did they all make such odd sounds?

The alley opened up to a large walk made of boards lined with more houses. Broken crates littered the wooden planks near the homes, and ruptured sacks of grain lay trampled on the ground. Water soaked a white powder leaking from some of the burlap bags.

More gulls picked at smashed fruit and vegetables on the boardwalk. Three large ships floated in the water nearby. Simon stood beside one of the ships that seemed to be made of a patchwork of metal and wood. He waved, walked up a wooden plank, and boarded the ship.

"That's your ship?" Monica paused for a step. The boat rocked back and forth as the water ebbed and flowed. Was it safe?

"Yes, she might not look like much, but she'll surprise you." Fahltrid mounted the plank, his boots thumping on the wood. "Now get on board before the crowd discovers where we've gone. We're lucky they've already finished ransacking the docks, or we'd find them here as well."

Monica scrambled after him, her bare feet slipping on the slick boards. "Aric isn't supposed to come with us."

"He's unconscious. He doesn't have a choice in the matter. Either we take him with us or the crowd finds him." Fahltrid laid Aric's motionless body on the deck. "Everyone knows this boy's face. It would be murder to leave him." He stood at the top of the gangplank and looked out over the docks. "Where is that girl?"

Monica knelt beside Aric. Fahltrid was right. They couldn't leave him, but would his family be safe without him?

A smoky haze filtered through the streets and alleys, drifting toward the docks. Monica laid her satchel beside Aric and stood. Simon appeared at Monica's side. "There you are. You should explore the ship when you get a chance." He shook his head as if in awe. "It's quite amazing, really. They have a steam engine!"

Monica nodded but kept her gaze fixed on the town. A steam engine wasn't important, whatever it was. Wheaten needed to get on board.

"I'm going to go look for Wheaten." Fahltrid tramped down the gangplank. "Stay here if you still want to go to Eursia. If you're not here when we return, we'll leave without you." He walked up the alley and disappeared behind a building.

Simon crouched beside Aric. "Well, I suppose it's you who needs the doctoring now, Aric? Fine time to go to sleep." He rose and rested a hand on the ship's wooden railing, his face a little pale. "What happened back there?"

"Someone recognized Aric." Monica rubbed her upper arm where a fist had connected with her skin. Aric's injuries were even worse, but what had knocked him unconscious? Had someone hit him in the head?

"He is the heir, after all." Simon waved a hand. "He was worried about that. Madam Veronica will be most upset when she figures out he isn't coming to New Kale."

"Probably." Monica stood on tiptoes, staring as hard as she could at the line of leaning buildings framing the docks, but there was no sign of Wheaten or Fahltrid. Fires burned in a few of the houses now, their flames licking at the roofs and jumping to nearby houses. She clenched her fists. The people did this to themselves. How could they react this way to freedom?

Wheaten darted out from the alley, her face pale. She ran up the gangplank, barreled past them, and scrambled down a flight of stairs. "They're coming! The mob followed me." Her frantic call sounded muffled.

Monica scurried after Wheaten. "What can I do to help? Where's Fahltrid?" She ran after Wheaten down a narrow hallway and into a room holding a black metal machine.

"Nothing. You can't help. You don't know how." Wheaten turned a handle that jutted out of the machine's side, and the ceiling opened above them. A black pipe crept up from the machine and entered the new hole. "The captain is coming." She turned the crank faster, tears forming in her eyes. "He'll be here."

"If you tell me what to do, I will know how." Monica glanced around the cramped room. Was this the steam engine Simon had mentioned?

Wheaten motioned to her and pointed at the crank. "Fine. Keep turning this, and when it won't turn anymore"—she pointed at a second handle near the base of the machine—"turn this one. I'll be right back." She ran along the hall and up the stairs to the main deck.

Monica grabbed the handle and started turning. It swung easily at first, but every turn became more difficult. A thump sounded overhead. Monica strained to move the crank, but it stopped and wouldn't budge.

"Now the other." She grabbed the second handle. As she moved the metal as instructed, the skin on her hands began to ache. The wounds had just scarred over from her run-in with the computers, and the new, soft skin wasn't ready for this kind of friction.

A hissing sound erupted from the machine, and wafts of steam issued from a crack in the side. Monica sucked in a breath and kept turning. Steam. It looked just like the gas used to terminate a city. She shuddered. It was silly to dwell on that. Of course this steam wasn't the deadly gas. This would help them escape death.

The engine chugged and spluttered. Scalding hot water dripped onto Monica's hands, and she jerked away. Was it supposed to do that? "Wheaten!" She tried to grab the handle again, but the metal burned her skin.

The ship lurched forward, throwing Monica to the floor. A riveted bolt in a plank dug into her hip, and another scraped her arm. She climbed to her feet and headed for the exit. "Wheaten!"

The ship lurched again, but Monica managed to stay upright. She ran up the steps to the ship's main deck. "Wheaten, is the engine—"

A burning torch fell on the ship's deck. Gasping, Wheaten snatched it up and threw it into the water.

She grabbed Monica's arm and hauled her toward the deck rail. "Help me get the gangplank in. The old man won't help. Something about his heart."

Simon sat on the deck nearby, his face gray, a hand resting on his chest.

Clutching a side of the gangplank, Wheaten glared at Monica. "Get over here!"

Monica scrambled over and grabbed the other side of the narrow plank. As her hands met the wood, one end of the walkway dropped off of the dock, jerking them toward the water as it fell.

The mob swarmed the docks yelling so many different things the words were almost indiscernible. A few phrases rose above the others—people calling for Aric's death.

"Pull it up!" Wheaten yanked on her end, but it didn't budge.

Monica braced her feet and pulled with her. They wrenched it onto the ship just as someone threw another torch.

"Watch out!" Wheaten grabbed for the torch, but it sailed past her fingers and rolled toward Aric's unconscious form.

Monica dropped the gangplank, and it clattered to the deck. "Aric!"

Fire licked at the boards near Aric's head. Monica dove and caught the unlit end of the torch. Hot wood met her palms, scorching her skin. Sucking a breath through clenched teeth, she hurled the flaming stick over the rail.

Wheaten stomped on the little fires that ate at the floorboards. The flames disappeared, leaving only smoky trails and black dots marring the deck.

The boat pulled away from the docks, distancing them from the jeering crowd and calls for Aric's death.

Monica blew on her stinging hands, but it did little to alleviate the pain. "Wheaten?" Monica glanced around the boat. Wheaten stood nearby, and Simon still sat near the railing. There was Aric, lying down, but … "Where's Fahltrid?"

CHAPTER SIX

"The captain stayed behind." Wheaten crossed her thin arms over her chest and looked away from Monica. "To help hold them off so we could escape."

"I'm sorry, Wheaten." Monica inhaled deeply. He didn't even know them. Of course, he was Wheaten's captain, but why should he sacrifice his life for a crew member? She rested her arms on the rail. The town grew smaller with every passing moment, and the people scurrying across the docks looked like the bugs that lived in the tunnels beneath Central.

As the ship pulled farther away, the water opened up, ripples of blue, gray, and green swirling together in myriad colors. She reached toward the waves, but the boat rode too high for her to come close to touching the water.

Wheaten joined her at the railing. "The captain isn't dead. I'm sure of it. He'll find me anywhere. He's proven that." Tears glimmered in her eyes, but she blinked them away. "Even if he has to row all the way across the ocean, he'll do it."

"How can you be sure he's alive? That mob was …" Monica shook her head. If she hadn't seen everything herself, she would have thought the recent events impossible. How could people turn so evil so quickly? "They threw a man into that fire. There's no telling what they'd do to anyone. They were even fighting each other near the end."

Wheaten picked at a splinter poking from the rail. "I saw that, but I know he's alive. If I can survive everything that I have, he can live through this. It's in our blood." She pried the splinter off and threw it into the water. "It's my fault he couldn't get on board anyway. He was here. He was fine." Tears streamed down her cheeks, and she made no move to wipe them away. "I was trying to find the crew. They don't know how to survive out there. They need to be here on the *Katrina*. Not out there."

"Do you think they'll be all right?" Frowning, Monica gripped the railing. Why wouldn't a ship's crew know how to survive in the city? Merchants knew all about cities, didn't they? According to Simon's commerce books, merchants went through cities transporting goods, interacting with field laborers, Nobles, and peasants alike. The merchants had the most freedom of anyone other than Nobles.

"They'll be fine," Wheaten said. "Fahltrid will find them and come to us." She walked away and headed down the stairs leading to the lower deck. "I need to check the engine."

Monica sat beside Simon. He still looked a little gray, and he hadn't interrupted even once. He really must not be feeling well. She touched his hand. "Are you all right?"

"Fine, fine." His other hand stayed on his chest. "A ship this size must have a place to lie down somewhere. Certainly they don't make their crew sleep on deck." He waved her off. "Go find a place for me to rest. I'm too old for adventures of this stress level."

Monica stood. "I hope you feel better soon." She skirted Aric's unconscious form. Should she try to do anything for him? They still had the first-aid kit from the train, but she didn't know anything about medicine. Maybe Wheaten would.

Monica glanced at the hatch leading to the engine room. There was no sign of beds down that way. Maybe the other hatch would reveal something suitable.

Viral Execution

She tromped down the flight of stairs to a dark passage below. The closeness of the ship's inner walkway felt similar to the cramped slave passages—similar to home. She ducked beneath a low-hanging beam. Glowing green balls of light shone from rusted lanterns hanging from ceiling beams, casting flickering shadows on the walls.

Monica pushed back a soft, blue sheet from a metal-framed doorway. She fingered the worn fabric for a second, so much like the wall slave bunk curtains. With a quick yank, she pushed it toward the wall. Metal hooks lining the curtain's top rattled and bounced across a copper bar overhead.

In the next room, six hammocks hung from more low-hanging beams. Three hammocks stretched out on one side of the cramped room and three on the other, creating an aisle that led to a metal wall.

She nodded. This would work for Simon. A hammock might not be very comfortable, but it was better than lying on the hard wood floor.

After running back up the stairs, she stepped onto the main deck. Wheaten crouched beside Simon who now sat with his eyes closed and head resting on the railing. "Monica?" she called.

Monica ran over and knelt at Simon's feet. "What is it?"

"His breathing is erratic, and he won't respond." Wheaten slid her arms under Simon's. "Help me guide him down to the deck. He'll fall over otherwise."

Monica laid her hands behind Simon's head and back, and she and Wheaten eased him to the floor. "I don't know what's wrong with him," Monica said. "He got hit earlier at the Cantral palace, but I didn't think it was that bad." She touched one of the small bandages covering a scrape on his forehead. "These cuts aren't very bad either. Simon's usually tougher than this."

Wheaten sat back on her heels. "I don't know what to do. I'm just a merchant's kid. I don't know anything about medicine. The captain knows some, but he's not here."

"Aric is a doctor." Monica edged over to him and shook his shoulder. "Aric, we need your help. I know you're hurt, but Simon needs you." Aric moaned and stirred. "Aric, please wake up."

His eyelids flickered open. He stared at her for a second before closing them again and groaning. "We're on the ship, aren't we?" He put a hand to his head and sat up. "I can feel it rolling."

"Yes, and Simon isn't waking up." Monica dug in her satchel and withdrew the metal first-aid kit. "That Seen back at the station must have hurt him more than we thought. Please, help him."

Aric opened his eyes. "You knew I didn't want to come aboard. I was supposed to go to New Kale."

Monica popped the latch and swung the box lid open. "I know, and I'm sorry, but there was a riot, and Fahltrid brought you here unconscious. We didn't know what else to do."

"Yes, well …" Aric took the first-aid kit. "Thank you for not leaving me behind, though now there's the problem of the boundary line."

"The boundary line?" Monica stood and offered him a hand.

"Never mind. I'll take care of it." Aric accepted her hand and crawled to his feet, shaking his head. "Someone's fist got me square in the temple. I'm still a bit foggy." Rubbing his brow, he shook his head again. "Now, what's wrong with Simon?"

"He won't respond or wake up, and he looks pretty pale." Monica motioned to where Simon lay. "Could it be his heart?"

Aric shuffled over to Simon and knelt beside him. "Wheaten, do you have a first-aid kit on this ship? And does it have a stethoscope? The kit we brought does not have one."

"I know we have a kit, but I'm not sure about the stethoscope." Wheaten rose to her feet. "I'll get it." She ran down the stairs toward the engine room.

"I'll try using just my ear for now." Aric leaned over and pressed his head to Simon's chest.

Monica held her breath. The ship's creaking and the snapping of the sails overhead seemed overly loud now as were the calls of gulls overhead. She sighed. Simon had to get better. They needed him. He was the only one who knew her mother, who knew all the parts of the plan. He couldn't die!

"Here it is!" Wheaten scrambled back up the stairs carrying a black satchel with a burgundy strip sewn across one side. She dumped the contents onto the deck. A wad of bandaging bounced toward the railing, and medicines rolled after them, followed by a rubber tube with a metal U at one end.

Monica stopped the medicines and bandages from rolling off the deck. "Is that the stethoscope?"

Aric snatched the tubing and inserted the two rubber-tipped ends of the U into his ears. "It is." He unfastened a few buttons on Simon's shirt and slid a metal pad against Simon's bony chest.

Wheaten started putting the medical supplies back into the bag. Monica helped her and added their kit from the transport to the pile. It'd be best to have all the supplies in one place. There was no telling when they'd need them again.

Aric leaned back and withdrew the two rubber stoppers from his ears. Shaking his head, he sighed. "His breathing isn't normal, like you said. I'm worried about something other than the blow he received. He's rather old, you know."Aric placed the stethoscope into the first-aid bag. "Do you know how old he is exactly?"

"No." Monica shrugged. "He never said. It's hard to tell slaves' ages. Work wears them down so quickly, and most people don't know exactly when they were born. We don't recognize birthdays like Nobles do."

"If you had to guess." He glanced at Simon, his brow furrowed. "Sixty-five?"

Monica widened her eyes. Sixty-five? If he were that old, that would mean— "But the chips don't work anymore! The systems are shut off. It can't be that. It has to be from when the Seen hit him."

"No, it doesn't have to be."

Simon grumbled something.

Monica flinched. "That's a good sign, right? He wasn't moving before. Maybe we can ask him. He would know how old he is. Simon's like that. He would keep track."

"Do you really think Simon would tell us his age if we asked?" Aric smiled. "You've known him longer than I, but I don't think he'd take kindly to that question."

Simon snorted softly, and his eyelids fluttered.

Monica laid a hand on his shoulder. "Come on Simon, wake up, please."

He stirred a little but didn't waken.

She sat back and pulled her knees to her chin. "Okay. If the system is down, then how could the chip kill Simon when he turns sixty-five? And if it is that, then why would he be acting like this? Doesn't the age limit just terminate someone on the spot?"

"One question at a time, please." Aric tapped his chin. "The chips are set for sixty-five years when they're implanted in someone. It's in the chip's inner workings. It has nothing to do with the main computer. The only way to shut it off is to reset the chip."

"Then you can do that! You did it with Regina!"

Aric sighed, a sound seemingly amplified in the darkness. "Not exactly. Regina's was a simple reboot, not quite the same. I just turned it off for a split second then back on. It happens sometimes if a chip malfunctions. People can live through that. When a chip reaches the time limit that's been programmed into it, it shuts down the body slowly over the course of about a month by sending electrical pulses to shut down the least important organs first."

Monica put a hand to her mouth. "That's awful! Terminating is bad enough, but this …"

Aric continued slowly. "Writing a code to reset the whole system is possible in theory, but there are sure to be firewalls, and it might not even work if we don't use the physical button. When a chip is refurbished and implanted in a baby, the doctors need only push the chip's reset button—it's no bigger than a pinpoint—and the chip is ready for another sixty-five years. At least that's how it is for slaves. Nobles' chips are never recycled."

Monica closed her eyes. "Then if Simon is sixty-five … Do you think you can save him?"

"I really don't know. The code I would write would be experimental at best. It could kill him."

"What choice do we have?"

"Before I write any code we should ask Simon what he wants." Aric opened Monica's satchel and withdrew the three computers that Simon had stowed there before they left Cantral's palace. "He's known since he was a child that he would die at sixty-five. All slaves know that." He turned his tablet on. "Don't they?"

"Yes, of course." Monica shuddered at the thought. No one talked much about the age cutoff. But they definitely knew.

"Then he might have come to peace with the arrangement. For all we know, he's looking forward to it." Aric laid his tablet on the deck.

"No. Not Simon. He wants to live." Monica picked up Amelia's tablet. Scratches covered the surface—scars of time, a testimony of what it had been through and what it had accomplished. "He loves life."

Simon's breathing sounded ragged now. She took Simon's hand. Age spots dotted his skin, and raised purple veins coursed up his arm. She rubbed a thumb over his wrinkled fingers. Could he really be sixty-five? What did that age look like, anyway? Most wall slaves didn't live to be much older than fifty before they were sent to the fields to wring the last drop of strength from their worn bodies.

She shook away those thoughts. They would lead only to thinking of lost family. "Simon?" she whispered.

He snorted loudly. "What? What is it?" Lifting his head slightly, he glared at her. "What's wrong with you two? Can't you let an old man sleep?"

"Are you feeling any better?" Monica whispered. "How's your heart?"

"Just skip to the point." Aric leaned forward and made eye contact with Simon. "Are you sixty-five, Simon? I have reason to believe you are, so don't try to worm your way out of answering."

Simon opened his mouth, then closed it again. "What an impertinent question."

"I'm a doctor. I'm allowed to ask impertinent questions."

Monica crossed her arms. "It's for your own good, Simon. Aric might be able to help. We need you. We wouldn't know what to do without your help."

Simon smiled. "Of course you wouldn't. I'm the mastermind behind all of this." He flicked a hand in Aric's direction. "And don't you forget it." His face turned pale, and he rested his head against the ship boards. "Anyway, yes, if you must know. I am sixty-five. Have been for almost two weeks now. I've survived longer than I expected to, actually. Started feeling it a day or two before the Cillineese computers were destroyed." Holding up a hand, he added, "Not that it has affected my brilliant plans. My faculties are still fully functional."

"Of course." Aric picked up his tablet again. "But that doesn't mean your chip won't terminate you at any minute. I think it would be wise to proceed quickly. It will take some time to write a program to safely reset your chip."

Simon sat straight up, eyes wide. "Reset my chip! That will kill me, you foolish boy. Perhaps I'll just take my chances with the chip as it is. I've been doing well enough."

"You're getting worse." Frowning at Simon, Aric turned his tablet on. "I listened to your heart while you were sleeping. It has an arrhythmic beat and a flutter. You must have noticed something different." He drew a finger across the surface of his tablet screen, and his eyes moved back and forth. "Have you felt sick lately? Nauseated? Dizzy? Short of breath?"

"Of course I've noticed." Simon closed his eyes. "I'm not an idiot. And yes to all those symptoms. It's quite aggravating. So if there is anything you can do to fix it, be my guest, but resetting my chip seems too extreme."

"If that's your wish, then it will be a last resort."

Simon's frown deepened. He closed his eyes and lay in silence. Monica crossed her arms, waiting for his answer. He had to agree. What else was there?

The ship continued its gentle creaking and swaying. Wheaten sat nearby, her eyes questioning, but she stayed silent.

Simon nodded. "All right. As a last resort. But only if I'm taking my dying breath."

"Of course." Aric typed something into his computer before turning it off. "Monica and I will brainstorm some other ideas, less drastic ideas. But we need you in Eursia. Like you said …" He winced. "You're the mastermind."

"I'm glad you agree." Simon raised his chin, and his eyes closed again. "Now I'm rather tired. I'm old, you know. You should let me rest while you muddle this out."

"That sounds like a good idea." Aric laid the tablets back into the bag.

Monica pressed a hand on Simon's forehead. Could he really be dying? He seemed so well just before they left—commanding the trials with such force. "Let's get him into one of those hammocks first. He might be more comfortable there."

Wheaten jumped up. "Good idea. I'll help carry him." She scurried over. "Are you up to helping, Aric?"

He rubbed the side of his head. "I think I can manage. But I don't think my heart would break if I accidentally tossed him overboard."

CHAPTER SEVEN

They settled Simon into one of the hammocks, and he fell asleep quickly. His soft snores echoed in the small cabin. Aric set a shushing finger to his lips and whispered, "Let's go back on deck to examine the tablets and discuss our options." He headed for the door without waiting for an answer.

Monica cast a look back at Simon, then followed Aric up the stairs. She laid a hand on the back of her neck. So all those people she freed … would they die at sixty-five as well?

She climbed onto the top deck, and Wheaten followed close behind.

Aric stood by the doorway, his computer tablet in one hand. "Is there any place to work around here, Wheaten? Perhaps your captain has some computer information we could use—something with a larger processor."

"Why would you think that?" Wheaten's face paled. "We— we're just merchants. We don't use computers much." She crossed her arms over her chest. "And the only place there's a desk or workplace is the captain's cabin or control room, and you can't go in there."

Raising an eyebrow, Aric settled onto the floor. "I don't see why not, but there's no time to argue about it." He turned on the tablet, and it blinked to life. "I should get to work before Simon deteriorates any more than he already has. I'm worried about him.

I hate to admit it, but we really do need him. I wouldn't know what to do when we arrive."

Monica sat across from him and folded her hands in her lap. "Right. He's the only one who really knows what my mother looks like, too. I have memories of her, but they're vague." She twisted her fingers together, feeling every scar embedded in her damp skin. "Very vague." She tried to bring up the memories—her mother's soft brown hair, brown eyes, kind words for her only child.

Shaking his head, Aric tapped some more at his computer, his face illuminated by the lighted screen. "I'm afraid I don't remember her very well either. It was a long time ago." He began typing quickly, his fingers moving rapidly for a few seconds, then pausing before beginning again as he muttered. "A blocking program, maybe? Turns off access to the brain stem? I don't know if it's been tried. And if that doesn't work … could the aging app be shut off without harming the chip? If he's the second owner then it will die soon enough." He continued mumbling to himself.

Wheaten sat beside them, her eyes wide. "Is there anything I can do?"

"I don't think so." Monica curled her knees up to her chin. Aric was the best suited for this task. He knew what was and wasn't possible. What help could she or Wheaten be, anyway? They both had lowly backgrounds, wall slave and merchant, neither of whom should know much about computers.

Closing her eyes, Monica inhaled deeply, blocking out Aric's soft chatter and feeling each rhythmic dip and bob of the ship. She reached under her collar and withdrew her two necklaces. Rubbing a thumb across the etching in Alyssa's medallion, she whispered, "I wish I knew what to do."

If Aric heard her words, he ignored them. His indistinct grumblings continued. She laid her head on her knees. Her fingers tangled with the two strings until she found the glass holding Amelia's chip. Amelia would be the best one for this job, but of course that was impossible. Unless …

Monica opened her eyes and stared at the thin chip in the glass vial. It looked no bigger than a bug in the center of her palm. She had been Amelia once, and it had been hard enough, but now … now they had her tablet—her ideas. Amelia would know what to do. *Did* know what to do, in the notes she left behind. "Aric?"

He flinched and lowered his computer. "I'm rather busy here."

"I think I might have something."

He turned back to his computer. "I'm sorry, Monica, but you've said yourself that you're useless with computers."

"Yes, but this isn't really my idea." She smiled and lifted the vial so he could see. "It's Amelia's. Well …" Her smile fell, and she clutched the vial in a fist. "It's really my father's, if what Amelia said is true. Anyway, what if we cloned your chip for Simon?"

Aric blinked. "Cloned my chip?"

"Yes. It makes the coding in the chips identical, right?" Her hands shook as she pondered the idea. Could it work? "Your chip is, what, nineteen? If we copied the program from your chip onto Simon's, then wouldn't his think he's nineteen, too?"

"Cloning …" Aric laid his computer on his lap and looked up. He stayed silent for a few long moments.

She rested her chin on her knees. "Well?"

Wheaten stared at her, her eyes narrowed. "Cloning is impossible and illegal." She clambered to her feet and walked away, calling back, "I have work to do."

Shaking his head, Aric smiled. "Cloning isn't impossible in theory. I suppose it could work. If I knew anything about cloning. It's an illegal procedure, you know. Imagine the havoc it would wreak if someone got hold of the code of an important Noble and pretended to be him. Research into it was outlawed about fourteen years ago, if I remember correctly. It was never interesting to me." He held up a hand. "Why would I want a different identity?" Staring at her, he shrugged. "Until now, that is. Being me could get me killed. The Eursians might think I'm coming to assert my power. Especially if they hear that Aaron's dead."

"Right." Images of Aaron's murder came to her mind—the Seen thrusting the glass into Aaron's neck and the blood—so much blood. Monica squeezed her eyes shut to stop the images. "So do you think it's possible or not? With Amelia's code, couldn't you figure it out? You know so much about programming." She opened her eyes again.

"It is a very good idea, except my chip has, well … Never mind." He opened the satchel and withdrew Amelia's tablet. "I'll need to look at Amelia's code." He turned the computer on and began scrolling and tapping the screen.

The tablet let out a long, low beep, and a short grinding noise. Aric's brow furrowed. "That's never a good sound."

"What's wrong?"

"I'm not sure. Maybe residual damage from the water." Aric ran a hand down the screen and issued more commands. It beeped again. "There." His brow relaxed. "It's working now."

Monica leaned closer. "What does it say?"

"There are a few notes, but mostly it's just the code. Well"— he scrolled the screen to reveal more text—"part of the code, anyway. She must have stored the rest somewhere else. If she finished it at all."

"She locked part of the tablet." Monica extended Amelia's chip to Aric. "We need this to unlock it."

He took the vial and turned it between his fingers. "Cloning code is illegal, you know. Citizens aren't allowed to possess or tamper with the chips' process codes without special clearance, and I never heard of Amelia receiving that clearance."

"It *was* illegal. Those laws are gone now." Monica shrugged and pointed at the tablet. "The code has to be complete. It has to be locked in there somewhere, like her journal entries were. She talked about using the code on chips she was experimenting on, and that it had worked, so the code exists."

Aric made a fist around the vial. "Then I'll search for some locked portion of memory, and we'll see where we can go from there." After typing for a few moments, he held the vial up to the tablet. The tablet beeped, and he began working again.

Monica stood. "If there's nothing I can do here, I'll go see if Wheaten needs help with anything."

Nodding, Aric kept his gaze on his tablet. "It could take me a while to do this. Working without distraction would be best."

Monica walked away, carefully adjusting her gait to match the gentle roll of the ship. The flow of the water around them seemed quieter now, and there was no sign of land in any direction. Inhaling deeply, she let the scent of salty air wash over her. A crisp breeze snapped the sails overhead, and the ship's wood and metal beams creaked and groaned as they passed over the waves.

"Did you figure it out?" Wheaten landed on all fours in front of her.

"Where …" Blinking, Monica stepped back and looked up. One of the ship's masts extended into the sky above them, and thick braided rope ladders led up to the sails. "You were up there?"

"Yes. There's no other way to get the sails out." She looked down at her hands, splaying her fingers, revealing tough, calloused palms. "It's hard work without the crew here." She clenched her hands into fists. "I hope Fern and the rest are okay."

Monica nodded. "I thought they would be on the ship when we got here. I've read a bit about ships, thanks to Simon's insistence."

"Yes, well." Wheaten's face flushed. "We were in the process of … recruiting two new members when we heard about the computers' downfall, and it got kind of messy around here for a little while. We sent our crew away for their safety, but now I'm not sure if that was the best idea."

"Since Fahltrid's there, he'll take care of them, won't he?"

"If he can find them." Wheaten shrugged. "They don't know how to survive out there. The new ones can barely manage getting on board a ship."

Monica studied the sails for a moment. The crew could barely manage getting on board a ship? But they were merchants.

Merchants were born merchants just like slaves were born slaves, so any merchant would have been in the shipping business his whole life, wouldn't he? She wrinkled her brow. It just didn't make sense. "Well, since they're not here …" Monica set a fist on her hip and pivoted. "Is there anything I can do to help?"

Wheaten glanced around the ship. Her gaze seemed to linger on a small door leading to a room with a black pipe protruding from the roof. After a moment, she shook her head. "Nothing right now. Maybe later." She headed for the door. "I need to take care of some things."

"Okay."

Wheaten jogged across the deck and went into the room, closing the door behind her. Frowning, Monica walked over to where Aric sat. What was that about? Were all merchants secretive? Maybe Wheaten was just nervous about being alone on her ship with three strangers. Who wouldn't be? Even if she were a capable sailor, she was still a young girl in the middle of the ocean with no one to help her if the need arose.

CHAPTER EIGHT

A few hours later, Aric still sat on the deck, bent over Amelia's tablet. "I think I have all of the code figured out now." He rose and held the tablet up to Monica. "And I combined all the code and Amelia's notes into one file so they'll be easier to read."

"That's great." She pulled the tablet close and tilted it until the screen became clear. Numbers and symbols jumbled together on the screen, but Amelia's notes came into view a moment later.

Test 6.4 partial success, but chip #2 held new coding for only 10 minutes before shutting down. Chip #1 had successful transfer. I don't understand how Joel accomplished what he did. In every one of my trials, the second chip has died. Even with the notes I found I haven't come close to replicating his conclusions. I'm beginning to believe a clone transfer really is impossible and that the information Veronica provided me with is false. Could she be holding some information back?

Monica ran her finger down the screen, revealing more text.

Test 7 was a complete success. I now have two chips sending the same signal to the computer with no adverse effects to the chips' circuitry. Veronica wasn't lying as far as I can see. I will have to show her if we ever get a chance to meet. There's no telling if the chips would harm a person if they were implanted, but I am not willing to test it on a human subject. Perhaps if I could find an animal test subject.

Viral Execution

I've heard that scientists of old used rats in some of their experiments. I could petition for one to be implanted with a chip, but it would most likely be too risky. Someone would wonder why and ask too many questions. I will just have to be content with these findings. The mystery of Brenna and Rose is solved. My only question now would be 'why?'—but of course Joel is no longer here to ask. I wish I could study these findings further. Maybe a Seen would volunteer to take a chance. Laney might be willing enough, and she would never betray me. It would only benefit her if it succeeded.

The text continued with more details and some scraps of partial code. Monica handed the tablet back to Aric. She had read it all before when she was trying to figure out how to shut down the Cantral computers.

Sighing, Aric scrolled through the text. "So cloning a chip is possible, but the computers would immediately terminate both signals if they sensed the same signal from two chips. Since Amelia succeeded, she must have gotten through our firewalls, and that's never been done before." He shook his head. "Then Amelia really was everything the Council believed her to be."

He fiddled with the tablet, as if not sure what to say next. "I wonder what my mother has to do with this. If I had known she was mentioned here, I would have certainly made sure I asked her more questions before she left for New Kale. Now there's no way to ask. And what's all this about my mother's sister?" Frowning, he placed the tablet on a barrel. "Her name is Brenna Rose, and she lives in Eurs—" He froze. "Is she why we're going to Eursia? This trip isn't just about stopping their fledgling independent computer system, is it?"

"Partly." Monica forced a nod. "We are going to stop them from fixing their system, but what really …" She winced. Could he possibly understand? "But what really drives me is that I want to see my mother. Brenna Rose is my mother." A tear trickled down her cheek. "I haven't seen her since I was four. All this time—all this time I thought she was dead."

Aric nodded, then shook his head, his brow furrowed. "I should have known. I haven't done much research into our family history, but I should have known. My mother went to Cillineese so often when I was a child. She never called Joel's wife my aunt, though. I heard about Brenna moving to Eursia because of the—" He met her gaze. "Well, I'll let her tell you what happened, if we find her."

"Right. We need to take care of Simon." Monica blinked away more emerging tears. "Do you think you can use Amelia's codes?"

"Yes. The codes are well written." He gestured toward her tablet. "It's a simple matter of running the program from one chip to Simon's." Aric withdrew his tablet from the satchel. "We'll need my tablet as well. I can set up a wireless communication between the two and have them linked so that each computer's sensor can be held next to each chip." He stacked the two tablets, then handed Amelia's chip to Monica. "Fortunately, both Amelia's and my tablets have chip readers in them."

Monica clutched the vial. "And those were illegal, too, right?"

"Exactly. It's a good thing neither of us was fond of rules."

Monica tied her necklace back in place, letting the glass vial lie out in the open. "Can we clone Amelia's or Fox's chip to Simon's? That would be safer than using yours, wouldn't it?" She laid a hand over the vial. "In case something goes wrong. This chip can't hurt me. Yours could kill you."

"Or worse." Aric tucked his tablet under his arm. "But no, we can't use them. A cloning would take a significant amount of power—power the chips get from the body." He dug into the satchel and withdrew a small plastic envelope with a tiny chip inside. "Both Amelia's and Fox's chips are the same version. They run off a small backup battery inside but receive most of their power from the body—power they can't get if they're not inside their assigned person."

"I see." Monica winced at the thought of a chip drawing power from someone's body. Of course they had to, but the newer chips ran off of someone's electromagnetic field. It seemed less barbaric that way—less invasive, but it really wasn't. It was still a parasite controlling a person's life. "We need to focus on Simon's chip. So we'll use yours, right?"

Aric nodded toward the door leading to the room where Wheaten had disappeared. "Yes. Unless Wheaten lets us clone her chip, we have to use mine if Simon's going to live."

"I don't think she'd agree to that." Monica pointed at Aric's hand where he still held Fox's chip. "And we need to figure out how Fox disguised his chip from the Cantral computers, and you're the only one here who can do it."

"Yes, I know that very well." Aric rubbed the back of his neck. "I need that code as much as Simon needs the cloning."

Monica raised an eyebrow. "Fox's program will save your life? You seem well enough to me."

"It's possible." Aric clenched his hand into a fist and blew out a long sigh. "I'm not allowed to go to Eursia without the right clearance codes and access permits." He pointed out to the ocean. "There's a boundary line—where the Eursian computers' reach meets the Cantral computers'. It's probably a four-day trip from here, and if I cross it, and the Eursian computers are up like you think they are, I'm dead."

Monica widened her eyes. The ruling Nobles' computers could kill them? "Then we need to work on Fox's chip. You can do that right after you clone your chip to Simon's. If there are four days to go to the boundary, there should be enough time." She frowned at the small chip in Aric's hand. "Shouldn't there?"

"Yes, I can probably figure it out in a day or so." He withdrew a third, smaller computer from the satchel. "We won't be able to clone my chip to Simon's until tomorrow, because that is my twentieth birthday. My protection code expires then and won't knock me unconscious if anyone fiddles with my chip."

Monica crouched beside him. A protection code? "What's—"

"I don't have time to explain it. All you need to know is I can't clone my chip to Simon's until tomorrow, so there's nothing you can do for now unless you can convince Wheaten to let us use hers." He nodded toward the door Wheaten had gone through. She stood just outside it now, a stack of papers in her arms.

Monica locked gazes with Wheaten. Would she let them clone her chip? She had no idea who they were or if they were trustworthy. Chip manipulations were off-limits. Even mentioning chip programming set some people on edge. No doubt a stranger would think they were out of their minds.

CHAPTER NINE

Wheaten carried a small stack of papers to the boat railing and placed them on the deck.

Climbing to her feet, Monica whispered to Aric, "I'm going to talk to her. We might as well ask if we can use her chip, right?"

"Sure, go ask her." He waved her away. "Let me concentrate on Fox's chip. My computer's having issues reading it."

Monica nodded and walked to where Wheaten stood. "Wheaten?"

She tore one of the pieces of paper in half, then in half again. "It's just Ten." She ripped the paper into eighths.

"Ten?" Monica wrinkled her brow. What was she talking about?

"Yes. I didn't really get a chance to tell you before." She ripped the page once more, then tossed the pieces over the railing. They fluttered into the water below, and the waves swallowed them. "My name is Wheaten, but everyone calls me Ten. It's easier." She tore another page into small sections and threw them overboard as well. "Unless you're the captain. He insists on Wheaten for some reason."

"Okay, Ten." Monica watched as another piece of paper met its demise over the ship's rail. How could she word her request so it didn't scare Ten or make her nervous about being on the ship with them? "Do you know anything about chip programming or the Nobles' slaves?"

"You mean like the Seen?" Ten stopped ripping a page mid-tear.

"Yes, the Seen." Monica smiled. So the merchants did know about the slaves. Sometimes the slaves speculated that no one knew about their misery, that they were just ghosts and rumors to be whispered about. "More specifically about their chips and the termination age."

Ten yanked the paper in half. One edge of the piece ran across her forearm, raising a thin line of blood. Inhaling sharply, she tossed the paper overboard without finishing the tear job. "Paper cut." She clapped a hand over the small wound. "I might know about the termination age. Why do you ask?"

"Simon's sick, and he needs medical attention." Monica's gaze wandered to the stack of papers on the deck. Ten's picture stared back at her. A metal clip held the photograph to a document with typed letters on it.

"Well, your friend is a doctor, isn't he?" Ten picked up the page. "Get him to help Simon. I don't know anything beyond first aid, and not much of that, either." She tore the page in half.

"He's working on it, but he can't help him right now." Monica eyed the newly torn paper. "What are you doing?"

"Something the captain told me to do if anything ever happened to him." She tugged the photo from the page and slipped it into her pocket before tearing the paper into smaller pieces and throwing them over the side.

Monica picked up the next page from the stack. Scanning it revealed a photo along with other facts about a woman whose picture was clipped to the corner—age, height, eye color, and more. At the bottom it read *Status* and beside it *Field Hand* along with two chip numbers.

Wheaten snatched it out of Monica's hands. "This is a job I have to do myself."

"Sorry." Monica scrunched her brow. The page had said a field hand. The woman it talked about couldn't have been a field worker. She was one of the crew members, wasn't she? If she was, she had to have been born a trader or she wouldn't be one now. No one with a chip changed classes. A legal class change wasn't possible for anyone but a Noble, and why would a Noble change class? They only ever did if they were forced—a disgrace to the family.

Ten finished ripping the page and then another. "Well?"

Monica brushed away the confused thoughts. Maybe the woman wasn't a crew member at all. "Anyway, Simon needs help. He's sixty-five years old, and—"

"So he's dying." Ten disposed of the last page and set her hands on her hips. "There's nothing you can do. You might as well let him sleep until his chip terminates him. Say your good-byes."

"No." Monica shook her head. "We can save him. If we clone someone else's, a younger person's chip to his, his chip will think he's younger again and reset."

"It's not possible." Ten rubbed at the paper cut on her arm. No more blood appeared. "Cloning is illegal, and no one has done it successfully before, so you shouldn't get your hopes up." Her face flushed red. "And even if you could, whose chip would you use? Aric's? He's not twenty yet, is he? You'd better not try it." She set her hands on her hips. "Or maybe yours? You certainly can't experiment with mine!"

"It is possible." Monica backed up a step. "I was hoping you'd let us use yours but—"

"Never in a million years." Ten's eyes narrowed, but something flickered behind the anger. Fear?

Monica held up her hands in a defensive gesture. "I'm sorry. I'm just trying to help Simon. He's going to die if we don't do something."

Ten crossed her arms and looked at the floor. "Then I guess he'll die. He's lived a long life. Longer than most Seen."

"I know, but …" Monica let her arms fall back to her sides. "How do you know so much about the Seen and the computers? You're a merchant."

Redness crept up Ten's neck. "And you're a slave. People can know more than what their work requires. It's natural for people to be inquisitive."

"How do you know I'm a—" Monica shook her head. That wasn't important. "Yes, people can know that, but *I* didn't know about Aric's protection code, and I've lived in the palace all my life. You're a merchant, but you knew. You knew about the age cap, too. Why? How?"

Ten shrugged and fingered the hem of her loose-flowing shirt. "I guess it doesn't matter who knows now." She rubbed the back of her neck, probably feeling the scar from her chip implantation. "If all the computers are down, then who can punish me?"

"Punish you for what?" Monica sighed.

"For my stolen identity." Ten turned her back to Monica. "I'm not really a merchant."

"What do you mean?" Monica glanced to where Aric sat across the deck, still working on Fox's chip.

"Technically, I am, but heritage-wise, no." Ten kept her gaze downcast. "It's a long story, but the captain rescued me from the fields. My mother was a Seen, and the captain knew her." Shrugging, she stuffed her hands in her pockets. "So the captain wanted to make sure I knew about Seen, Noble, and slave life since it's all part of my heritage."

Monica shook her head. Ten's story was making less sense every minute. "Rescued you from the fields? No one leaves the fields once they're sent there. Their chips won't allow it."

Ten turned back toward Monica and kicked at a stray piece of paper that had escaped being thrown overboard. "Every one of our crew had another identity before they were brought aboard. All of them used to work in the fields—demoted Seen, wall slaves, or convicts."

Viral Execution

Inhaling sharply, Monica stepped back. How could that be? Everyone had chips. No one could escape. Could they? If what Ten said were true, then there were other people working to free the slaves and defy the computers. All this time she and the slave council thought they were working alone, that she was their only chance. But here was someone else who had taken up the call.

"It's hard to believe, huh?" Ten scooped the scrap of paper off the deck and tossed it into the breeze. "I was nervous about telling you before, but then I figured you couldn't do anything about it now. The computers are down. I saw the evidence of that myself."

"It's not as hard to believe as you might think." Monica touched Amelia's chip hanging from the cord around her neck. "I'm the reason the computers are down. I'm not a Seen like Simon and not a Noble either, really." She took a deep breath. "I don't have a chip at all. I was able to sneak into the Cantral computer room and take it down."

Ten's eyes widened. "That's why you're on the run?" She looked over her shoulder at the sea, though the city was long gone. "But I think anyone would want to get out of there."

"It's not exactly why we're leaving Cantral." Monica let her necklace fall back into place. It would probably be all right to tell Ten about their plan. After all, she and the captain had been working to free people already, so she would probably want to help. "Eursia has its own computer system that they're starting up. They're trying to make it independent of Cantral's." She shook her head. Did that make sense? She didn't fully understand the plan or how it worked, so how could she explain it to Ten? "Simon knows the details. That's one reason it's so important that he lives. If he dies, the plans are lost, and we won't be able to free the Eursians."

"I see." Ten's gaze seemed locked on something past Monica. "But that doesn't make me willing to let you use my chip for this experiment. I've been cloned once, and it's not happening again."

"What?" Monica's jaw slackened. "You said it was impossible a few minutes ago, and now you're saying it's been done to you?"

Ten's cheeks reddened, and she looked away. "Yeah, well, I still wasn't sure if I should tell you then. I don't really know you. I only decided to tell you now because, like I said, I figured there wasn't anything you could do about it."

"No, there's not, and I'm happy that you and the captain are saving people from the fields. My adoptive mother was sent to the fields when I was eight." Monica suppressed any questions about Emmilah. That wasn't important right now. Simon's life was. "What program did the captain use to clone the chips? Can we use it now? We have only one that Aric modified from our cousin Amelia's notes on her computer. We could use something safer."

"You're moving way too fast." Ten inched backward a step, holding her hands up. "I have no idea who this Amelia is or what you're talking about other than the clone program." She crossed her arms. "And we can't use the captain's program. He keeps it on a memory stick on a necklace that he wears all the time. He couldn't leave something like that lying around the ship."

Monica sighed. "Of course not." She looked over at Aric, who still sat on the deck, typing away at his computer. "We'll have to use Aric's chip. His security code wears off tomorrow, so we can clone his chip to Simon's then. If he survives that long." She clenched a fist. Wasn't there anything else they could do?

"I'm sorry." Ten averted her gaze.

Monica nodded and turned away. *Sorry* wouldn't help Simon. She jogged over to where Aric worked. Ten still had some answering to do about the captain's rescues. Monica crouched beside Aric. He looked up from his computer. "What did she say?"

"No." Monica sighed. "Like we thought she would." Aric nodded and began typing again.

Monica rested her chin on a hand. "Why is it taking so long to read his chip? It didn't take this much time with Regina's."

"Fox's chip went into hibernation mode at some point." Aric punched in a few commands on his hand-held computer. "Normally only chips made within the last eight years can tell when their owner has died, and they send a beacon message to the computers to report it. Versions any older than eight years have to have someone find the body and report the death, which is easy enough, since we always knew where every chip was. But this one"—he shook Fox's chip in his cupped palm—"has had its coding tampered with so much, there's no telling what it knows and what it doesn't. If he did all this coding himself, I'd be surprised."

"Why? Did you know him personally?" Monica shuddered. Who would want to be acquainted with someone as evil as Fox?

"Yes, I knew him." Aric slid the chip back into its plastic envelope. "The computer has all the code on its hard drive now. Finally." He handed the envelope to Monica. "Hold this."

"How did you know him?"

He withdrew his tablet from his bag and plugged it into the smaller computer. "Fox was head of Cantral security for many years, and besides that, he's my—" He looked up. "Well, actually, I guess it's 'our.' He's our uncle. My mother's twin brother. Or was, anyway." He stared into the distance and spoke softly. "I wonder if she heard about his death."

Monica gulped. Uncle? That man was her mother's brother? How could siblings turn out so different? One so loving and the other so cruel. Her mother had mentioned Fox in one of her journal entries and that she knew him. But her brother?

"Surprised?" Aric punched the On button at the top of his tablet. "I suppose living life as a wall slave has kept you in the dark about all the Noble family connections."

She nodded. "It did, but we need to concentrate on Fox's program before it's too late."

"I can work and talk at the same time. The computer is doing most of the processing anyway." Aric tapped his computer. "Did you know your father's older sister is Aaron's wife?" He grimaced. "And he's dead now, too. You're going to have quite a few people upset at you, you know. Fox's wife and daughter, my mother,

Aaron's wife …" He typed in a few more commands. "Fortunately for you, Melody wasn't very fond of Aaron. It was a match for power, not for love."

Monica gasped. "I didn't have anything to do with Aaron's death!" Would she be blamed for that? "Let's not talk about this, please." She shuddered. Trig and Garth had died, too, but Aric didn't seem at all concerned about them.

"You had nothing to do with his death?" Aric laughed softly, shaking his head. "If you hadn't shut down the computers, this would never have happened. It would have been impossible."

Monica stood, her fists clenched. There was nothing she could say that would make him understand. "I'm going to go see how Simon is doing."

"Fine. I'll keep working." Aric waved her away.

She trotted down the stairs to the deck below. The ship creaked all around, louder than it had when they were in port. She swept aside the curtain that hid the hammocks from view. A groan came from the back of the room. Monica stepped forward. Was that Simon or just the ship? She scurried to Simon's hammock. The bed swayed in time with the ship's sounds. "Simon?" She crept up to his side. "Are you all right?"

He snored loudly, inhaling a gurgling breath.

Laying a hand on his shoulder, she squinted at his pale, wrinkled face. The green light from the lanterns lining the hall did nothing to help his skin's sickly appearance. His mouth hung open, and his deep, irregular breathing continued.

"Simon?" she whispered. He didn't even flinch.

With a quick turn, she dashed back upstairs to the deck. "Aric." She crouched beside him. "Simon's breathing strangely. I've heard people breathe like that before, when they're taken to the infirmary. They never come back. You need to check on him. He's getting worse."

Aric continued scrolling down the tablet screen. "What does it sound like?"

"Sort of gurgling, like there's water in his throat." Monica glanced back at the stairs. "He didn't respond when I called him, either. You're the doctor; you need to help him."

"If he's doing badly, then this code can't wait." Aric tapped on the screen, faster and faster. "I have to have Fox's code pulled out and deciphered so that if this cloning knocks me out you can transfer it to both of us before we cross the border."

"But he's dying!" Monica chewed her bottom lip.

"Then let me figure out this code!" He waved her away again.

She set a fist on her hip. "At least come check on him."

"Not right now." Aric glared at her. "I'm still not sure the cloning will even work. You might remember from Amelia's notes that both chips died in her first trial runs."

"But she fixed that."

"So she said." He breathed a heavy sigh. "We'll try it tomorrow, as we had scheduled, after I get Fox's code transferred to my chip. Then the cloning will put it on Simon's chip as well, and we won't have to worry about the Eursian border."

Monica nodded, but Simon's ragged breathing kept nagging at her. "Can you please come check on him anyway? Maybe you can slow down the chip's program or something?"

"Very well." Aric gathered the computers and slid them into the satchel. "I doubt there's anything I can do, though."

Monica scurried down the stairs ahead of him. "At least we can let him know we're working on the program."

"As you wish." Aric strode to where Simon lay in the hammock. He took one of the lanterns from its hook and held the green light close to Simon's face. After staring at him for a moment, Aric set the lantern back and drew the stethoscope from the first-aid satchel they had left near the hammock. He set the flat end of the scope against Simon's chest and listened for a moment.

Simon's breathing sounded just as harsh and watery as before.

Aric withdrew the stethoscope. "His heart sounds worse. I'm not sure how much longer he'll—"

Simon gasped. His eyes jerked open.

Monica stepped forward, but Aric grabbed her wrist. Simon's eyes closed, and he stopped breathing.

"Stand back." Aric pushed Monica away and rolled Simon out of the hammock. He fell to the floor, though Aric kept his head from hitting the boards.

"What can I do?" Monica pressed herself against a support beam out of Aric's way.

He positioned Simon onto his back and started pressing down on his chest in a steady rhythm. "Go ask Wheaten if the ship has a defibrillator on board. Quick as you can!"

Monica dashed up the stairs. "Ten!" She clambered onto the main deck, looking this way and that. "Ten!"

Ten appeared at the top of the stairs leading down to the engine room. Dirt smudged her face, and soot marred her scowling brow. "What?"

"We need a defibrillator. Do you have one?" Monica rushed to where Ten stood. "Simon's heart stopped!"

Ten whirled around and disappeared down the stairs to the engine room.

Monica started to follow her, but Ten yelled, "Wait there!"

Monica bounced on her toes, switching from one foot to the other. "Please hurry," she whispered.

A moment later, Ten reappeared carrying a small plastic box. "Got it." She rushed past Monica and ran down the steps toward Simon and Aric.

Monica sprinted after her into the dark room.

"He's lucky we have one. They're not standard, you know." Ten held the box out to Aric, who still pushed down on Simon's bare chest.

"Yes, yes. Thank you." Aric nodded to Monica. "Come here, Monica. Keep pressing on his chest like I am. And Wheaten, do you know how to charge it up?"

Ten nodded.

He continued his steady pushing. "Do it."

Monica slipped past Ten, knelt, put her hands on top of Aric's, and copied his rhythm.

Aric pulled one of his hands out from under hers. "Got it?"

"Yes." Monica kept up the pressing.

He pulled his other hand away and turned to Ten, speaking softly to her and fiddling with the plastic box.

Monica focused on Simon's face. His eyes remained closed, and he didn't seem to be breathing, but how could he breathe with her pressing on his chest? She continued as Aric had instructed. He was a doctor. He knew what he was doing.

A low beep sounded from somewhere. Aric pulled two metal squares with rubber handles from inside the plastic box. "Ready?"

Monica lifted her brow. "What do you want me to do?"

"Stand back and don't touch him." Aric rubbed the two paddles together, smearing something across the metal surfaces. "Now."

Monica leaned away and held her hands up. "Ready."

Aric placed the paddles on Simon's chest, the metal touching his skin. "Punch that button, Wheaten."

Ten pressed something on the box.

Simon's body lifted and bounced, then lay motionless on the floor again.

Aric let the paddles clatter to the floor and held a finger to the side of Simon's neck. Aric's shoulders sagged, and he sighed. "A pulse. That was easier than I thought it would be." He nodded at Ten. "Pack that up, please."

Monica's head pounded from the rush of emotions. "What now?"

"We're going to have to do the cloning." Aric withdrew his smaller computer from his bag.

"Now?" Ten folded the two paddles back into the plastic box. "But you'll get knocked out."

Aric flinched and looked at Monica. "You told her about that?"

"She already knew." Monica held up her hands. "But she's right. How can we decipher Fox's chip without you? And how will we get you to wake up again?"

"Either I do this or Simon dies." Aric clicked a few buttons on the computer, and two green lights blinked on the console. "First, I need to scan my own chip, get a reading of all the code, and copy it onto the hard drive."

Monica shook her head. "If you do this you will both die once we cross the border."

Ten inhaled sharply. "You don't have travel codes?" She smacked her forehead with the palm of her hand. "Of course not. The computers are down."

Aric held his small computer to the back of his neck. The lights flashed twice then turned orange, red, and finally green again. Wincing, he scrunched his eyes closed. When a sharp beep sounded from the computer, he pulled it away from his neck, his eyes opening once more. "You and Wheaten can figure out Fox's code. My computer will do most of the work anyway. Simon can help you once he recovers." He held the computer up. Text scrolled quickly across the square screen.

"Okay, but how will we wake you up again?" Monica gritted her teeth. This was a bad plan, but what else was there?

"You need my Key-Keeper code." Taking his tablet in one hand and the smaller computer in the other, Aric brought them together and shoved a prong on the smaller computer into an opening in the tablet. "Brenna is probably one of my Keepers. My mother is one, and there are always three."

"Who's Brenna?" Ten's gaze traveled from Monica to Aric. "And what's this about Fox's code?"

"No time to explain." Monica sat on her heels and watched as he tapped the screen. "You don't *know* who the Keepers are?" Lights flashed on the two computers, and the word *Syncing* appeared on both screens. "What if my mother isn't one?"

"No, I don't know, for my own protection. And if your mother isn't one, then I'll have to be unconscious until we get back to Cantral." Aric frowned. "But considering she's my mother's sister, it's a good bet that she is."

Simon groaned, his eyes opening slowly. "My head hasn't hurt this much since I was punished for protesting that transfer," he muttered.

"You're awake!" Monica scrambled to her feet.

"I need some peace and quiet." Simon waved her away. "It feels like my skull is being drilled into."

Aric unplugged the smaller computer from the tablet and handed it to Monica. "Here. You'll need to hold this to the back of my neck. I have the devices synced now, and I put in an override so we could copy my code more thoroughly."

"Okay." She clutched the thin computer in both hands. This was it. They'd either make Simon well, or … She nodded firmly. No. They would make him well.

Aric turned to Simon. "I know you're in pain, but you're going to have to turn onto your stomach so we can access your chip more readily."

Groaning, Simon turned over, folding his arms in front of him to keep his face from touching the floor.

"All right." Aric pulled Simon's collar back and laid the tablet on his bare neck. "Monica, I need you to hold that computer to my neck." He motioned to Ten. "If you could help, I'd appreciate it." He guided Ten's hand to the tablet on Simon. "No matter what happens, make sure this stays in contact with his skin until the cloning is finished." Turning to Monica, he whispered, "The same goes for you. If either computer loses contact, Simon's chip could short out, and he'd be a vegetable for the rest of his life."

CHAPTER TEN

"Now I activate the program. Aric swallowed hard, his Adam's apple bobbing. "These computers have a wireless capability to talk to each other, but it's more reliable to plug them in. Unfortunately, that's not possible in this case."

"Can't you get on with this?" Simon muttered. "My head is killing me."

"Yes, of course." Aric leaned over Simon and typed something on the tablet that rested on his neck. "We'll know the process is finished when the computers beep loudly. Also, Simon's headache should go away. At least, it won't be as bad." He pointed to the tablet's screen. "Wheaten, please tap this once I'm situated, and the program should run."

The ship lurched to the right. Monica steadied herself as did the others in the cramped room.

Ten knelt beside Simon and poised her finger over the screen. "A storm is brewing. I noticed it earlier."

"Then we have to hurry." Aric lay on his stomach, then Monica rested the computer against his neck.

"Here goes." Ten tapped the tablet's screen.

A low whining noise emitted from the computers on the men's necks. Aric stiffened. His head turned to the side, and his cheek rested on the floor.

Monica tightened her grip on the computer. She couldn't let it slip now.

Aric's eyelids clenched tightly. His fingers twitched. Monica glanced from one man to the other. No one could stop the process now.

The computers flashed and emitted grinding sounds. Simon's hands clenched into fists, and his thin arms tensed. Monica tensed her own arms. How long could this go on?

Seconds ticked by, each feeling like an eternity as the two men lay twitching beneath the computers. The ship rolled to the right, then to the left. Monica battled each shift as she steadied Aric's computer. Sweat trickled down her forehead in spite of the cool musty air permeating the ship's quarters.

The creaking outside amplified, like wood ready to snap. Ten's breathing quickened. "I have to secure the lines and sails!"

"No! Not yet!" The ship tilted once more, but Monica held her ground. Her knees ached. Her toes cramped. As she shifted to a crouch, she sucked in a hissing breath. When would that beep come?

A moment later, a low beep sounded from both computers. Finally! She laid the computer on the floor. "Aric!" She pushed his shoulder and rolled him onto his side.

"I'm going up on deck." Ten balanced the tablet on Simon's neck and raced for the stairs. "Come up as soon as you can. I need help."

Monica managed a weak, "I will."

Aric's eyelids remained closed, though looser now, and his breathing stayed even, his voice silent.

As rain pattered on the planks above, Monica rose and whirled toward Simon. The elderly Seen lay on his stomach and groaned softly. He turned over, toppling the tablet to the floor. "That certainly took long enough. Knocked me out, too. I don't appreciate that one bit, you know."

"You're okay." Monica breathed a long sigh. "Do you feel any better? Is your headache gone?"

Simon sat up and frowned at Aric. "What happened to him? Exhausted from all that coding?" He shook his head and let out a tsking sound. "Young people just aren't built like they used to be. Of course, Nobles aren't very sturdy to begin with."

Monica put her hands on her hips while balancing against the constant rocking. "Aren't you going to answer me?"

Furrowing his brow, Simon stared ahead for a moment before nodding. "I feel like a new man. Even my heart seems to be behaving now, though I'm still a bit queasy from someone shocking me." He eyed Aric's motionless form. "So, I have his chip coding in my head."

"Yes." Monica raised her voice to compete with the pounding rain and whistling wind. "The computers would think you're a Noble now."

Simon rose to his feet. "A deserved promotion, I think."

"I'm sure you won't let it swell your head."

"Of course not. I am the humblest man on earth." Simon bent over Aric. "He's unconscious. Did he mention this as a possibility?"

She nodded. "It's some sort of protection code. We need his Key-Keeper to wake him." Again balancing against the rocking ship, she picked up the two computers along with Amelia's and set them in the satchel. "And according to him, my mother is one of those Keepers."

"Well, then we'll have to make sure she inputs this key, won't we?" Simon nudged Aric's limp arm. "In the meantime, you'll have to force a bit of food and water into him."

The ship rocked to the side. Simon fell backward onto a swinging hammock. Monica grabbed a rope to steady herself. "I have to help Ten. I've already waited too long."

"Oh, yes. The young ship maiden." His brow wrinkled. "What a strange name for a girl."

"Her real name is Wheaten. Maybe she'll help me lift Aric into a hammock."

"Go on, then. I am strong enough to keep him from rolling, that is, if you can keep this bucket of a ship from capsizing."

"Thank you, Simon." Monica slid the curtain across the entryway to the hammock room and ran up the stairs. When she walked out onto the deck, her feet slid on a slick portion of metal, but she quickly righted herself. Windswept rain splashed her face and arms, leaving wet trails across her skin that dripped to the deck.

"There you are!" Ten shouted from one of the rope ladders leading to the top of a mast. "We need to get the last sail in."

Balancing against the rolling motion, Monica inhaled a sharp breath of the salty, wet air. "I've never been in the rain before."

"Well, you're going to be in it for a long time now." Ten dropped to the deck with a splash and ran to her, apparently unaffected by the tossing ship. "I hope you're not afraid of heights."

"No, not afraid."

Ten helped Monica walk to the rope ladder. "You'll have to climb this."

Monica blinked through the veil of rain. The large canvas cloths snapped in the wind. The bottom half of the sail had come loose and flew freely. Only ropes at the top of the mast held it in place.

Ten looped an arm into one of the ladder's holes. "If I'm reading the signs correctly, this is going to be a bad storm. We have to bring the sails in now, or we could flounder." She stepped up two feet on the ladder. "We have to do it before the weather turns worse."

A huge wave splashed over the railing. The ship lurched, forcing Monica to grab the ladder. Water rolled over her now-frigid feet as she hung on. "Worse than this?"

"A lot worse." Clambering higher, Ten shouted, "Now come on!"

Monica climbed after Ten. The wind tugged at Monica's hair and clothing, trying to rip her from the ladder and toss her to the deck below. She clutched each section of rope and she forced herself to stay just a few feet behind Ten. Monica kept her gaze focused upward, blinking against the constant onslaught of rain. They climbed to the top of the rope ladder where it met a horizontal wooden post that held the large sail taut.

Ten gestured toward the flapping cloth, again shouting. "We have to get this rolled up and secured. I already released its lower ropes."

Monica brushed water from her eyes. The sail extended twenty to thirty feet wide. How were two girls their size supposed to get this done?

"Ready?" Ten sidled off the rope ladder onto a thin line running the length of the beam. Her bare feet gripped the braided fibers with ease, and she leaned over the post and reached forward, dragging the sail and drawing it up toward them. "You have the easy part!" The wind beat against the canvas, making her words sound choppy and far away. "You get to stay on the rigging. Just do as I do!"

Monica copied Ten's motions. The rain-slickened sail tried to evade her fingers, but she brought the coarse cloth up and tucked it into itself. With each tug on the sail, the wind whipped her hair into her face and eyes, and rain pounded her head as friction from the material gnawed at her vulnerable skin.

"Last one over here!" Ten tied a knot on a rope that kept the sail secured to the post, but the other half of the sail still flapped free.

Blood-tinged water trailed down Monica's wrists. Pain ripped through every nerve. The driving rain grew colder, drawing a hard shiver.

Ten slid her feet along the rope leading back to the rigging. "Now the other side!"

Viral Execution

"The other side?" Monica started down the rigging. Each rope rung of the ladder dug into her palms, but she kept going. If she looked at her hands, she might stop, and if she stopped …

"Come on!" Ten scrambled to the opposite side of the mast where another rope ladder led upward into the swirling gale.

Monica followed her up the rigging. Chills shook her arms, but she pressed on, climbing hand over hand. Just one step at a time. Soon the torture would be over and she could check on Aric and Simon. But she mustn't worry about them right now. The slightest distraction could send her flying into the raging waters. Then all would be lost.

CHAPTER ELEVEN

Wind battered Monica as she clung to the sail and hauled it up hand over hand. With every second, the canvas grew heavier, weighed down by rain and her own exhaustion.

A few feet to the right, Ten fought with another section of the sail. She shouted something, but the wind batted her words away.

Monica focused on Ten's lips, trying to read her commands, but driving rain swept between them and blurred every movement. Ten fastened a knot in a thin rope, latching her portion of the sail to the wooden beam she leaned against. She edged over to Monica. "There's a ship!"

Monica's fingers slipped as she tried to tie the final knot. She dared not look away. "Where?"

"Off our stern." Ten took the cord from Monica and finished the knot. "Let's get down before we get killed."

"Our stern?" Monica started the climb down. She shot a quick glance around, but dizziness forced her to focus on her descent.

When they were just a few feet from the deck, Ten jumped and landed on all fours. "Stern's the back end of the ship."

Monica dropped to the deck, still clinging to the rope ladder as she scanned the sea and the ship rode its heaving waves. "I don't see a ship."

"I got a glimpse. It's hard to see." Ten motioned toward the hatch. "Go below deck and stay with your friends. Get some rest."

Monica shivered. It would be nice to get out of this wind, but she couldn't leave Ten to work by herself. "Are you sure?"

"I'm sure." Ten shielded her eyes with a hand and stared over the stern. "If I'm right about who's on that ship, I'll have all the help I'll need very soon."

"Monica." A finger prodded her shoulder. She blinked and lifted her head. "What?"

Ten stood beside Monica's hammock—her hair and clothes now dry. "The storm's in a lull. It calmed down soon after you went below."

"I guess that's why I was able to sleep." Monica swung her feet to the floor. "What happened to that ship you saw?" She rubbed the grit from her eyes and suppressed a yawn.

"I never saw it again. Lost us in the storm, I guess." Ten sighed. "I was hoping it was the captain."

"It could still be him, couldn't it?" Monica glanced at the hammock beside her. Simon lay snoring in the canvas bed, and Aric rested on the floor nearby.

"Yes, it could be." Ten pulled a black garment from behind her. "I didn't have time to get this before, but here's a rain cloak for you. It's coated with something to keep the wool from absorbing water."

Monica drew the large, coarse garment onto her lap. Flecks of gray speckled the black fabric, including its hood. She held it out, and the hem dragged the ground. Without armholes, it seemed like an odd piece of clothing.

"It keeps us from freezing to death in the winter." Ten displayed an identical garment. "Everyone on the crew has one."

"Thank you." Monica stood and tucked her cloak into the hammock. "Do you think you could help me with a program now that the storm's calmer?"

"That depends on the kind of program." Ten looked over at Aric. "I'm not as good at programming as the captain, but I know some things."

"Just a second." Monica grabbed the satchel and withdrew Fox's chip and Aric's tablet. She held out the chip in an open palm. "This is Fox's. He used to be head of Cantral's security team, and he had a code that hid him from the computers."

Ten nodded. "Interesting."

Monica examined the chip more closely, staring at the dots and rivets that marked the metal surface. "Since Fox is dead, we can't ask him how he created the program, but if we can replicate it, we can put it onto Aric's and Simon's chips so they'll be hidden from Eursia's computers."

"I see. Then they can cross the control line without getting terminated." Ten turned on Aric's smaller computer and started typing in commands. She then plucked the chip from Monica's hand and placed it on top of the tablet. After a few moments it let out a low beep, and she handed Fox's chip back to Monica. "I think I got the code copied, but the chip's low on power. If I keep trying, it'll shut off completely."

Monica put the chip into the vial containing Amelia's and let it hang from her neck. "Aric said it was low. That's why we couldn't use it to clone to Simon's chip."

"Cloning does require a lot of energy." Ten frowned at the computer screen. "I won't know if I got everything I need until we look the code over."

Monica shook her head. The cloning program was her father's design, wasn't it? How could Ten know about it?

Ten adjusted to a cross-legged position. "A chip can't be cloned unless the person has been dead only a few minutes. Otherwise the power gets too low."

Monica nodded. That made sense, but … "And you know this, how? Cloning chips is banned technology, and supposedly no one ever really got it to work."

Grinning, Ten passed the computer to Monica. "But you just did it to Simon. Where did *you* get your cloning program?"

"My father." Monica looked down at the dozens of lines of codes streaming across the screen. None of it made any sense. "And my cousin."

"Then we have something in common." Ten tapped the computer. "There's some odd code in there that I don't recognize."

"Something in common?" Monica let the computer rest in her lap. "Who taught you about cloning?"

Ten sighed. "Maybe we should get our stories out in the open before we work on this code. It's still a few days to the border."

Monica handed the computer back to Ten. "Okay."

Ten turned the computer off and stowed it in the satchel. "You want to go first?"

"I guess so." Monica clasped her hands in her lap. "My father came up with the first cloning program I ever heard about. It had something to do with my mother." Closing her eyes for a second, she took a deep breath. It might take all day to tell the tale.

While Monica talked, Ten listened silently. Only the ship's gentle creaking and Simon's snoring interrupted the story's cadence.

Monica spoke of her escape from the Cillineese termination, her life as a wall slave in Cantral, and the fall of both cities' computers. As she remembered each loved one lost, tears came to her eyes, and her throat tightened, making her voice pitch higher at times. She told the story up to when she met the crowd near the docks in Cantral and saw the security guard get shot. "And you know the rest from there."

"Yeah, I guess I do …" Ten stared at her. "Some of your story sounds pretty unbelievable."

Monica slumped her shoulders. Her throat hurt, and tears threatened to fall. "But you've probably been through some unbelievable things, too, if you weren't originally a merchant."

"I said it *sounds* unbelievable." Ten sat up straighter. "But I do believe you. My story is similar, but without the tearing down of our government computers." She splayed her sun-browned, calloused hands. "No scars except rope burns and old splinter marks. Makes me feel like I've had a pretty easy life."

"I doubt that you have," Monica whispered. Her throat ached for water, but she stayed seated. "Now your story."

"The captain could tell it better than I. He's the one who saved me." Ten rose and headed for the stairs. "I need to go check on some things. The ship won't sail itself."

Monica scrambled to her feet. "You're not going to tell me?"

"I will." Ten jogged up the stairs, calling back, "Just not this minute."

Monica shook her head and crossed the room to where a bucket of water stood near the door, a dipper resting within. She couldn't force Ten to tell her anything, though she would probably open up soon.

Monica drank from the dipper. The water tasted stale, but at least it quenched her thirst. She turned back to the hammocks. Should she wake Simon? He seemed to have slept the entire time she had, and he still hadn't stirred. Was sleeping this long natural after going through such an ordeal?

She backed away. It was probably best that he sleep. She swirled her cloak around her shoulders and tied the black cord at her neck. Warmth encircled her arms and torso, though the fabric scratched her skin.

She climbed the stairs and stepped onto the cold, damp deck. Rain continued to patter softly, as if defying clouds in the distance that started to break apart, revealing blue-tinted sky.

A loose sail flapped in the wind. Ten struggled with a rope attached to a corner of the canvas, pulling it toward a beam of wood connected to the mast.

Monica grabbed part of the rope and helped Ten guide the sail's corner to the beam and tie it in place.

"Thanks." Ten fiddled with a piece of metal near the knot. "Some of the sails came loose during the storm. We couldn't secure them tightly by ourselves, but it worked well enough." She stepped away from the rope. "We weren't driven far off course."

"That's good." Monica played with the tie of her cloak.

"Yeah." Ten jogged to the other side of the sail and began securing it. "I just hope the captain catches up soon. I don't know the docking codes, and we'll be in trouble if we arrive without them. Fox's code won't hide a ship from the port authorities."

Monica helped Ten with the sail. "Maybe your captain kept the codes hidden somewhere." She tugged on the rope, tightening the knot. "He kept other valuable information on board. Those crew profiles could have gotten you all killed."

"It's not the same." Ten's face flushed. "And besides, that information was safe. That room was rigged to blow if we saw any sign of trouble."

"Blow?"

"Explode. Gunpowder kegs in strategic places." Ten ambled to the room where she had retrieved the files. "That reminds me ..." She drew a key on a chain from under her collar and inserted the key into the door's lock. "The codes change with every docking. I don't think he would write them down, and he doesn't tell me. They're too valuable to trust to a fourteen-year-old."

"I really wouldn't know."

Ten opened the door and hid the key back under her shirt. "No fault of yours, since you were a wall slave most of your life." When they entered, Ten closed the door behind them. "We have complicated rules and regulations. I don't even know them all."

Ten crossed the room in two steps and stood in front of a rolltop desk. "No merchant needs to. Merchant is a classification for our caste, but ..." She pushed the desk open and punched some raised buttons on top. "There are hundreds of jobs and titles inside the class of 'merchant.' "

A rumbling filled the room. A pipe, large enough for a person to fit inside, protruded from the floor and inched higher and higher every second. Another hole opened in the ceiling, revealing the swirling clouds. The top of the pipe fit through the opening and blocked the view once again.

More shudders ran through the floor, vibrating Monica's feet. A hissing noise raced up the pipe. She backed toward the door. "What's that?"

Ten tapped a knuckle against the metal. "Steam port. I started the engine again. It shut down during the storm for safety. Fortunately, it was still primed." She pulled open a drawer and rummaged through it. "We need to leave the room soon, though. It gets hot in here pretty quickly."

After a few minutes of searching, Ten slammed a drawer shut and shook her head. "Can't find the codes. Just old inventory and shipment logs." She tugged on the end of her braid. "It could be in his tablet, but he has it on hand or hidden at all times. Not in here, though. It gets too hot for a computer."

Ten opened the door, letting in a cooling breeze. "Let's go."

After they exited to the frigid deck outside, Ten locked the door behind them. "I guess I don't have to lock this anymore, now that I disposed of the crew's files, but it's a habit."

"Speaking of the crew's files …" Monica looked down. Should she bring it up again? What was the harm? Ten could just not answer. "When will you tell me more about them? The stolen identities. I still don't understand how you know about the cloning program that my father supposedly invented."

Ten's mouth formed a tight line, but she nodded. "We can talk while we search for the captain's tablet."

CHAPTER TWELVE

Ten led Monica into a cramped room beside the engine area. "These are the captain's quarters. He sleeps near the engine room so he can access it quickly if there are any problems." She lifted a thin mattress from a narrow cot and pulled it from the metal frame. "So you really want to know why the captain saves people from the fields?"

"Yes, of course." Monica ran a hand over the top of a desk. The legs swayed, and she jerked her hand back. "I've been fighting for people's freedom my entire life, thinking that the slaves and I were alone in the cause. We never considered people outside our walls even knew about us. I want to know everything about the captain's work."

While they continued searching, Ten told her story. At one time, the captain was a Noble. He and his brother Drehl went to Cantral to study, focusing on computer programming. While there, Drehl met a Seen girl named Katrina and got her pregnant. The captain was furious with Drehl, but Drehl said he would marry Katrina, a promise he wouldn't keep since the children of a slave mother automatically become slaves themselves.

Drehl's father arranged for Katrina to be demoted to the fields. Drehl then left the Noble caste and became a merchant of agriculture so he could look for her. After just six months at sea, he disappeared somewhere near Penniak. Although the captain also left the Noble caste and often searched for Drehl, all he ever found was this discarded and damaged ship, named after the woman Drehl apparently never located.

While repairing the *Katrina*, the captain discovered Drehl's notes about a computer program that disguises and clones chips, which led the captain to discover Drehl's attempts to rescue field slaves.

When Ten finished the story, she shrugged. "That's about it. The captain used what he learned to continue the rescues."

Monica inhaled a cleansing breath. "How long ago did all of this happen?"

"Almost fourteen years."

Monica let out a low whistle. Fourteen years! It had been twelve years since her father had died, twelve years since that fateful day the toxic gas snuffed out his life and ended his research on cloning. "That's a long time."

Ten squared her shoulders. "And the captain has made good use of it. He has saved two hundred slaves, including getting them jobs on other ships, but …" Her shoulders sagged. "The biggest problem is that if people keep disappearing from the fields whenever we come into port, we will be found out."

"True," Monica said. "What do you do?"

"We find some citizen who just died and whose chip number hasn't been catalogued yet. We give the chip a jolt of energy to recharge it and then reprogram it. If not for that need, we could save a lot more people." Ten sighed. "The captain made me a permanent crew member and let me in on some of his secrets. Just a few days ago, we had heard about someone's imminent death, so I went on a scouting mission to find him. Then the mobs broke out, and the riots came next. I barely got away with my life."

"The riots ruined your operation, but maybe now the slaves are freeing themselves. The computers can't stop them."

"Maybe." Ten brushed a foot against the lighter-colored wood floor where the trunk had stood. "This is interesting." She knelt and pried up a loose floorboard, revealing a small hole beneath.

She reached in and pulled out a palm-sized watch, a small book, and a handful of coins. "Maybe the codes will be in this book."

Monica crouched beside Ten. She had said she was fourteen years old, the same number of years since her story began. Monica whispered, "The captain found Katrina, didn't he? The girl, I mean."

"Yes, but not until after Drehl had been declared dead." Her cheeks flushing, Ten flipped through a few wrinkled pages of the book. "There's not much in here, just expired codes and numbers and logs."

Monica half closed an eye. "You're Katrina's child, then, aren't you? That makes you the captain's niece. That's why you're a permanent crew member."

"I thought you'd put it all together." Ten turned a few more pages and shook her head. "According to my chip and our logs, I'm here as an apprentice. I'm another merchant's child." She closed the book and settled it back into the hole. "There's nothing in here. He must have switched to using a computer when Shal got him the tablet."

"How did Katrina survive the fields?"

Ten shrugged. "She was stubborn, I guess. The captain found her just days after I was born. Since there's no medical attention given to any of the workers, if he hadn't found us, we both likely would have died in a few days. He was only able to get me out. She had to stay behind."

"But he never stopped trying to rescue her, right?"

Tears glittered in Ten's eyes. "He finally stopped a year later when word of her death came."

Monica let her head droop. "I'm so sorry."

"It's the way of slaves. You of all people should know that." Ten brushed a tear away. "Sometimes I wonder what it would have been like if I had been born a Seen." She fingered the small gold watch before putting it back in the hole with the book. "I've never even been inside a palace, but I sometimes imagine what it's like. It helps pass the long hours when I'm on night duty."

"The palaces are beautiful. There's no denying it."

"I'll just have to keep imagining." Ten laid the coins back into the hole and pushed the board back in place over it. "I'm not a Seen or a Noble. That will never change."

Monica shook her head. Ten's feelings about a different life were all too familiar, imagining how it could have been. If her own parents had chosen differently, where would she be now? Had they ever imagined that she would succeed, that she would actually fulfill their dreams?

"Let's check the storage room now." Ten rose and walked out of the quarters.

Monica followed but paused by the door and glanced around at the captain's belongings, most of them dark, rough, and leathery, symbols of his apparent strength and endurance. He had been rescuing slaves all this time and even had a cloning program, maybe before her father had his. Who could have imagined that there were others out there trying to do the same work? Trapped in the walls of Cantral, it was easy to forget anyone outside the palace existed, at least anyone who cared about the suffering of those in bondage.

She nodded firmly. But they did exist. This rescuing mission included good, strong people from all classes, not just a wall slave who didn't have a chip. As if guided by a greater power, they all had done their parts and were now coming together to complete their common cause. And this wall slave, though battered and bleeding, would march with them no matter what.

CHAPTER
THIRTEEN

Ten opened the door down the hall from Fahltrid's cabin. Stacks of objects unidentifiable in the dim lighting lined the room, and a ladder near the middle led up to a closed hatch.

When she yanked on a cord by the ladder, a string of lights flickered on, illuming three support beams from where the lights hung. "This is where I sleep, along with any other female crew members. The captain might have kept the tablet here, but it's a long shot."

Monica blinked as she adjusted to the new light. Wooden and metal crates of all sizes, some strapped to the support beams and others bolted to the floor, were piled all around.

Ten crossed the room in three strides and stood over two thin mats rolled out in the floor's center. "We'd better get started."

"Right." Monica's mind whirled with all the new information —former slaves now merchants and Nobles who renounced their positions, risking their lives for a seemingly hopeless cause, just as she and other Seen and wall slaves had.

"You're rather deep in thought." Ten shoved a crate to the side. "It's a lot to take in, I guess." She moved a box out of the way and tapped on the wall behind it. "Just don't feel sorry for me, okay? This is my life, and what could have happened won't change it, and that's all there is to say about the matter."

After an hour of moving crates and sacks, Ten sat on one of the boxes and rested her chin on a hand. "I don't know where else to look."

Monica sat on a crate across from Ten. "Then we can work on Fox's code now?"

"I suppose we'd better." Ten rose from her seat and clambered up the ladder.

When Ten and Monica emerged onto the deck, Ten slid the hatch cover back into place. They crossed to the other hatch and descended the stairs to the hammock room. Simon still slept, and Aric lay motionless on the floor, his chest moving up and down in a steady rhythm.

When Monica walked closer, a floorboard creaked under her foot.

Simon snorted and sat up. "What? Who's there?"

"It's just us, Simon." Monica stepped over Aric's body and laid a hand on Simon's shoulder. "Ten and I are going to work on Fox's program now."

"Excellent." Simon lay down again. "Get to work, then, and wake me when you're done." He closed his eyes and sighed heavily. "Dying seems to have worn me out."

Monica and Ten settled on the floor across from each other. Ten retrieved Aric's computer from the satchel, set it on her lap, and began entering commands with the tips of her fingers.

Monica hugged her knees to her chest. "Is there anything I can do?"

Ten shrugged her thin shoulders. "Just give me a few minutes."

Monica rested her chin on her knees. While Ten worked, the ship creaked all around, adding to the somber mood. Aric's steady breathing meant that he still lived, but how long would he last?

Ten's fingers danced across the tablet screen. She said nothing, just sighed in exasperation now and then.

Minutes turned into hours. Monica's limbs hurt from being still for so long. Ten hadn't asked her to do anything, not even take a quick look at the sails. The ship seemed to be sailing itself, and there wasn't anywhere else to go.

After a few more moments, Ten set the tablet down and rubbed her eyes. "This is taking longer than I thought it would."

Monica nodded. "I guessed as much. Fox would make his coding difficult to understand."

"Difficult is putting it lightly." Ten rose and stretched. "I need to check on the engine." She patted her stomach. "And find something to eat. Are you hungry?"

"Yes." Sighing, Monica stood. "Maybe I could work on the program while you're gone. I don't know much about computers, but I might be able to help."

"We're still at least three days out from the computer control line." Ten nudged a tablet with a toe. "We have plenty of time." She headed for the stairs. "Come on. We'll bring something for Simon to eat, too."

As Ten led the way, Monica followed. They worked their way to a small kitchen complete with stove and sink on one side of the room. Sacks of supplies stood on the other.

They quickly ate meal bars and took one back to Simon. With Ten's help, Monica managed to get Aric to take a few sips of water, though he remained unconscious even as he swallowed.

The hours passed with Ten and Monica both leaning over the tablet. Ten gave Monica a rudimentary lesson on computer programming so she could help figure out Fox's code. When evening came, Ten set a lantern on deck in hopes that Fahltrid would see it if he happened to be following in the ship she had spotted earlier.

Monica and Ten took turns sleeping, keeping watch, and poring over the tablet. Simon rested peacefully in his hammock while Aric lay on the floor. Earlier, Ten and Monica's efforts to lift him into one of the hanging beds had failed.

Another day passed much the same as the first, and they didn't seem any closer to cracking Fox's code. The ship sailed along smooth waters, needing only a little assistance from Ten to keep it on course.

On the fourth day at sea, Monica sat on deck with Aric's tablet in her lap, shielding the screen with a hand to ward off the glare from the afternoon sun. "Ten?"

Ten looked up from where she sat nearby mending a tear in a small sail. "Made any progress?"

"I think so." Monica squinted at the screen. "I've isolated the code that seems to be the disguise sequence, but I guess we can't be sure until we put it on a chip and try it."

Ten jabbed her large sewing needle into the sail and scurried over. "Great. Let me double-check your work." She took the tablet and used a finger to scroll through the code.

Monica furrowed her brow. It had seemed correct, but it was safer to make sure.

Nodding, Ten tucked the computer under her arm. "It looks fine. Good job." She offered a hand up to Monica. "Let's go try it on Simon, if he's willing. We're traveling faster than I first estimated, so the sooner their chips are hidden, the better."

Monica took Ten's hand and jumped to her feet. "How soon do you think we'll get to the control line?"

"Tomorrow afternoon." Ten led the way down the stairs to the hammock room. "And we may even see the Eursian coast in two days if we keep up this speed."

As they descended the stairway, darkness enveloped them. Ten pushed the curtain aside, letting light filter into the room. The small green lanterns hanging from the support beams flickered listlessly, their chemical lights almost worn out after three days of constant use.

Ten held the computer at arm's length, letting its glow shine across the room's patchwork metal-and-board floor.

Monica hurried to where Simon slept. "Simon?" Laying a hand on his shoulder, she called again, "Simon! We think we have the code ready."

Viral Execution

His eyelids fluttered open. "Ready for what?"

"For copying code to your chip," Ten said as she stepped over Aric's unconscious form. "Then you should be hidden from the Eursian computers. After that, we can copy it to Aric's chip, and you'll both be safe."

"Yes, yes, I know all that." Simon swung his feet over the side of the hammock and let them rest on the floor. His hair stood on end, and redness rimmed his eyes despite the many hours he had slept. "But I have Aric's chip coding now, so won't the program knock me out like it did to him?"

"No," Monica said. "Aric said his code expired, since the day before yesterday was his birthday."

"Then why is he still asleep?" Simon pointed a bony finger at her. "Answer me that. You're not experimenting on me until you're certain this program works." He raised an eyebrow. "Ten should try it. She's younger than I, less at risk of complications."

Ten held up her hands in a defensive gesture. "My chip is permitted to travel, so it doesn't need to be hidden." She looked at Monica. "Don't tell me we did all that work for nothing."

Monica sighed. "Simon's being his usual stubborn self."

Simon wagged his finger at her. "You would be stubborn too if it was your chip on the line. Of course, you don't have a chip, but my point is still valid."

Ten picked up Aric's second computer from the floor and withdrew Amelia's tablet from the satchel. "While you two argue, I'll make copies of this program in case anything happens." She snapped the computers together at their connection points.

Monica pursed her lips. How to get Simon to comply? "Simon, if you don't do this, then the Eursian computers will kill you. Don't you realize that?"

"Yes, I certainly do." Simon wrinkled his nose. "But I'm not so certain I want some amateurs meddling with my chip, not after what I've been through."

Amanda L. Davis

"It's either that or death, Simon, and death is not an option I'm willing to choose." Monica crossed her arms and tried to stare him down, but he wouldn't meet her gaze.

Heaving a long sigh, Simon shrugged. "All right. All right. I suppose facing death one more time this week won't hurt." He lay down again and waved a hand. "Very well. Proceed, but if you do manage to kill me, I will come back as a ghost and haunt you for the rest of your days, which likely won't be many since you would have no intelligent life remaining on this ship."

Monica smiled. "You're too stubborn to die just yet."

"I think we're ready to go." Ten detached the computers and lifted one of the tablets. "Turn onto your stomach please, Simon."

Sighing again, Simon rolled onto his stomach, making his hammock sway. Monica steadied it with a hand.

Ten selected something on the tablet screen and pressed the computer's edge to Simon's neck. "Here it goes."

A moment passed, and Simon twitched. "I felt something."

The tablet popped and sizzled. Simon's head jerked to the side, and a shudder ran through his body. Ten jerked the tablet away and let it clatter to the floor.

Monica bit back a squeak. "Simon!"

He lay motionless.

Ten pressed a finger against his neck. After a few seconds, she exhaled. "He'll be all right, I think." She opened her hands, exposing her palms. Angry red marks marred the skin in the center. "The tablet short-circuited. Shocked us both. I think it didn't have a large enough power supply to run the program properly."

Monica winced. "Those burns look nasty."

"I'm fine." Ten furrowed her brow. "But I don't know why he's unconscious."

"Do you think Aric's protection program activated?" Monica whispered.

"I don't know." Ten picked up Aric's computer from the floor and pressed it to Simon's neck before tapping a few buttons. The computer beeped once and flashed a yellow light. "I'm not getting any reading."

"Get that thing off me." Simon's eyes opened, and he reached back and batted at the computer. "That was a terrible jolt. Of all the possible outcomes, I did not expect that one."

"You're okay!" The temptation to hug him swept through Monica, but she held it in. He probably wouldn't respond well to that.

Ten backed up a step, holding the computer close. "Is it all right if I try to read your chip again?"

Simon sat up and swung his feet to the ground. "Very well. As long as I don't get shocked."

"No worries about that." Ten pressed the computer to the back of his neck. When the computer buzzed and the yellow light flashed on, she pulled the computer away. "No reading."

Monica let out a long sigh. "It worked."

"Good. I'm never letting anyone run any programs on my chip again. I went sixty-five years without it having problems, and now you've meddled with it twice in one week." Rubbing the back of his neck, Simon scowled. "And both times it has given me a horrendous headache."

Ten picked up the tablet computer from the floor and drew it close to her face. "This is shot. Circuits are completely fried. We'll have to use the same code on Aric, but we'll need more power somehow."

Monica knelt and rolled Aric onto his stomach. His nose pressed against the floorboards, but he made no noise. "Do you have any ideas?"

"Not without hooking it directly to the ship's communications battery, and that would probably lead to even more problems. Too much electricity could fry his brain."

Monica pushed away the short hairs at the back of Aric's neck, revealing the small scar from his chip insertion. "How close are we to the computer control line?"

"I would have to check. Why?"

Monica rolled Aric onto his back again. "If that ship you saw was Fahltrid's, maybe we can wait for him to catch up and help us. You said he was good with computers."

"He is, but …" Ten laid the fried computer on the floor. "I suppose you're right. There's no use risking Aric's life before it's necessary."

"Of course not." Simon sniffed and lay back in his hammock. "Now go find out where we are."

"All right, but it might take awhile." Ten started up the stairs. "You can stay here, Monica. I don't need help."

Simon closed his eyes and in moments started snoring.

Monica curled her knees to her chest and recalled Ten's recent lessons about how the charts worked. The various instruments and calculations were as confusing as the computer programs. The ship had a navigational computer, but it worked only half the time, so all the crew had to be well versed in charting a course on a physical map.

Twenty minutes later Ten galloped back down the stairs. "We're about three hours from the control line. I keep underestimating how fast we're going."

Simon snorted and sat up. "Three hours?"

Ten nodded. "And there's another storm coming. I think it's going to be worse than the last. We need to start preparing now, before we take care of Aric's chip."

Monica rose to her feet and ran behind Ten up the stairs. A storm even worse than the last? How could they possibly manage the ship on their own?

CHAPTER FOURTEEN

The first drops of rain began to fall as Monica finished tying off the last rope to restrain the sails. She scrambled down the rigging and met Ten on the deck. "All set, I think."

"Good." Ten wiped at some grease on her arm, but it just smeared across her skin. "I shut the engine down for now. It'll give us more time to work on Aric's chip. We're only an hour from the border."

"Then let's go!"

"I need to do one last thing." Ten picked up a small lantern from the deck and shook it. A bright green glow emanated from the holes in the metal sides. "A signal. So the captain can see us." She clambered a few feet up the rigging and secured the lamp to one of the rope rungs. As it swayed in the strengthening breeze, it cast an undulating glow on the deck.

After climbing down the ropes again, Ten ran to Monica. "Ready."

They scrambled down the stairs into the darkness of the hammock room. "Simon?" Monica called.

Soft breathing sounded. Ten followed close behind. "Still sleeping?"

"I think so. He hasn't done much else for three days." She crept up to the hammock where he usually lay. The outline of Aric's motionless form on the floor was barely visible in the dim glow from the waning lanterns. "Simon?"

He sat up in his hammock. "You're finally back?"

"We're an hour from the line." Aggravation laced Ten's voice as she jerked the satchel open to pull out the computers. "And a storm's coming. A bad one. We had to prepare."

Monica helped Ten with the satchel and took Aric's small computer. "We have to try to hide Aric's chip now, even if it's dangerous."

Sighing, Simon nodded. "Of course. Carry on with it then, but don't be surprised if he doesn't survive."

A lump formed in Monica's throat, and her gaze drifted to the first-aid bag. "Ten, could you get the defibrillator ready? Just in case."

"Sure." Ten opened the bag and drew out the box and paddles.

While Ten worked on preparing the defibrillator, Monica switched on Aric's computer and pulled up the program she and Ten had worked on for so many hours. The lines of code on the screen were understandable almost at first glance now—streams of letters and numbers that had made no sense before Ten's many patient lessons.

Monica turned Aric onto his stomach. "If something happens to him, we'll have to be ready to flip him back over."

"Don't worry. He'll be fine." Ten set the defibrillator to the side and bit her lip. "I hope."

Monica set the computer's edge against the scar at the back of Aric's neck. "Here it goes." She pressed the Run option on the screen.

For a few moments, nothing happened. Then a short buzz sounded, and the smell of burning plastic issued from the computer. Heat pulsed through Monica's hands, but it didn't burn.

A soft groan came from Aric's motionless form.

Ten grabbed the defibrillator, but Monica waved her away. "I don't think we need it." After a few seconds of silence, Monica breathed a long sigh. "Let's try to get a reading with my cousin's tablet."

Ten picked it up and turned it on. "Does it have a chip reader?"

Nodding, Monica took the tablet, brought up the reader program, and held the edge to Aric's neck.

The computer beeped once, and Aric's chip number appeared on the screen. Monica shook her head. "It didn't work."

Ten's shoulders drooped. "Then should we try again?"

"Not unless you know how to get around a protection code." Monica set Amelia's tablet on the floor and turned Aric onto his back. "What good would it do?"

Ten crawled to her feet. "No worse than just waiting for him to die when we cross the border."

"That's true, but …" Monica brushed hair back from Aric's forehead. Ten was right. They couldn't just give up. "But it doesn't make sense to keep trying something that failed."

"The very definition of insanity," Simon muttered. "But miracles do happen." He lay back down in his hammock. "Knowing your experience with overcoming impossible situations, I wouldn't doubt you're being watched over by a miracle worker."

The sound of rain broke overhead, pounding against the ceiling.

Ten exhaled long and loud. "Here it comes."

Monica stared at Aric's closed eyes and listened to his breathing. Simon was right. So many of the situations she had escaped from had been supposedly impossible. She should be dead many times over, but here she was, alive and well and continuing her mission.

Looking up at the ceiling, she sighed. *Please let the program work. Let us save Aric.*

The ship swayed to one side. A crash sounded overhead. Monica flinched.

Ten ran for the stairs. "I have to check out that noise. I'll be right back."

The wind howled, making the ship creak and shudder. Simon clutched the sides of his swinging hammock. "She wasn't joking about that storm!"

Monica grabbed Amelia's tablet. Was it the only computer they had left? They had never found the captain's. She jumped to her feet. The navigation computer! "I'll be right back." She darted after Ten and dashed up the stairs two at a time.

Wind and rain ripped by the open hatch. Water splashed into the stairwell. Ten struggled with the hatch's wood cover, ready to close it from the deck level.

"What are you doing?" Ten's words sounded faint, though she appeared to be shouting. "What about Aric?"

Monica tucked Amelia's tablet under her bodice, climbed out onto the main deck, and stood next to Ten. She grabbed the other side of the hatch and helped Ten drag it into place. She grasped Ten's arm and spoke directly into her ear. "Can we use the ship's computer on Aric? That will give us more power."

Ten put a hand to her eyes, shielding them from the driving rain. "It might kill him!"

"He'll die if we don't!" Rain plastered Monica's hair to her head and her clothing to her skin. She wrapped her arms over her chest, trying to protect Amelia's computer from the wet onslaught.

"Fine! We'll set it up, then go get him." Ten pulled Monica toward the wall where the navigation computer was hidden. She yanked open the door to the file room, pushed Monica inside, and slammed the door behind them, dampening the noise from the storm.

The engine's steam pipe still protruded from the lower deck and into the ceiling. Heat emanated from the metal, warming Monica's frigid skin and calming her shivers. "If we have enough power, we might be able to reset his chip. Trick it to take him out of the lockdown."

"We have enough power. Like I said, enough to kill him."

Monica yanked Amelia's computer from under her shirt and held it close to the warmth. Water droplets beaded on the glass screen. As she wiped them off, she murmured, "Can you access the computer from in here? Or do we have to go back out?"

Viral Execution

"We can access it here." Ten scooted to the wall farthest away from the engine pipe and flicked open a latch. A large panel about two inches thick swung open, revealing wires and blinking lights. Ten reached inside and pulled a bundle of five wires from the back. She held a hand out to Monica. "The tablet. We're running out of time. We still have to get Aric up here once I get the programs copied over."

Monica gave her the computer. "I'll go get him. I might be able to drag him to the base of the stairs at least."

"Right." Ten popped the back off of Amelia's tablet and tinkered with the wiring. "Get Simon to help."

"If he will." Monica shoved open the door. Wind tried to rip the knob from her hand, but she held it tightly and forced the door closed again. Rain buffeted her from all sides. As she ran for the hatch, something rolled across the deck and hit her feet.

She snatched it up. Bent metal caught on her hands, leaving behind a glowing green residue. The lantern Ten had hung? A faint glow still pulsed through the holes in the metal, but dimly. She set it down and forced the hatch open. The lantern falling must have been the crash they had heard earlier.

The hatch slid open more easily this time, and she ran down the stairs. "Simon! I need your help!"

"Again with needing my help?" Simon stood next to his hammock, holding one of the lanterns. "I was just wondering if you two had gotten swept overboard."

"I need help getting Aric to the main deck." She threw the strap of the first-aid satchel over her head and secured the bag at her hip. "We're going to try to write Fox's program onto Aric's chip using the navigation computer." She tucked her hands under Aric's arms. "But first we have to get him there."

Simon sniffed. "As if my heart is strong enough to carry a man of his size. I did just die, you know."

"You've been sleeping for three days." Monica gritted her teeth and pulled. Aric slid forward an inch. She tugged again, her muscles burning. He moved a little farther.

"Three days is hardly enough time for recovery." Simon bent over and picked up Aric's feet, but his efforts made no difference.

Water cascaded down the stairs and trickled over their feet, wetting Aric's clothes. Monica let go for a moment and tossed the satchel containing her mother's diary onto one of the hammocks, out of the water's reach.

"I saw the ship!" Ten's shout sounded distant.

Monica grabbed Aric's arms again. "Great!" The water helped Aric slide a little easier, but every foot of progress was a struggle. "I need help!"

Footsteps pounded down the stairs. Seconds later, Ten's hands joined Monica's, and together they dragged Aric to the base of the stairway.

Frigid water pouring down the steps made Monica's feet cramp, but she and Ten kept going, dragging Aric up one stair at a time. Her injured hands screamed at her to stop, to let go, but she kept hold of Aric's arms. "The lantern fell. The ship won't be able to see us."

"I know." Ten grunted with each pull. "It's too dangerous to hang it up again."

They emerged at the top of the stairs and laid Aric flat on the rain-swept deck. Bracing against the rocking ship, Ten forced the hatch closed behind them while Monica kept Aric from rolling.

Ten and Monica dragged him into the warm file room. The ship pitched to one side, throwing Monica against the door. It swung open, and she tumbled headlong into the rain. She slid across the deck and slammed into the railing.

She scrambled to her feet, staggered back, and caught hold of the knob. When she dragged herself back into the room, she slammed the door and shoved the latch into place. Gasping for breath, she brushed water from her eyes. "That was close! I nearly fell overboard!"

"I saw." Ten stood holding a rope and a circular tube that looked like a doughnut. "I was about to come after you."

"Thanks." Monica shook water from her hands. "Any idea how much time we have?"

"Just soon is all I know." Ten laid the rope and tube down and knelt next to Aric. Water ran down her cheeks, dripping from her hair and eyelashes. "I can't see the control line's warning buoys in the storm, so even when we get close, there's only one way to tell." She wiped a hand across her forehead. "I'll feel a tingle in my chip when we cross, but by that time, it'll be too late for Aric."

CHAPTER FIFTEEN

Ten picked up Amelia's tablet from beside the computer access panel and tugged away wires protruding at the back. "I have the program copied over now, so we'll just be using the ship's computer." She withdrew a small screen from somewhere inside the panel. Green numbers and letters flitted across the black screen in quick succession. "It has limited power because of all the problems we've been having with it, but in our case, that's a good thing. We don't want to fry Aric's brain."

Monica hugged herself. Shivers ran up and down her entire body despite the warmth from the engine's pipe. "That little thing has a chip reader?"

"No, but it can send signals." Ten opened the back of the screen and pulled out two wires. "This is riskier than using Amelia's tablet. Are you sure you don't want to give that another try?"

Monica pushed Aric's hair away from his chip scar. "I'm sure. All it would do is ruin the tablet. We already know it doesn't have enough power. This is the only option we have left."

"Right." Ten pressed the two wires against Aric's skin. "This will send a shock through him, so don't touch him, okay?"

The ship swayed suddenly, making them lurch to the side. Monica steadied herself and nodded. "Go ahead."

Ten held the wires by their protective rubber coating with one hand and typed with the other. "Here it goes."

Short sparks flashed from the wires. Aric's head jerked up and to the side.

Ten yanked the wires away and turned off the computer. "Roll him over!"

Monica pushed Aric onto his back.

His eyes stared up at the ceiling, wide and twitching. His head jerked from one side to the other, and saliva oozed at the corner of his mouth.

Monica gulped. "What do we do?"

Ten pulled one of Aric's shoes off and then his sock. "I think he might be seizing." She pried open his mouth. "Have to keep him from biting his tongue." She stuffed the sock into his mouth. His eyes rolled up until only the whites showed.

Monica clenched her hands into fists. "Can I do anything to help?"

"Not really." Ten sat back on her heels and shrugged. "He just has to get through it himself."

As Aric's arms and legs twitched, tears rolled down Monica's cheeks. She wiped them away and whispered, "Come on, Aric!"

The ship jerked to one side and then the other. Monica threw a hand out and caught herself against a wall.

Aric rolled across the floor, but Ten grabbed his arm and stopped him.

Something crashed outside, making the ship shudder. Monica scrambled to her feet and caught hold of the desk to steady herself. "What was that?"

The crash came again. The ship moaned above the howling of the wind. The noise sounded a third time and a fourth before starting a rhythmic thumping. Monica laid a hand on the wall and felt the pulses through the wooden boards.

"Cut it away!" The shout sounded muffled, but it was definitely male.

Ten released Aric. "The captain!" She jumped to her feet and grabbed the doorknob.

"I said, cut it!" the voice called again. The thumping stopped.

Ten glanced from Aric to the door. "The captain might need me. It's hard to come alongside another ship to board, let alone in the middle of a storm."

Aric's back arched, and he groaned.

Monica knelt beside him and yanked open the first-aid satchel. "What do I do?"

"I don't know." Ten rushed over and pulled the sock from Aric's mouth. "I thought it might be a seizure, but I don't know. I'm not a doctor. I was just going by what I've seen before. The captain used to—" She slapped a hand to her head and closed her eyes, wincing.

A burning pain seared Monica's chest. Gasping, she tore at her necklaces, ripping Amelia's chip away from her skin. Sparks flew inside the vial. Heat emanated from the glass. She threw it across the room, and it bounced off the wall.

Aric lay silent, his breathing almost imperceptible.

Dizziness washed over her. Laying a hand to her chest, she wished the burning sensation away, but it clung to her skin, feeling as though it drilled deeper with each second. "The control line?" The words came out ragged.

"Yes. That chip didn't have authorization, so it terminated." Ten touched Monica's shoulder. "Are you all right?"

"I think so." Monica blinked back tears. "Did the program work?"

"If it didn't, he would be dead." Ten waved a hand over Aric's mouth. "He's breathing."

Monica picked up the vial, then untied Alyssa's medallion necklace and slid them both into her pocket. Her chest hurt where the chip had burned her skin, and wearing the necklaces would only make it worse.

Ten stuffed the computer parts back into the compartment and closed the access door. "You know, I don't think this power boost should have worked on Aric, but"—she flipped the latch to secure the door in place—"I guess we should be glad it did."

Monica closed her eyes for a moment, trying to quell the pain. Maybe she *was* being looked after by a miracle worker.

"Wheaten!" The hoarse cry sounded somewhere close, but the wind and rain muffled it again.

"Oh!" Ten jumped and opened the door. The wind jerked it from her hand and banged it against the side of the room. "Captain!" Ten dashed out, and a suction slammed the door behind her.

Monica knelt beside Aric again. Had the seizure done permanent damage? She had seen a slave fall victim to one but never heard it called by that name. A small boy in one of her old dorms had the attacks so often that he couldn't work, and he was terminated.

She touched Aric's shoulder. "Can you hear me?"

His respiration continued at an even pace, though it grew stronger with each breath. She withdrew her hand. He was alive. Nothing else mattered. Even if the lockdown was still in effect, at least they had made it across the border. Now they just needed the KeyKeeper's code from her mother.

"I'll be right back." Monica opened the door and braced herself. Inhaling deeply, she stepped out into the cold rain and closed the door securely behind her. "Ten?" The wind swept the word away so quickly it barely reached her own ears.

A new lantern hung from the rigging, swaying and casting a dim circular glow on the deck. Water washed over the ship's rail and tugged at Monica's feet, urging her to come closer to the edge.

She grabbed hold of the rope rigging. "Ten!" Shielding her eyes with a hand, she glanced around. The deck seemed deserted. Had Ten gone below? The ship pitched to the side, trying to tug her from her spot. "Ten!"

Monica inched her way to the hatch leading down to the hammock room. The ship's swaying threatened to knock her feet out from under her, and each new splash seemed bigger than the last.

A strong hand gripped her upper arm. Gasping, she whirled around.

A large man with black hair held her arm in an iron grip. The green lantern light cast a sickly glow across his skin. "You should be below decks!"

She jerked her arm away. "Let me go!"

He stepped back and held his hands up. "Suit yourself. I'm just trying to help."

"Monica!" Ten appeared at her side. "Come back to the file room for a minute."

As Monica staggered after Ten, wind battered every step, making her feet slide on the wet deck. Now it felt stupid to refuse the man's help. He was probably one of the captain's crew.

Ten opened the door and pushed Monica in. The wind slammed the door behind them, almost catching Ten's hand as she reached for the knob.

Another large man knelt beside Aric's motionless body. Water dripped from his curly black hair and landed on Aric's already wet clothes.

"Captain, I found her." Ten hugged herself, swaying back and forth as if trying to get warm.

Shivers ran up and down Monica's spine. "How did you sneak past me? I didn't see you on deck."

Fahltrid laid a calloused finger on Aric's neck. "Storms can cause confusion. We did not sneak." He held Amelia's tablet in one hand. Its screen glowed a bright blue, and some text flashed across it. "You're correct, Wheaten. It appears the code is in place, though his lockdown is still active." He held the tablet out to Monica. "We'll carry him to the bunk room. He'll rest there until we can wake him."

Monica took the tablet and held it close. "How did you find us? And in this storm? I can barely see across the deck out there."

Viral Execution

Fahltrid glanced at Monica before taking hold of Aric's shoulders. "Wheaten, his ankles please." He waited for Ten to pick up Aric's feet before continuing. "We'll discuss technicalities once we get this man situated." Fahltrid hooked his arms under Aric's and backed up to the door. "Where's Yerith?"

"He was outside a minute ago." Ten's wiry arms strained under Aric's weight.

Monica opened the door and tried to take hold of one of Aric's ankles to help lighten the load, but Ten shook her head. "Just get the door and then the hatch."

After waiting for Fahltrid and Ten to shuffle through with Aric, Monica stepped into the beating rain and closed the door. She stuffed Amelia's tablet under her shirt and staggered ahead.

She knelt beside the hatch leading down to the hammocks and shoved it forward a few inches, but it refused to move any farther. She braced her feet against the deck and pushed. The wooden door moved another inch, then wouldn't budge.

The man who had grabbed her earlier appeared and forced the door open the rest of the way. "It sticks sometimes." He turned and met Fahltrid and Ten. "Captain?"

"Get everyone organized, Yerith. See that they're on task." Fahltrid and Ten descended the stairs to the hammock room.

The rain lessened in intensity, but the ship still pitched wildly, throwing Monica off balance. Yerith helped her down the stairs, then bounded back up and closed the hatch, shutting out the frigid rain.

Monica jogged into the hammock room. Ten and Fahltrid swung Aric into one of the hammocks. Simon stood nearby, muttering something indiscernible.

The hammock rocked back and forth from Aric's momentum. He lay motionless despite the swaying. Fahltrid pressed a finger to Aric's neck, then stepped back. "He'll be fine." He gestured to Ten and marched toward the exit. "Come, Wheaten. There's a lot to do to get the ship back in good condition, though considering your

resources, I'd say you've done an adequate job in my absence."
He mounted the stairs and left.

Simon raised his eyebrows. "Not one for hellos and good-
byes, is he?"

"Yeah. At least he'll have the docking codes we need." Ten's
shoulders sagged, and she scurried up the stairs. "I'll be back
when I can. Stay here. It looks like the whole crew came, so we
have plenty of help."

"Okay." Monica pulled Amelia's tablet out from under her
shirt. Hopefully, the water hadn't damaged it. It couldn't take
much more abuse. She dried it off with the edge of the cloak Ten
had given her. Monica sighed. In her rush to help Aric, she hadn't
even thought to put it on.

She sat on a hammock near Simon's and filled him in on
what had happened to Aric and on the captain's arrival. While
she talked, the hammocks' swaying eased, a physical echo of the
ship's settling. The storm had ebbed.

Later, Ten joined them, wearing dry clothes and wrapped in
her cloak. "The captain wants to see you in his cabin, Monica. The
engine is running again so it's too hot in the file room."

"All right." Monica followed Ten up the stairs and into the
dusky evening. Pink and orange clouds decorated the sky, reflecting
the waning sun's light in brilliant array.

Yerith and another dark-haired man stood nearby, winding
a coil of rope as thick as their arms. A slender woman dressed
in loose pants and shirt passed by, carrying a large sack on her
shoulder.

Ten sidled up to Monica and pointed at the man beside Yerith.
"Laek." She pointed at the woman. "And Fern. There are three
more crewmen, but I'm not sure where they are."

She led Monica down the stairs toward the engine room. When
they stopped at the captain's cabin, Ten knocked lightly on the
door. "Captain?"

"Come in, both of you."

Viral Execution

Ten swung the door open and ushered Monica inside.

Fahltrid sat at his desk, a small tablet in front of him, its screen glowing brightly. Bruises marred his tanned face, and his shoulders drooped. He turned off his computer and faced them, though he remained seated. "Monica, if you would please be so kind, I would appreciate it if you would fill me in on all that has happened that led you to being here on the *Katrina*. Wheaten has told me some of it, but I would like to hear it from you."

"Yes sir." Monica glanced at Ten. How would the captain react to her story? It was unusual, to be sure, but certainly he would understand what she had been through, considering his own past. She inhaled deeply and started at the beginning.

CHAPTER SIXTEEN

When Monica finished telling Fahltrid about her past, he leaned back in his seat and said nothing for a few moments.

She closed her eyes. How many times would she have to relive that story? She inhaled deeply. Probably many more to come.

"Thank you for telling me." Fahltrid clasped his hands in front. "I'm guessing Wheaten has filled you in on our history by this time."

Redness tinted Ten's cheeks. "I thought it would—"

Fahltrid held up a hand. "It's fine, Wheaten. I trust your judgment." He picked up his tablet. "Much of the time."

Monica nodded. "She did tell me, but that doesn't explain how you found us. From what I've seen, the ocean is a pretty big place."

"Indeed it is." Fahltrid tapped his computer against one hand. "But the lantern Wheaten hung was quite useful until it went out, and the ship we commandeered from the Cantral docks had some adequate tracking equipment." He stood and opened the door. "We left it to board the *Katrina* from the lifeboat. Isale and Krath, two of my crew, stayed behind to sail it back to Cantral."

"I see." Monica followed Ten and Fahltrid from the room.

"You may go about your duties." Fahltrid walked ahead and turned the corner into the engine room. "We'll be in port in two days."

"Yes, Captain." Ten gestured to Monica. "Come on. I'll introduce you to the crew."

Two days passed quickly aboard ship. Monica helped out when she could, but Ten insisted she not do much—to give her hands more time to heal.

She took a turn every day sitting by Aric's hammock, though he never stirred and seemed to grow thinner despite the liquid food mixture one of the crew had concocted for him. Fahltrid said it was dangerous to feed an unconscious man, but Aric would starve or dehydrate if they didn't.

Simon's health improved rapidly, and he was soon back to giving orders and making demands. He was insufferable, as usual, claiming that if not for his advice, they would all have surely died.

On the third day, Fahltrid announced they would be coming into port in a few hours.

Monica sat by the ship's railing, her mother's journal in hand along with Simon's dictionary pages. It was still a struggle to translate even one word, but trying to figure out her mother's entries helped pass the time.

Ten leaned on the railing nearby and stared into the fog. "I think it's clearer now. I can see the shore."

Monica squinted at the never-ending mist. "I don't."

"Huh." Ten rested her chin on a hand. "Seems clear enough to me. I can't wait to get there. The port cities are so much fun. You'll see—places to explore, people to meet, exotic foods to try."

"That does sound exciting, but I don't think I'll have much time for fun."

"I suppose not. You'll be sneaking around like a rat." Ten ran a finger along the ship's rail. "If you succeed, the captain will have to look for a new way to use the *Katrina*. We won't have a sponsor anymore, and we'll have to find some source of income, but …"

Shrugging, she let out a short sigh. "That's the way of things. It's for the best, I know."

"He'll find something. He's obviously a resourceful man."

"I have an idea!" Ten stood straight, a twinkle in her eye. "Maybe we can be pirates!"

Monica frowned. "What's a pirate?"

"Never mind. It was just a joke." Ten stepped away from the rail and gave Monica's braid a gentle tug. "Now let me fix your hair so you can be presentable when you meet your mother. You want to make a good impression, don't you?"

Monica ran a hand over the loose strands that had come free. Soon after the storm Ten had braided it in the merchant's style to help keep it in check. "Yes, I do." She gripped the ship's railing. Would meeting her mother be anything like she imagined? Would she even recognize her? She fingered the vial holding Amelia's chip, once again resting against her chest. It was harmless now, just a hunk of metal, but it was a reminder—a symbol of the past. Tucking the vial back beneath her shirt, she sighed. A symbol of another person who had to die.

"It would be amazing to get to go to the palace and explore." Ten's nimble fingers made quick work of taking out Monica's hair and braiding it again. "I've never been to the Penniak Nobles' district, let alone the palace, though I've seen them from afar. Unlike in Central, they're visible from the port. I've never seen Central's pal—" She tied off the braid with the bit of string. "Actually, I guess I have, since the fields are in sight of it, but I don't remember, so it hardly counts."

"You could come with us, couldn't you?" Monica turned and faced Ten. "We might need someone who's good with computers. We wanted to bring Aric, but …"

Ten's expression turned downcast, and she laid a hand on the back of her neck. "I don't think my chip would let me into the Noble section. I'm just a sailor. The captain is allowed, but only for a short time."

Viral Execution

"Couldn't we hide your chip, too?"

Raising an eyebrow, Ten smirked. "You have another tablet lurking somewhere? I don't want to try the ship's computer method, and you said Amelia's computer was off-limits."

Monica put a hand to her side to reach for her satchel before remembering she'd left it in the storage room where she and Ten slept. "Right. We can't lose Amelia's information about chip cloning."

Ten fiddled with the hem of her long, wool cloak. "No, I guess not." She pointed toward something behind Monica. "Look! If you can't see the land now, then you're blind as a bat."

Monica spun. The mist cleared around them, disappearing as they advanced on a stretch of white sand. Cliffs rose high and chalky to the left, and more ocean stretched to the right. The water seemed to grow bluer as they approached the coast, and a large dock came into view, abruptly cutting the beach short. She took in a deep breath. The same salty air that they'd been experiencing all week enveloped her senses.

Wrinkling her nose, she glanced back at Ten. "Other than those cliffs, it doesn't look much different than Cantral, does it?"

"It will once you get farther in." Ten waved a hand as if to clear the lingering mist. "The palace is modeled after Cantral's, though. They like to keep up with the central continent. It's the city and the Nobles' district that are really interesting, so the captain tells me." She pointed toward the water again. "There's the buoy line marking where the dome would rise if there's a termination command."

Orange balls bobbed in the water, one spaced every hundred feet or so from the other, curving a dozen yards off the shoreline.

Monica shuddered. A line of death. The dome's reach included all the ships in the harbor. Fortunately, the dome wouldn't rise anymore, not with the Cantral computers cut off. No one could send termination signals to computers.

She fingered the glass vial at her throat before untying it. It could stay here on the ship where she slept. There was no need for it anymore. If anyone noticed her wearing it, it would just raise more suspicion. Alyssa's necklace could stay with her, though. It had proved too useful in the past to leave behind.

"I'll be right back." She jogged downstairs and tucked the glass vial beneath some supplies before rejoining Ten at the railing.

The now familiar thrum of the engine below deck stopped abruptly, and the pipe, protruding tall and black above the communications room, began to descend.

"Are you ready?" Simon appeared by their side, holding a folded gray cloth.

Monica jumped, her heart skipping a beat. "Simon!" She laid a hand on her chest. "You shouldn't sneak up on people like that. And ready for what? It'll be awhile before we dock, won't it?"

"We must prepare and pack. It won't be very long now." Simon unfolded the cloth to reveal one of their cloaks. "The captain says a storm is approaching, and we'd best take these with us when we leave."

"Okay." Monica folded the cloak over an arm.

"Wheaten!" Fahltrid's voice boomed out from somewhere nearby. "All hands are to be working. You're not a passenger!"

"Right." Ten sighed and whispered, "I'd better get going. It takes a lot of work to come into port." She scurried off, joining the bustle of the other crew members rushing back and forth across the ship.

Monica took two steps to follow her before Simon's bony hand gripped her arm. "You'll stay right here, young lady. You'll only get in their way."

As Simon's grip tightened, Monica winced. "Ten showed me how to do everything."

"Sailing in the open water is much different than navigating into a port, and last I read, Port Kennit is a rather busy one."

He released her and pointed toward the port. "You can see for yourself."

She edged away from his fingers and turned her gaze toward the docks. They loomed ever closer now, and small boats drifted all around the *Katrina*. A few larger sailing ships and one giant metal ship with no sails lurked nearby, their decks alive with activity. "How many do you think are out there?"

"A few dozen." Simon sighed. "I'm sure rumors have kept most of the merchants away. According to accounts I've read, there should be dozens of ships waiting their turn to reach a dock. Penniak has a very small port, though very active. Makes it more defendable."

"Penniak?" Monica squinted at the name painted in blue letters on the closest ship, but it was too far to make out. Ten had mentioned Penniak, too. "I thought this was Port Kennit. And aren't we in Eursia?"

"So many questions." Simon wagged his finger at her. "Yes, we are in Eursia. I said that's where we were going, didn't I?"

"Then what is Penniak? Another city-state nearby?" She folded her arms beneath the cloak, looking up at him with what she hoped was a no-nonsense stare.

He let out a long-suffering sigh. "Of course, of course. In a way, Penniak is the capital of Eursia as Cantral the city is the capital of Cantral the continent. Penniak just wasn't named the same thing as its continent like Cantral was. Less pretentious, I suppose. Kennit is just the name of this port. There are other ports around as well; Kennit is the main one. Is that clear?" He smiled brightly without pausing long enough for her to answer. "Excellent. Now we must plan our mode of attack."

Monica's mind whirled at the barrage of information. Kennit was in Penniak and Penniak was in Eursia, and she and the ship were in all of them at once. And mode of attack? "What do you mean? I thought we were sneaking in."

Simon eyed her with an exasperated glare. "Yes, of course I meant sneaking. A sneak attack. It would be foolish to barge in making demands. We'll use the wall slave entrances." He rubbed his hands together. "I've always wanted to explore them and the messenger tunnels."

Shaking her head, Monica suppressed a smile. "I seem to remember that not going well last time you tried it. You were disgusted at the cobwebs and close spaces."

"Actually the last time we tried it, we were running from a mob." Simon wrinkled his wiry eyebrows. "And besides, the time you were referring to, that dormitory had been ransacked and rendered uninhabitable. It could be expected. These tunnels will be well traveled, I'm sure."

As one of the sailors ran by, a heavy coiled rope slung over his shoulder, Monica pressed herself against the rail. "I don't think it will be very different from the dormitories." She shrugged and watched the activity on the deck. Nothing would change his mind, and did making him see really matter? It was the Nobles whose opinions needed to be swayed.

They slowly drew nearer the great stone dock in the harbor. The smaller ships skittered out of the *Katrina's* way, sails raised high. Shouts echoed all around from the *Katrina* and other boats—not angry or excited shouts, just raised voices, loud enough to be heard, though their words still scattered in the distance.

The sun peeked out from behind the mist, but a cold chill hung in the air despite the glow. Simon huffed loudly. "They certainly are taking their time. The dock isn't but a few yards away, and we're inching along."

"They're just being careful." Monica's gaze flitted back and forth along the dock. Sharp-looking, odd-shaped things clung to the dock's side where the water lapped against wood. A green residue marked where the water would rise no farther before splashing back into the ocean. Vendors manned stalls across the street from the landing, hawking their wares to the throng of passersby.

Viral Execution

Large crates partially covered with tarps lined the dock, and a long metal arm stuck into the air above them, thick wire ropes attached here and there, letting a huge hook dangle from the arm's end.

"What is that?" Monica pointed at the contraption. If anyone would know, it would be Simon. At least he'd claim to.

"That?" Simon furrowed his brow, squinting against the sun. "That, my dear, is a loading crane. They use it to ferry the heaviest parcels to and from the ships."

A loud clanking sounded nearby. Monica turned and caught sight of two sailors, walking around the capstan with slow, labored steps, lowering the anchor from its storage house and into the water below.

Ten and Fern stood by the side of the ship, gripping the gangplank and lowering it toward the dock. Sweat beaded on Ten's forehead, but she and Fern brought the gangplank to meet the shore's edge without trouble.

Ten straightened, wiped her hands on her cloak, and jogged over. "Ready to go ashore?" A wide smile lit her face. "I'll show you all the best shops to go to. Even though our sponsor is here in Penniak, we haven't been to Port Kennit in almost a year. Still, the onshore merchants should remember us. They're eager to talk to anyone they think is a potential customer."

"We have no time for such things." Simon started for the gangplank. "We must find an entrance to the palace and meet with Madam Rose as quickly as possible. The sooner this is finished, the sooner we have time to explore this new country."

Monica grabbed his sleeve. "What about Aric? We can't just leave him here."

Simon plucked her fingers from his sleeve and pushed them away. "Why not? He'll be perfectly fine. We can't be encumbered by a comatose body. Are *you* volunteering to carry him? I certainly can't."

Monica shook her head. "Not by myself."

Simon turned to Ten. "*She* probably could, though." He lifted his brow. "Are you accompanying us on this expedition? With Aric down, we likely have use for a computer technician."

Ten backed up two steps. "I'd love to come, but I can't. My chip wouldn't allow it. I already told Monica that." She shrugged. "And as for Aric, he'll be fine here. The captain won't let him be neglected, and we're staying in port until you're ready to leave."

Simon stroked his chin. "We could hide your chip the same way we hid mine, though not with Amelia's tablet."

The captain hurried over, a scowl etched on his forehead. "There you are, Simon. We're ready to begin unloading. We have a buyer for most of our cargo, and we'll be ready to depart tomorrow, so I suggest you accomplish your mission as quickly as possible. We won't want to linger here any longer than necessary. It will raise suspicion. Sailing under Cantral's identification signal is dangerous right now."

"Then change it." Simon waved a hand with a flourish. "And while we would like your niece to come with us to help in case we run into any computer problems, we realize that is impossible, and Madam Rose won't be able to help much, since she can't compromise her position any more than she has." He raised an eyebrow. "Perhaps *you* can come with us."

"I can't do that."

"Why not? I'm sure your crew is perfectly capable of running this business by themselves." Simon gestured to Yerith who passed by at that moment.

Fahltrid sighed and shook his head. "Yes, they're capable, but it's not safe. They're too new. Too fresh from the fields. If something were to go wrong and they were to panic and get caught, I'd never forgive myself."

"Not to mention we'd all be terminated," Ten muttered.

Fahltrid turned Ten around to face him and released his grip on her shoulder. "Wheaten, if you're willing, I could find a way to hide your signal so you can accompany them, but if you don't want to, don't let them pressure you. You never have to leave the ship."

Ten started to nod, then stopped. "Except when you need me as a scout. Then I don't have a choice."

Drawing back, Fahltrid blinked at her. "What do you mean? I thought you wanted to do those trips, for your mother's sake."

"Yes, but you never asked. Just commanded." Ten held up both hands. "Never mind, I don't want to talk about it. I'll go with them." She dropped her hands back to her sides. "Where can we find another tablet to hide my chip?"

"Shal, of course. There's no one I trust more to get us one safely. " Fahltrid turned and started walking away.

Ten shrugged. "I just thought that after Shal said … I thought you didn't want to do business with her anymore."

"Wheaten." Fahltrid spoke without facing her. "That is a situation you know nothing about. Just do as I say."

Ten clenched a fist. "Yes sir."

CHAPTER SEVENTEEN

Monica jogged beside Ten, their cloaks fluttering behind them as they darted down the cobblestone street. Ten ducked beneath a passerby's arm and wove in and out of the crowds with ease. Monica followed as best she could, but people kept stepping in front of her. As yet another person stood in her way, Monica slowed her pace and dodged to the side, muttering, "Excuse me."

Sights and sounds danced around in a dizzying pace as she quickened her steps to catch up with Ten. People jabbered in some foreign language, every word sounding harsh and guttural. A few spoke with a more nasally accent, and their words blended with the others in a nonsensical swirl.

Ten turned down a narrower alley, her bare feet making no noise as they struck the packed dirt. Monica stepped off the cobblestones and into the alley a second behind Ten. The crowd continued to swarm past the narrow opening without a glance her way. A putrid odor hung in the air, making her cough.

Monica backed away from the busy street. Her foot landed in a brown puddle. She hissed. Hopefully that was just water.

Grabbing Monica's arm, Ten whispered, "Come on. We can't stay long. We don't want to draw attention or suspicion. This is the entrance to a small-time tar and sealant factory. I'm picking some sealant up for Fahltrid. We use it in hull repairs."

Viral Execution

"Are we getting the tablet somewhere else, then?" Monica whispered, shaking drops of dirty water from her bare foot.

As they approached a shabby door in the side of the alley, the rancid scent increased, turning Monica's stomach.

"No, this is Shal's place. The tar and sealant are a front. It's a real business, just not their main one." Ten laid a hand on the door, her palm resting on a ragged board riddled with holes. She knocked with a knuckle twice, stuck a finger through one of the larger holes, pulled her finger back, then knocked three times before coughing loudly.

Monica stared at her. "What—?"

"Shush," Ten whispered.

The door jerked open, and a short, middle-aged man peered out. His brown hair stood on end as if he'd received a shock from his chip. "Yes, what is it?"

"We've come for some supplies." Ten raised an eyebrow and nodded toward the shop entrance. "For... for our ship. Captain Fahltrid of the *Katrina* sent me."

The man narrowed his eyes. "Wheaten, isn't it? Grown up a bit, haven't you?"

"Yeah. That tends to happen to most people my age." Ten crossed her arms over her chest. "Is Shal here?"

"Wouldn't you like to know?" The man's gaze slid to Monica, making her shiver. "Who's your friend?"

Glaring, Ten stepped forward until she stood right under the man's chin. "I want to talk to Shal. We don't have any business with you, Chrom."

"Of course you don't," he muttered. "You never do."

"We don't need explosives on a merchant ship." Ten tossed her head and deepened her glare. "Now let us in."

He jerked away from her and huffed loudly. "Fine, get inside." He motioned to Monica. "You, too, hurry up. Average transaction time is five minutes. Can't have you staying here any longer than that."

"And you just wasted one," Ten grumbled, but she followed him into the store.

Monica tiptoed after them. The door slammed behind her, and she flinched. Ten reached out and held Monica's hand.

Darkness closed around them. Only a little light issued from the holes in the door. The stench grew until Monica's stomach heaved and she struggled not to gag. "What is that smell?"

"The glue cooking," Ten said. "It's a terribly smelly process, and Chrom's other concoctions don't help the odor, either."

A soft voice came from somewhere in the darkness. "Chrom, why do you insist on keeping the lights off in here? We are open for business, aren't we?"

Chrom grumbled. A cranking noise sounded near the door, and blue sparks leaped from the wall, illuminating Chrom as he turned a metal handle in a circle. He turned the handle faster, and the sparks dissipated.

A soft light appeared overhead, strengthening with every passing second. Long strips of glowing plastic lined the rotten ceiling boards. They brightened until they illumined the entire room and pulsed in a steady rhythm.

Chrom stuffed his hands into his greasy-looking pants pockets. "Shal, what're you doing out here?"

A dark-haired woman stood in front of a moth-eaten curtain near the back of the room. Her brown-eyed gaze flitted around, as if making sure nothing had gone missing. "I heard the knock. An outdated one, Wheaten." She let a pair of leather goggles dangle from one hand. "We changed it six months ago, but it will do nonetheless."

After setting the goggles on a black table, she opened her hands toward them. A silver ring glittered on her left hand "So, what can I do for you?" She smiled, revealing teeth too straight and white to belong to anyone but a Noble. "You're obviously not here just for sealant."

Viral Execution

Monica backed up a step. This woman's speech and manners were too fine. And jewelry? This wasn't right. She couldn't be just some peasant merchant. "Ten," she whispered.

Squeezing Monica's hand, Ten smiled. "Of course, Shal. You know the captain's needs pretty well by now. We need a new tablet."

"Already?" Shal's eyes narrowed. "I replace your relic that Fahltrid managed to keep alive for decades, and you need to replace one of my masterpieces in only a year?"

"Yes." Ten nodded firmly and tapped her bare wrist. "We're running short on time. Chrom here"—she jerked a thumb at the man—"held us up by asking stupid questions. Do you have a tablet to sell or not?"

"Pushy, pushy." Shal drew a sturdy, burn-scarred chair away from the table and sank into it, propping an elbow on the back. "I might happen to have an old tablet I don't need anymore, but the question is…" She picked at a sooty spot on her pants and shrugged. "Do you have the money to pay for one?"

"I have our ship's charge ID." Ten pushed a flap of her cloak to the side and pulled out a thin, plastic card. "Trust me, we can afford it."

Shal drummed her fingers on the tabletop. "I see Fahltrid didn't come with you. He hasn't found your father yet?"

"No." Ten's cheeks reddened. "How much for the tablet?"

"Of course not. If he had, he would be here." Shal sighed and rubbed the ring on her finger, turning it around and around. "Five thousand and you give me the old tablet back."

"Five thousand?" Ten's jaw muscles tightened.

Monica glanced from Shal to Ten. Was that a lot? Five thousand what? If this woman was a Noble, why was she selling to merchants?

"And you give me back the old tablet." Shal stood. "If that's too much, you can find some other smuggler to do your dirty work, but you and I both know you'll be out of port before you can even begin to establish trust with a new mule, so you'd better take my offer or resign yourself to the *Katrina* being just a sailboat for the rest of your career."

"Right." Ten's hand slid back into her coat. "Let's go, Monica."

Monica turned to the door that Chrom now held open. Ten walked out, and Monica hurried after her.

"Wait!" Shal called, stalking toward them. "We'll come to a deal."

"Will we?" Ten paused a step." How can I trust you not to rip us off?" Ten continued walking. "We'll all be in trouble if we stay too long and the authorities look into it. Your computers aren't sanctioned."

"Get back inside." Shal rushed out the door and grabbed Ten's arm. "We don't discuss business outside. Do you want to get me killed?"

Ten scampered back into the building. Heart thumping, Monica darted after her. What was going on? Mule? All these new words and phrases made no sense.

As soon as the door closed behind them, Shal nodded to Chrom. "Go get the sealant."

Glaring and muttering something in the guttural language Monica had heard in the streets, Chrom shuffled to the curtain hanging on the opposite wall. He pushed it to the side, revealing a passage leading into darkness. He disappeared within, and the curtain fell back into place.

"Now." Shal set her hands on her hips and kept her voice low. "You obviously don't want to give the tablet up. Which means you've been participating in illegal activity, and that's something I don't want any part of. The only illegal activity I want a hand in is my own. So I'll make you a deal." She eyed them for a moment before letting out a long sigh. "Seven thousand. Take it or leave it."

"The old tablet isn't worth two thousand!" Ten snapped, folding her arms over her chest again. "Captain Fahltrid would never approve of that deal. Besides, our daily charge limit isn't that high. You want me to get fired? I have to bring this tablet back."

Smirking, Shal shook her head. "Don't play games with me, Wheaten. I know your uncle would never abandon you, no matter what you did. The two thousand is for risk, not for cost of the old tablet. Besides, this one has much better specs than the last."

Ten flinched. Her mouth opened and closed, as if she wanted to retort with a comeback but couldn't think of anything.

Monica stepped toward the door. This probably wasn't going to end well. They were taking too much time here.

As if on cue, Ten laid a finger on the back of her neck and closed her eyes for a second. "There's the warning buzz, Shal. I have to go." She turned on her heel and stormed out of the smelly building.

"Wait!" Shal called.

Monica scurried after Ten and closed the door behind them. "That was useless. Now what are we going to do?"

"Come on." Ten jogged a few paces from the store.

As they entered the crowded street, the strong odor cleared, and the salty breeze from the harbor wrapped around them. Monica pressed her back against a damp, wooden wall, keeping out of the crowd's way. "You're not allowed to stay in a shop for more than a few minutes?"

"Right. Different time allotments for different shops. It depends on what they sell." Shaking her head, Ten winced. "We stayed a little too long." She thumped the back of her head against the wall and slid to the ground, crouching over the cobblestones. "And I didn't even get the sealant. Shal is normally trustworthy. I don't know what has her trying to get such a high price. Tablets are not worth that much, even the ones sold on the black market. Our whole cargo isn't worth more than ten thousand, and that's six months' worth of work." She rose and brushed some dirt off of her cloak. "Let's get back to the ship. You and Simon will have to go by yourselves." She grabbed Monica's arm. "And don't worry about Aric. We'll take care of him."

Monica tore away from Ten's iron-fingered grip. "Isn't there someone else we can get a tablet from? Somewhere legal?"

Ten raised her eyebrows. "Not with a chip reader."

Monica blew out a long breath through gritted teeth. "I'll get the tablet from Shal, then. I can do the transaction. The computers can't track me."

Withdrawing the plastic card from her cloak, Ten shook her head. "But they can track this, even if you use it instead of me. All transactions are sent to the computers for approval."

"That won't matter for much longer." Monica held out a hand for the card. "By the time they have the opportunity to look into it, we'll …" She glanced out into the crowd. "We'll be done and on our way back to Cantral."

Ten placed the card in Monica's palm. "Fine, but don't accept any offer over five thousand. Even that is a terrible price, but since money isn't going to mean much after this, we'll take it."

"Right." Monica closed her fingers around the card and stuffed it into a pocket. "I'll see what I can do."

"Thanks. I'll be walking up and down the dock in the meantime." Ten gestured to the crowd. "I have to pretend to be shopping. Just standing around draws suspicion, too. Don't be gone long, okay?"

"I'll be as quick as I can." Monica trotted down the alley.

"And don't forget the sealant!" Ten called.

CHAPTER EIGHTEEN

B reathing through her mouth to avoid the odor, Monica walked to the door and poised a hand over the rotten boards. How had Ten knocked? Twice and then stuck a finger, then … Monica rolled her eyes up and brought the images of the past minutes back to mind. Yes, that was it.

She tapped the door twice with a knuckle and copied Ten's procedure. With a final rap, Monica stepped away and coughed.

The door swung open, and Chrom's scowling face peered out. "Oh, you're back, are you? Forgot your sealant. I knew you'd return, but I thought it'd be a little later." He glanced up and down the alley. "Where's Wheaten?"

"She's not coming." Monica firmed her stance and lifted her chin until she looked him in the eye. "I want to talk to Shal."

Chrom smirked. "She's not coming. She doesn't have time to deal with the likes of you." He looked her up and down. "Skinny as a stick, frightened, and don't want to show it. You remind me of a Slink."

Monica clenched her fists. Whatever a Slink was, it probably wasn't nice. "Let me see Shal. You don't want to lose a sale, do you?"

"Chrom, let her in." Shal's call came from the shop. "You'd think she was a security agent, the way you carry on."

"Fine." Chrom pushed past Monica into the alley. "I'll leave you biddies be, since you're sure to throw me out anyway. A man knows when he's not wanted."

Monica ducked into the room, and Shal closed the door behind her. The strips of light on the ceiling pulsed brightly.

Shal held a tablet under her arm. "So you're back. A little more quickly than I expected. You're not trying to get me in trouble by staying longer, are you? That will cause you quite a lot of pain, I can assure you, and it will do little good. My computers are well hidden."

"I'll be fine." Monica fingered the plastic card in her pocket. "I just want to buy the sealant and tablet and get out of here. I have places to be. I'm sure you do, too."

"I'm not sure I'm willing to work with you." Shal laid the tablet on the table and reached a hand into her own pocket. "I have to be careful whom I trust. I've never seen you before. You could be a Noble spy, for all I know."

Monica withdrew the card. No need to make the woman nervous by leaving her hand in her pocket. Shal might think she had a weapon. "And I'm not so sure you're not a Noble. I've never seen a commoner with such perfect teeth or diction."

Her gaze narrowing, Shal nodded. "And I've never seen a Slink with such a tan or haughty attitude."

"A Slink?" Monica forced herself to keep a blank expression. Chrom had mentioned a Slink, too.

"Yes." Shal's hand slid deeper into her pocket. "A slave from the palace. I've seen some working in the fields when I've had reason to go there. They never last long, and they all have your look about them. Skinny, haunted, and frightened."

Monica held the card out to Shal. "Do I look frightened to you?" She narrowed her eyes to match Shal's expression. "I'm prepared to pay five thousand. That's what you first offered, and I'm sure you wouldn't want anyone around here to know you're a Noble, so you'd better take it."

Viral Execution

"I am not a Noble." Shal snatched the card from Monica. "But I can tell that's all you're going to give me, so I'll take it. Wheaten's daily credit limit probably isn't much higher than that anyway."

"So you're not a Noble, and I'm not a Slink." Monica let out a long breath. "And thank you."

"Don't mention it." Shal pulled open a drawer in the table and yanked out a small box. She slid the card into a thin slot, punched some numbers on a keypad on the box's front, and pulled the card back out. "If anyone asks, you just purchased a few thousand pounds of ship sealant." She shoved the card back toward Monica. "And please tell Fahltrid he could have had the tablet for free if he weren't so stubborn."

Monica took the card back and frowned. What did that mean? Shal picked up the tablet and a small black jar. "If anyone catches you with this tablet, you had better have an explanation that doesn't involve me, or you'll regret it. I might not be a Noble, but I happen to know a few." She shoved the two items into a rough burlap sack, drew the top closed with a drawstring, and handed the bag to Monica. "Now get going. That tablet should last at least five years, and I won't replace it any sooner unless Fahltrid comes to his senses."

Monica held the scratchy drawstring in a death grip. "Thank you again." She rushed from the room before Shal could raise any more objections or ask any more questions. What did it matter if the woman was a Noble or not? Soon enough the chip and computer class system would be gone for good. Besides, Fahltrid seemed to trust her, and he had proven himself to be reliable so far.

She dashed into the street and leaned against the building wall just outside the alley. The tablet was hers. Ten could come with them. Tucking the bag under her arm, she breathed a sigh of relief. Now to find Ten so they could head to the palace. Simon and Fahltrid would be wondering what was taking them so long.

Rising to tiptoes, she scanned the crowd. If only she weren't so short.

"Monica!" Ten's voice called out over the bustle, and her golden hair bobbed in and out of the crowd. She elbowed past a large man who carried a crate smelling of fish. "You get it?"

"Yes." Monica dug into her pocket and handed the card to Ten. "She took five thousand," she whispered. "I threatened to tell people she's a Noble, and then she claimed she wasn't, but she said she thought you couldn't give more anyway."

"I think she's half, and either way, mules don't like to have their reputation tainted." Ten shrugged and waved a hand. "Let's get back to the ship and hide my chip."

Monica jogged after her. "What's a mule?"

Ten glanced over her shoulder but didn't miss a step in her steady lope. "A mule's a smuggler or shipper of illegal stuff. Shal's a mule. So's Chrom." She stepped onto the thick boards of the gangplank leading to the *Katrina*. "Tablets aren't really illegal, but the ones we get from Shal are. They have too many features for a ship's tablet." She tapped the back of her neck. "Chip readers, for one. Which definitely *are* illegal."

Monica halted at the first board and gazed at the masts and sails tied tightly up in their proper places. "I guess you could say Fahltrid is a mule, too."

Pausing at the top of the gangplank, Ten frowned. "Yeah. I guess you could say that."

"Wheaten!" Fahltrid's voice rang out. "I see you there. Hurry up and come aboard. Where's Monica? Simon's badgering me more than seagulls after we bring in a fresh haul."

"Coming!" Ten disappeared onto the ship.

Monica raced after her, her bare feet striking board, then metal, then board as she passed over the patchwork planking. Simon could drive even steady-tempered Fahltrid to distraction. She hugged the burlap bag close as she jogged to where Fahltrid and Ten stood near the main mast. Monica lifted the bag. "We got it."

"Perfect." Fahltrid laid a hand on her and Ten's shoulders and guided them to the communications room. "We'll have this done in moments, and you three can be on your way."

Ten slid into a seat at the desk and held the armrests. "I'm ready."

Monica dug into the burlap bag until her fingers met smooth, cool metal. She withdrew the computer and held it out to Fahltrid. "Here's the tablet."

"Shal's price was robbery," Ten muttered, "but I didn't know where else to go."

Fahltrid clasped the tablet in his calloused hands and turned it on with a press of his thumb. "It's fine. We have plenty saved, and money won't be worth anything much longer." The tablet screen flickered to life. Fahltrid began typing with quick, precise strokes.

While Monica watched him work, Shal's words rang in her head. "Fahltrid, Shal said something about you getting the tablet for free, if you came to your senses."

"Ah." As he shook his head, a hint of red tinged his cheeks. "Wheaten, my tablet please."

"Okay." Ten looked at him a long moment before hopping to her feet. She unlocked the rolltop desk with a key he handed her. After flinging a small drawer open, she snatched out the captain's tablet and handed it to him.

Monica shrugged. Whatever was between Shal and Fahltrid was their business.

He pressed the two tablets together. "I'm downloading the program to the new tablet."

Settling back into her seat, Ten grimaced. "Let's get this over with."

"It shouldn't hurt much." Fahltrid pressed the new tablet to her neck and tapped the screen.

Ten closed her eyes. She gasped, then opened one eye. "That stung. Is it done now?"

Fahltrid drew the tablet away. "Yes. Though the tablet seems to be fine. That's surprising."

"Great." Ten jumped out of the seat. "So I'm hidden now?" She pushed two fingers against the back of her neck. "It feels just the same as before."

"We'll test it. If it worked, you three need to be on your way." Fahltrid waved the computer over her neck, and the computer made no noise. "You're all set." He plunked it back into the drawer. "But I'm not sure why the new unit didn't overload like the others."

Then massaged her neck's scar. "Shal said it was better than our last one. She's always looking for ways to upgrade her products." She yanked open the door and pulled Monica through. "Let's go. I know the way to the palace."

Monica handed Fahltrid the bag with the sealant, then stumbled after Ten, allowing her to take the lead. "But there's more to do. I still have to get my things, and where is Simon? We can't leave him. He's the only one who knows anything about Eursia's palace and Nobles."

"I know about the Nobles. They're a bunch of over-lording snobs." Ten released Monica's hand. "But I suppose we need him, and really …" She plucked at her loose-fitting shirt. "We'd stick out pretty badly in the Noble sector. We'll need to figure out disguises."

"I have that covered." Simon tromped up the stairs from the lower deck, two satchels in his arms. "And we're ready to depart. I assume you figured out Ten's chip problem and have that resolved." He shoved the satchels into Monica's arms. "Here are our Seen uniforms and your mother's diary, as well as Amelia's tablet with that ingenious sleeper code Aaron came up with. It might come in handy. Infiltration is a tricky business."

Monica hugged the bags to her chest. "It turned out to be a good thing I went, or we might not have gotten the tablet."

"Of course it was a good thing." Simon grinned. "I suggested it."

Viral Execution

"I can take one of those." Ten grabbed a satchel from Monica and slung the strap over her head. "Let's go."

Monica slipped the other satchel strap over her shoulder and hid the bulk with her cloak. "I assume we'll change once we get nearer the palace."

"Of course." Simon marched to the gangplank and waited at the top. "Come along, now."

Monica trotted after him. "Are you sure Aric will be okay while we're gone?"

"Yes, yes. Fahltrid has promised to give him excellent care. He might be rather thin and atrophied when we finally return to Central, but it will be good for his character in the long run."

Ten joined them. "This will be quite an adventure, won't it? Finally going into a Noble palace, I mean." She gripped the strap of the satchel in both hands and bounced on her toes. "What's it like?"

Monica frowned. This wasn't an exciting adventure. It was a dangerous mission, something to be feared, approached with caution. "You'll see." She toed the gangplank's first board. The next leg of their journey was about to begin.

CHAPTER NINETEEN

"No sense dawdling!" Simon marched quickly down the gangplank. Ten trotted after him, and Monica brought up the rear with firm steady steps. When her feet met the dock, she held her breath and glanced around. The crowd still shuffled through the streets going about their business, completely unaware of the life-changing events that would take place. She squared her shoulders. They would learn soon enough.

"Wheaten!" Fahltrid called from the ship. Ten and Monica whirled around.

Fahltrid stood at the gangplank and jogged down. He held out a hand to Ten.

She shuffled up and met him halfway. "What is it?"

He pulled her into a fierce hug and whispered something into her ear. He then released her and gave her a tablet.

With the tablet in hand, she galloped back down to the dock, her forehead wrinkled. She hooked an arm around Monica's and steered her down the street toward Simon, who had already walked nearly out of sight.

Monica studied her for a second. Maybe she shouldn't ask, but it might be important. "What was that about?"

"This." She released Monica's arm and handed her the tablet. "He gave us Shal's new tablet in case we need it. He still has his old one." She jogged to catch up with Simon.

Viral Execution

Monica tucked the new tablet into her satchel and followed Ten's lead. As her bare feet slapped the cold, damp cobblestones, her calloused skin barely registered the small pebbles scattered here and there along the road.

They wove silently through the crowd, following Simon up the main street, down narrower side roads, and into a wide, almost deserted street farther into the city.

Simon held up a hand. Ten and Monica stopped. As a light drizzle started to fall, he raised an eyebrow and lowered his hand. "Lovely." He pushed Monica against a wall and motioned for Ten to stay against the bricks as well. "If we were traders, we would already be out of our district. We need to be careful."

Ten inhaled sharply. "This is exciting. Where are we going now?"

Monica cast her a sideways glance. She needed to calm down. This wasn't a game. Monica looked up and down the street. As the rain intensified, splattering large drops on their heads, the few wandering people scattered. She raised her cloak's hood to protect her face from the downpour.

"Hmmm." Simon seemed perfectly content ignoring Ten's question. He flipped his collar up and held it close. "Much too damp for an old man like me." Eyeing Monica for a second, he shivered. "Must be nice to have a cloak. I couldn't find a third. But you know me. Always thinking of others first."

Monica dropped her mouth open. "Simon!" She reached to untie her cloak. If he wanted it, he could have it. She was much more accustomed to poor conditions than he was.

He waved a hand. "No, no. You keep it. We'll be inside soon. I just had to stop and get my bearings." He marched off into the rain.

"Okay …" Ten hopped into a large puddle, splashing water all over their cloaks. "Let's get going then."

"I'm coming." Monica pulled her cloak tightly around herself and trotted after Ten.

"Hurry up," Simon called from across the street, now standing under a narrow awning.

They ran to the awning and ducked under it. The rain thrummed on the canvas material, making it hard to hear anything else.

"After we go down this side street," Simon said raising his voice above the strengthening storm, "we will be in the Nobles' district. If we can find the delivery entrance to the palace, we should be able to enter from there. If anyone stops us, tell them that's where we're headed." He shivered and rubbed his arms. His shirt stuck to his skin, revealing the outline of thin limbs beneath. "With this rain, it is unlikely anyone will want to question us closely. Merchants know and follow the rules. No one wants their license revoked."

Ten nodded. "There's nothing worse than that."

Monica untied her cloak. "Simon, don't make any objections." She shoved the dripping fabric at him. "You need this more than I do. It's dry on the inside." Forcing a smile, she shrugged. "We can't have you catching a cold and dying on us. We need your expertise."

"Of course you do." He swept the cloak over his shoulders and tied it in place. The hem reached only partway down his calves, but it would protect his head and body well enough.

She handed him her satchel. "But it will be your job to protect what's in here."

"I was just about to suggest that." He tucked the satchel under the cloak.

With the wind now tearing at Monica's shirt and pants, she folded her arms across her chest. "Let's get going then. I'm starting to welcome the idea of being in the messenger tunnels. It's better than being out here."

As soon as they stepped out from under the awning, rain pelted them with a stinging ferocity that took Monica's breath away. She bowed her head and followed Simon, barely paying attention to where he was going, just making sure she placed her feet where he had stepped.

Something gripped the back of Monica's shirt. Ten whispered, "It's just me. I don't want to get lost. I can't see a thing!"

Monica nodded, though Ten probably didn't notice. The rain seemed to be falling at an angle now, stinging her cheeks.

"There's the palace." Simon's voice sounded distant, though he stood only a few feet ahead.

Monica forced herself to look up and caught a glimpse of the building. The rain obscured the features, but the faint outline of an enormous, square building with dozens of windows shimmered through. Raindrops stung her eyes, and she turned her gaze down again.

"Amazing," Ten whispered. "It's so big. Bigger than a fleet of ships. *Two* fleets of ships!" Her grip tightened on Monica's shirt, pulling her collar back against her neck. "You used to live in one of these?"

"In the walls of one, anyway." Monica bowed her head and continued the slow trek behind Simon. The palace might be beautiful inside and out, but it hid something ugly. The walls held secrets and whispers of the dead.

Simon circled the front of the palace, skirting far away from giant doors, a huge porch, and a long access road in front. As Monica followed, she risked a glance around. No one else lingered outside the palace. They must all be inside, safe from the storm.

Beside the palace, a thick cluster of trees lined a gravel road that stretched into the curtain of rain and disappeared in the distance. "That could be it," Simon called. "They would want to put the slave entrance out of the way yet make it easily accessible."

They shuffled to the gravel path. The small road continued to the palace wall where a side door stood, but that couldn't be the entrance, could it? The Nobles wouldn't want slaves and merchants trudging in and out for all to see.

Simon gestured to the left. "We'll go that way."

Monica looked in the direction he indicated. Yes, the path turned to the left, the rocks coming right up to the wall. They quickened their pace. She sucked in a breath and swallowed some raindrops. Coughing, she hurried despite the rocky trail. The path would be plain dirt inside the palace. It would be dry and warm in there, too.

An opening came into view on their right—an indentation in the stone carved in the palace's side. A sheet of metal stood within the indentation, sealing off whatever lay behind. Simon set a hand on her shoulder and Ten's and guided them under the overhang.

Breathing heavily, he threw off his hood. "Quite a storm, isn't it?" He turned to the door and ran a finger down the smooth metal. "Looks rather like a delivery door, doesn't it? It's the right size, anyway."

Monica laid a hand on the cold, wet metal. It extended above their heads a few feet and was wide enough to allow four people to pass through standing side by side, arms outstretched. "I suppose so. I've seen one only once before, in Cillineese. It was a bit smaller than this."

"I've never seen one before." Ten pushed her hood from her forehead and let it fall to her shoulders. "But fortunately, the captain gave me the code to get in, if we can find the keypad." She ran a hand over the metal, but it was one smooth sheet with no indication of a hidden number pad.

A small slot opened at eye height, revealing a piece of dark glass, and a muffled voice issued forth. "Enter your pass code if you want in." The voice muttered something about new merchants not having sense to come out of the wet, but his exact words were lost in the thunderous rain.

Monica turned to Ten. "Should we ask him where the pad is?"

"That could raise more suspicion," Ten whispered, her words almost inaudible. "But I've never done this before. The captain usually does the transactions with a middleman merchant, and besides, we usually avoid working with palaces."

"We'll have to find another entrance." Simon started to raise his hood again, but Ten caught his wrist.

"No." She ran a hand along the wall. "The keypad has to be somewhere. Help me look."

Monica touched the stone entryway. What would it look like? Her fingertips rubbed against the gritty white wall until she came to a palm-sized section that dipped into the surface, creating a square divot. She pressed her hand on the spot. It flipped outward, revealing buttons with a number on each. "Here." Motioning to Ten, she stepped away from the box. "Here it is."

Ten rushed over and held the flap open as she typed in a ten-digit number. "We'll see if that works."

"What code was that?" Simon peered over her shoulder. "I didn't get a good look."

A beep sounded, and a green light flashed above the keypad. Smiling, Ten let the keypad cover fall back into place. "The *Katrina's* identification number."

The metal door ascended toward the ceiling and disappeared into the stone. A large, dark-skinned man stood on the other side, arms crossed over his broad chest. "New merchants?" His voice sounded rough and gravelly.

Ten stepped forward, a small plastic card in her hand. "We're from the ship *Katrina*. We've been trading for quite some time." She passed the white card to him. "See for yourself."

Nodding, he turned the card over. "That seems to be in order." He pulled a small box from his pocket and held it beneath the card. "How did a bedraggled crew like yours get a sponsorship from such a prominent Penniak Noble? He must be desperate to get his business going." Grinning, he nodded to Ten. "No offense."

Ten's jaw flexed, and her hands clenched into fists. "That's none of your concern. Are you going to let us by?"

Monica glanced at Simon. His wiry hair lay plastered against his head, making him look older and thinner than usual. Moving slowly, he reached into the satchel hanging at his side.

"Don't be so hasty." The man slid Ten's card into the box and pulled it out. "I have to see what you're scheduled for." He stared at a screen on the box. "Of course anyone can see from your lack of carts that you're not delivering, but it's protocol."

"Of course." Ten shot a worried look at Monica.

Monica returned the glance. They didn't have clearance. He would stop them and raise the alarm. Simon had Amelia's tablet; would he know what to do? Sometimes he seemed so oblivious. Would he realize—

The man frowned. "You're not showing as scheduled for a pickup today."

"I have what you need right here." Simon pulled out Amelia's tablet and turned it on with a stroke of his thumb. "It's a completely new program." He tapped the screen a few times. "North Cantral ruler, Aaron Markus himself, designed it."

Handing Ten's card back to her, the man shook his head. "I'm sorry, but I can't accept any new pass codes without hearing about it myself from the security crew. If this new program is coming into use, they'll let me know when I can accept it."

"You have no choice." Simon pressed the tablet with a finger.

The man blinked rapidly and stumbled forward a step. "What?" He fell to the ground with a thump and curled to the side. Within seconds, his breathing became soft and steady.

Simon slid Amelia's tablet back into the satchel. "Good to know that still works. I was afraid its trip down the Cantral waterways might have damaged it too much."

Ten reached over and tapped a button on the wall. The door behind them slid closed. "What did you do to him? That can't be legal."

"He's only asleep," Monica whispered. "Don't worry."

"Of course it's not legal, my dear. If I thought you had any qualms about defying a totalitarian, enslaving government, I would have left you behind. But considering your history, I thought it safe to bring you." Simon stepped over the man with one long-legged stride. "Now let's be off. These tunnels can be treacherously maze-like."

Ten's expression turned somber, and she squared her shoulders. "Right."

A draft whispered around them and headed down a tunnel nearby. Monica shivered and followed Simon and Ten along the passage leading straight ahead. Her clothes clung to her limbs, chaffing her legs with every step. This was going to be a long walk.

CHAPTER TWENTY

Simon stopped in the middle of a long, dirt-floor tunnel. "This is as good a place as any." He untied his cloak and let the still-damp garment fall to the floor.

A small globe light buzzed above. Monica rested her head against the wall. "For what? We haven't seen an entrance anywhere."

Ten fingered the ties on her cloak. "I'm starting to get the feeling that we're lost."

"No, no. Just pausing for a quick costume change." Simon dug into his satchel and removed rolled-up black fabric. "I didn't want to risk the doorman waking up while we were still nearby." He handed a black dress to Monica and another to Ten. "This should fit you well enough." He shook out a pair of pants and a shirt. "Now turn around and get changed, and I'll do the same. There's no time to argue. If someone sees merchants wandering the halls, they're sure to raise alarms."

"Great." Ten held the dress up to herself. "I've always wondered what it would be like to be a Seen. Maybe I shouldn't have wondered so hard."

Simon started unbuttoning his shirt and turned to face down the hall. "Stop yakking and hurry up."

Monica quickly changed into the Seen dress and discarded her merchant's clothes into a soggy pile.

"Done," Ten called.

"As am I," Simon muttered. "It's nice to be back in the uniform."

Monica spun on her heel to face them. "I am, too."

Simon slung his satchel strap back over his head. "Wheaten, if you'll kindly stow the clothing in your satchel, we'll be on our way again." He patted his bag. "I don't want the computer or my papers to get wet."

"Sure thing." She snapped open her satchel and started shoving the clothes inside.

As Monica helped her pick up the items, water squished out around her fingers. She pushed the clothes into the bulging bag and wiped a hand on her dress. "It's good to be dry again. I thought that rain was going to rip us to shreds. I've never been in a storm that heavy. Well … until I got on the *Katrina* I had never been in a storm at all, but I never imagined one could be so fierce."

Ten refastened her bag. "Just wait until it's storm season. What we saw out there is nothing compared to some squalls we get."

"Squalls?" Monica hurried after Simon who had started walking again, apparently oblivious to their conversation.

"You know. Storms. Really bad ones." Ten patted her bag. "We have to take off our cloaks before climbing the rigging, or we'll get blown overboard. Sometimes there's even hail."

Monica forced a smile. Would Ten think she was stupid if she asked what hail was? The girl already found her strange, so what could it hurt? "What is hail, exactly?" She hurried to add, "I read about it in a book once, but I've never seen it or had it explained to me."

"Hail is nothing more than chunks of ice…" Ten launched into an explanation about weather patterns and hailstorms and how the sky turned green. She shifted to talking about hurricanes and tornadoes and the difference between them and waterspouts, barely pausing for a breath between topics.

The flood of information made Monica's head spin, a good feeling, really. Learning new things was one of the best parts of freedom.

A few minutes later, they arrived at two passageways, one leading straight ahead to a metal door and another leading to the right, up a flight of stairs. Monica smiled. Just like home. Though she had been to only two other palaces, it seemed that the designs in all of them were pretty similar when it came to wall slaves' entrances and exits.

Simon marched to the stairs and rested a hand on the battered railing. "Up we go, then."

Ten gripped Monica's arm. "It feels so close in here, like the walls are pressing in on us. It's nothing like the sea."

Monica slipped her fingers into Ten's hand and gave it a squeeze. The poor girl had been used to open spaces her whole life, yet she could potentially have been born here, sentenced to a life of confinement. She had escaped that fate only because of other people's mistakes and sacrifices.

They continued up the stairs in silence until Ten broke the quiet with a whisper. "You used to live here?"

"The walls were my home, yes. But not these walls." Memories resurfaced with each step—uneven walls marked with graffiti and dents from the years of people traveling past without a sound but who still let their thoughts be known through the damage they inflicted with their tools and the tortured words scrawled by angry hands. *Death to Nobles. We will be free.* Curse words crossed through some of the lines, and sketches marred others.

She fingered the bare spot on her wrist. Without her band to tell her the time, it was difficult to know for sure, but it must be a little past noon. The wall slaves would be having a short respite to wolf down their meager meal bars before heading back to work.

Stopping in front of a passage that led to the left, Simon raised a hand. "This entrance will do as well as any. We can't risk being seen by wall slaves." He kept his voice low. "We don't know if the wall slaves and Seen live together in the dorms as they do in some palaces. They might raise an alarm."

Ten edged against the wall, her eyes wide. "What's down there? It's too narrow to go very far, right?" She touched the intersection's corner. "It looks like we might have to walk sideways to get through."

"We probably will." Monica stepped into the hall. "We don't know exactly where it leads yet, but it has to go to a room, or they wouldn't have it here." She sidled along the wall, deeper into the tunnel. Light from the main corridor dimmed.

As Simon followed, he sniffed loudly and muttered something about being too old for this.

Shuffling in place, Ten looked up and down the hall. Monica beckoned to her as best she could from the narrow walkway. "Come on. The wall slaves' lunch break will be done soon, and they'll be getting back to work. We don't have much time."

"I know, I know." Ten edged into the opening and followed them.

As Monica inched along, dust swirled around her feet, tickling her toes. A soft, almost imperceptible buzzing filled the air, as if a hundred voices whispered in the corridor nearby. Could there be that many Nobles in the room outside?

They passed a hallway leading off to their right, but a few feet in, a wooden board blocked the way. Monica frowned. A blocked passage? Why? It would only make it more difficult for the slaves to do their jobs.

As they continued, they walked past another blocked-off passage. Monica shook her head. Something odd was going on.

Every few yards, finger-sized white lights shone on the wall. Marking an access panel maybe? Monica approached the first one and crouched, splaying her knees out to the side so she could fit in the narrow space. A wooden switch poked out of the wall beside the light. "Definitely an access panel."

When she flipped the switch, a fist-sized hole opened. Soft music filtered in from the room—flitting silvery notes that died out quickly only to be replaced by a swift, lyrical sequence that completely drowned out the nearby vibrations.

Monica peered into the hole. A young girl with dark brown shoulder-length hair sat on a bench in front of a large, oddly shaped black box that stood on three legs. Was it called a piano? It seemed like someone had mentioned that name as a musical instrument before in a distant memory.

"What is that?" Ten's whisper barely rose above the music.

"Someone playing piano, of course." Simon tapped Monica on the head. "We certainly can't go through this one. It wouldn't do for a Noble to see three Seen sneaking in from the wall-slave passage."

"Right." Monica studied the girl for a second longer. Something about her face seemed familiar, but—

Simon hooked a hand under Monica's shoulder and hauled her to her feet. "Come, come. The next room might be empty."

She flicked the view port switch closed and continued down the passage. He was right, as usual. They couldn't appear in front of a Noble.

With every sidestep, the next white light drew nearer. When Monica arrived in front of it, she crouched again and looked through the port. A wide hallway opened up, expanding to the left and right and out of view. Straight ahead, a window looked out over a white stone railing and into a garden, though the heavy rain disguised a blur of greenery growing there.

"It's an empty hall," she whispered. "It should be fine to go out here." She laid a hand on the panel and pressed. The door swung open slowly and silently. Letting out a short sigh, she climbed through. At least it didn't require a chip. Some of the newer access doors did, and if they were to come upon one of those, they might be in trouble.

Viral Execution

She scooted out into the corridor. Dusting off her dress, she straightened. Paintings covered the ceilings, crystal chandeliers hung from golden chains, and other crystal fixtures stood on pedestals beside each of the dozen or so windows lining the hall.

The smell of fresh paint and plaster assaulted her nose, making her sneeze. Her muscles stiffened, and she glanced around. Piano music drifted in from the other room. At least the girl had stayed put. Simon crawled from the passage, and Ten quickly followed, shoving the door closed with a foot. Her bare toes left smudges on the glass panel.

"We can't leave any sign that we were here." Shaking her head, Monica used the edge of her skirt to wipe the mark away. The panel was part of a ceiling-high mirror made of twenty-one glass pieces that reflected the windows and the garden.

"Sorry." Ten held up her satchel. "What should we do with our bags? Seen don't have anything like this, do they?"

"No, we'll have to hide them somewhere." Monica pressed on the glass panel, careful to keep her fingers on the edges. The glass sprang open, revealing the wall-slave passage again. She held her hand out to Ten. "Quick, we'll hide them in here. A wall slave will find them, but it's unlikely they'll report clothes. They'll probably keep them for themselves."

Ten handed Monica the bag, and she stuffed it inside. Turning to Simon, she nodded at his satchel. "Yours, too."

He held the bag to his chest. "We can't risk losing the tablet and the journal."

"All right, but if someone sees you carrying the bag, they might ask questions." She shut the panel and wiped off two fingerprints she had left.

He opened the bag. "That's a chance we'll have to take." He reached into the bag. "And before I forget. You two need shoes and wristbands."

Monica wiggled her bare toes against the polished wood floor. She and Ten hadn't worn shoes at all on the ship. In fact, as far as she could remember she hadn't ever had a pair of shoes before she posed as Amelia.

He withdrew two pairs of black socks and flat, thin shoes and tossed them to Monica. As she fumbled with the shoes, the socks drifted to the floor.

"Simon!" she hissed. "The shoes could have made a lot of noise." Handing a pair of shoes to Ten, she glared at him. The piano music continued. The girl in the room nearby likely hadn't heard them yet.

"I had complete confidence in your abilities." Simon withdrew three plain gray wristbands and closed his bag. "Now hurry. Someone could come along at any time."

Monica slipped the socks and shoes on, then tied the laces with deft fingers. Just a few weeks ago she would never have managed to get the ties secured correctly, but thanks to Ten's knot-tying lessons on the *Katrina*, it came easily now.

"These aren't comfortable." Ten shuffled her shoe-clad feet, her nose wrinkled. "They seem dangerous. I can't get a grip on the floor."

"No one expects you to climb rigging or other such pursuits while wearing them." Simon glared at Ten and Monica and handed each a wristband. "These don't work, but they are an essential part of your costume. Now let's go. We need to figure out this palace before anyone asks why three Seen are wandering around aimlessly." He marched off down the hall.

After sliding her wristband in place, Monica hurried after him. Ten did the same and followed, pausing every few steps to glance down at her feet. Monica tried not to smile. Ten would have a lot of new things to get used to in a very short time.

Monica's mood quickly darkened. How would Ten react when given orders by a Noble? She was accustomed to taking orders from Fahltrid, but a Noble?

Monica fell into step with Ten. "We might get stopped and ordered to do something, you know."

"I know." Ten shrugged.

"And we'll have to do it, even if we don't want to." Monica stared at one of the statues as they passed—a man holding some sort of weapon in one hand and the horns of an animal in the other. What would these Eursians be like? These people of Penniak could be very different from people in Cantral. What if they tried to talk to her in that language she had heard in the streets? Of course everyone had to know the Cantral language, but what if they preferred to speak in this other language? She wouldn't know what they were saying.

They walked in silence for a few minutes until they came to another hall. The smell of paint grew stronger, and some of the walls looked wet. As they approached, the buzzing noise intensified.

Simon walked to one wall and peered at it closely. "Someone has been remodeling. I wonder why. This place certainly has enough room. Not only that, the architecture is stunning without any modification. And what in the world is that buzzing noise? It sounds like a ventilation fan malfunctioning."

"Where are we going?" Monica tugged on his sleeve. Penniak's palace modifications weren't important. "We can't just wander around aimlessly. I think this place is bigger than Cillineese's palace. We'll get lost."

"We're looking for another Seen." Simon peered around the corner down the adjacent corridor. "Someone who can tell us where the main rooms of the palace are located. Once we learn that, we will know where the best place to wait and watch for Madam Rose is." He tapped his chin and looked up and down the hall. "I suppose we could split up."

"Split up?" Ten's words came out in a squeak. She cleared her throat, as if to hide her nervousness. "Like Monica said, we could get lost. This place is big." Her cheeks flushed red. "I mean, I'm used to wandering around new cities and figuring out roads and such, but what about you two? You're used to staying in a palace all the time."

"Nonsense." Simon stepped into the side corridor, his brow wrinkling. "Monica is quite adept at memorizing routes, thanks to my amazing memory drills."

Monica nodded. He had drilled her enough times with mazes and fact sheets that she could memorize most things without a second thought. The memory drug Aric had given her when she was posing as Amelia had also helped tremendously. "I don't mind splitting up, if it means finding my mother faster. I want to get this over with."

Simon patted Ten's head. "Don't worry. You can stick with me. If anyone asks, I'm training you. Plenty of younger Seen have mentors to help them learn the rules."

"Sounds good to me." Ten's shoulders relaxed, and she held her head a little higher.

Monica bit her lip to hold back her objection. Seen were assigned to a mentor only if they were eight years old or younger. Someone Ten's age wouldn't need one anymore, but saying so would only make her nervous.

Hooking his arm around Ten's, Simon gestured down the hall. "After you, Mademoiselle."

Ten smiled and raised an eyebrow. "Mademoiselle?"

"It's old French." Simon guided her down the hall to the left. "They still use a form of it here in Penniak."

"Bye, then," Monica called, giving a short wave. She might as well go to the right. The other hall dead-ended, so there weren't many other options.

The air still vibrated with the soft noise coming from every wall, and her footfalls echoed from the domed ceiling. She quickened her pace.

A large opening stood to her right, revealing a parlor sitting room. Three windows lined one wall with creamy translucent curtains draping them. Rain spattered the windows, and wind rattled the panes. A couch with a deep purple cover looked inviting to her weary limbs, but she bowed her head and passed the room. The torturous walk through the driving rain had sapped her energy, but there would be time to rest later.

She broke into a trot and passed the next few rooms with barely a glance inside. Where was everyone? Shouldn't the palace of Eursia's capital have more people? She came to a staircase cut into the wall to her right. Dashing up, she ran her hand along the curved metal railing. There weren't even any noises of wall slaves. Certainly there had to be hundreds in a building this large.

As she put her foot on the last step, a woman rounded a corner, coming out of a nearby room. The woman held a few papers in her hands, and her gaze never left them. Her knee-length skirt swished as she approached the stairs.

Monica gulped. The woman's finely tailored brown skirt and colorful blouse proclaimed her status as a Noble. Everything in Monica told her to run, but that would draw more attention.

The woman looked up and met Monica's gaze with wide brown eyes. "Oh, I'm sorry. I didn't see you there."

"That's all right, ma'am." Bowing her head, Monica took in a deep gasp. It couldn't be, could it? The woman's face shape, her eyes. They were so familiar, like something out of a dream.

The woman patted Monica's shoulder with a gentle touch. "Are you new? I don't think I've seen you here before."

Monica forced herself to look up. "Yes ma'am. Brand new." She met the woman's gaze again. Could this be Brenna Rose? Could she really be her mother?

CHAPTER TWENTY-ONE

The woman squeezed Monica's shoulder and gave her a tight-lipped smile. "Then you need to know you don't have to be afraid. We don't have as many strict rules as the other city-states." She touched Monica's still-wet braid. "I see someone already told you you can style your hair outside of the standard regulations."

Monica widened her eyes. Her hair! She and Ten had forgotten to put their hair in simple ponytails like all Seen women wore.

"I'm sorry." The woman released her, a puzzled expression on her face. "I'm scaring you. I'll let you get back to your duties now." The woman's gaze searched Monica's face one more time, her puzzled look turning into a frown before she headed down the stairs.

Putting a hand to her thumping chest, Monica blinked rapidly. Her mother hadn't recognized her? Tears welled in her eyes, but she wiped them away. How could she expect her to recognize someone after so long? Still, she had to talk to her. But how should she address her? Only one choice was available. She would just have to go for it.

As the woman reached the last step, Monica called out, "Madam Rose?"

The woman grabbed the handrail, her knuckles white. She turned and faced Monica, her skin pale. "What did you just call me?"

The blood drained from her face, but Monica forced herself to whisper it again. "Madam Rose."

The woman mounted the stairs two at a time and took Monica's wrist in a firm grasp, her gaze a mixture of anguish and concern. "Who are you?" Without waiting for an answer, she guided Monica to a side room and closed the door, bolting it with a quick flip of the latch. She turned to Monica again and laid a hand on her own chest. "I'm sorry, I'm not …"

Fear raised prickles on Monica's neck. She wasn't Rose? Then why had she reacted so forcefully to being called that? "You're not Rose?"

"I'm not used to being called by that name."

"Oh. Right. Simon said Rose was your preferred name, but you're also called Brenna Rose."

"Simon?" The woman's gaze pored over Monica again. She reached out and brushed a cool hand across Monica's cheek. "Who—" She gulped, and tears welled in her eyes. "Who are you?"

A stab of sorrow pierced Monica's chest. Her mother didn't remember her. "M—Monica." She shook her head. No, Rose might not know that name. "I mean—"

"Sierra?" Rose drew her hand back and cupped it over her mouth, blinking against the tears filling her eyes. She dropped her papers and held out her arms.

Monica hesitated. This was her mother—the woman who gave her up so she could live, but calling her "mother" seemed strange. Unbidden tears blurred her vision. She took two steps into Rose's embrace and wrapped her arms around her waist. Laying her head against her mother's chest, she breathed the faint scent of perfume.

"I'm sorry." Rose choked back sobs. "I'm so sorry. My little girl, to see you again …" Her fingers trembling, she gently ran a hand over Monica's head. "Sierra, Sierra, what have you been through?" She caressed Monica's scarred arms. "I can see it in your eyes, the tortures you've endured. I didn't know how bad it would be. I could only imagine, but ..."

Sobs erupted from Monica's chest, welling up from the innermost corners of her heart. As she reveled in her mother's strong, loving embrace, memories of past tortures came afresh to mind. How had she survived all those years in the walls? Could anyone explain it? She should have been dead a dozen times over, yet here she was.

Monica hugged Rose tighter. What if she disappeared? What if this was just some vivid memory coming back to life for an instant and her mother was actually far away or dead?

"I won't ever let you go again," her mother whispered. Her lips pressed to Monica's head, moving her hair and sending a tickling sensation down her scalp.

Pulling back, Monica wiped her eyes, a flash of fear worming its way back into her chest. "You can't promise that." Her words came out cracked, and her throat ached from crying. "I can't either." She inhaled a sharp, shaky breath. "We don't know what's going to happen in the next few days, or even hours."

"Whatever happens, I'll stick with you to the end, even if it means my death." Rose caressed Monica's cheek again and shook her head. "I have thought of you every day. I regret not taking you with me. I should have insisted. We should have found a way."

She gripped Monica's arms, turning them over to reveal the worst of her scars, thin white and pink lines crisscrossing her skin all the way up to her hands and her shortened finger. New tears trickled down her mother's cheeks. "I can't imagine what you've gone through." She ran a hand over Monica's forearm. "I'm sorry. Can you ever forgive me for leaving you?"

Monica grasped Rose's fingers. "There's nothing to forgive. We both had our missions to fulfill." She touched a scarred forearm. "These are just testimonies to what I've gone through, to the people I've helped save, and ..." Reaching beneath her collar, she withdrew Alyssa's half-circle medallion necklace. "And those who've died for me."

She looked up and searched Rose's face, the faint lines around her sorrowful brown eyes and forehead barely concealed by a thin layer of the facial powders and paints Noble women often used. "You've been through a lot, too, I'm sure." Monica tucked the necklace away again.

"It's nothing compared to your pain." Rose turned her head and closed her eyes for a second. "There's so much to say, but how can I say it? How can I fit twelve years into a few sentences?"

Monica nodded. She had so much to tell about her life—what happened, the news of Cantral and of the life she lived there. But did it really matter? It would only make Rose feel worse and wouldn't change the past. "We have too much to discuss about your programs and what we have to do now, in the present."

Rose stooped and gathered her papers. "Oh, Sierra. It's so complicated. The past is intertwined with the present, and the present wants to take a life of its own until it's completely out of our control. Yet, we still have to trust in God, because it's not out of His." She set the papers on a side table.

Widening her eyes, Monica shook her head. God—someone she only knew about in passing. How could she trust someone she didn't know? "How is it complicated? We just have to shut down the computers. I've done it twice now, and with your help, it should be even easier."

"I'm afraid it's not as easy as you may think." Rose rested her hands on Monica's shoulders. "I'd love to hear of your accomplishments. You've shut down two computers?" She shook her head. "Amazing. And I've taken all this time to partially disable some systems."

"You've had to be more careful." Monica clasped her mother's hand. How good it was to feel a loving touch. How long had it been since someone had shown her real love? She placed a hand on the back of her neck. "Your chip doesn't allow you near the computers, does it? I can go wherever I want to."

Rose laid a hand over Monica's, covering her neck. "Joel's plan worked." She drew her hand back and blinked rapidly. "It came so close to failure, and he sent me away before …" Inhaling, she shook her head. "A doctor in Cillineese knew about you and wanted to give you a chip before your birthday because of the rumors about your father's plans, but I see Joel was able to hold him off."

"I—I didn't know." Monica wiped away a pooling tear. She could have been chipped. Her father had saved her more than once. If she had had a chip, her nurse, Faye, would never have been able to get her out of Cillineese. The computer wouldn't have allowed it. "Faye got me out, and I lived in Cantral all this time, using other people's chips." She reached beneath her dress to pull out the glass vial containing Amelia's chip before remembering she had left it on the ship. "I often carry a dead one with me, but I left it behind this time."

Rose nodded. "So many people killed by this system. We have to stop it."

"Do you know where the computers are?" Monica searched her mother's face. She still hadn't explained why it was more difficult. "I can just sneak in and tear them apart like last time. I gutted the computers in Cillineese and Cantral. The Seen have posted guards to make sure the Nobles or anyone else won't rebuild the computers. We can do the same here."

"I do know where the computers are." Rose leafed through the pages. "In fact, I was drawing up plans for some codes for them."

Wrinkling her brow, Monica asked, "To shut them down? Then you don't need my help?"

Rose folded the papers and tucked them under an arm. "As I said. It's not that easy. I wish it could be, but there are too many lives at stake. We have to move carefully. Penniak is in a transition period, and everything is in limbo until these codes are in place."

Viral Execution

Monica stepped back from her mother. "You're working for them? But Simon said—Tyrell—the codes—the viruses." She tried to collect her thoughts. What was happening? Her mother worked for the Nobles?

Rose shook her head and held up a hand. "Sierra, please, don't think badly of me. I'm doing what I can. Every program I write, there's a glitch, a bug. I've kept Penniak from having its own system for as long as I can. I even kept us linked to Cantral's system for as long as possible, hoping, praying that we would hear of its downfall and ours as well, but there was only so much I could do without being caught. There are other programmers there to fix every error I write. Fortunately, they miss some. Your father taught me well. I would never betray him." She reached out and drew Monica into a tight hug. "Or you."

Monica relaxed in Rose's arms, all doubt fading away. Of course she had to be careful. She had a chip, a constant monitor of her whereabouts. If she were discovered and terminated, then she wouldn't be able to do any more good, and whatever she had broken would be fixed. Then where would they be? "I think I understand."

"Thank you." Rose stroked Monica's hair. "I still can't believe you're here, that you're even alive. I've prayed for this meeting ever since we were parted. I have so many things to tell you." She drew away and held Monica at arm's length. "Most importantly, I—"

A knock sounded at the door. Rose's face drained of color. She released Monica's shoulders. "The meeting."

"What?" Monica whispered.

"Please, pretend to be a Seen, just for a while longer." Rose wiped her eyes free of tears, straightened, and walked sedately to the door.

Monica wiped her own tears away. If Rose could act at a time like this, then so could she.

After unlatching the door, her mother opened it, revealing a young man dressed in a Seen uniform. He bowed his head slightly. "Madam Brenna, I was told to inform you that the meeting is about to start, and Master Dedrick requests your presence. He also requests that you bring your program plans."

"Thank you, Felix." Rose offered the young man a small smile. "Please tell him I'll be there shortly. With the plans."

The man bowed again, stared at Monica for a second, then backed out of the room. Letting out a long sigh, Rose closed the door. "Sierra."

Monica studied Rose's worried expression, the taut line of her mouth. "What's this meeting about? May I ..." She squared her shoulders. This was her mother. She would listen to a reasonable request. "May I come with you? As a Seen. We're—I mean, the Seen are all but invisible to most people. No one would even notice."

Rose smiled but shook her head. "I'm afraid not. Only Dedrick and the five head programmers are allowed in these meetings. I wasn't even promoted to a head programmer position until three years ago." She opened a drawer in the side table and withdrew a tablet. "They don't fully trust me even now." Tucking the tablet under an arm alongside the papers, she nodded at the door. "It's a long walk to the meeting room. Will you come with me?"

"Of course." The urge to take Rose's hand and hold it tightly was almost overwhelming, but she held back. She was a Seen again. Rose—or Brenna, as they called her here—was a Noble. Seen and Nobles didn't hold hands.

CHAPTER
TWENTY-TWO

Monica and Rose entered a corridor where Felix waited by a closed door. He opened the door for Rose then closed it again after she entered. The latch clicked loudly in the stillness. He looked at Monica, both dark eyebrows raised. A garbled, guttural sentence came out of his mouth, and he nodded.

Taking a step back, she gulped. That was that language she had heard in the streets.

"No, no," he whispered, switching to the official Cantral language. "I only asked if you understood me. I didn't mean to frighten you. Most new Seen speak Gervanian best, so I thought I'd try that first." He beckoned to her. "You're Madam Brenna's new assistant? She hasn't had one since she first came to Penniak, so I wondered."

"Uh, yes." Monica wrinkled her brow. So this Felix wasn't as ominous as he seemed. "I'm sorry, I speak only the Cantral language and a little bit of Cillineese."

He raised his eyebrows again. "Really? Usually assistants must speak at least five languages to even be considered. I speak no fewer than six, with a smattering of Latin." He lifted his chin, as if it were an accomplishment to be proud of.

Monica nodded. What was Latin? She couldn't ask. It would only make her seem more ignorant. "That's quite impressive. So you're an assistant?"

"Yes, to Master Dedrick himself." Felix edged toward her, away from the door. "Don't worry about them hearing. That room is almost soundproof, to keep their meetings secret, of course."

"Of course." Monica sidled away from Felix. With his quick smile and thin, clean-shaven face and easy manner, he seemed too friendly, too eager. And who was this Master Dedrick? Penniak's ruling Noble? It seemed the most likely explanation. And who was he to Rose? When she said his name, it … it was something she couldn't put her finger on.

"You're a quiet one, huh? We assistants don't have to be as silent as average Seen, you know. I guess you were recently promoted." Felix took another step toward her. "How long have you been in Penniak? Not long, by your accent. I'm pretty good at figuring out where people are from by their mannerisms and accents."

Monica concealed a grimace. More questions to answer. At least he was willing to talk enough for both of them. "I guess you've been an assistant for a long time then?"

"Oh, yes." He smiled, as if enjoying a pleasant memory. "I was apprenticed to Dedrick's assistant when Madam Brenna first came to Penniak, and that was twelve years ago. I was made Master Dedrick's assistant when I was fifteen, so I've been an assistant for four years. You'll find out soon enough that that's a long time for an assistant to last. Most don't last longer than two years. You have to have a tough personality and be willing to be outspoken to be an assistant. Most Seen are too timid. It's an honor to have this job and be a Seen, anyway. There are plenty of lower Nobles who'd love to take my place."

He retrieved a palm-sized computer tablet from a satchel that hung near his waist. "You're going to have to be very careful about your job. Madam Brenna is …" He lowered his voice and stepped even closer. "Well, don't tell anyone I told you, but she reminds me of a Seen sometimes, and she doesn't like to be around the other Nobles or have an assistant. You probably won't last long in this position."

"You won't either, if anyone hears you talking about Madam Brenna like that." Monica stepped back. Her mother was a Noble, and maybe the only one out there who actually deserved the title. "You shouldn't be so trusting with someone you don't know. As far as you know, I could be a lower Noble."

Felix laughed softly, then cast a glance at the closed door leading to the meeting room. "It would be hard for you to pass as a Noble. While your facial features have classic Noble lines, I see a lot of Seen in your ancestry, and your build is much too slight. You could almost pass for a Slink, but I wouldn't be so rude as to call you one."

"You basically just did." Monica's cheeks burned hot. This man seemed perfectly willing to push her in all the wrong ways. Did he even realize how he sounded? Did Dedrick let him speak to him that way? But what did Felix know anyway? She *was* a Noble. Being a wall slave and Seen might come naturally now, but she wasn't born as either.

"Yes, well"—Felix started typing on his computer—"my apologies."

Monica sidled farther away until she stood only a few feet from the intersecting hallway. The buzzing in the walls seemed to grow louder in the silence. Where was it coming from? She could ask Felix, but a question would just draw more attention. And where were Ten and Simon? They could be wandering anywhere, getting into all sorts of trouble. At least Simon's satchel might not be noticed, since Felix had one as well.

Breathing out a long sigh, she fiddled with her blank-faced wristband. Felix seemed content to leave her alone for now. Good. She had barely had time to think about what just happened. Her mother was in that meeting room, separated by only a wall of stone and plaster. She had hugged her with all her might and said she loved her.

Monica wrapped her arms around herself, remembering the embrace. How good it felt to be loved, to know someone truly cared. Certainly Tresa cared for her, and Simon did as well, in his own way, but neither could compare to a mother's love—something she hadn't experienced since her adoptive mother, Emmilah, had been taken to the fields eight years ago. Yet, it was difficult to call Rose "mother."

Frowning, Monica let her arms fall back to her sides. She hadn't seen Rose in twelve years, and besides the journal entries, knew nothing about her.

Monica watched the closed meeting room door for any sign of movement. There had been plenty of times that she never spared Rose a second thought during the years within the walls. Hunger pangs and dizziness often drove out other thoughts. Monica grimaced, remembering those times—aching hunger gnawing at her stomach with no hope of food in the near future. It had been easy to forget about that while on the ship, eating meals cooked by Fern or Ten and ration bars especially formulated for the sailors. There was no hunger on the *Katrina*.

Felix met her gaze for a second, then looked down at his computer again. After typing something, he looked at her once more. "I, uh—I am sorry—if I offended you." Ducking his head, he turned his attention to his computer.

She narrowed her eyes. "I'll be fine. I'm used to it." Simon did it often enough, and he didn't even bother apologizing. Still, it was decent of Felix to try to be nice. "I forgive you."

"Great. So." He smiled. "What's your name, anyway? I'm Felix."

Monica nodded. "Right, Moth—Madam Ro—I mean—" Heat rose to Monica's cheeks. The correct name finally came to her tongue. "Madam Brenna mentioned your name when you delivered the message about the meeting."

The heat in her cheeks intensified. How could she have been so careless? Rose was Madam Brenna to her. She repeated the name in her head a dozen times, trying to get it to stick. Another mess-up like that could be very bad.

"Okay, so she did." He slid his computer back into his bag. His gaze seemed to pierce her, figuring out all her secrets. "But she didn't mention your name."

The meeting room door opened. Perfect timing. She could figure out what name to use for herself later.

Felix jerked to attention, standing straight and tugging on his black shirt to align the buttons in a perfect row down his chest. Monica straightened as well and checked her dress for wrinkles. There were a few from being stuffed in Simon's bag, but they weren't too bad.

Two older men exited the room, talking heatedly in the nasally language Monica had heard on the streets. One of them, with hair whiter than the other, held a computer tablet between them and gestured at it as they walked down the hall and turned into the side corridor.

A dark-eyed woman emerged, her face lined with the ghosts of past glares and her jaw clenched as she marched down the corridor. A middle-aged man sauntered from the room, his hands jammed in his pockets. His dark hair and compact build raised reminders of Fahltrid, but this man was younger, paler. He nodded at Felix, paused half a step as he passed Monica, then nodded again and went on his way.

Monica frowned. What was that for? Nobles generally ignored Seen. Maybe Felix was right about assistants being different from other Seen.

Rose came out next, her papers and tablet held close, her features perfectly schooled to show no emotion. After a tall, broad-shouldered man exited behind her, Felix closed the meeting room door.

The man placed a hand on Rose's shoulder and said something in the nasally language, smiling as he spoke. Rose said something in the same language.

He motioned to Felix and strode down the corridor with long easy steps. Felix jogged after him and gave Monica an almost imperceptible wave as he passed.

Rose lingered in the hall, walking slowly. She reached out and grasped Monica's hand, gave it a squeeze, then stepped away again. She said something in an odd language.

Monica blinked. Was she supposed to understand that?

Rose's expression turned downcast. "Do you speak only Cantral's language, then?" She held up a hand. "Please, don't take that the wrong way. I'm only wondering."

Regret pricked Monica's heart, and she shook her head. Had she let her mother down somehow by not learning other languages? They had never come easily. "I'm afraid I only know Cantral's language and a few words from others I picked up while living in the wall slave dorms. We had transfers from other cities frequently, and they often didn't speak the main language very well."

"Lower your voice, please," Rose whispered, casting a look up the hall. "It would be easy for others to overhear us." She glanced back at the meeting room. "We'll have to find someplace private to continue our discussion. Unfortunately, all conversations in that meeting room are recorded, since they're official business."

"Then where can we go?"

Rose laid a gentle hand on Monica's shoulder. "The library will most likely suit. There are plenty of private rooms for study and programming use." She fixed her gaze straight ahead and walked down the corridor with a determined stride.

Monica hurried after her, adding a little quick-jog step every few feet to keep up. As they made their way down the hall, taking a half dozen turns, they passed a few more Nobles and Seen who seemed to take no notice of this new assistant. And that was just fine.

Glancing all around, Monica quickly memorized the route in case she had to return by herself. There was no telling what could happen in the next few minutes. It felt wrong to be walking out in the open like this while Nobles and Seen went about their business as though Cantral's computers were still up and running and everything was normal.

But everything wasn't normal. And soon, if all went well, nothing would ever be normal again.

CHAPTER TWENTY-THREE

Rose stopped in front of a tall, narrow wooden door and whispered to Monica, "We'll have to be cautious in here. This is the library side door, and the meeting rooms are close by, but we're still likely to run into people who know me and might want to discuss business matters. They'll wonder about you and might ask questions since I usually don't have an assistant."

"I understand." Monica met her mother's brown eyes. Too many questions could get them in trouble. If someone tried to look up her chip number, she would be discovered in an instant. "Should I use a different name, then?"

"Monica should be fine." Rose smiled. "Now let's not speak again until we find an empty meeting room." She turned the large brass knob and swung the door open. She slipped through the gap with the practiced ease of someone accustomed to small spaces.

Monica followed and closed the door softly behind them. Really, if they wanted to keep up this guise, she should have opened the door for Rose, but her mother was obviously not used to having a Seen around to wait on her.

They entered a brightly lit aisle lined with bookshelves that touched the curved, paneled ceiling. Rose rushed ahead, and Monica jogged after her. They moved so quickly she didn't have time to read any of the titles or memorize the room.

The odor of cleanser and perfumes wafted through the air, much different from the musty, old smells that lingered in the

Cillineese library, thanks to Simon's hobby of collecting ancient books. As they entered the library's main walkway, Rose slowed her pace. Monica followed her example and kept a few steps behind, her head bowed.

Buzzing whispers floated around the library—so different from the Cantral library which was often void of life—as the Nobles there cared more for computers and politics than reading. Someone stopped in front of Rose and spoke in the odd guttural language that sounded like the one Felix referred to as Gervanian. Monica kept her head down.

Rose responded in the same language, an exasperated edge creeping into her voice. They spoke for a few moments before she continued down the hall, Monica again trailing. When they arrived at a door off to the side, Rose motioned toward it.

Monica stood still for a second before realizing she was supposed to open it. Of course. There were other people around, and she had to play the part. She grabbed the knob and swung the door open. Rose strode through, and Monica entered after her, closing the door behind them.

"Finally." Rose reached around Monica and snapped a lock into place. "We can stop acting now. These rooms are for private study. They're unmonitored, and they don't even have time limits, so they're only for the highest-ranked Nobles."

Breathing a sigh of relief, Monica looked around the simply furnished room. Dark wood panels lined the walls, and an even darker desk and chair stood at one end of the small room.

Rose flipped on the light switch, and a lamp blinked to life, aiding the small globe lights in the ceiling. "We still won't have much time. I'm expected to deliver the final fix for a computer systems error in a few hours. We're implementing the last phase of a program to make the Penniak computers stable. We can't let that happen." She drew a chair away from a small table in the room's center. "Please, sit."

"Can't you just stall until we take the computers down?" Monica slid into the seat and tucked her feet under herself.

"I'm afraid not." Rose claimed a second seat and folded her hands on the shiny tabletop. "It's imperative that I write the program. If I don't, someone else will, and I won't be able to write in loopholes in case we can't take the system down in time. The other programmers are just as skilled as I am, and they would easily be able to keep me from changing the programs in the future. Jacob is especially good at it. I'm afraid he might even try to take over leadership if things go badly. He's been causing trouble ever since he was promoted to programmer eleven years ago. He wasn't even in Penniak but a few years before he got his promotion." Rose reached across the table and held a hand palm up. Monica slid her hand into her mother's, and Rose continued, "Now there's something important I need to tell you. I don't want you to learn it from someone else."

Monica squeezed her mother's hand and searched her face. Worry lines creased her forehead. "What is it?"

"I'm not sure how to say it." Rose's face flushed pink, then turned a little pale. "So I'll just tell you straight out." She inhaled deeply. "The only way for me to escape Cillineese's termination was if Joel and I were divorced and the computers no longer recognized us as family. We didn't want to do it. I said I would rather die in Cillineese with him, but he told me it was for the greater good. He couldn't escape, and he wanted us to, and that was the only way he knew how to do it."

Monica frowned. Divorced? Was that some Nobles' term?

Her mother continued. "He arranged for me to live with my sister, Veronica, in Cantral a week before the termination. Of course at the …" Tears welled in her eyes, and her words came out choked. "At the time, we didn't know how long it would be until the termination. His sources told him it wouldn't be long, and he should get me out while he could. We would have gotten you out then, too, but it just wasn't possible. Then suspicion about the reasons for our divorce was raised, and people questioned my loyalty. Veronica heard that the ruler of Penniak was looking to marry someone well connected to the Council of Eight, to strengthen ties."

She clasped and unclasped her hands and inhaled deeply. "Since my father was the southeast wing ruler at the time, I was a good candidate. Veronica and Joel agreed that if the termination were to happen, it would be safest for me if I were engaged to be married to someone whom the Council thought completely loyal."

Blood drained from Monica's head, making her dizzy. She pulled her hand from Rose's grip. "How long did you wait until you married him?"

Tears coursed down Rose's cheeks. "I refused to marry Dedrick until I knew for certain Cillineese was fallen and Joel was dead. I mourned for him and you for a month. I wanted to die, to leave this world of slavery and misery, but I knew what I had to do. I knew I had to marry Dedrick and reestablish my position in the Noble world for the good of all the slaves. Sierra ..." She gazed pleadingly at Monica. "You have to understand. I couldn't let Joel die in vain. He knew the risks. People died so I might live, and even though it hurt, I had to do what was necessary."

"I ... I see." Monica looked away from Rose's piercing stare. Of course she had to. It wasn't much different from the trials Monica herself had been through. She too had to suffer for others, to survive uncertain times and risk life and limb. Others had died for her, too. She couldn't let them down. "I understand." She met Rose's gaze again. "I'm sorry, I ... it was just a surprise, though I guess I should have realized you couldn't come here and attain such a high position without some sort of deal." Breathing a long sigh, she folded her hands on the table. "So you married Dedrick."

"Yes." Rose withdrew a small white cloth from her pocket and dried her eyes. "Which leads me to another revelation you might find difficult. Dedrick and I have two children—a daughter and son." She twisted the cloth between her fingers. "Faye and Alex."

Monica gripped the edge of her seat with both hands. Two children? That meant she had a brother and sister—a whole family here in Eursia, and she had had no idea. "Faye and Alex," she whispered. "You named Faye after my Seen nurse?"

Rose's shoulders relaxed, and she leaned back in her chair. "Yes, because I was hopeful that she would save you, and she was so kind and loyal."

"She did save me. My adoptive father in Cantral told me about her. She came all the way to the Cillineese walls to save me, even though it caused her immense pain." Monica turned her head from the memories, though they stayed in her mind's eye—brief flashes of images of Faye and that nightmarish day.

"I wish I could thank her." Rose fingered a lock of her loose-flowing brown hair. "I know well the pain caused from being out of bounds." She pointed to the papers and tablet she had been carrying on the table. "This program will only make things worse—more unbeatable, but how can I get around writing it? Dedrick trusts me. He counts on me to do this correctly, to stop people from overthrowing him, to help establish our government."

Monica tried to read her mother's forlorn expression. Did she actually love Dedrick? If he wanted the system to stay alive, then he had to be evil. Who could force people to live like the wall slaves and the Seen—or the peasants, fearful to even stay in a shop too long? "He believes in the chip system? How can he not know how you feel about it?"

Rose nodded, her eyes downcast. "He—he's a good man, just brought up to believe in the chips. He was groomed from an early age to assume this role, while you and I know better. I've tried to discuss it with him, but he won't hear me out. He thinks the system is fine and will be even better with our improvements."

Reaching across the table, Monica held her hand palm up. "Then what are you going to do?"

Rose's hand met Monica's, and their fingers intertwined. "What I know is right." She rubbed a hand over the tablet. "Things could get very difficult very quickly if we don't proceed with caution."

"Trust me, I know how to handle difficult." Monica smiled and released Rose's hand. "So what do we do first? You said we can't just destroy the computers, so what do we need to do to stop them?"

"So much courage." Rose's gaze searched Monica. "The computers reach everywhere in this palace." She gestured to the dark paneled walls that emitted a low vibrating noise. "There are systems built in every wall, redundancies around every corner, and there is only one terminal where master commands can be input. You can hear the systems in the walls everywhere you go. Some technicians were even putting in new ones this week, though they're finished now. If you tried to rip out every system, you'd bring the palace down around our ears, and it would kill many Slinks who wouldn't be able to escape."

"Then what about the main terminal?" Discouragement pricked at Monica, but she shoved it away. There was still a chance. Any access was a weak point they could exploit. "You could write a program to wipe out the computer. It's still possible."

Rose twisted a thin gold ring on her left hand. "I'm afraid only Dedrick can get in that room. It requires chip identification. Not even I can get in unless an emergency protocol is activated, and that would only happen if the computer thought Dedrick was dying or compromised." She stopped fiddling with the ring. "And before you ask, no, we can't break the door down. The room would be flooded with knockout gas, and we would be caught and probably executed. There is an emergency oxygen tank inside, but you have to have the right chip number to access it. Also, there are no Slink doors to the room. Dedrick takes care of everything himself."

A knock sounded at the door. Monica flinched.

Rose wiped her eyes one more time with her white cloth before stuffing it into a pocket. "Would you please get that, Sierra? I think it would be best if we keep up the Seen act for a while longer."

Monica slid out of her seat and pushed it back into place. "I think so, too. We can't very well tell Dedrick that I'm your daughter, can we?"

"No, I'm afraid not. I wish I could, but—"

"I know. I wasn't trying to make you feel bad." Monica smiled. "I understand the situation."

The knock came again. Monica unlatched the bolt and swung the door open.

Simon stood outside, a fist raised to knock once more.

Ten peeked around his shoulder. "We found you!"

Simon's bushy eyebrows turned down, and he swatted Ten lightly on the head. "Be quiet, young lady. Don't you know we're in a library?" He peered into the room, brushing Monica out of the way.

"What is the meaning of this?" Rose pushed back her chair and marched to the door. When Rose and Simon locked gazes, her jaw dropped. "Simon?" Taking a step back, she beckoned to him. "Come in, quickly, please. Did anyone see you?"

Simon gave Ten a quick shove, and she trotted inside. He shut the door with a jerk. "Doubtful. It's wonderful—the Nobles here actually seem interested in books. How did you ever manage that, Madam?"

"I'm sure I had nothing to do with it." Rose grinned and held out a hand. "It's so good to see you again, Simon."

"Handshakes, what nonsense." He waved her hand away and gave her a quick hug. "I've known you since you were a young—"

"Simon," Rose's voice took on a warning tone. "Please. I think I know what you're going to say." She pulled away from him. "And I haven't told Sierra yet. Let me tell her in my own time."

Monica wrinkled her brow. A Noble hugging a Seen like an old friend. That was a sight many wouldn't believe. But tell her what? What else could her mother be hiding? Wasn't being remarried and having two children enough of a surprise?

CHAPTER TWENTY-FOUR

"I see you've reunited with your daughter." Simon sank into one of the seats at the table. "So we've started calling Sierra? That or Monica is fine with me. She's changed names so many times. We could even call her Amelia, and she would still answer."

Her face growing hot, Monica shook her head. "Simon, please."

"Amelia?" Rose slid back into the other seat. "Amelia is Gerald's daughter's name. Why—"

"We don't have time to get into that," Monica said. "I'm sorry, but we really need to start on this plan. We don't have much time before … before Mother has to deliver a program to Dedrick and the other programmers."

Ten leaned over and whispered, "I am incredibly confused. I don't know who any of those people are."

Simon pointed at Ten. "Ah, yes, I forgot. Madam Rose, Wheaten, from the merchant ship *Katrina*." He then gestured at Rose. "Ten, Madam Rose, Monica's mother."

Rose nodded to Ten. "It's nice to meet you, Wheaten, even under these circumstances. And please, Simon, here in Penniak I'm Brenna."

"Oh, yes, of course." Simon muttered something under his breath about people in her family changing their names too often.

Monica sighed. "It would take a long time to explain who everyone else is. We've figured out that I can't just tear up the computers like last time. It's impossible here because of their layout and expansive reach." She withdrew Alyssa's medallion necklace and brandished its sharp edge. "This is useless here."

"And we can't access the master panel to install a virus, either." Rose ran a hand through her hair, pushing the long locks away from her face. "It feels hopeless. Before Dedrick installed the system, I thought I had a chance. I even have a virus mostly written that could wipe out the computers for good, but I haven't finished it yet. I didn't want to risk anyone using it for ill. There were a lot of rumors and accusations flying when we received news of Cantral's fall and Tyrell's death, too. I couldn't work for a while—it was too dangerous."

"I guess we should just give up, then?" Ten squeaked as she said the last word.

"Give up?" Simon half rose from his chair. "We can't give up! It's not in our nature. We Seen are a hardy bunch. We adapt to our situations. We just have to think of a plan. Something I'm rather good at. So you're in luck."

"Yes, Simon." Rose ran a finger around her tablet. "I've been grateful for your plans in the past. You and Joel were always able to come up with some of the best solutions to our problems, even when you were far away in Trentin."

"How kind of you to say so." Simon rested his folded hands on the table. "Could we perhaps just blow the computers up? If they are throughout the palace, a few well-placed charges would do the trick. We would evacuate everyone, of course."

Ten's eyes lit up. "I know just the person to get us the explosives!"

"While it would work …" Rose shook her head. "No. Evacuating all the Slink, Seen, and Nobles would be next to impossible without more help. We couldn't do it with just us four, and what if someone didn't get out in time?"

"Well, we'll think of something." Simon furrowed his brow. "On a different note, there's another matter we need to discuss." He turned to Monica and Ten. "Be thinking about the computer plans while Madam Ro—Brenna and I explore options for unlocking Aric's chip. We have no current solution for the computer, so we might as well help where we can."

Monica crouched by the door and rested her back against the wall. Think of a plan? That was going to be difficult.

"Aric is here?" Rose asked. "Veronica's little boy?"

"Indeed. And close by."

Rose's eyes took on a faraway look. "Of course, he must be twenty by now. I remember when he was just …" She frowned. "What do you mean his chip is locked? How did that happen? Is he in any sort of danger?"

"Madam Brenna." Simon blinked at her. "I've never known you to be this flighty or anxious."

Rose laid a hand on her forehead. "Yes, I know. I'm sorry. This has been a lot to take in, and everywhere I turn someone I care about is in danger or could be in danger."

"Yes, well." He cleared his throat and told her how Aric's chip had been locked down, and how they used Fox's program to disguise themselves from the computers.

"Foxlar?" Her face turning white, Rose laid her hands flat on the table. "He's here? He's helping you? I thought he left Eursia for good."

Monica tensed her muscles. Fox. The name brought a flood of fear.

"Madam, you wound me." Simon tapped his heart with a bony finger. "I? Work with Foxlar? Never! In fact, he's dead." He waved a hand dismissively. "But his program has proved to be helpful."

"Dead." Rose let out a long sigh, the word flowing out on the breath in a soft mutter. "Now he can never repent." She closed her eyes for a second, then opened them again, her jaw tensing. "About Aric's lockdown. You need his Key-Keeper to free him."

"Exactly."

"Then it's a good thing Veronica had me named a Keeper before I came to Penniak. Assuming she didn't revoke my codes, they should still work." Rose turned on her tablet and began typing.

Monica scrambled to her feet. "Then you can wake him!"

Simon glared at her. "You're supposed to be thinking of plans, not eavesdropping on our conversation. I said we would sort this out."

"Yes. I can wake him." Rose continued to type. "Veronica and I are sisters and were best friends growing up, so she gave me his Keeper's code shortly after he was born and named heir." She handed the computer to Simon. "I just typed the codes into this document. I didn't save them anywhere, for Aric's safety." She opened a drawer in the table and withdrew a sheet of paper and pencil. "Write them down. I can't risk a note being found with my handwriting on it. As soon as you have them entered into his chip, you must destroy the paper."

Simon bowed his head. "Of course, Madam. Ten can take the numbers back to the ship and use them while we continue our mission."

"Are you sure?" Rose's hand stayed extended, as if she wanted to take the tablet back. "If those numbers are lost ..."

"Yes, yes, someone could do him great harm, but that won't happen." Simon started copying the numbers onto the page. "Ten is trustworthy, aren't you, Ten?"

Ten stood and squared her shoulders. "Of course. The captain has had me running errands with people's lives in my hands since I was eight years old. I can do this."

With a quick stroke of his pencil, Simon finished the numbers and handed Ten the paper. "Yes, I'm sure. And you don't owe the Nobles any favors either, do you?"

"I apologize, Wheaten," Rose murmured.

Folding the page, Ten shrugged. "It's okay. You don't have a reason yet to trust me, but you will soon, when I return with Aric.

I'm an expert at changing people's chips and whisking them to safety. With the captain's help, of course." She tucked the page into her pocket, unbolted the door, and slipped out.

Monica got up and relatched the door.

Rose's hand fell to the table, and she looked at Simon questioningly. "Who is this Wheaten? Since when do you know merchants? I seem to recall you hardly ever leaving the library."

"She's a friend." Simon tilted back his seat. "I've come a long way since you left Cillineese." He snapped his fingers and let the legs of his seat bang back to the floor. "That reminds me." He raised an eyebrow, dug into his satchel, and withdrew Amelia's tablet along with Rose's worn yellow journal. "We thought you might like to have this back, Madam." He handed the journal to Rose and the tablet to Monica.

Running a hand over the binding, Rose held the book close. "So you did receive it." She closed her eyes and murmured something too soft to hear. "But." She opened her eyes again and looked from Monica to Simon. "Sierra—Monica doesn't know Cillineese, and I know you don't either, Simon, so don't try to con me into thinking you do. How did you know what it contained?"

"Con you?" Simon closed his eyes and inhaled deeply. "I don't know what you're talking about." He peered at Monica. "And I do know Cillineese. Just not Old Cillineese. After the termination they introduced a new population, so now 'Cillineese' is something entirely different than what you knew it to be, Madam."

"Ah, yes, I should have specified." A small smile played at the corners of Rose's lips.

Monica's own lips twitched, threatening to break her somber mood. It was good to see Simon and Rose happy, and maybe even content, but there were important matters at hand. Had they forgotten? At least Ten could awaken Aric and bring him. His presence might encourage them to stay on task.

Monica cleared her throat. "Simon managed to translate a few pages so I could read them. It was nice to get a glimpse …"

She trailed off, heat rising to her cheeks. It felt odd to admit her connection with Rose through those pages, as if the person in the journal was different than the woman who sat in front of her. "I—I enjoyed reading them."

Rose's gaze locked with Monica's. She seemed to ask questions with her eyes, as if trying to read her mind. It felt good in a way but too intimate, too probing.

Monica broke the connection and laid Amelia's tablet on the table. "We also brought Amelia's tablet with her programs on it. She was working on replicating Joel's—my father's cloning program. Apparently, Veronica told her about it or hinted at it in some way."

"May I see?" Rose reached for the tablet, and Monica pushed it toward her.

After Rose thumbed the tablet's corner, the screen came to life. Fuzzy blue horizontal lines danced across the screen, obscuring some of the text. Rose squinted and tapped a computer folder. "This has seen some heavy use?"

"Yes." Simon let out a long, burdened sigh. "Someone saw fit to lose it down Cantral's computer room river. We almost didn't recover it. Aric was able to get it working despite the water damage."

Monica frowned at him. It couldn't have been helped. She and Felicia almost died in the floodwaters beneath the Cantral palace. They had no time to think of the tablet.

"It's all right, I can still use it, but I would be careful with it if I were you. It could die at any time." As Rose's gaze darted from one end of the screen to the other, she drew a finger slowly down the side of the tablet, scrolling to read more text. Her face paled.

"What's wrong?" Monica stepped toward her.

Rose laid the computer on the table and closed her eyes. "I can't believe Veronica would do that." She pointed to the computer. "You've read Amelia's notes? About my name and the cloning?"

Nodding, Monica crossed her arms over her chest. Another mystery about to be revealed. "I wondered about that. She never explained anything. Amelia made it sound like Veronica had told her about Joel's cloning program, but she didn't go into details or tell what he did with the program."

Rose picked up the tablet, looked at it again, and murmured, "Why would Veronica do that? Why would she tell Amelia? Veronica had a hand in the whole plan. She, Joel, and Brenna were the ones who made it possible. I just had to agree."

"You're not making any sense." Monica searched Rose's face. She spoke of Brenna like she was another person. Fear churned Monica's stomach. Had she opened her heart to some stranger, an actress who only wanted her mother's identity? But Simon trusted her. He knew her. "Aren't you Brenna Rose? Aren't you my mother?"

Rose shot a desperate look at Simon. She folded her hands on the tabletop, and her fingers turned white. "I am your mother, Sierra, Monica—whichever you prefer. I am your mother. I carried you inside of me, I gave birth to you, and …" Rubbing a hand on the journal, she sighed. "And I wrote every word in this book. But I am not who most people think I am. I am not a Noble." She met Monica's gaze. "I am a Seen."

CHAPTER TWENTY-FIVE

"A Seen?" Monica sucked in a deep breath. How could her mother be a Seen? She was a Noble, Veronica's sister, and the wife of a prominent city-state ruler. She walked freely among other Nobles unquestioned. "That can't be true … can it?"

"It's true." Rose kept her gaze downcast.

"Well, not entirely." Simon shrugged. "It's technically only half true."

"Station is determined by the mother." Rose frowned at him. "My mother was a Seen, so I am, too."

"But then how…" Monica's gaze locked on Amelia's tablet. The cloning program. Joel had turned a Seen into a Noble by cloning her chip with a Noble's. Just like she and Aric had done for Simon. "Then you're not really Veronica's sister? Who let you clone her chip?"

Rose handed the tablet back to Simon. "I am Veronica's sister, as well as Foxlar's and Brenna's."

"But again." Simon held up a finger. "Only by half."

Letting out a long sigh, Rose nodded. "Unfortunately, yes. My—"

A knock sounded at the door. Monica clenched her fists. Not again! Couldn't they have a discussion in peace?

Rose twisted her wristband. "I'm not due to deliver the program for another two hours. Who could that be?"

Monica grasped the doorknob. "Should I answer it?"

"Yes. If you don't, it will look suspicious."

Grumbling about his age, Simon eased out of his seat and stood by the wall, hands folded in front of him. "I was never very good at this subservient Seen posture."

Monica unlocked the door. "I can imagine." Keeping her facial expression blank, she swung the door open.

The young girl who had been playing piano stood outside. She peered up at Monica and inched a step back. Her gaze flitted from Monica's face past her shoulder. "Momma?"

"It's all right, Faye." Rose called. "You may come in."

Faye cast Monica another long look before stepping inside. She ran across the room and climbed into Rose's lap without invitation. Monica closed the door and locked it again. So this was Faye.

She studied the little girl sitting in Rose's lap. Her dark brown curls matched Monica's own, and her high cheekbones and pointed chin were similar, too, though not as similar as Amelia's had been. Maybe those features were common in Noble families. But Amelia and Monica had green eyes while Faye's were brown, just like her mother's.

"Daddy said you were working on a new program." Faye leaned her head against Rose's chest, apparently oblivious to Monica's and Simon's presence. "I looked for you in your usual room, but you weren't there."

"No." Rose stroked Faye's hair. "I decided to work in here today." She set Faye back on her feet. "And unfortunately, I must get back to work. Daddy's waiting on me to finish a program, so you need to finish your lessons."

Letting out a long, exaggerated sigh, Faye nodded. Monica unlocked the door, and Faye slipped out of the study room. Seconds later, the door clicked softly closed behind her.

Rose picked up Amelia's tablet. "Now we must form this plan. We have less than two hours to complete it and put it into action."

She turned to Monica. "I hope you have a real chance soon to meet your sister, but for now—"

Monica shook her head. "I understand. It's dangerous for them to know about me."

Her mother's body seemed to relax. "I'm sorry."

"You've said that a lot today," Simon said. "And you still haven't explained your heritage to Monica." He reclaimed his seat and settled in. "Much better for old bones than standing at attention."

"It's all right," Monica said. "I've waited this long. I can wait a little longer." She walked to the table, her hands folded behind her back. "We need to get to the terminal without setting off the gas and without getting caught. And only Dedrick is able to do that."

"Then it's simple." Simon formed a steeple with his fingers, resting his elbows on the tabletop. "Convince him to shut it down. It will be the easiest takeover yet. Perhaps even better than blowing the place up." He eyed Rose. "Certainly he can't resist your charms, Madam Brenna."

Rose's cheeks flushed. "Actually, he can. He's quite set in his beliefs. I've tried to show him the truth before, but he won't budge. He believes that control is the best option. He thinks that ruling by fear is the only way to control so many people."

Monica reached across the table and picked up Amelia's tablet. Running a hand over the cool metal frame, she stared at the blank screen. What if the computer only thought it was Dedrick opening the room? She squeezed the sides of the computer. It could work. Couldn't it?

Simon tapped her on the head. "What ideas are brewing in that odd little brain of yours?"

Monica ducked away from his finger and slid the tablet back to Rose. "I was just wondering. What if we tricked the computer into thinking that it was Dedrick coming to the access room when it was really one of us?"

Rose picked up the tablet. "The cloning program?"

"Exactly. We know it works. We used it to copy Aric's chip signal to Simon's, since Simon's was shutting down. That's why Aric's went into lockdown. But Dedrick is an adult. He wouldn't have any Keeper's lockdown on his, would he?"

Rose shook her head. "They expire when the chip turns twenty. All potential heirs to city-states have them, supposedly for their own protection, but it never seemed like a good plan to me. Alex, your brother, has one as well."

"The codes do their job." Simon shrugged. "It keeps people from tampering with the chips and codes. Inheritance of a ruling position in a city-state is a high prize. Some are willing to kill for it."

Monica tapped the tablet's corner, bringing the screen to life. "The point is, we can clone Dedrick's chip without harming him. Then we could put the signal on yours or Mother's chip and we could get into the access room without releasing the gas, and then we could install a virus that kills the computer."

"The virus I haven't finished writing." Rose drew her tablet toward her and let it rest beside Amelia's. "It's in here. Bits of code hidden here and there in all of my other programs, each nonfunctional, undetectable to the untrained eye, but once I put them together and add a few more commands, it should be able to wipe out the entire system and leave a blank slate. The chips would be free from commands, and the slaves could leave the palace. I'm just afraid that someone might write on that slate and use it for their own purposes. There have been whispers about some of the other programmers. They've been questioned again and again but been cleared every time. Yet I have my doubts."

Simon raised both hands. "It's a risk we must take. I have complete faith in your skills, Madam. If anything like what you described does happen, we'll fix that, too."

"Thank you, Simon." Rose smiled weakly and turned on her tablet. "I guess I should get to work. I'll need this code ready and the plan executed before Dedrick wants the program I'm supposed to write."

"What should we do in the meantime?" Monica glanced at Simon. They couldn't just sit here idly.

Picking up Amelia's tablet, Rose stood. "I think you two will have to take care of the difficult part." She pressed the tablet into Monica's hands. "Dedrick's chip will have to be cloned, just as you said. I would be willing to be the one to carry his signal, but I need to write this program, and the cloning has to be done with the recipient and donor present."

"Did you help Joel write the program?" Monica's fingers touched her mother's as she took the tablet.

Rose released the computer and stepped away. "Not now. That question must wait for another time."

Simon shoved back his chair and saluted Rose. "I volunteer for this dangerous quest." He grinned at Monica. "First a Seen, then a Noble, and soon to be a ruler of a vast city-state. Who knew someone like me could rise in the ranks so quickly?" He shot a look at Rose. "Besides you. But my chip was trying to off me, and yours wasn't."

Smiling, Rose shook her head and guided them toward the door. "No one is doubting you, Simon." She gave Monica a tight hug and whispered in her ear, "I'll be praying for you. This won't be easy."

Monica pulled away and nodded. "But Simon, your chip is hidden. Even if we put Dedrick's number on it, won't you still be invisible to the computers?"

"No, of course not." Simon waved a hand. "Cloning a new number on it will reset those protocols." After taking the tablet from Monica, Simon tucked it into his bag. "Madam, you do realize we're going to have to render your husband unconscious, don't you? I doubt he would respond well even to 'pretty please' if we ask to clone his chip."

Viral Execution

Rose nodded. "Just please don't hurt him too badly. I don't even know how you're going to manage, but ..." She laid a hand on Monica's shoulder. "But if my daughter can take down Cantral single-handedly, then she should have no problem doing this."

"Single-handedly?" Simon bristled. "I should say not."

"Simon helped tremendously, Mother." Monica smiled at Simon. He wouldn't let anyone take credit for work he did, no matter how slight. "But don't worry. It will be simple to knock Dedrick out. We have a program Aaron Markus created that puts people to sleep through their chip. We'll be able to wake him up again, and he won't know what happened."

"Good." She squeezed Monica's shoulder, then released her and stepped back. "God be with you."

CHAPTER TWENTY-SIX

"Come, come, apprentice," Simon called over his shoulder. "We assistants cant' be late."

Rolling her eyes, Monica fell into step with him. He was taking this assumed assistant's role much too seriously. At least being able to tell people that they were assistants to Madam Brenna cut out a lot of questions. They could even ask others if they knew where Master Dedrick could be found without arousing suspicion.

They wove through the crowded main foyer. Monica glanced at every man they passed, checking each face and comparing it to the mental image she had of Dedrick. She had seen him for only a few seconds, but his chiseled jaw and dark features were easy to remember.

Simon's steps slowed, and she matched her pace to his. They passed a dozen or so Nobles, some with light-colored hair, some with darker, but none looked much like Dedrick. A few Seen stood here and there in corners, waiting to come alive at the call of their masters.

Monica studied the taciturn face of a man in Seen uniform. He stared straight ahead, unlike the other Seen man next to him, who kept his gaze downturned. Maybe they would know where Dedrick was lurking. It probably wouldn't hurt to ask.

She approached the first Seen in silence. When she reached his side she cleared her throat.

He turned and looked down at her. "Yes? What is it?" His words came out clear and crisp though spoken in tones no louder than a whisper.

Simon stopped and backtracked, a deep frown furrowing his brow.

"Could you tell me," Monica whispered, "where I can find Master Dedrick? Madam Brenna sent me to find him."

The man gave a short nod. "I saw him pass by earlier. I believe he was heading for his office." He glanced at his wristband. "He usually reads petitions during this hour."

"Oh." Monica nodded. But where was his office? She should have asked Rose that before they left. If she asked the Seen, it might raise suspicion. "Thank you."

"You're quite welcome." The man inclined his head toward her. "Always willing to help a new transfer."

She smiled and nodded back to him. If he thought she was new, then it wouldn't be odd for her to ask directions. "Can you— can you tell me where his office is exactly? I haven't been to all the rooms in the palace yet."

Simon sighed and tapped his foot.

The Seen eyed him for a second before turning back to Monica. "Certainly, though I'll tell you now that you'll likely never go to every room in the palace. There are over two hundred, and most Seen don't have a reason to visit many." He pointed past a group of Nobles to a wide staircase that led to an upper floor. "Take those stairs and you'll come to a receiving room. There is a hall branching off to the right. Follow it and knock on the first door on your left. That is Master Dedrick's main office. He should be there."

"Thank you very much," Simon said as he grabbed Monica's wrist and ushered her past the two Seen.

"Yes, thank you," she called over her shoulder in a whisper.

Simon led her to the stairs, dodging past the group of Nobles. He mounted the gleaming wooden steps and released her wrist. "Come, come."

Sighing, she followed him up the stairs, taking them one at a time and pressing close to the railing. Simon charged ahead, a spring in his step, as if he were ten years younger than he actually was.

Monica sprinted after him. Was he excited about this? They came to the top of the stairs and entered a large room with a domed ceiling. A long wooden desk stood at one end with three chairs behind it. Another stair opened to the left, leading down to a room below.

"There." Simon pointed to the right where a door-lined corridor led into the unknown. "I believe that is the hallway the Seen indicated." He withdrew Amelia's tablet. "We must be ready to knock Dedrick out as soon as the door opens."

"Can't we knock him out before we go in there?" Monica licked her lips as she looked at the wide, dark door. It would be better that way. Then Dedrick wouldn't know who did it.

Simon looked at her, his eyes narrowed. "No, of course not. What a foolish notion."

"Why?"

After turning on the tablet with a flick of his thumb, Simon approached the office. "Because the door might be locked, and then we would be stuck out here."

"Oh." Heat rose to Monica's cheeks. "Don't forget to knock out Felix, Dedrick's assistant. He's probably in there."

Simon tapped on the computer, then looked up at her. "Very well."

She sidled up to him and peered over his shoulder as he selected two numbers to put to sleep.

Simon glanced back at her. "Stop hovering. Need I remind you that I know more about computers than you do?" He frowned for a moment before turning back to the computer. "You and your mother are both acting unusual—flighty and nervous." He raised a hand over the door, poised to knock. "It's time to shape up or this mission will be over before it begins." His fist connected with wood, and a loud knock reverberated through the hall.

She stepped behind him. But wasn't nervousness to be expected? She and her mother had just met each other, essentially for the first time. How did he think they should react?

When the door opened, Felix appeared in the gap. He frowned at Simon, but then his gaze met Monica's. "Ah, you again. I didn't catch your name before."

"Simon," Monica hissed. He should have run the program by now.

Simon tapped the computer frantically, and it made a short buzzing noise.

"Simon?" Felix glanced from Simon back to Monica. "I'm assuming that's this man and not you. What do you want?"

"Who is it, Felix?" someone called from within.

Felix ducked back inside, but his words passed through the opening. "Madam Brenna's assistant as well as another Seen, sir. I'm not sure what they want."

"Simon." Monica's heart rate increased with every second. "What's wrong?"

He shook his head. "The water damage seems to be hampering the system."

"Brenna's assistant?" Dedrick's voice sounded annoyed. Wood scraped against wood. "Brenna doesn't have any assistants."

"Simon!" Monica hissed.

Simon shoved the tablet at her. "Then *you* try to make it work, Miss Know-it-all."

She fumbled with the tablet and scrambled with the keys. Fuzzy lines danced across the screen, blurring the words and two chip numbers that had been there moments ago. "Come on," she whispered. *Please.*

The door opened again, and Dedrick stepped out. His gaze locked with Monica's. Brows drawing together, he shook his head. "Who are you?"

Her heart leaped into her throat. What to do? The fuzzy lines continued. When the "run" button appeared between the fuzzy lines, she tapped it.

Simon stepped in front of her, pushing her back with one arm. "Excuse her sir, but she's still in training. We're new assistants to Madam Brenna, sir. She must not have informed you yet."

"Not informed me yet?" Dedrick looked down at them, his frown deepening. "That would not happen."

Monica punched the "run" button again, but it did nothing.

He stared at Monica. "You look familiar." He reached for her tablet. "And what are you doing?"

She jerked away from him. This had to work! She smacked the tablet with a hand. The lines cleared for a second, and she slapped the "run" button.

"I asked you a question." Dedrick grabbed her shoulder and snatched the tablet. "What are you doing?"

"Sir?" Felix stumbled and shook his head. After staggering for a moment, he fell to the floor in a heap.

Dedrick's grip tightened on Monica's shoulder, sending spasms of pain down her arm. He blinked, then toppled to the side. His hold slackened, but he pulled her down with him.

Gasping, she hit the floor, and the tablet skittered down the hall. Simon scooped it up. As Dedrick's hold loosened more, Monica shook free of his grasp.

"We should put the sleeper program on Shal's computer next time so we can avoid such troubles." Simon dusted off Amelia's tablet and slid it into his satchel. "And you really need to stop abusing this one if you want it to continue working. That won't be for much longer anyway, from the looks of it." He slid his hands under Felix's arms. "Come, come. Get his ankles. We can't leave them out here for someone to see and raise an alarm."

"No, I guess not." Monica grabbed Felix's sock-covered ankles and helped Simon drag him into the office.

They returned to the hall and pulled Dedrick inside as well. Inside the office, the buzzing coming from the walls seemed more intense.

Simon rolled Dedrick onto his side. "For such a tall man, he's not very heavy."

"That's fortunate for us." Monica closed the door and flipped the lock. "Let's get this over with."

Simon picked up a tablet from the desk. "Interesting. This could come in handy." He turned it on and pulled Amelia's tablet from the bag. "Now would be a good time to transfer all of Amelia's files. We don't want to risk losing them in a hard drive failure. That would be quite unfortunate."

Monica double-checked the lock and crossed the room, stepping over the sleeping Felix. "You can't take Dedrick's tablet. He'll know it's missing."

"We're going to leave him here sleeping peacefully. We can't have him waking up when he knows that we were the reason for his sudden bout of sleepiness." After plugging the two computers together, he shrugged and grinned. "And besides, depending on the way you look at it, soon *I* will be Dedrick, so it is my tablet anyway."

"What will we do with Amelia's tablet, then?"

Simon typed some commands onto the tablet. "We'll keep it. Just in case. We don't want to be foolhardy, and there's no reason to dispose of it." He gestured to the men lying on the floor. "Search Dedrick and Felix for a key to this office. We'll need to lock them in here after we're done."

"Maybe on a chain?" She knelt beside Dedrick and turned down his collar. Nothing hung around his neck. She turned out his pants pockets and then his shirt pockets as well as those in his jacket, but found only lint. It felt odd searching him. He was her mother's husband. Did that make him her father?

After copying Amelia's files to Dedrick's computer, Simon unplugged them from each other and repeated the process with Amelia's and Shal's computers.

Monica scooted to Felix and started turning out his pockets as well. When she came to his shirt pocket, her fingers hit something hard and metallic. She withdrew a small key. "I found a key. Dedrick didn't have one."

"Yes, that's not unexpected." Simon held up Amelia's and Shal's computers. "Done. Now the hard part. Dangerous, anyway. I wonder how many changes my chip will take."

Monica pocketed the key and stood. Simon handed her Shal's and Dedrick's tablets then put Amelia's back into his bag.

Simon lay prostrate, his cheek on the floor as he looked at Monica, sweat glistening on his upper lip. "Well, get on with it."

"Okay." As Monica turned on the cloning program, her hands trembled. When the computer signaled its readiness, she powered up Dedrick's as well.

She nestled a computer at the back of Dedrick's neck before pressing the other to the back of Simon's. It touched his skin, resting on his vertebrae. She leaned over to see the screen more clearly and programmed it to clone Dedrick's chip code to Simon's. A message flashed across the screen, something about it talking to the computer at Dedrick's neck, then it said, "Program in Progress."

Simon shuddered and closed his eyes. "What an odd sensation."

The tablet beeped once, and the message "Program Complete" flashed across the screen. Monica pulled the tablet away and laid it on the desk. She smiled. "Looks like it worked. Neither of you are dead yet."

Simon climbed to his feet. "Most fortunate Amelia figured out how to get the computer not to kill an identical chip number— unlike your father." He toed Dedrick's shoulder. "Thank you kindly for your identity, good sir." Simon slipped Dedrick's wristband off and snapped it onto his own wrist next to his plain Seen band.

Viral Execution

Toeing Dedrick's shoulder again, Simon frowned. "Do you think I should switch clothing? It might do well to dress as a Noble." He fingered the gold wristband. "Especially while wearing this gaudy thing."

"No." Monica handed Simon the two tablets. "Let's just leave. We need to get this done before someone misses them. Rose said it was two hours until the meeting, and that was a while ago."

Simon slid the tablets into his bag. "Exactly. I suppose Seen are more invisible anyway." He took the gold wristband back off and put it into the bag. "And it wouldn't do for me to be seen wearing a Noble's band." After flipping the bag closed, he headed for the door.

Monica unlocked it and stepped out. "Now to meet with Rose again and see if she has that program ready."

"Indeed, and get to the control room as quickly as possible." Simon closed the door. "And you need to start calling Madam Brenna 'Mother.' She deserves it, you know."

Monica locked the office and slid the key into her pocket. It wasn't that easy. Of course Rose deserved it, but after so many years of being motherless, it was hard to accept someone she barely knew filling that role.

CHAPTER
TWENTY-SEVEN

Simon knocked on the library study room door, glancing back over his shoulder every few seconds.

"No one followed us," Monica whispered, standing behind him. "You can stop worrying."

"It's not a matter of worry. I am merely—"

The door jerked open to reveal Rose, her eyes wide and cheeks pale. "You made it." She put a hand to her chest and closed her eyes for a second. "Thank you, Lord." Opening the door wider, she beckoned. "Come in quickly."

Monica and Simon slipped inside, and Rose closed and locked the door. "You did it?" She laid a hand on the door's polished wood. "Is—is Dedrick all right?"

"Certainly. He's sleeping soundly and locked in his office." Simon withdrew Dedrick's wristband and the three tablets from his satchel. "I took the liberty of relieving him of his wristband and tablet. I thought we might have use of them." He laid the items on the table.

Monica sidled along the back wall to a good observation position. Rose was taking this rather well.

"We just might. Good thinking." Rose aligned her tablet with the others and claimed one of the seats at the table. "I wish I could go with you two, but my chip won't allow me near the room."

Stepping forward, Monica raised a tentative hand. "Could we hide your chip like we did Simon's? We explained that before. Then you could come with us."

Rose fingered the back of her neck, a contemplative look on her face. "Foxlar's program? In my head? I shudder at the thought, but it may be for the best. I could be of use to you if things go wrong." She tapped her tablet, and the screen came to life. "I finished the virus program, and I believe it will wipe the computer correctly. I've never seen the control room or the mainframe, but I've written programs for it before."

"And—" Simon began, but Dedrick's wristband began to beep. Simon snatched it off the table and squinted at the small screen. "Oh, dear."

Monica stepped forward, and Rose leaned in. "What is it?" they said at the same time.

Rose held out a hand for the wristband. "I think that's a security alarm. May I see?"

"Certainly, Madam." Simon handed the wristband over, and it continued its shrill song.

Clicking a button on its side, Rose held the wristband closer. It silenced. Her eyes moved back and forth as she read whatever text marched across the screen. "Oh, no."

"What is it?" Monica's words came out in a gasp. Had someone found Dedrick and Felix already?

"It seems some intruders knocked out a guard at the delivery door." Rose flicked on Dedrick's tablet. "I'll need this for more details. They can fit only so much on the wristband screens." She selected some options and began to read again, her lips moving silently. After a moment, she looked up, her brow furrowed. "They were discovered and detained when the guard's replacement came for the shift change. They're in custody now—a young girl, a young adult man, and a middle-aged merchantman, all with nonexistent chip readings."

Monica gulped. "Ten, Aric, and Fahltrid?"

"Oh, that is certainly problematic," Simon muttered, shaking his head. "What will they do with them?"

"It's—it's likely they'll be terminated." Rose fisted a hand and put it to her lips. "Chip anomalies are always treated with the utmost caution, and with the rumors abounding, they'll likely be thought of as spies from Cantral."

Dryness spread through Monica's mouth. Terminated? Aric and Ten? "Can we stop it?"

"Not if you want to get to the computer control center in time." Rose covered her face with her hands. "They're expecting Dedrick to answer this call. A breach like this is important enough for him to handle. They'll be checking his office if he doesn't respond soon." She uncovered her face. "I'll answer it using his tablet. I think I can manage to write like he does."

"Excellent idea." Simon nudged the tablet closer to her. "I'm sure you can fool them long enough for us to plan a rescue."

She began typing on the tablet. "I see there are some new files on here from Amelia's computer."

Monica kept her back to the wall. "Simon thought it would be best to transfer them in case Amelia's died."

"That was probably wise. I want to keep the cloning program, if possible. I doubt I could replicate it." Rose stopped typing. "I've become proficient at programming over the years, but I'll never be the programmer Joel was, or Amelia, apparently." She slid the tablet back to Simon. "I might be able to stall the termination, but I can't clear them of all charges. Only Dedrick can. I told them to wait for Dedrick to come, that he wants to interview them. What do you suggest we do now?"

"Do I have to do all the thinking around here?" Simon eyed Monica. "What do you think we should do?"

Monica approached the table with tentative steps. Simon had to be the one to access the main control panel to put in the virus. She could go to Ten and Aric, but what help could she provide? Put everyone to sleep with the program? Then what? There would be even more people looking for them. Maybe Mother could go. "If only Dedrick can free them …" She tapped the back of her neck. "Couldn't you be Dedrick, too?"

"I'm afraid not. People accused of treason must be cleared by Dedrick, and he must be there in person." Rose ran a hand through her hair. "I would have to convince people, not computers, that I'm Dedrick, and people are much harder to fool when it comes to identities." She smiled. "I wouldn't make a very good man. Your friends and Aric will be guarded by a member of the security team."

"Then I suppose trying to delay them further is the best option." Simon shoved back his seat and rose. "Madam Brenna, you are obviously best suited for that task. Monica and I will go shut down the computers."

"I doubt it's going to be so easy." Rose stood and handed Simon her tablet. "The virus is ready to be installed, but I hope you're prepared to deal with the potential consequences. If something goes wrong, things could turn out even worse than they are now."

"Of course it will be easy." He pointed at Monica. "She and I have done this twice already. Third time's the charm!" Taking the tablet under his arm, he rocked on his toes. "And we can put any upstart Noble to sleep if we have to. Unless they have Fox's program, but that's highly unlikely. It's not something he would share with the general public." He made a shooing motion toward the door. "Madam, I believe it's time for you to go save our friends' lives. It wouldn't do to lose them, now would it?"

"Of course not." Rose picked up Dedrick's tablet. "Do you want to take this or should I? I might be able to put in some commands to help Aric and your friends' cases, but I would be found out quickly."

Monica shrugged. "We could take it in case there's need of it at the control panel."

"That's an excellent idea." Simon stacked Amelia's tablet on top of Rose's and handed Shal's tablet to Rose before taking

Dedrick's. "But you might like to have a tablet for emergencies. This one is supposed to be top-notch."

Rose tucked Shal's tablet under one arm. "Thank you."

"Three tablets to lug around," Simon mumbled. "Seen aren't really supposed to have even one. How exciting." He slid them into his satchel. "Let's go, Monica." He grabbed the doorknob, then turned back to Rose. "Now, where is this control room?"

"Oh, right." Rose laughed nervously. "Unlike most computer rooms, it's on the top floor. When you reach the top of the staircase, turn right and walk until you come to a dead end. There's a door on the right. Inside is the main control center. I can't tell you more than that; I've never been inside."

"Thank you very much, Madam." Simon unlocked the door. "Are we finally ready to depart?"

Rose circled around the table and hugged Monica. "I know it seems silly to say, but please, try to be safe. I'll be praying for you."

Monica returned the hug. "Thank you."

"We don't have time for these sappy good-byes." Simon jerked the door open and stepped through. "Women these days."

Monica glanced at the open door. People could see them! She ducked out of Rose's grasp and backed away. "I'll see you later, then."

"Yes." Rose followed them out of the room and closed the door.

"Well, Brenna." A Noble man, one of the head programmers—the one who raised reminders of Fahltrid—appeared from behind an aisle of books. "I was just looking for you."

"Jacob." Rose stepped back and put a hand to her chest. "You startled me. What do you need?"

Simon continued walking down the aisle, already past Jacob and heading out of the library. Monica sidled after him, but Jacob grabbed her arm.

She froze in place. He was a Noble. She couldn't just jerk free. She had to stand still until he released her.

Jacob smiled at her, then turned back to Rose. "I thought the rumors were false. Certainly the illustrious Brenna wouldn't stoop to having a Seen assistant, and two of them! But your daughter was quick enough to blab about it to me. Such a talkative thing."

"You leave her alone." Rose's gaze strayed to Monica.

His dark eyes followed Rose's line of sight. "My, things are getting interesting around here." He released Monica's arm and tapped his wristband. "I'm sure you've heard about the alert. I know Dedrick would have informed you about it already."

Rose's eyes narrowed. She grabbed Monica's wrist and drew her away from Jacob. "What I would like to know is how you knew about it. It came only to him. You're only a second-class programmer. You don't have security clearance for this message."

"Really?" Jacob smirked and looked at his wristband, eyebrows raised. "The alert was coming across loud and clear on my wristband. How could that be if I'm not supposed to hear it?" His gaze strayed to Monica and stayed on her for a moment before turning back to Rose.

Monica shuddered. He didn't seem at all like Fahltrid now. Fahltrid would never be so cold and calculating.

"I know very well what you're up to, Jacob, even if the others don't see it. I've read your programs." Rose pointed down the hall. "Monica, you're dismissed. I have things to discuss here." She turned back to Jacob. "And then I must check on this alert. We can't allow a breach like this to go unattended."

Monica nodded. "Yes ma'am." She trotted away, fear twisting her stomach. What was that about? What if Rose didn't finish talking to Jacob quickly enough, and Ten, Aric, and Fahltrid died? But her mother knew what was at stake. She would know when to cut the conversation off. There was obviously something else going on in Penniak's Noble world, and it didn't bode well for Rose and Dedrick.

Simon waited for her outside the library, arms crossed over his chest and a scowl growing on his wrinkled face. "There you are. We haven't time, my dear." He hurried to a stairwell and began a quick climb.

She followed him up to the next floor. "I'm sorry, but I couldn't get away. That Noble man—Jacob—came and stopped me."

They headed up another flight of stairs. As they reached the third flight, two Noble women walked past them. Monica clamped her mouth shut, and she and Simon walked in silence up two more flights. When they turned right down a long hall, Simon's frown deepened. His hand clutched the satchel at his side.

Monica looked down the corridor. Black carpet with swirling beige and green designs lay on the floor, and gold light fixtures hung on the wall, illuminating the long passage.

They jogged down the hall and came to the door on the right, just where Rose had said it would be. Simon stopped and opened his satchel. "Are you ready for another adventure, Monica?"

She stood a little behind him and stared at the red wood door. What would they find? "I—I guess so."

Simon withdrew Dedrick's wristband and slapped it on before pulling out the tablet. "If Madam Brenna doesn't answer that alert in time and Dedrick's sleeping state is found out, we'll be in a pretty pickle."

Monica wrinkled her brow. *Pickle?*

Simon turned on the tablet and laid a hand on the doorknob. A light blinked on above the door, and Simon pushed it open. He nodded to Monica. "After you."

Taking a deep breath, Monica walked inside. As her foot touched the floor, a light flickered on, illuminating a small room with a computer console taking up an entire wall. Red, blue, and green lights flashed. A monitor about two feet wide hung in the console's middle, text flowing across it in an unending display of white and black.

Viral Execution

The door closed behind her with a loud thump. She jerked and whirled around.

Simon released the knob. "It's just me. Don't be so jumpy."

Shuddering, she stepped toward the console. Below a line of lights stood three metal panels with black latches holding them onto the wall. She knelt and ran a hand over the small rivets where a patch had been welded into place. "If I were doing this the old way, I'd rip these off and be done in a few minutes."

"Thanks to the paranoid Penniak Nobles who built this place, that isn't possible, so don't mope about it." Simon handed her Dedrick's computer and retrieved Rose's from his bag. "Now for the virus."

Monica clutched Dedrick's computer tightly and looked around the room again. Soon this would be over. The white ceiling and floor reflected the clear, bright lights, making her squint. After this was done she could be with her mother again without worry about ranking. They could go back to Cantral. She could meet her brother and get to know her sister, and maybe even Dedrick, if he would let her. There was no telling how he would react when his empire was brought down, especially since he seemed so sure he had broken free from Cantral and established his own rule.

"Are you ready?" Simon held Rose's tablet up to an open port just below the computer monitor's base. Despite the cool air circulated by a pair of fans embedded in the ceiling, sweat glistened on Simon's forehead.

Monica nodded. "What if installing this virus does create an opportunity for another Noble to step in and take over, like Rose said?"

"Then we'll kill whoever it is." Simon plugged the computer into the port. "I have complete faith in your mother's programming abilities, but there's no use throwing caution to the wind." He typed in a command.

"Kill him?" Monica gulped. "I think that's a little drastic. There has to be another way."

Amanda L. Davis

Red lights flashed across the computer console. A beeping sound came from somewhere in the room. Simon released the tablet and backed toward Monica. "I hope that's a good sign."

Hissing noises filled the walls, and the lights grew hazy. An acrid smell tickled Monica's nose. "What is that?"

Simon turned, his eyes wide. "It smells like the termination gas." He ran for the door and pulled on the knob, but it wouldn't budge.

"Termination gas? Not sleeping gas?" Dots spotted Monica's vision. She grabbed the doorknob as well, covering Simon's hands with her own. They tugged together, but it didn't even rattle. Monica pounded a fist on the wood. No! What had gone wrong? How could they fail after coming so far?

White mist filled the room, blocking the computer from view. Only the blinking red dots showed through the haze. Monica tried to draw in a breath, but something seemed to be pressing on her chest. This couldn't be happening.

Her knees buckled. The floor came up at her, and she crashed into the tiles. Pain flashed through her body. A thump sounded nearby. Simon? She reached out a hand, but her fingers touched only mist. "Simon?" She couldn't keep her eyes open. She struggled to gather her thoughts, but they all slipped away in a jumble of pictures and words, floating on the mist and disappearing in the white clouds.

CHAPTER TWENTY-EIGHT

"**I**s she awake yet?" The impatient, grinding voice drilled into Monica's head. She groaned. The pounding sensation and voices floating around were all too familiar. At least she wasn't dead.

"It would appear so." Another voice spoke. It sounded familiar, almost like Fahltrid's.

Monica tried to sit up, but something jerked her wrists and shoulders down. She tugged her hands back and forth, trying to free them. Metal bit into her skin, and she let her arms rest again.

Something prodded her side. "Open your eyes, Seen. We know you're awake."

She forced her eyes open against the drowsy feeling that weighed down her lids. Dryness coated her tongue. She tried to swallow, but it hurt too much. Bright lights shone on her, and metal bracelets held her wrists to the railings on the side of a bed. A strap ran across her chest and shoulders as well.

Jacob stared down at her, and the dark-eyed woman she had seen leaving the programmers' meeting stood nearby.

Monica turned her head from the bright light. "Where's Simon? Is he okay?" The words rasped in her throat and forced her to cough.

"Simon?" The woman looked at Jacob.

"Is he the old Seen we found with you?" Jacob leaned over her bed, blocking some of the bright light.

"Yes." Monica managed to glare up at him despite the pounding in her head. "Where is he?"

"In another room. He may or may not survive. Such a powerful gas is difficult for the elderly to recover from. Especially without the aid of oxygen therapy." Jacob pulled away. "Now you're going to tell me what you were trying to accomplish in the control room, or I will terminate your friend without giving him a chance to recover." Jacob threw Simon's satchel onto her stomach, but the bag felt light—empty.

Monica glared at him again. He would probably kill Simon no matter what she said. A darkness seemed to glint in Jacob's eyes, something that made her shudder. "How'd you find us? You can't get into that room."

"I'm asking the questions here." He held up Rose's and Dedrick's tablets. "Brenna is conspiring against Dedrick, isn't she? That's why she finally agreed to a Seen assistant, too cowardly to risk her own life by sneaking into the control room. And all this time …" He turned to the woman standing nearby. "Brenna is a sly one. She would have been a great asset to us if we had gotten her on our side in the beginning. I shouldn't have listened to Foxlar." Setting the tablets down again, he shrugged. "On second thought, before you answer the first question, I want to know how you got into the room. It's theoretically impossible."

"You'll just kill Simon and me after I tell you, so why should I answer?" Monica turned her head. When she moved, the metal braces on her wrists pressed cold against her skin, but they weren't very tight. Her wristband sat higher on her arm than did the metal. The braces had plenty of free space around her wrist. The only thing keeping them from sliding off were her hands. Maybe …

"I give you my word I won't." Jacob paced beside her bed. "And if you don't answer, I can make your life a living hell."

"You think you can convince me through torture?" Monica grimaced and pulled at the cuffs. Her hands were just too big to fit through. There was nothing this man could do to hurt her more than what she had already suffered. She splayed her hands palms up and raised her arms as high as the short chains on the cuffs would allow. "I've been through what you couldn't even imagine."

Jacob grabbed her braid and pulled her head farther back, pointing her chin toward the ceiling. Pain wrenched through her neck, and a gasp escaped. "I can imagine quite a bit," he whispered. "So I wouldn't suggest trying my patience." He released her, then turned to face the woman. "Jareasa, is Brenna still with the intruders?"

"I've been here with you. How should I know?" Jareasa shuffled to the side and nudged something on the floor. "She certainly doesn't know about him yet. Otherwise there would be an uproar throughout the whole palace."

Monica strained against her bonds to try to see what lay on the floor, but the straps held her fast. "What are you going to do with me?"

"I'm not sure yet." Jacob picked up the tablets, crossed the room in a few strides, and stood by a door. "But I thank you for getting me access to the computer console room. I could never have gotten in without activating the emergency protocols. And with Dedrick out of commission, Brenna is the next in command, and she will be much easier to control."

He turned and stared at Monica for a moment, his gaze searching her face. A moment later he smiled, but his eyes stayed cold. "I wonder if Dedrick knows about you. And a Seen, too. How interesting." He opened the door. "Jareasa, don't touch her bonds. She's to stay here until I come back."

Jareasa grabbed his wrist, pulling his hand away from the doorknob. "We're in this together. You're not going near that console without me."

He shook her off. "Of course. How could I have done this without you? I'm not going to the console yet. I'll come back for you when I do. I'm going to check on those prisoners. I'm assuming Brenna's still with them." He stepped through the doorway. "Now guard our little Seen and make sure she doesn't wriggle away somehow." Without another word, he disappeared down a hall.

Jareasa slammed the door and muttered something too low to hear.

Monica tugged on the bonds again. She tried to squeeze her hand flat to slide it out of the metal ring. It budged half an inch then caught on the heel of her hand.

"You might as well give up." Jareasa lowered herself into a straight-backed chair and sighed. "Where would you go if you're free? Jacob will make sure you don't get out of here alive. He's been waiting for an opportunity like this for a long time."

"An opportunity like what? He can't even get into the control room. He'll be gassed, too." Monica continued to strain at her bonds, though it was probably useless. Even if she got away, Jareasa was too big to overpower.

"Not once the emergency protocol has been activated." Jareasa shrugged, a smile slowly growing. "Of course he couldn't have done that himself. His chip would be on record, and Dedrick was never out of the way, but now ..." She nudged whatever was on the ground again. "You've taken care of that. He'll easily be able to get Brenna to do what he wants. All he has to do is threaten Faye."

Faye! Monica gasped. How could he be so evil? How could power be so important to people? She flexed her shoulders against the confining strap. "So what's in it for you? Why are you helping him? You have a good job—you're a head programmer. What more could you want?"

"To be co-ruler." Jareasa glared at her. "A little Seen like you would never understand what it's like. You don't even know how to think for yourself."

"Ha!" Monica spat out. "As if he will keep his end of the deal." She relaxed her arms. She had to distract this woman, make her angry enough to leave. "Power-hungry people never do what they say. He'll terminate you as soon as he has the ability to do so."

"That's not true. We've worked together for years now. He transferred here from Cantral as a nobody, from a family with too many sons and not enough connections. We worked our way up from the bottom." Jareasa crossed the room to the door and opened it. "I have to find someone to transport Dedrick and Felix to the holding cells." The door slammed closed behind her.

Monica strained, yanking her hand against the metal ring. It dug into her flesh and sent tendrils of pain through her hands. With another tug, she slid her left hand free, ripping some surface skin from both sides. Inhaling sharply, she tried to do the same with her right, but it wouldn't budge.

With her free hand she fumbled with the straps across her chest and shoulders and unbuckled them. The cloth straps fell away easily. She sat up and slid from the bed, though her right arm was still attached to the railing.

Giving it one final jerk, she sighed. Maybe there was a key somewhere. She swept a quick look around the room. Dedrick and Felix lay in a heap on the floor near the foot of her bed, breathing softly, their eyes closed.

She edged to the side table and opened its single drawer. A few pens rolled around inside, and a pad of paper skidded from the back of the drawer to the front. She closed the drawer. Jacob wasn't stupid enough to leave the key anywhere nearby. He probably had it in his pocket.

Monica reached into her own pocket. The key to Dedrick's office was gone. Jacob must have taken it. How else would Dedrick and Felix have gotten here?

She felt at her neck. No leather cord rubbed against her skin. Jacob had even taken Alyssa's necklace. She leaned against the bed. Now what? Who knew she was in here? Simon? She jerked against her bonds. Simon could die! He could be dead even now if no one was helping him. His heart had been through so much already.

She inched to the door, stretching out her arm as far as she could, the cuff on her right wrist holding her back.

Her fingers brushed the doorknob, not quite reaching far enough. "Help!" She stamped a foot on the ground, but it didn't make much noise. "Somebody help me!"

She stood still for a second, but the only sound in the room came from the buzzing computer in the walls. She kicked at the door. *No! It can't end like this!*

Closing her eyes, she knelt beside the bed, her cuffed arm raised above her head. There had to be a way to help Simon. Squeezing her eyes more tightly closed, she whispered, "Please, help me." Didn't Rose say there was a God who heard their prayers? He had listened when Felicia was drowning, but what about prayers for Simon? Maybe he was too old to be worth saving. He had lived a good, long life. He was already living on borrowed time. But did that really make a difference?

No. Every life was valuable—Simon's, Rose's, Fahltrid's, Wheaten's, even her own, as well as every wall slave, Seen, and Noble. If there was a God who listened, He would know that better than anyone. "Please," she whispered. "Help us. Help us all."

CHAPTER TWENTY-NINE

Monica rested her chin on her knees. Her wrist ached from pressing against the cuff so long, and her head still pounded from the effects of the gas.

Time ticked by in uncountable minutes. Dedrick and Felix remained sleeping as she sat staring at their motionless bodies. How long could the program keep them in that state? It seemed like they would have to wake up eventually, program or no.

"Monica?" The call sounded distant.

She perked up and inched as close as she could to the door, her arm stretched out behind her. "I'm in here!"

"Monica?" The voice called again, soft and feminine. Ten? Giving a fierce tug on the cuff, she managed to slide the bed forward an inch. A foot smacked against Felix's head, but he remained motionless. Monica stretched her arm farther out and grasped the doorknob. "I'm here! In here!" She turned the knob and tugged, but the door didn't budge.

"Hold on!" a second voice called. Fahltrid?

"I can't get the door open!" Monica banged a fist on the wood.

"Stand back." Fahltrid's voice came through muffled.

Monica jumped away from the door just as a loud thump sounded against the wood. The frame rattled and shook but held firm. Another thump rippled across the wood. Splinters popped out around the knob and lock.

Clenching her hands into fists, Monica held her breath.

A thump came again. More wood splintered around the knob. With yet another blow, the door burst open, and Fahltrid stumbled through. He quickly recovered his footing and nodded at Monica. "Palace doors are sturdier than most."

Ten peeked inside. "Monica! We thought we'd never find you."

Monica stretched toward them, but the wrist cuff stopped her. "You got away! How did you ever manage it? Dedrick …" She glanced over her shoulder at the sleeping Noble. "Dedrick couldn't clear you."

Fahltrid pushed the door closed, though the damage wouldn't allow it to latch. "Your mother came and talked to our guard, but then …" His expression deepened to a glare, and he growled, "Jacob got her to go somewhere with him. They were whispering, and your mother appeared to be in deep distress. They left us alone with the guard, and I thought it would be a good time to leave. Before your mother arrived, we stayed put because we didn't know what else to do."

Ten peered around Fahltrid's arm and grinned. "The captain is excellent at executing a sleeper hold. He knocked out the guard, stole his keys, and got us out of our cell. He's too humble to tell you that part."

"I'm glad you're okay." Monica let out a sigh of relief. Whatever a sleeper hold was, it was a good thing Fahltrid knew how to use it. "Is Aric all right? Did my mother's code work?"

"It did, and he's with Simon." Fahltrid lifted a large silver ring that held at least a dozen keys. "Now let's see if any of these will work on that cuff." Fahltrid tried several without success. Only a few remained.

Ten poked Dedrick's shoulder. "Did you knock these guys out?" She winked. "I'm impressed. Who taught you the sleeper hold?"

"A computer program did that." Monica smiled. "If Simon were here, he might have claimed credit."

Viral Execution

One of the final keys scraped into the cuff's lock. As Fahltrid turned it, something clicked inside. The cuff sprang open, releasing Monica's hand.

She yanked away and rubbed her wrist. "Thank you!"

"You're welcome. Now we had better get back to Aric and see if he needs help with Simon." Fahltrid tucked the key ring into his pocket.

Ten nudged Dedrick again. "Are we just leaving these guys here? What if they wake up?" She wrinkled her nose. "I've had enough of Nobles catching us and locking us up."

Monica nodded. "Jareasa, the other programmer who was here, said she would be sending someone to take them to holding cells. I just hope she doesn't come back with that someone."

Fahltrid stepped out of the room. He paused just outside the door, looked both ways, then beckoned to them. "It's clear. Simon's down the hall two rooms. We found him first."

Monica slipped out after Fahltrid and followed him down the hall. He knocked twice on a large wooden door, then opened it without waiting for an answer.

Aric stood over a narrow bed, hands pressed against Simon's chest, pumping rhythmically. He looked up at them, his eyes wild. "He stopped breathing!"

"What?" Monica rushed forward. Simon's pale face stared up at her, his expression blank. "No!" She grabbed his hand. "Simon!"

A strong hand jerked her away. "Let him work," Fahltrid whispered.

Aric continued pumping Simon's chest, up and down, up and down.

Ten clutched Monica's arm but said nothing.

"Simon." Monica closed her eyes. "We can't lose you! *I* can't lose you! You're my … my friend."

Fahltrid whispered, "Pray, child. Pray. It's all we have left."

Monica nodded, though each push from Aric's hands seemed like the scoop of a burial shovel. "God. Please. Please help Simon. Help Aric. Please."

"If only I had a defibrillator!" Aric sucked in a breath. Then, balling his hand into a fist, he punched Simon in the chest. "Come on, you ornery old Seen! Wake up!"

When Aric lifted his fist, Simon gasped and caught Aric's wrist. He groaned and inhaled again, ragged and slow. "I thought I was a Noble now. … And who's ornery?"

Aric shook off Simon's hand and slapped a plastic mask over his face. "You only get to be a Noble if you live." Tubes ran down from the mask to a large green tank. Aric spun a dial on the tank. "Now keep breathing, or I'll have to hit you again."

Tears streamed from Monica's eyes. "Simon!"

"Yes, what is it, girl?" His voice sounded muffled underneath the mask. "Stop saying my name over and over! I heard you the first time."

"Actually." Aric pressed two fingers to Simon's neck. "You were dead, so you couldn't have heard her the first time. Now settle down. You're going to hurt yourself."

Monica cupped her hands over her mouth. Simon was going to live. He would be all right. She closed her eyes for a second. *Thank you.* Maybe they were being looked after.

Simon plucked at the mask on his face, but Aric pushed his hand away again. "You'll leave that on until I say you may take it off. You asphyxiated."

"I suppose Ten and I should return to the ship," Fahltrid said. "I've gotten Aric here safely. It could be dangerous for so many of us to be wandering these halls."

"No, please stay." Monica reached toward him but stopped short of touching his shoulder. "Can you tell me more about what Jacob said to my mother? Did you hear anything? Where did they go?"

Fahltrid held up a calloused hand. "Slow down. Give me a chance to answer. We were in a holding cell, and the guards were threatening to terminate us, but I wasn't worried, since I had hidden my chip using the ship's computer, and I knew I could overpower both guards with little trouble. When Rose arrived, the security guards spoke with her about our sentencing and wondered when Dedrick would arrive." He shrugged. "Then Jacob came and said there was an emergency and he needed Brenna to come with him immediately. He—"

The lights dimmed, then blinked off, plunging them into darkness.

Monica gasped. What happened?

"Well." Fahltrid's voice came from her right. "That was unexpected."

A strange, garbled sound emanated from all around, like a machine powering down all at once.

"What's that?" Ten whispered.

Monica strained to see in the darkness. "Did the computers shut down?" The vibrations from the walls had stopped. Someone took hold of her arm.

"It would seem so," Aric's voice sounded close to her ear. The hand released her. "Do you know anything about this?"

"I think Jacob has something to do with it. He wants to take over Penniak, he and a Noble woman named Jareasa."

"A coup. I see." The lights flickered on then off again. Aric stood beside Monica. "We'll have to stop him. He must be doing something with the computers. Is he a programmer?"

Distant shouts echoed through the halls. The lights came on again and glowed brightly.

"Yes." Monica gave him a quick rundown of all she knew about Jacob and his plans and how the computers of Penniak were set up, but as she explained it, the information felt like too little, and they had no way to fight him.

Aric's brow furrowed, and his gaze grew dark. "There's only one main access?" He walked around Simon's bed and picked up the first-aid satchel from the floor, something he must have brought with him from the ship. "That seems unlikely."

"You're saying my mother is wrong?" Monica breathed deeply. Her lungs still burned from the encounter with the gas.

"In a way." He pulled Amelia's tablet from his satchel. "If Dedrick can make it so there's only one central control panel, I can make it so there's more than one." Turning the computer on, he sighed. "I wish I had my tablet, but someone seems to have fried it. This one will have to do."

Ten inched closer to Fahltrid. "We should just get back to the ship."

"No. Especially since Jacob …" Fahltrid trailed off and laid a hand on Ten's shoulder. "We need to help. If this succeeds, our jobs will be done forever. No more field laborers to save."

Monica peeked at Amelia's computer. "What are you planning, Aric? Something is going on up there in the computer room. We need to hurry."

Aric tucked the computer back into the bag. "I need an access point to the central computers. If I can hook this computer up, I should be able to hack into the mainframe and see what's going on. I hope Amelia's damaged computer can take the strain."

Motioning toward the walls, Monica shrugged. "Pick a wall, any wall. My mother says a portion of the computer is just about everywhere. Here is as good as the next place."

Aric tapped the wall with a knuckle. "Tearing into stone is not easy. Have you noticed any wooden walls?"

"Let me think." Monica closed her eyes for a second and went over the routes she had taken during the past few hours, imagining every hall and every turn. Where had there been wood? She opened her eyes again. "There's a hallway near where we first came in. It smelled of paint, and Simon said it had recently been built. It was where we first noticed the humming, too. I think it's wooden."

Smiling, Aric closed his bag and headed for the door. "I guess that's the Antrelix working, isn't it? I knew it would enhance your memory for a long time to come."

"No, it was my training." Simon sat up and ripped the mask off. "And you two are not going anywhere without me. I wouldn't miss this for anything."

"Simon." Fahltrid grabbed Simon's wrist. "I don't think it would be wise for you to attempt walking just yet." Fahltrid motioned to the bag hanging at Ten's side. "I slipped my older tablet into the satchel as we were leaving the cell area. It should work better than Amelia's. It is not damaged."

Ten dug into her bag and handed Aric Fahltrid's computer. "Thank you." Aric took the tablet and jerked open the door. "And Simon, I agree with the captain about you staying here. Besides, I'm your doctor, and I order you to stay put." He strode out of the room.

Simon slid from the bed and pointed at Fahltrid. "If you don't want me walking, you're going to have to carry me, because I'm going. I will not miss out on breaking down a wall."

Just as Fahltrid opened his mouth to speak, Monica slipped out of the room and jogged after Aric. He walked quickly ahead, first-aid satchel tucked under one arm. She caught up with him just as he turned into another hall. "You know where you're going?" She fell into step with him.

"I have an idea." He gestured to the hallway. "When we were escorted in by the guards, we passed a hall similar to what you described, but if you would like to lead the way, that's fine with me."

Monica leaped ahead and strode a few steps in front. "Whether it's the Antrelix or Simon's training, I can probably find it faster. We have to stop the computers before Jacob does something irreversible."

CHAPTER THIRTY

They reached the remodeled corridor in a few minutes. Gesturing to the newly painted wall, Aric looked at Monica. "Is this it?"

"I think so." She tapped the wall with a knuckle. With each tap, she pulled her skin away from tacky paint. The wall echoed slightly. "It sounds wooden to me. The walls being full of wires must make it difficult for the slaves to get around. I guess that's why some of the passages we saw were boarded off."

"Of course that's why." Fahltrid appeared in the hallway, but the voice sounded like Simon's. Ten jogged behind him.

Simon peeked over Fahltrid's shoulder, riding piggyback style, his arms wrapped around the captain's neck.

"Fahltrid," Aric called, "come help me with this." Aric dragged a statue of a man riding a horned animal.

Fahltrid frowned. "You can let go of my neck now, Simon."

"Oh, of course." Simon slid to the floor and patted his chest. Coughing, he crouched against the far wall. "Well. Get to work."

Aric pulled the statue closer, grunting. "This is heavier than it looks."

"You're weakened from so many days of sleep." Fahltrid hoisted the statue onto his shoulder. "I'll take a whack at that wall."

Monica scrambled out of the way and stood beside Simon. The lights flickered again. A cry came from somewhere nearby.

Viral Execution

Monica jerked around and laid a hand on the wall. This one didn't vibrate beneath her touch. Another cry sounded—no more than a whimper. A wall slave? The lights flashed again.

"What is that?" Fahltrid let the statue slide to the floor and winced. "There's something with the chips ..." He slapped a hand across the back of his neck. "It's like a pinching sensation."

Ten squeaked and closed her eyes. "I feel it. I thought our chips were hidden!"

Fahltrid grabbed the statue again and smashed it into the wall. The statue's body plunged into the boards, splintering the wood. Sparks flew, and the animal's horns snapped off in Fahltrid's hands. Shaking his head, he flung the horns to the floor. "No time to waste, Aric. This is quite painful."

"Indeed." Simon closed his eyes and rested his head against the wall. "Almost as painful as Aric punching me in the chest."

"I know, I know." Aric tore at the splintered boards. Monica rushed to join him. The splinters dug into her fingertips, but she kept digging, exposing wires and small metal plates with blinking lights.

"That's enough." Putting out a hand, Aric stopped her. "Monica, can you see any green and white wires?"

Monica tugged out a bundle of wires. White connectors snapped them together every few feet, holding them in place, but the wires were blue, purple, red, and other colors. No green or white. She tugged out another bundle. Thick green wires and two thin white wires twisted together and led deeper into the wall. The wires stopped short from coming out of the wall, and she had to maintain a grip on them to keep them in view. "Here!"

He pulled a knife out of his pocket and pressed the blade against the plastic.

Monica slid her hands out of the way but held on to the wires. "If I let go they'll pull back in the wall. They're not very long."

"Keep hold of them, then." He re-gripped his knife.

"That's going to hurt." She took a second look at the blade. "The guards let you keep that?"

"I took it back after Fahltrid knocked them out." Aric snapped the knife through the wires. Sparks flew. His hands shook as he picked up Fahltrid's computer. With his jaw clenched tightly, he hissed through his teeth. "Monica, hold this while I strip the wires."

She clutched it tightly in one hand, the other still holding the wires. Ten whimpered. Simon moaned. Aric needed to work faster! Their friends were hurting.

Sweat beaded on Aric's forehead as he used his knife to strip bits of plastic from the wires. "Now open the back panel, if you can." Blood oozed on his fingertips as he stripped another wire.

Monica turned the tablet over with one hand and located two clips holding the panel in place. It popped off easily, revealing a metal plate covered with raised dots and a few wires running from soldered points on the plate. She laid the cover on the ground. "Ready."

He handed her the knife and took the tablet.

Fahltrid groaned and clapped his hands around the back of his head. "I'd help if I could, but it's hard to concentrate."

Aric pulled two wires from the tablet and twisted one with the wall's white wires and one with the green. "I don't know if this tablet has enough power to talk to the computer through a rigged setup, but we'll see."

Monica set the knife on the floor and tried to pull the wires farther from the wall, but they held fast. "What are you planning?"

He started typing what seemed like random numbers and letters onto the black screen. More text flowed into view—thousands of nonsense words skittering by too quickly to read. "Hack into whatever this stuff is and stop it. If I can. Someone …" His brow furrowed, and his fingers quickened their pace. "Someone is writing code into the computer this minute. Jacob must have been able to get into the computer control room."

Monica clenched her hand into a fist. He got in? That meant her mother had bowed to his pressure. Was she all right?

Viral Execution

Aric cursed under his breath and continued typing.

"Aric!" Simon moaned and held his head. "Completely uncalled for, my boy. If anyone were to curse, I would suspect Fahltrid. He's the sailor."

"Then plug your ears." Aric shook his head and continued his frantic typing. "This guy knows I'm here now. I'm trying to write faster than he is, but he's experienced. I don't know if I can."

Fahltrid crawled forward on hands and knees. "The pain is easing. Let me have a look."

Aric edged to the side but continued typing.

Monica looked for a way to secure the wires so they would stay without her holding them. "What can I do?"

"Just stay there and keep hold of those wires." Fahltrid stared at the tablet. "That's going by quite quickly, but I think I have an idea of what he's doing." Rubbing his eyes, he sighed. "He used your mother's program to wipe the system and then input his own code. That's what we're feeling. The chips are being rewritten."

"I thought so. I was trying to stop him." Aric touched a line of text, but it disappeared under his finger and was replaced by more and more words. "Rewriting the chips? He could kill half the people in the city!" He shook his head. "And why isn't it affecting me as much?"

"Probably because of your rank," Simon muttered. "Less coding to work through."

Fahltrid growled and pointed at the screen. "The command codes. Jacob is putting locks on them. We need to break into the system before he finishes locking it. What do you suggest?"

Monica edged out of the way as far as she could and still hold the wires.

"If he's recoding the chips, just commandeer some," Simon muttered. "Specifically ours. I want this headache gone."

"Perfect." Fahltrid closed his eyes, shook his head, then opened his eyes again. "I'll isolate our signals and wipe them from the computers. Our chips will still be running, but the computer won't accept their signals. We'll be invisible." He typed some words. "Aric, Simon, what are your numbers? I have mine and Ten's."

Simon and Aric rattled off their numbers, and Fahltrid typed them in. "I'll have this done in just a moment. Security systems are being rewritten so it should be pretty easy to get in right now." Monica studied Ten's pained expression. Ten and Simon couldn't stand much more of this—especially Simon. He had already died twice! "Why didn't my mother think of getting to the computers this way?"

"Bashing through walls?" Aric yanked his smaller computer out of his bag. "I can't imagine my mother's sister even thinking of such a thing. And the reprogramming wasn't possible until now." He turned on the computer. "Fahltrid, I think I have something to add to your idea. Any of you know Jacob's chip number?"

"No." Monica reached farther into the wall. Maybe there was something inside that would help her secure the wires.

Shaking his head, Simon let out a long sigh. "There should be a database somewhere, though if he wiped the computers, it could be difficult to find."

Fahltrid tapped a few keys. "There. That's the last one. I have it entered." He set the tablet down and clapped a hand on Ten's shoulder. "Are you doing any better?"

She wiped her eyes and nodded. Her breathing turned shaky. "Yes sir."

Monica's fingers met with more wires. Were any others safe to pull? She tugged some of the longer ones to the forefront. "What's your idea, Aric? Why do you need Jacob's number?"

"Just a minute." Aric held up a hand, his forehead wrinkled. "You don't know any of the head programmers' numbers, do you? Maybe your mother's?"

"No, sorry." Monica wrapped some of the longer wires around the wires connected to the computer. "I just met her today."

"I know it." Simon raised a trembling hand. "Now that that headache is receding and I can finally think again."

Viral Execution

"How do you know her number?" Aric kept his fingers poised over the number pad. "Seen don't know Nobles' numbers."

"Does that really matter?" Simon snapped. He laid a hand on his head. "Do you want it or not?" He whispered a seven-digit number before closing his eyes again.

Aric's fingers flew into action, and his eyes roved across the diminutive text that scrolled by on his screen.

Monica finished wrapping the wires securely together, then ran her hand up and down the wall. Maybe she could find a nail somewhere. What was Aric considering? Why couldn't he just let them in on his plans? Maybe they could even help. "What are you thinking?"

"I said just a minute." Frowning, Aric kept up his typing. "It's hard to talk and figure out this code at the same time."

"Sorry." Monica's fingers hit something sharp on the wall. There! A nail. She wrapped the longer wires around the protruding metal, keeping them and the shorter wires in place. As she inched away, the wires stayed put. She nodded. Good.

Standing, Ten shuddered. "The pain is almost gone. Thank you, Captain."

Fahltrid nodded, a hint of a smile playing at the edges of his mouth.

Aric clenched a fist. "Got it!"

Monica's heart jumped. "What?"

He pointed at the tablet and motioned to Fahltrid. "With a good deal of help from our captain, we're going to kill some Nobles."

CHAPTER THIRTY-ONE

"**K**ill some Nobles?" Monica gasped. They couldn't do that. The point of this mission was to free people!"

"May I remind you—" Simon started to stand, but Fahltrid laid a hand on his shoulder, keeping him down. Simon flicked Fahltrid's hand away. "May I remind you that *you* are a Noble? Really the only one here, if you don't count Monica, and I usually don't."

Aric shook his head. "I might be a Noble, but I've gotten into this too far to back out, so I might as well keep going, right? And besides, I need to protect my family." He typed on Amelia's computer. "I have to wipe this computer so there will be room on the hard drive for my virus. Some of the memory is corrupted, and it won't store as much information as it used to."

Monica raised her brow. "Your family is back in New Kale."

"Part of it's here." Aric nodded at the computer. "Now, Fahltrid, if you'll please assist me, I'd appreciate it."

"Wait!" Monica crossed her arms. "You still haven't explained your plan!"

Aric pointed at the wires in the wall. "The plan is to put Jacob on a termination schedule. If he doesn't agree to our demands, I terminate him from where we're sitting. We can do the same to the other programmers if we need to, though Jacob seems to be the head of the takeover. If he won't listen to our threats, we can still take out the computers once the programmers are dealt with."

"What?" Monica felt the blood drain from her face as dizziness washed through her head.

Fahltrid took Amelia's computer. "It seems a bit extreme, but if it will work … I for one wouldn't mind seeing Jacob dead, knowing …" Shaking his head, he sighed. "Never mind." He picked up his own tablet and plugged it into Amelia's computer. "I think we should risk it. The safety and happiness of everyone in Penniak, and possibly all of Eursia, are in danger if Jacob's program goes through."

"But we don't even know his number." Monica shook her head. "It's not possible."

"I know it." Fahltrid pointed at the tablet screen and murmured something about a code.

"How do you know his number?" Monica furrowed her brow. "Besides, we can't kill anyone. There has to be another way."

Aric turned to Monica. "We won't kill him or any of the other programmers if he cooperates, but we have to make sure he knows we're not bluffing. We can send a non-lethal zap to his chip to let him know we're serious."

"Never mind how I know. I just do." Fahltrid typed something into the computers. "With Brenna's, Dedrick's, and Jacob's numbers we should be able to find the rest of the programmers' numbers grouped together somewhere."

Monica gritted her teeth. "I still don't like it. I don't want anyone killed."

Simon huffed. "Since when do you make the decisions?" He raised an eyebrow and stretched his long, thin legs into the hall. "We tried it your way, and now we'll try Aric's. Hurting Nobles has never seemed to bother you before."

"I like Aric's idea," Ten whispered.

"I was never the one hurting Nobles." Monica stood and edged away from the computers. "If someone got hurt, it was always their own fault."

Fahltrid turned to Monica. "Jacob will stop at nothing. It's either him or your mother."

Simon frowned. "You're just going to have to accept the fact that you're not the only one who gets to make decisions. And besides, you need me to shut down the computer system."

Monica looked from Simon to Fahltrid to Aric. "You're right, Simon. I really could use your help. I need Dedrick, and you're as close as we'll get."

"Of course I'm right." Simon closed his eyes and rested his head against the wall. "Now get to work. We haven't got all day. Jacob will have you locked out if you keep dawdling."

Aric pointed at the tablet attached to Amelia's computer. "Fahltrid, if you'll assist me. I need someone to keep this access in the code open while I try to insert this virus. It could be difficult."

Fahltrid knelt beside Aric and started typing on the tablet. "I see what you mean. Jacob is countering your efforts. I'll try to put an obstacle in his way."

Aric jabbed a finger at Monica. "You and Ten guard the hall. If someone comes down the corridor, try to redirect them. If they won't leave, yell, and Fahltrid or I will come and help persuade them."

"Okay." Monica rose with Ten, and they jogged to the hall intersection. Monica pointed to the right. "You keep an eye down that way. I'll keep an eye down the other. If someone looks like they're going to walk by without stopping, don't say anything. They might not even notice a couple of Seen."

"Okay." Ten's words came out shaky, and her hands trembled as she pressed them against the floor where she knelt. Her bright blue eyes looked too large for her face, and locks of hair had escaped from her neat braid.

Monica stared down the hall. Being thrown into the Nobles' world headfirst and expected to land on two feet was difficult. She knew that firsthand, but it had to be even harder for Ten. She had sailed free all of her life, her chip a barely noticeable bump on the back of her head, and now a violent surge from the computers forced it to the forefront of her mind.

Clenching her fists, Monica closed her eyes for a second. Who knew how many others were out there experiencing the same pain because of Jacob's program? She again stared down the corridor. "Ten?"

"Yeah?" she whispered.

"Are you feeling okay now? I mean … that reprogramming looked like it hurt."

Ten shifted in place, her dress rustling. "I'm okay. It did hurt, but the pain is mostly gone. I just have a headache now. I think the captain cut us off completely from the computers this time."

"Good." Monica glanced down the hallway again. No sign of anyone coming. "I'm not sure why Fox's program didn't work. It should have."

"Jacob's program probably set new scanning protocols when it reset everything. Fox's program wouldn't be prepared to handle that."

They sat motionless for a few minutes, the sounds of Aric's and Fahltrid's murmurs interrupting their solitude. Simon's barking orders punched in every few minutes and grated against Monica's ears. Footsteps sounded nearby a couple of times, but they continued down another passage without approaching Monica and Ten's hallway.

"Monica?" Ten let out a long sigh.

"Yes?" The hard marble floor started to make Monica's knees ache.

"Did Jacob look familiar to you?"

Monica stood and rubbed the ache. "Familiar?"

"Yes. Like someone we both know." Ten scooted over and pulled her knees up to her chest. "He looks like a younger version of the captain to me. He even sounds like him."

Monica sat down, still across the hall from Ten. "I noticed something about his voice, but wouldn't Fahltrid have mentioned if they were related? Besides wanting him dead, I mean." She curled her knees to copy Ten's position. "Why do you ask?"

"My father disappeared in Penniak, you know. The captain found his ship in port here."

"Oh, I see." Monica rested her chin on her knees. Ten thought Jacob was her father? That would be terrible. Could someone change that much over the years? He had loved Katrina, hadn't he? He had forsaken his Noble title in Cantral to search for her … Or had he? Monica shook her head. "But isn't he too young? He's much younger than Fahltrid."

Ten blinked her eyes rapidly, as if keeping back tears. "The captain is younger than he looks. The sun does that to you. And Drehl is younger than the captain anyway."

Monica scooted to where Ten sat and grasped her hand. There was nothing to be said. If Jacob was Ten's father, could he be made to stop the takeover?

Releasing Ten's hand, Monica stood. "I'll be right back. Keep watch, okay?"

"Sure." Ten shrugged, her face now somber and still. "It takes only one person to watch."

Monica jogged back to where Aric and the others sat, their voices raised in an almost unintelligible argument.

Aric's voice rose above the rest, "That won't work, Fahltrid. If we kill him now, we'll have no idea how to undo this mess he has written in here. Another wipe could kill everyone! Without Jacob, this system he installed will stay for good!"

As Monica drew close, Simon's voice became clear. "You aren't listening to me. Just do what you did with our chips. Taking them out from the computer's manifest worked for us. It will work for the others, too."

Monica crept up to the trio huddled around the hole in the wall.

"That won't work either." Fahltrid's words came out in an exasperated sigh. "We have to know each chip number in the first place, and there are thousands, millions of chips to write out!

Besides, the system has locked us out of that section. Without Jacob's codes to unlock it, we're lost." His jaw flexed. "We could just kill him and get whoever was working with him to let us in. She'll know the codes."

"Maybe." Monica eased up to them. "Jareasa didn't seem to know as much as Jacob does."

"She's a head programmer. She's knowledgeable enough to get promoted that high." Aric pointed at Fahltrid. "I think that your suggested course of action is not a wise one. Regardless of whether or not his partner knows coding, he will know this code best and will be able to undo it with the least amount of damage."

A hoarse yell echoed through the hallway. "Let go of me!"

Monica spun. A blond man held Ten around the waist and dragged her down the hall away from them. She kicked and hit him, but her fists didn't seem to lessen his hold.

"Ten!" Fahltrid dropped the tablet, and it clattered to the tile. He leaped to his feet and dashed toward them.

Monica scrambled after him, her heart thumping wildly. *Ten!*

The man halted, yanked a knife from a leather sheath at his side, and held it at Ten's throat.

She stiffened, clamping her arms to her sides. "Captain," she whimpered. "Help."

Fahltrid thundered to a stop a few feet away, his hands raised. "Please, don't hurt her."

Monica clenched her fists. Fahltrid could beat this smaller man in a fight, if not for the knife.

"I won't hurt her unless you make me." The man pressed the blade close to Ten's skin. "I have a message for you from Jacob."

A red tinge crept up Fahltrid's tanned neck. "What does that traitor want?"

The man's scowl deepened, his brown eyes flashing menacingly. "He wants me to ask if you thought he wouldn't recognize you even after so many years. He knew it was you the minute he saw you in the holding cell."

"Captain." Ten's eyes filled with tears.

"If Jacob wants to speak with me, I'll go with you peacefully." Fahltrid held his hands open and above his head in a sign of surrender. "Just leave Ten alone. I'll go with you."

"He doesn't want you." The man edged down the hall toward the offices and meeting rooms. "He says to tell you that she has Katrina's eyes."

"I'll kill him," Fahltrid whispered.

Monica glanced at him. Did the man hear that threat? What if he killed Ten?

"If either of you try to follow me, you will regret it." The man dragged Ten farther down the hall.

"You won't harm her." Fahltrid stepped tentatively toward them. "Jacob wants her alive."

The man pressed the knife harder against Ten's neck. Blood trickled down to her shirt. "Alive yes, but he didn't say anything about maimed." He again pulled her farther down the corridor, and they disappeared around a corner.

Fahltrid gripped a handful of his hair and groaned. "Ten!" He fell to his knees and pounded a fist against the floor.

Crouching beside him, Monica shook her head. What could they do? That man would hurt Ten if they tried to follow.

Fahltrid climbed to his feet, his shoulders slumped and his head bowed. "I promised her mother I would protect her."

"It's not your fault." Monica blinked back tears. "I shouldn't have left her alone. He would have hurt her if you had tried anything."

Aric walked up and gestured back at the computers plugged into the wall. "I'm sorry, Fahltrid. I tried to isolate his chip signal and knock him out, but with the other programs running, the computers couldn't find him in time."

Fahltrid's jaw tightened. "I'm going after her. You and Aric can figure out this program Jacob is concocting. I have to know where he's taking her."

Viral Execution

"Just remember," Aric said. "If you find Jacob, you can't kill him. We need him alive."

"I'll do whatever it takes to rescue her." Fahltrid stared down the corridor. "I'll be back with Wheaten no matter what. She's what matters."

Monica reached out to take his arm but drew back. "What about the slaves you've freed over the years? Don't they matter? This is what we're working toward. We have to get this shut down. Ten knows that."

Fahltrid shot her a stony look, then jogged down the hall, his boots making barely any noise on the tiles.

Monica clenched her hands into fists. He had to remember the mission. He just had to. If Jacob died, all could be lost. And what if Jacob really was Ten's father? Could Fahltrid kill his younger brother?

Monica watched as Fahltrid turned a corner and disappeared. If it meant protecting the niece he had raised from infancy, the answer was probably yes.

CHAPTER
THIRTY-TWO

Monica crouched by Aric as he continued working on the two computers still plugged into the wall. Several minutes had passed since the man had captured Ten with no news. "What if Fahltrid's in trouble? They have no way to contact us."

"He can take care of himself." Aric continued typing without looking up from the screen.

Simon reclined against the far wall, snoring softly, his mouth hanging open. He hadn't seemed at all concerned about Ten's captivity and fell right to sleep just moments after Fahltrid left.

Monica picked up Amelia's tablet and scanned the screen, watching for the bits of code Aric had assigned her to look for. The green numbers flashed by almost too quickly to read. How did Aric get any information out of this jumble of letters and numbers? And how could he concentrate with Ten and Fahltrid in danger?

Blowing out a long sigh, she tried to focus on the screen again. A familiar-looking line of text popped up then off again in a split second. That was it! "Aric! I just saw it. What you said you were looking for!"

Aric took Amelia's computer and handed Fahltrid's to Monica. Aric used two fingers to open a blank box on the screen and began typing. "Not good."

"Why?" Monica held Fahltrid's tablet so tightly her thumbs began to ache. "I thought you were looking for it."

"I was watching for it, but I didn't really want to see it." He slammed a fist against the floor. "No!"

Monica flinched.

The humming in the wall quieted.

Simon coughed and spluttered. "What's this?" He sat up, rubbing his eyes. "They didn't agree to our terms?"

"We haven't told them the terms yet." The computer screens dimmed, and Aric unplugged them from the wall. "Jacob found us and shut down this section of the computer. We're locked out. Guards might already be on their way here."

Monica sucked in a deep breath. "So Jacob won? He has Ten, he has my mother and sister, and he has us locked out."

"We need a new access point." Aric tucked the computers into his bag. "Are there any other places with wooden walls? Somewhere Jacob wouldn't know where to look for us?"

Footsteps sounded down the corridor. Monica tensed. "The security team?"

"Probably." Simon pressed his palm against his chest and shook his head. "Ten's captor must have told them where we are, and his coming with a knife means they know our chips are not vulnerable. We're lucky he didn't have a gun."

"No time to talk!" Aric handed Monica his bag and draped Simon's arm over his shoulder. "Come on, you crusty old Noble."

The footsteps sounded closer, though slower, perhaps more cautious. "Monica …" Aric growled out her name. "You've evaded Nobles your whole life. Where should we go?"

Monica edged toward the walls, her instincts flying back to mind. "The walls. We go to the walls."

"A temporary respite." Simon coughed, his face looking even paler. "The computers allow security teams into the walls."

"Temporary respite will have to do." Monica knelt by the wall opposite the one filled with the computer's workings. She ran her hands down the wood paneling until her fingers slid into a crevice.

She popped the access panel open, revealing a dimly lit, narrow corridor.

Aric helped Simon get to his knees and guided him through the hole. A loud bang sounded, and something whizzed by her cheek. Gasping, she clamped a hand to the side of her head. "What was that?"

"A gunshot!" Aric grabbed her wrist and yanked her to the ground. "Stay low."

Now on hands and knees, she peeked around the open access panel. Two men charged down the corridor toward them, each pointing a gun.

Another bang sounded, and something thunked into the wood by her hand.

"Do you have a death wish?" Aric shoved her into the access and tumbled in after her.

Her hands scraped against the wood floor, and her chin knocked on a support beam in the opposite wall. Pain shot up her jaw. Her heart thumped wildly as Aric latched the door. Rubbing her chin, she winced. "Gunshots? Like on the docks?"

"Yes." He took her hand and hoisted her to her feet. "Those bullets can probably pierce the weaker spots in these walls."

Monica pushed his hand away. "We need to get farther into the passage, maybe even to the main dormitory. It's probably near the upper level."

Aric shook his head. "Simon can't take the stairs."

"Nonsense." Simon climbed to his feet. "I can take the stairs."

Something pounded on the panel. "We know you're in there," a man's deep voice called. "You might as well come out. It will go easier for you."

Monica hissed, "We have to go!"

"Give us a moment," Aric called. "The girl is hurt. I'm a doctor, and I need to make sure moving her won't cause any further injury."

"Hurry it up!"

Viral Execution

"I will." Aric stood with his back to Simon and whispered, "We'll have to do it piggyback like Fahltrid did. I'm afraid your heart might give out again otherwise. You shouldn't even be standing."

"Very well." Simon clambered onto Aric's back and wrapped his arms around his neck.

Monica motioned them down the passageway, her voice low. "Try not to make a sound. They won't know which way we've gone."

They trotted down the dim hall, ducking under support beams and weaving around pipes, small white lights in the ceiling their only guide. As they turned into a side passage, a loud crash sounded behind them. Monica racked her brains for past hiding places. But the security team could go anywhere.

She led the way up the main stairs. The security team had even sneaked into the Cantral wall-slave dorms when she was eight in an effort to find her after drugging all the occupants with meal bars laced with some kind of sleep inducer. She was lucky to have escaped that time.

Shouts echoed up the corridor, floating toward them. Monica took the stairs two at a time. With every footfall, the scar on her leg pulsed. When she reached a landing, she whirled around.

Aric labored up the stairs a few steps behind. Sweat glistened on his pale forehead. "Where are we going?" His breathing sounded ragged.

"To the wall-slave dormitory." She laid a hand on her chest and breathed deeply. "Do you need help?"

Aric quickened his pace, a deep scowl etching his brow. "No, I'll be fine."

Monica trotted down the steps and grabbed his arm. "We don't have time to spare. If Simon doesn't walk, we could all die."

"And …" Simon slipped from Aric's back and laid a hand on his shoulder. "My life is up to me, isn't it? You two should go on without me."

Monica tugged on his hand. "We're not leaving you, and we're wasting time discussing it."

Aric supported Simon on one side, and Monica moved to his other, but the narrow passage left no room for her to help. Aric dragged Simon upward, Monica close at their heels.

A crowd of people huddled in the stairway just ahead, murmuring among themselves. Someone gasped, and the whispers stopped. Every slave turned and looked at the trio, their eyes wide. Monica froze. The Seen uniforms were a dead giveaway that they shouldn't be here, and Aric's Noble features would make him stand out as well.

She shook her head. What now? Images of the past flashed by in a dizzying array.

"Monica." Aric grabbed her arm. "We have to get out of here. Where can we go?"

Shouts sounded from farther down the stairwell. The line of slaves moved up the stairs a few feet, and the murmuring started again.

"I don't know." Monica pointed at a side passage to the left. "They'll just follow us wherever we hide, and I don't think you two will even fit through some of these hallways."

She pressed her hands to the sides of her head. Think! She mentally scrolled through the past few minutes—the shots, ducking into the panel. "Simon, you got into the wall first. They haven't seen you." She drew her hands away from her head and gently pushed him up a stair. "Go with the wall slaves to the dorm. Blend in. Your Seen uniform might stand out, but they probably won't search the dorms if they see Aric and me going down the other hall. They're only looking for us. Not you."

"And abandon you?" Simon crossed his arms over his chest. "I should say not!"

"She's right." Aric laid a hand on Simon's shoulder. "Monica will be my lookout while I try to hack into the system again."

Simon frowned for a moment, then nodded. "Very well." He turned and joined the flow of people heading up the stairs.

Two men appeared at the bottom of the steps. One shouted something in an odd language.

A wall slave let out a short shriek, and a child wailed.

"You two!" the man called in the Cantral language. "Stay where you are. The rest of you—" He switched to the guttural language and barked a command.

The crowd scurried up the stairs and began filing into the dorms farther up.

Aric grabbed Monica's arm. "Where do we go?"

The two men charged up the stairs.

She glanced around. The narrow passage on the left looked promising. She pointed at it. "Can you fit?"

"No choice." Aric pulled her toward the opening.

A shot rang out from below. A sickening thud and a scream echoed through the hall. Monica jerked around in time to see a woman collapse to the floor, a pool of red spreading across the back of her dress. She tumbled down the stairs, tripping one of their pursuers. Another wall slave screamed, and they started running, scrambling over each other.

Aric shoved Monica into the opening and pushed his bag into her hands. "Go!"

She trotted down the dark, narrow corridor. Another shot rang out and thunked into the wall somewhere behind them. A hand touched her back, prodding her forward.

"Faster!" Aric whispered. They turned sharply to the left. The passage stopped at a dead end. "Now what?"

Monica reached out and brushed her hand along the dead end. "There should be …" Her fingers struck a wooden beam. "A ladder." She started climbing hand over hand. "This is a doorway in the Nobles' rooms. That's why the wall dead ends. We have to climb up and over. There will be another corridor on the other side."

The thud of footsteps grew louder behind them. "They're catching up," Aric said. "Go!"

Monica crawled across the hidden door opening and scrambled down the ladder on the other side. When her toes touched the floor, she backed away a few steps. "Hurry!"

At the top of the doorway, Aric turned around, his back and legs scraping against the sides of the tunnel. When his foot hit the first rung, a muffled bang sounded. He grunted and fell backward. Monica raised her arms. He slammed into her, knocking her to the narrow strip of floor where they both settled in a crumpled heap.

"Aric!" Her body aching, she crawled out from under him and helped him rise.

He took a moment to balance himself. "Come on." Clutching a hand to his shoulder, he jerked his head toward the passage. "We have to keep moving."

Blood appeared beneath his fingers, illumined by the ceiling lights. Redness spread across his shirt.

Monica gasped. He'd been shot? "Better if we get out of this passage and into another. They can't track us." She edged away from the ladder and searched the wall with her hands. There had to be a crevice—a sign of a door somewhere. Her fingers slid into a small divot in the wood. She yanked on the hidden latch. A panel sprang open into the hall outside.

She entered the Nobles' corridor on hands and knees. Aric crawled out into the hall, his face pale.

Monica shut the panel without a sound and led the way down the hall. "You got shot?"

"Yes, I got shot." Aric walked beside her, limping every few steps.

"In your leg and arm?" Monica searched for another panel on the opposite wall.

"No." Aric shook his head, a grimace forming. "I got shot in the shoulder. The leg got hurt in the fall. I'm surprised I didn't crush you."

She knelt beside a latch barely concealed near a statue. She tugged on it, but it wouldn't budge. "It's sealed."

Monica rose and walked farther down the hall. "Is the wound bad?" She turned a corner and glanced back.

"Yes, it's bad. Getting shot is always bad." Still holding a hand to his shoulder, Aric glared. "Now where are we going?"

"Not sure yet." She scampered to another panel farther down the hall and yanked it open. It revealed a cramped slave's passage. "This will do."

Aric joined her and peered inside. "It will have to."

She looked up at him. "When we came into the palace I noticed some slave passages blocked off for the computer's use. If we can find one of those …"

"That could be a good access point." Aric glanced over his shoulder. "They're going to find us if we don't get out of here." More blood seeped through his clenched fingers. "Especially if I start leaving a trail."

Monica shoved the satchel through the opening and scrambled in. "Will you be all right?"

Aric squeezed in next and closed the door. He grunted, and his footfalls sounded heavy behind her. "I'll be fine. Let's keep going. Those security guards wont' stop looking for us."

Monica watched him for a second before hurrying on. Would he really be all right? The woman who had been shot had dropped like a stone. Monica focused straight ahead walked farther down the corridor. Now to find an access to those computers. Without that, they were stuck, and her mother and sister would have no one to rescue them.

CHAPTER
THIRTY-THREE

Monica turned down another passage, the satchel of first-aid supplies and tablets still clutched tightly in her hand. How many turns and twists had they taken? Ten? Twenty? She had lost count as they jogged, desperately trying to put space between them and the security guards.

Aric's soft footfalls continued behind her, a constant reminder that he still followed. She stopped in front of another junction in the wall passage. A corridor jutted off to the right and another started to the left, though it ended after just a few feet. "I haven't heard a sound from those guards in at least ten minutes." She turned and faced Aric. "I think we've lost them."

Nodding, Aric grimaced and pulled his hand away from his wounded shoulder. "Now we can concentrate on finding someplace to plug back into the mainframe."

Monica entered the left passage and ran a hand along the wall. The computer's steady vibrations echoed in this wall just as loudly as any other. She pressed her fingers firmly against the wood. But maybe …

She crept a few more feet into the corridor and knocked on the dead-end panel. It echoed softly beneath her knuckle. Smiling, she beckoned to Aric. "I think the computer comes out into here."

Aric strode over, his face pale in the dim light from the passage ceiling. He stood by the wall and ran a hand down the smooth wood, keeping his injured arm pressed close to his chest. "I think whoever built this computer used some of the slave passages for the larger components. That's good news for us."

Monica wiggled her fingers into a small crack between the side wall and the wood panel. She tugged on the board. A groan sounded, like nails pulling out of wood. As splinters dug into her fingers, the board moved an inch.

"Here, I'll help." Aric slid his good hand into a crack on the other side of the panel and yanked. A hiss escaped his clenched teeth. Muttering something under his breath, he yanked again, and the board popped loose.

A cloud of dust burst from the opening, carrying a warm, musty smell. Tangles of wires lay inside along with three metal boxes, each the size of a child, lights blinking on the surfaces.

"Ah!" Aric said. "Three computers. We're in luck."

Monica grabbed the board and laid it out of their way. "Now what?"

Aric pointed at the bag. "The tablets."

She dug out the two computers and offered them to him.

He took Fahltrid's tablet but shook his head at Amelia's. "I don't think I can handle two at a time. It's going to be hard to keep up with the program typing with only one hand." He settled the tablet onto the floor and knelt beside it, his injured arm still pressed against his chest. "You said you've never done any programming, right?"

Monica touched one of the computers in the once-blocked hallway. "Only a little. Ten taught me some while on board the ship."

Aric gripped his shoulder again, sweat beading on his lip. "Yes, she told me that." He nodded at the wall computers. "Get those open so I can see what we're dealing with."

Monica located a small black pull tab on the closest computer box and tugged on it. The tab popped up, and the metal sheet covering the computer's front wiggled loose, but another tab held it in place farther down. When she unlatched the second tab, the sheet pulled free, revealing more blinking lights along with small green metal disks with raised dots covering their surfaces.

Setting the sheet to the side, she glanced over her shoulder at Aric. "Is this a good enough access?"

He drew his hand away from his shoulder, his fingers and palm now completely covered with blood, both dried and fresh. "Yes. This one is better than the last. There are some hard drives here." Nodding, he inched forward. "It should be simple enough. I have already written the code to attack Jacob's chip. All we have to do is hack in and run it."

"Good." Monica picked up a tablet and held it out. "Just tell me what to do. I'll be your other arm."

Pointing at a palm-sized piece of metal with raised dots, Aric smiled, though it looked almost like a grimace. "Pull the red wires out of that one. It's just a wireless range booster. There will be a redundant one close by, so the computer won't go berserk."

Monica yanked the bundle of red wires out and held them tightly. "Okay."

"Take the back access off one of the tablets." Aric continued giving orders until Monica had Fahltrid's tablet connected to the red wires and plugged into the system. Soon, green letters scrolled across the tablet screen.

Aric's face seemed to grow paler by the minute, but it was difficult to tell for sure in the dim lighting.

"See that string of code?" Aric pointed at a stream of numbers just before they disappeared from the screen.

"I think so." The numbers stayed in her mind's eye. "But they disappeared. What am I supposed to do?"

"They'll come around again in a moment." Aric's breathing changed. It became more labored and ragged as he leaned over the tablet. "It should run by every half minute or less. The computer is constantly using that command. It's a string that allows access to the chips. The computer uses it to send assignments and messages. Wall slaves, Seen, and everyone else." He nodded. "There it goes again. Tap it next time and drag it across the screen to this box. We can work with it, rewrite it to accept my program that talks to Jacob's chip."

Monica's head swirled, but she nodded and watched the screen. Aric would talk her through it, and everything would fall into place. No need to worry about the programming part. He would take care of it.

"See it yet?" Aric blinked and shook his head, his hands trembling.

"Not yet."

He inhaled sharply and blinked a couple of times. "On second thought, I think I'm going to need your help."

"With what?" She glanced up from the tablet.

Aric's eyes looked glassy now, not quite focusing. "I was hoping the flow would stop on its own." He drew his hand away from his shoulder, revealing a bloody mess of cloth and exposed skin high on his upper arm. "But I think I'm going to need a tourniquet. I'm feeling rather faint."

"Aric!" She jumped to her feet and glanced around the narrow hallway. "What can I do? What's a tourniquet? How do I get one?"

"A tourniquet will cut the blood flow to my arm, to stop the bleeding." Using his uninjured hand, he fumbled with his shoe laces. "We can tie a lace around my shoulder, then we just need something to tighten it. I'll explain as we go." His fingers fumbled with the knot.

Monica brushed his hand away. "Let me do it." She made quick work of the knot and jerked the lace free from the shoe.

"Cut away my sleeve now."

Monica rummaged in the first-aid satchel and withdrew a tiny pair of scissors. With a few snips she cut away the sleeve and pulled it from his arm.

As the fabric scraped over his wound, Aric hissed through his teeth and closed his eyes. "Now tie the lace under my armpit and over my shoulder. Tight as you can."

She plunked the scissors back into the bag, then did as he instructed, knotting the lace at his back. The thin cord dug into his skin, making white marks near the wound. "Now what?"

"Now ..." Aric groaned and opened his eyes. "We need a stick of some sort to insert in the tourniquet and tighten the lace."

Monica ran her hands along the rough wood floor. There had to be something! Her fingers hit against dirt and pebbles, but the floor was mostly free of debris. The board they'd pulled from the wall was much too big, and so was the metal panel. But maybe ... She dug through Aric's bag and pulled out the scissors once more. "Will these work?"

He nodded before squeezing his eyes shut again. "Keep them closed and push them between my arm and the shoelace. Then twist them to make the knot tighter."

She inserted the scissors as instructed and turned them in a circle, allowing the lace to bunch in a knot. The skin around the bandage puckered and paled. Aric groaned.

After tucking the scissors so the twist wouldn't come undone, Monica sighed. "Is that better?"

Aric's head lolled, and his breathing turned deep and steady.

"Aric?" She reached out to touch his arm but drew back. Any touch might cause him more pain. "Aric? Are you all right?"

His breathing remained unchanged, and his eyes stayed closed.

"Aric!" She laid a hand on his uninjured shoulder. Had he fainted?

He gave no response.

Monica sat back on her heels. Now what? She couldn't do this without him! She didn't know enough about programming. Closing her eyes, she rested her head on her knees. She had to think. There had to be something she could do. Rose depended on her, and so did Faye and Ten. Simon, too.

Opening her eyes again, she sighed. Simon. Was his heart holding up? Had he escaped from the guards? If so, would he be able to stay hidden? What would he say now if he were here? He would probably be brimming with confidence, as usual. He would pump her up and insist that she do whatever was necessary to save lives.

Monica's gaze strayed to Fahltrid's tablet lying on the floor amidst a mess of wires. The string of code Aric had pointed out flashed across the screen again. She picked up the tablet and poised her hand over it. Soon, the number string drifted down the screen once more. When she tapped it with a thumb, it appeared in bold in the screen's lower left corner. Taking a deep breath, she pulled it into an open file and picked up Amelia's computer where Aric had stored his program. She could do this. She had to.

No one else could.

CHAPTER THIRTY-FOUR

Monica stared at the computer code filling Fahltrid's tablet screen. She held the tablet tightly in one hand while supporting Amelia's computer in the other, pressing them tightly together end to end so the connection between them stayed strong.

Aric remained motionless beside her, the tourniquet wrapped snuggly around his shoulder. Purple blotches ran up and down his bare arm, probably because of the cutoff blood flow, but she couldn't remove the tourniquet. He would bleed to death.

"Please be okay, Aric." Monica watched him for a second before turning back to the computers. Poising her fingers over the tablet screen, she inhaled deeply. This was it—a challenge that was certainly almost unattainable for her fledgling computer skills, but she had to try.

Pulling the string of code over to the program, she integrated the two, manipulating the original string to accept Aric's virus. The motions seemed to come instinctively, like she knew what to do just from watching Aric and Fahltrid work in the hall. Her fingers flew as if working on their own. Aric's memory drug and Simon's drills brought back every moment she had worked with computers, every code she had ever seen. All of Ten's instructions flooded in. Monica sorted through them, wading in the stream of information and putting it into use with this new program.

Viral Execution

The code now finished, she drew it back into the stream of words and numbers flowing across the tablet's background. The new program flashed once then sank into the stream, almost indistinguishable from the rest as it flew by every few seconds.

Monica laid the tablet on the floor. Had it worked? After transferring a copy of the code and program to Amelia's computer, she unhooked it and laid it on the floor. She would need evidence of the program's presence and abilities to convince Jacob to let Rose and Faye go.

She looked at Aric again. Could she leave him here? What if a wall slave found him and reported him to the security team? She shook her head. They probably wouldn't do that. Since his Seen uniform was torn and dirtied now, they might think it a cast-off garment. They would more likely assume he was a wall slave and take him to an infirmary for treatment.

She laid a hand on his good shoulder. "Aric? Please, wake up."

He moaned softly and opened one eye. "Amelia?"

"No, Monica. Remember?"

He opened his eyes wider and sat up with a start.

Pushing his shoulders, she forced his back against the wall. "No. You'll hurt yourself."

"I'll hurt myself?" he hissed, grabbing her arm. "You're the one pressing against my wound."

She jerked her hands back. "Sorry, I was trying to get you to stay put."

His face paled. "I've lost a lot of blood." He turned his head to the side and probed his wound with his good hand. Taking his hand away again, he heaved a sigh. "The bullet went straight through. Most fortunate for me." He pointed to the first-aid satchel. "Give me my supplies. I'll stitch this up now that the flow of blood has stopped, and we can finish that program."

"I think I already finished it." Monica shoved the bag to Aric's side.

Aric rummaged in his bag, his brow furrowed. "Really?"

"Programming is in my blood, you know." Monica picked up Amelia's computer and held it against her chest. "Will you be able to come with me to threaten Jacob with our program?"

Threading a needle with a length of thick black thread, Aric shook his head. "I'm afraid you'll have to do it yourself. I don't know that I'll be able to stand. Blood loss makes one very weak."

"Yes, I know." She looked down at the computer in her hands. "So if I did it right, will this virus terminate any of the programmers on my command?"

"Not exactly." Aric pressed the needle into his skin beside the wound, his teeth gritted. Drawing the needle across the wound, he made the first stitch to close the bullet hole. "Every programmer but your mother has their number in there, but it doesn't kill them on the spot. I got the idea for the program from Simon's chip." He drew another stitch across the wound. "It will slowly shut down Jacob's chip, as if he were a slave turning sixty-five. The symptoms should convince him to do what you ask."

"Then at least I can use the sleeper program." She shuddered. It was better than killing the programmers, anyway.

"You can try, but with how the computer has been acting , I'm not …" Grimacing, Aric shifted in place and adjusted his grip on the needle. He grunted and looked down at his hand.

Monica followed his gaze. His fingertips and hand appeared mottled and purple, and the color seemed to be creeping up his arm. "Why is that happening?"

"Loss of blood flow. Now be quiet. We need to get this done. If I don't get circulation back soon, I'll lose my arm."

"Right. Sorry." She inhaled deeply. "What if Jacob takes the computer from me? He's much bigger than I am, and he could overpower me without much effort."

"He can't overwrite the aging program with so little time. He would have to figure it out in an hour or less." As Aric drew another stitch through his wound, a sharp hiss escaped through his clenched teeth. He let the needle rest in his palm before answering. "Which I doubt he can do. I'll be down here with this tablet, and I can write commands from here. If you're not back in an hour, I'll start terminating a head programmer every ten minutes—Jacob last, of course, so he can take down the programs he enacted."

"Kill them?" Monica shook her head. "I—"

"It's the only way." Aric closed his eyes, a pained expression increasing. "Now get going. I'll take care of everything here. Fahltrid and Ten are counting on you, not to mention your family." He resumed stitching on his shoulder. "Just make sure you get back here in time to stop me from killing anyone if Jacob acquiesces to our plan."

Monica nodded and ran down the dim corridor toward an access panel, Amelia's computer tucked under an arm. She knelt beside the narrow wooden hatch and glanced back at Aric. He kept his head turned to the side, still stitching his wound.

Biting her lip, Monica swung the hatch open. He would be all right. After all, he had awoken from his faint, and he could remove the tourniquet soon.

She crawled on hands and knees into the Nobles' hallway, the floor changing from wood in the slave passage to marble in the Nobles' section. She scrambled to her feet and looked every which way. No sign of the security team.

After taking a deep breath, she broke into a jog down the wide, silent corridor. Jacob would have taken Rose to the computer room to work under his watchful eye.

She ran faster, sprinting up a flight of stairs and dodging past a small cluster of Nobles who stood wide-eyed, whispering among themselves. Had they noticed the computer change as well?

Bowing her head, she plowed forward. Of course. Who could have missed it? The pain Ten and the others felt must have been similar for the Nobles. How could Jacob risk so many lives just for his own power? If not for him, this would have been so much simpler. The computers would be destroyed already, and none of her family or friends would be in danger.

She clutched Amelia's computer in both hands and turned down the final corridor. A large man in a Seen uniform stood outside the computer room, his arms crossed over his chest and his back resting against the wall. His dark hair and plain features made him look similar to any other Seen. The man who took Ten had blond hair, so he wasn't the same man. At least this Seen probably wouldn't recognize her as a rogue slave.

As she drew closer, it became clear his eyes were closed, and a grimace marred his features. She slowed her pace and quieted her steps. This guard standing at a computer room door was a familiar scene, but this time she was alone, unarmed.

Holding Amelia's tablet close, she shook her head. Mostly unarmed. All she had was a computer program that might not even work. What if she hadn't integrated it correctly?

The man opened his eyes and looked at her, his dark eyes piercing. "What are you doing here, Seen? You have no business being here. Haven't you felt the change?"

She continued her silent march, tablet held out. "I have an important message for Master Jacob. He'll want to hear it, and he won't be happy if you don't let me deliver it."

"I can easily deliver it for you." The man stood straighter, his shoulders squared. "He doesn't wish to be disturbed."

Monica drew herself up to her full height, but she barely reached the man's elbows. "I'm Madam Rose's personal assistant. She needs me in this time of crisis, and she'll want to hear this message as well."

The man half closed an eye. "I'll have to check with Master Jacob."

"I'm an assistant. If it's improper for me to interrupt, I'll be the one punished." She slipped past him and took a step toward the door. Would she have to use the sleeper program? "You'll have nothing to worry about."

The man backed up a step. "Fine. But if you do get me in trouble, I'll make you regret it."

Viral Execution

Monica opened the door and stepped in. With the emergency protocols active, she probably wouldn't get gassed again even if she had a chip.

Rose stood by the wall-sized computer, her fingers poised over one of the control panels. Jacob loomed over her shoulder, a tablet clutched in one hand.

Stepping back, Rose glared at him. "It's done. Now tell them to let Faye go."

With a wave of his hand Jacob shooed her away from the console. "After I check that you haven't written any bugs into this. I know you, Brenna."

Monica closed the door softly behind her and waited silently.

Rose kept her gaze on Jacob. "You think I would risk my daughter's life by inserting a bug?"

"I wouldn't put it past you. Considering my recent revelation about your character, I'm not sure you're the woman any of us thought you to be." Jacob tapped some controls on the keyboard, a smile growing.

"I don't know what you mean." Rose turned toward the door. Her gaze met Monica's.

Monica gulped. Should she give the message now?

Rose's mouth dropped open, but she quickly closed it and turned to face Jacob again. "Dedrick never fully trusted you, and neither did I, and now you're proving we were right to keep you at arm's length."

"Yet it did you no good. I have the upper hand now and will keep it until this program wipes Dedrick's power from the system and you're both nothing but Seen. Unfortunately, changing his status will revive his chip from that program someone put on him, but since he's in holding, I'm not concerned." Jacob looked up from the computer. "I believe he'll be rather surprised when he wakes up from his chip-induced sleep. Especially concerning your daughter."

"You said you would release her!" Rose snapped, her face turning red. "What are you planning?"

"Not Faye, you foolish woman." Jacob backed away from the control panel. "I was referring to your other daughter, the one who has been sneaking around causing trouble. Where have you been hiding her all this time?" His gaze bore into Rose, and she shrank away. "Does Dedrick know about her?"

"I haven't hidden her anywhere." Rose straightened, her facial features hardening. "I wouldn't say she's hiding at all." She turned and locked gazes with Monica. "Isn't that right?"

CHAPTER THIRTY-FIVE

Monica held Amelia's computer at the ready. "I'm not going to hide anymore. It's time to finish this."

Jacob pivoted, his fingers clasped around his wristband. "Brenna, what are you planning? I will tell that Seen to kill Faye if you force my hand."

"Monica ...," Rose whispered. "Don't let Faye die."

"If anyone's going to die, Jacob ..." Monica firmed her voice. "If anyone's going to die, it's going to be you." She held up her computer. "You know Aric? The heir to Cantral's north wing? He's here. He wrote a virus that will terminate you if you don't do what we say. I don't want it to be this way, but ..." Licking her lips, she inhaled deeply. "I know it's for the best. The system has to fall, and this is the last stronghold. These people deserve to be free."

"Brenna, is this some sort of bluff?" Jacob fiddled with his wristband. "Do you expect me to believe Aric, Rian's son, is in on this? He is set to inherit the most powerful position in the world. Why would he help the illegitimate child of a rebelling city-state programmer destroy his power?" Jacob laughed, but a hint of sweat glistened on his brow. "It's ridiculous."

"You know nothing about me or about Aric." Monica smiled despite the growing dread in her stomach. Could she go through with this? If Jacob didn't acquiesce, he would die. "You already feel the effects of his program, don't you? It's similar to the one that shuts down a slave's chip at age sixty-five, but faster. It will have your organs shut down in an hour instead of days."

"You're lying." Jacob turned back to the computer. "I'd have noticed the code."

Rose walked over and laid a hand on Monica's shoulder. "My daughter knows what she's talking about, trust me. And Aric is here; I know that to be true. I would believe her if I were you. I imagine it's not very comfortable to have your heart slowly stop beating." Rose pursed her lips. "I've seen it happen many times in the slave dorms. I think it's time a Noble experienced what they've put the slaves through."

Jacob sneered. "You can't do this. You can't program a Noble's chip like that." He stalked across the room and snatched Amelia's computer from Monica. His gaze darted up and down the screen.

"You can when the system's been compromised and when you have an expert programmer on your side." Monica clenched her fists, willing herself to keep from taking back the computer. Aric was the one doing the programming. He would stop Jacob if necessary. She inhaled softly. But what about Faye? Where was she? "The effects of the program are reversible. That is, if you accept our demands quickly enough."

Jacob growled something under his breath as he stared at the code. "You haven't given me any demands, so how can I act?" His gaze slid to his wristband. "All I can do is retaliate."

"No!" Rose hissed.

Monica shook her head. "If you hurt Faye, you won't have a bargaining chip anymore, and Aric will just kill you."

"Then what are your demands?" Jacob grimaced. "I'll see if I can even consider them."

Monica narrowed her eyes. Consider? He had to do more than consider. He had to agree. Wasn't his life worth more to him than the computers and power? "We want you to let Ten and Faye go and allow my mother to shut down the computers."

"Ten?" Jacob frowned. "I don't know who that is, but as for Faye, I can't let her go. She's the only means I have to keep you from using this program to kill me anyway." He gestured to Amelia's computer. "I am more apt to believe you about Aric now. I know someone like you wouldn't be able to write this, and ..." Nodding at Rose, he shrugged. "It's not Brenna's style."

"What do you mean you don't know who Ten is?" Monica glanced at Rose. Asking for Faye had been a long shot—of course he wouldn't give her up—but he wouldn't hurt Ten. "She's your own daughter."

"My daughter?" Jacob inhaled deeply, then coughed. "Oh, I didn't know her name. It doesn't surprise me, though—Ten—rather slavish. I suppose I shouldn't expect anything different from Katrina. She couldn't help being nothing but a Seen."

Clenching her fists, Monica inhaled sharply. Hadn't he loved Katrina? What had happened to make him so uncaring? "We haven't much time. If you don't let my mother shut down the computers and the program you installed, then your chip will kill you. If you kill either Ten or Faye, then the virus will kill you. As soon as you shut down the computers, I'll have Aric terminate the program."

Jacob tossed Amelia's computer at her, and she fumbled to catch it. He turned to the main computer console in the wall. "I suppose I have no choice, then. But your mother cannot shut down the computer." He began typing on the computer but kept glancing over his shoulder every few seconds. "Only I can."

"It's true." Rose's shoulders slumped. "He wrote his chip into Dedrick's place. According to the computers, he's the new ruler of Penniak. He only needed me for part of the emergency protocols."

Monica tightened her grip on Amelia's computer. "Fine, then he can do it. As long as it's done, it doesn't matter whose fingers do the typing."

Rose edged even closer to Monica's side. "I'm proud of you," she whispered, her breath tickling Monica's ear. "God has given you great strength and courage. I had been praying for help, and then you opened that door …"

Monica nodded, keeping her gaze on Jacob. He didn't seem nearly worried enough about this situation. If he tried to free himself, Aric would be able to stop him, wouldn't he? Or had he fallen unconscious again? With that much blood loss, it would be difficult for him to stay awake.

Jacob continued typing something into the main computer. Monica craned her neck, but his shoulders blocked her view of the screen. How could he really be Drehl? Fahltrid had painted Drehl to be a good man, someone who cared about the slaves, but Jacob spoke so harshly about Katrina and Ten.

Jacob muttered something. The overhead lights flickered, as if on cue.

Monica flinched, and Rose's grip on her shoulder tightened. "Just the system reconfiguring," Jacob whispered. He glanced over his shoulder again, but his gaze seemed to go past them. "Nothing to worry about."

Monica watched him closely. Was he expecting that guard to help him? He shouldn't. A Seen wouldn't budge unless he was summoned. "Nothing you can say will reassure me," Monica said. "I won't be satisfied until this is finished."

Rose crossed the room in three steps and stood beside Jacob. "Don't think of trying to trick us."

"I wouldn't dream of it." Jacob cast a withering look at Rose before turning back to the computer. "We all know your skills by now."

As his fingers continued moving across the console, entering different commands and skittering from one control to the other, Rose's gaze narrowed. "What are you doing? You're going about that the long way. You're stalling!"

Monica looked from her mother to Jacob. "Jacob, I wouldn't advise that. The longer you wait, the worse your symptoms will get."

"The program isn't that simple, Brenna." Sweat beaded on Jacob's forehead as he continued typing. "I wrote in safety protocols to the program I downloaded. You didn't see them. If I were to take the shortcut, it would only complicate things."

"I don't believe you." Rose turned and met Monica's gaze.

Monica shrugged. There wasn't anything they could do to safely test his word. If he was telling the truth, then people's lives would be at risk if the computer retaliated. Rose's chip had no protections on it, nothing to stop the computer from terminating her. "We'll just have to trust him," Monica whispered. They had the virus to keep him in check. He wouldn't risk his life just to keep the computers running. Would he?

"Jacob." A new voice came from behind them. "What's going on?"

Monica whirled.

Jareasa stood in the doorway, her dark eyes narrowed.

The Seen guard towered behind her, his eyes wide and fearful. She pointed at Rose and then Monica. "What are they doing here? You're deviating from the plan!"

"Jareasa," Jacob's voice carried a warning tone, but Jareasa continued, wagging a finger. "I knew I should have come to check on you earlier, but the Seen"—turning slightly, she shot the guard a death glare—"were in a panic about the changing chip signals and needed calming. I can only assume you were successful with the programming, since even I felt it."

"Jareasa, perhaps if you gave me time to answer your questions, I would." Jacob coughed again, and his skin took on a sickly pallor, but he kept working.

Monica looked from Jacob to Jareasa, her heart racing. She tried to select the sleeper program on Amelia's tablet, but it wouldn't respond.

"Then answer!" Jareasa shoved past Rose, who stood motionless by Jacob. Jareasa sneered at her. "I thought you were going to get rid of her, Jacob." She motioned to the Seen guard, who shuffled into the room.

Monica widened her eyes. Could Aric tell what was going on here? They didn't have any way to defend against these people. Jareasa wouldn't care about the virus they'd inflicted on Jacob. In fact, she might even use it to her advantage.

"Jareasa, this is not the best time." Jacob resumed his work on the computer, a wince twisting his lips.

Rose stared Jareasa down. "If Dedrick were here, you would never dare do any of this. You're both cowards."

"We're not cowards," Jareasa said, "but we're not foolish, either. Of course we waited for Dedrick to be out of the way." She motioned to the Seen guard. "Take her to a holding cell. She's a traitor."

The guard stepped forward, though he glanced around the room warily. "I'm sorry, Madam." He clasped Rose's arm. She stiffened but made no move to shake him off.

Monica backed up. The tablet still wasn't responding. It had frozen again! What should she do? Find Fahltrid? This guard would be no match for the merchant's sea-hardened muscles.

"Jareasa!" Jacob turned from the computer, his face ashen. "You are not the one giving orders here. You know nothing of this situation."

Monica gripped Amelia's computer. Turning to the guard, she whispered, "You don't have to do what Jareasa says."

He shook his head, and his fingers around Rose's arm turned white. She winced. "She's right, Cole. You don't have to."

"Stop talking." Jareasa pointed at the door. "Take her out of here, Cole, and lock her in a holding cell near Dedrick. They'll have plenty of time to discuss each other's betrayals."

"Are you not listening to me?" Jacob whirled around and faced them, his fists clenched. "Cole, release her and stand down. Jareasa, you have no power here. You might as well leave."

Viral Execution

Monica stared at Jacob's sweat-covered, pale face. He panted heavily as he stood firm before the computer. Was Aric's program working that quickly?

"No power?" Jareasa fiddled with her wristband, her gaze never leaving Cole. "You think I would come unprepared? I didn't write my portion of the program without adding some hidden touches. I knew I couldn't trust you. You can't trust anyone in this business." She punched some commands into her wristband. Cole flinched but kept hold of Rose's arm. "Now you know, Seen, you do have to obey me, or you'll get more of the same."

Cole nodded and led Rose toward the door. Monica stepped forward. She had to stop this!

Rose held out her free hand toward Monica. "No. I'll be fine. Remember, we're not alone. Things will work out for the best."

The guard led her from the room.

"Stop!" Jacob stumbled forward, blinking rapidly.

Jareasa caught his arm and steadied him. "What's wrong with you? She's nothing. She has no power with the new program in place. The girl we can handle ourselves."

Monica backed away, holding Amelia's computer like a shield. She needed more time. If only she could warn Aric.

She ran for the door, but Jareasa darted over and caught her wrist. Jareasa snatched Amelia's computer and held it out of reach.

Running a hand through his hair, Jacob shook his head. "Jareasa, do you want me dead?"

"How could you ask such a question?" Jareasa's grip tightened on Monica's arm, sending a prickling sensation up her skin. "Of course not. We're in this together."

"Are we?" Jacob turned back to the computer. "Then what about the power you kept aside for yourself?" His fingers hovered over the console. Shaking his head, he blinked again. "If only I could concentrate!" He began typing again. "If you want me to live, then let the girl go."

Monica's fingers tingled. She needed to go tell Aric to stop this virus. "Jareasa, you have to release me."

"Why should I listen to you?" Jareasa dragged Monica to where Jacob stood. "You're ruining everything, Jacob. You can't back out of the plan now."

"If you don't let me go," Monica hissed the words through clenched teeth, the ache in her arm growing, "then Jacob will die. There's a virus running through his chip. It will kill him if I don't get it reversed."

Jareasa muttered something under her breath, then shoved Amelia's computer into Monica's hands. "Then reverse it!" Releasing Monica's arm, she turned to Jacob. "How could you let this happen?"

"Let it happen?" Jacob leaned against the computer console, his breathing heavy. "I didn't see it coming! You wouldn't have either." Laying a hand over his heart, he closed his eyes. "Whatever your name is, Brenna's daughter, you had better do something about that program quickly, or I won't be able to wipe the computers. I'll be dead."

"Fix it!" Jareasa shoved Monica toward the door. "Make him well." She clamped a hand on Monica's shoulder, her fingers once again digging in.

Monica gritted her teeth. "No." She ducked out of Jareasa's grip. "I'm in charge here, Jareasa, not you." She held up Amelia's computer. "Do what I say or you'll be next. The virus will infect you as well."

Like a striking snake, Jareasa slapped Monica. Pain lanced through her head. She fell to the ground, and the computer skittered away.

Gasping, Monica sat up and reached for the computer. Maybe the sleeper program …

Jareasa slid it away with a foot and grabbed Monica by the braid, yanking her to her feet. "Who's in charge here?" She hissed. Pain ripped through Monica's scalp, and tears sprang to her eyes.

"I don't know how to fix it."

Jareasa jerked on the braid. Monica's knees buckled, and she slumped to the ground, her head held up by Jareasa's hold on her hair. Throbs pulsed through her head and down her neck, aching in each vertebra. "You created a program without a way to stop it?" She scooped up the tablet and looked at the screen. "You're not even the one running this program. Who's behind this?" She raised her hand, ready to slap Monica again.

Monica tried to crawl away, but pain throttled her limbs. Every inch was torture.

Jareasa jerked Monica back. "Tell me!"

Monica closed her eyes and tried to steady her breathing. "Aric is controlling it. He's hiding somewhere." Her chest ached with every breath. "He can stop it."

"Then take me to him." Jareasa pulled Monica up by her arm and pushed her toward the door. "And we'll have him put a stop to this nonsense."

Stumbling, Monica started for the door. At least the pain was starting to ebb.

"And girl." Jacob's heavy breathing sounded louder. "Just know that if you don't return in time, I will kill your sister. If I feel I'm about to die, I have nothing to lose."

"No!" Monica turned, pain flaring.

He stared her down, though a glazed look covered his eyes. "Don't put it past me. If you kill me, I'll want you to always remember it, to haunt you forever. Killing Faye would be my only way to accomplish that."

Jareasa grabbed Monica's arm and dragged her out of the room.

Her heart thumping loudly, Monica took in a deep breath and hurried down the hall, the pressure of Jareasa's fingers on her arm a constant reminder of the fatal threat hanging over her head.

CHAPTER THIRTY-SIX

Monica limped to the wall entrance across from Aric's hiding place. Every inch of her body ached, and Jareasa threatened to slap her every time she slowed. But maybe this would work. If she went in a wall nearby, she could circle around and find Aric after she lost Jareasa.

Monica glanced over her shoulder. "We're here." She knelt by the hidden panel. Whispers sounded somewhere nearby. Was someone in the other wall with Aric?

"Good." Jareasa stood over Monica, her arms crossed. "If Jacob dies without carrying out his threat, I'll kill your sister myself, so you'd better not think about stalling."

"You're in the program as well, so you'd be dead, too." Monica laid her computer on the floor, then pressed on the wall's access panel. The door swung open, and Monica pointed at the dark hole. "After you?"

"You expect me to expose my back to you?" Jareasa shook her head. "Climbing headfirst into a Slink hole with a traitor is foolish at best."

Gritting her teeth, Monica let out a long sigh. "How am I supposed to keep Jacob from dying if you don't come with me?"

Jareasa crossed her arms, her lips forming a thin, tight line. "Call your friend out here."

Viral Execution

"He's hurt. He's in no condition to crawl through this opening." Monica started to enter the slave access. "I'll go in there by myself, then."

Jareasa yanked Monica's arm and pulled her to her feet. "I can't let you sneak away. Don't think I didn't notice your chip isn't in the computers. I don't know how you did that, but I'm not letting you out of my sight. Call your friend out here. If he cares about you enough, he'll come, injured or not."

Holding back a gasp of pain, Monica glared. "He's not able to crawl." She gritted her teeth. Maybe, if she could get Amelia's tablet back she could run the sleeper program. She just had to stall and look for an opportunity. "Aric! Please come out here." She turned and looked at Jareasa. What else to say?

A groan sounded from inside the opposite wall, followed by more whispers.

Anxiety crept into Monica's throat unbidden. She swallowed to quell the feeling, but it bubbled up again. Jareasa still held the tablet, mere inches away. Monica clenched her hands into fists. She could try to overpower the woman, but it didn't seem like a good option.

Jareasa gasped, and her grip on Monica's arm tightened, sending prickles of pain up to her shoulder.

As the pressure slackened, Monica jerked away, then leaped for the tablet.

Jareasa batted Monica's hands away. "What are you doing?" She dropped the computer and punched something into her wristband.

"No!" Monica snatched at Jareasa's hand, prying her fingers away from the wristband's screen. "Stop!"

Jareasa's eyes rolled up until the whites showed, and she stumbled.

Monica jumped out of the way. Jareasa crumpled to the floor. Twitches shook her arms and legs.

"Aric!" Monica knelt beside Jareasa's body, clenching her fists. Had Aric sent a termination order to Jareasa's chip?

Ten popped out of the slave access on the other side of the hall, her blonde hair completely loose from its braid. "Monica?"

Monica's breath caught in her throat. "Ten! You're okay." As relief washed in, fear crept in right behind it. "Is Aric in there?"

"Yes. The captain sent the termination order for Jareasa for him." Ten crawled to her feet and pushed her hair out of her eyes. "He's finishing bandaging Aric's wound. He was unconscious for a while, but he's awake again."

"How'd you get away? And how did you find Aric?" Monica unclasped Jareasa's wristband and slid it off her wrist. No use checking her pulse. If Jareasa was dead, that was a tragedy she couldn't repair.

"A wall slave found Aric and told us where he was when we asked around. And as for getting away, that was easy." Ten traced a finger-length cut on her neck, brushing off flecks of dried blood. "The captain saved me."

"I'm glad you're okay." Monica lit up Jareasa's wristband and scrolled through the list of previous commands. "I can only hope Faye is. We have to stop Aric's program from killing Jacob, or he'll kill her before he dies."

Ten scrambled back through the opening, calling, "Captain!" The rest of her words came out too muffled to understand.

Monica continued scrolling down the wristband's screen. The commands ranged from orders to Seen to delivery notifications and messenger tube pickups, but the most recent blinked red—a security alert. The guards would be here any second! But at least there was no termination order.

Gulping, Monica slid the wristband on her wrist next to her other one, then grabbed Jareasa's ankles and dragged her down the hall, away from the panel.

"Do you need help?"

Viral Execution

Monica released Jareasa's ankles, and her feet thumped on the floor.

Fahltrid appeared beside her, his shirt torn and hair mussed. "Aric is working on reversing the program. I'll go make sure Jacob doesn't harm your sister."

"Right now we need to take care of Jareasa." Monica glanced down the hallway. "She ordered security guards before she was knocked out. We need to hide her."

"No time." Fahltrid clasped Jareasa's hands, dragged her about ten feet from the access panel, and let her fall to the floor. "They'll eventually guess where we went, but leaving her here will buy us some time. At least she's not dead. She had a protection on her chip."

Running footsteps sounded nearby. Fahltrid jogged back and motioned to the opening. "Hurry. They're coming."

Monica snatched Amelia's computer from the floor, ducked inside the wall, and crawled up the passage toward where she had left Aric semiconscious. The door closed behind her, shutting out the light from the Nobles' hallway.

"I saw one coming around the corner," Fahltrid whispered from somewhere behind her. "I'm not sure if he noticed me or not. We need to get moving."

Aric lay by the exposed computer systems. The blinking lights from its console illuminated his pale face. Ten crouched next to him, bending over the glowing tablet that rested on the floor, still hooked to the tangle of wires protruding from the computer.

She whispered something to Aric. He nodded, making a vague, waving motion with his uninjured arm.

Monica crawled closer and stowed Amelia's computer in the open first-aid satchel before moving the bag out of the path. Shouts echoed in the hallway nearby.

"Wheaten, pack it up." Fahltrid's voice drifted through the passage.

"But Captain." Ten looked up. "I'm not done. Jacob isn't safe yet."

Kneeling beside Aric, Monica laid a hand on his arm. "The guards found us. Jareasa sent a security call through her wristband. We need to get going. Can you stand?"

"I have to try," Aric whispered.

Fahltrid joined them and started unplugging the tablet from the wall. "It doesn't matter, Ten. Finished or not, there's no time."

Ten stared at him for a moment before nodding. "How are we going to get away?"

"Through the slave tunnels." As Fahltrid packed the computer into the first-aid satchel, he let the wires fall to the floor. The bare ends touched each other, emitting sparks and flashes.

Flinching, Ten whispered, "At least I got his chip to stop progressing, but he won't get better until we fix it."

Fahltrid helped her to her feet. "We won't be able to fix it if we're dead."

Monica hooked an arm under Aric's. "Ready to try to stand?"

"You can't carry him on your own." Fahltrid wrapped an arm around Aric's waist and lifted him to his feet.

The talking outside grew quieter. As Fahltrid swung Aric's injured arm over his own shoulder, Aric moaned softly.

Someone spoke just outside. Ten snatched the bag from the floor and crept forward.

"We need to run," Fahltrid whispered. "Monica, you and Wheaten take the tablet to Jacob. If he does what we want, do what you can to save him. Perhaps the cloning program will work on him like it did Simon." He adjusted his hold on Aric as his head lolled to the side.

Ten held the satchel to her chest. "I don't know how to run that program."

Taking Ten's hand, Monica nodded down the corridor. "It's okay. I used it on Simon once already. I can do it again."

Viral Execution

"Hurry and get out of here." Fahltrid eased Aric forward a step. "They'll find the panel at any moment."

"Thank you, Fahltrid. For taking care of Aric." Monica tugged Ten down the hall. "Let's go."

"Wait." Ten shook free of Monica's hold and ran to Fahltrid's side. She wrapped her arms around his waist and laid her head against his chest. "I love you, Captain."

He stiffened and nodded. "We'll see each other again in a few minutes, Wheaten. I'll just be slower than you two. Now get moving." Ten pulled away and ran back to Monica's side, blinking hard.

"Are you okay?" Monica jogged down the passage.

"Fine." Ten tagged at Monica's heels, her breathing ragged, though they weren't running very fast.

The voices on the Nobles' side of the hall seemed softer. As they approached the panel, the words grew louder once more.

Muscles tensing, Monica held up a hand to Ten and slowed her pace. She crept by the panel on silent feet.

Just as she passed, the panel swung open, hitting her heels. Gasping, she jumped forward and turned back. A man poked his head into the opening, blocking Ten's path.

Ten backpedaled a few steps.

"You there!" the man shouted. "Seen, what are you doing in here?"

Ten skittered backward a few more steps, then abruptly started forward again. She gathered speed and leaped over the man's head, barely clearing the access panel door.

"Stop!" The man started crawling through the opening. "Both of you. I demand you stop, or I will be forced to terminate you!"

"Run!" Monica grabbed Ten's hand and pulled her down the hall, racing through the dim corridor. They had to lead the security guard away from Aric and Fahltrid. But could they outrun a grown man?

CHAPTER THIRTY-SEVEN

Monica's breaths came in ragged gasps, her grip tight on Ten's hand. They raced down yet another slave passage, the shouts of a security guard growing louder with every step. Only her familiarity with slave life and the way their corridors worked had kept them out of the guard's reach even this long.

"You can let go of my hand now," Ten gasped. "My fingers are numb!"

"Sorry." Monica let Ten's fingers slide away without slowing her frantic pace. "I don't want you to get lost." She jumped over a protruding pipe, and they pounded into a wide, open stairway. The thumping footsteps of the guard sounded nearby.

Gulping, Monica turned in a quick circle. "The main staircase. The dormitory is at the top. This isn't good. I don't know how to get to the computer room from here without going back into the Nobles' halls."

Her face pale, Ten stepped out of the narrow side passage, the first-aid bag still held against her chest. "What are we going to do?"

"Find another hall and backtrack, skirt around the guard." Monica trotted down a few stairs, glancing over her shoulder. Ten followed a few steps behind, her face pale and her bare feet keeping time with Monica's quick pace.

Heavy breathing issued from a passage to the side. Monica gulped and accelerated. "Ten, hurry!"

Monica looked forward again and turned down another side passage, narrower than most.

A squeal sounded behind her. She whirled around. Something thumped loudly. "Let go of me!" Ten's shrill call sounded close by.

Monica dashed back out of the hallway and onto the main staircase.

A security guard held Ten in a tight grip, her legs kicking uselessly in the air. The satchel lay open a few feet away on the stairs.

"Let her go!" Monica tried to sound fierce, but the words rasped in her throat.

The man looked down. Ten went limp and began sliding through his grip. Monica dashed up the stairs toward them.

In a split second, Ten started fighting again. The man's eyes widened, and he dropped her. She landed on the step just below his grasp.

Monica ran up the last two stairs to reach Ten's side, her heart pounding. She grabbed Ten's arm. "Run!"

Ten jumped to her feet, but the man's hand tangled in her free-flowing hair. He closed his fist around the locks and jerked. Ten's head snapped backward, and she let out a sharp cry.

Monica dove at the man and pummeled his chest with clenched fists. "Let her go!" Creaks sounded on the stairs above them. No time to see why. Monica continued her assault on the guard—punching and clawing, but he blocked her blows with a powerful arm.

"I'd terminate you both right now if I could." The man shoved Monica away and threw Ten to the floor. Ten's head bounced on a stair with a sickening crack, and she lay motionless.

Her breath catching in her throat, Monica stumbled back a step. "Ten!"

The man reached for her, but she ducked out of his grasp. He fumbled in his jacket and withdrew a gun.

"No!" Monica turned and skidded down two more steps.

A loud crash sounded, followed by a deafening bang that reverberated through the halls. Roaring pain ripped through her side. Black spots danced in her vision, and a falling sensation took over her mind.

The hard edge of the stairs pressed against her back. Waves of pain ebbed and flowed with every breath. She squeezed her eyes shut, but tears leaked through and trickled down her cheeks. She had failed Faye—again. Jacob would kill her. And Ten ... Poor Ten.

Monica reached out a trembling hand. She had to make sure Ten was okay. She hadn't moved since the guard threw her down.

Wrinkly hands clasped her arm and held it tight, cold skin pressing close.

"Came just in time, didn't I?" The crackly voice hissed in her ears, jarring her nerves, but soothing at the same time.

"Simon?" The word brought a fresh wave of pain.

"I thought I heard a commotion. I've told you before. I might be old, but I'm not deaf." His arms hooked under hers and dragged her to her feet, sending flashes of pain through her side and chest.

Gasping, she opened her eyes and pushed him away. "I think I got shot. Like Aric."

"Aric was shot? My, my, you really do need me. I knew it all along." Simon helped her lean against the wall. "And you're shot as well?" He looked her over. "Where?"

She put a hand to her side. The pain had already subsided. "I guess it just grazed me." A spot of blood stained her hand, though the wound had almost stopped bleeding.

"All right, then." Simon patted her shoulder. "Stand still while I check on Miss Ten. She doesn't look well. I missed what happened to her."

Viral Execution

Monica clasped a hand to her side again. "Please, hurry." She glanced around. The guard lay crumpled on the stairs, broken pieces of a slave's storage box littered around his head. Blood oozed from a wound on his forehead, and the gun lay on the stairs near his hand.

With a long sigh, Simon crouched beside Ten and laid two fingers on her throat. "She's alive, but she might have a severe concussion."

"Okay. Partial good news." Dizziness stirred again, almost overwhelming. Monica closed her eyes for a moment. *Please be okay, Ten. God, please help her.*

"Time to wake up, Ten." Simon shook her shoulder. "We can't leave you here, and we need to go." He looked up. "Where did Aric and Fahltrid get to?"

Groaning, Ten shifted her head, revealing a mark of blood just above her temple. "The captain ... is helping Aric. They were ... behind us."

Pain shot through Monica's wound. "Ten! You're okay!"

Ten sat up, a hand pressed to her head. "I'm not so sure."

After a quick pat on Ten's back, Simon stood. "Well, no time for lollygagging. Jacob is most likely scared, if his chip was doing to him what mine was to me, so there's no telling what he will do. I wasn't scared, of course. Since I have more experience with pain from a chip, I am accustomed—"

"Simon, please, there's no time." Monica helped Ten to her feet and held her arm. "My sister and mother are in danger. We have to get to the main computer room. Now!"

"Yes, yes, of course." Simon tapped the guard on the head with a boot. "I hope this one stays unconscious a while longer, but there's no way to be sure. Unless we kill him."

Monica and Ten started down the stairs, Monica keeping an arm around Ten's shoulders. "We're not killing anybody, not even Jacob."

"Very well." Simon snatched the first-aid satchel and the gun from the steps and jogged after them. "At least my heart is cooperating again. A kind wall slave allowed me use of his bunk for a catnap. It did me a world of good."

"I'm glad you feel better." Monica helped Ten ease into a side passage. "I just hope there weren't more of those guards. If one of them went after Fahltrid, I don't know if he could fight him with Aric to look after."

They shuffled down the wall-slave hall until they came to a panel. Shoving it open with a foot, Monica nodded to Ten. "You first."

After Ten crawled through and Simon scooted after her, Monica followed and closed the door behind them. As they walked through the Nobles' halls, she frowned. If only she could get to the computer room faster, but running ahead would do no good. Simon and Ten were in no condition to run with her. Faye and Jacob would have to wait.

Monica pressed a hand to her wounded side and tightened her grip on Ten's shoulders, helping her walk faster. They would get this done. They had come much too far to fail now.

CHAPTER THIRTY-EIGHT

Monica limped toward the main computer room, still propping Ten under her shoulder, Simon on Ten's other side. Monica halted in front of the door. "Okay, we're here."

"Good." Ten breathed a long sigh. "My head is killing me. It feels like it's going to explode."

"I hope not. It would be quite messy." Simon pushed the door open, revealing the brightly lit computer room. A whirring sound vibrated the air, and fans cooling the computers stirred up a soft breeze. A red light flashed above the console—a foreboding sign.

Jacob sat against a wall of the computer, his eyes closed and fingers pressed against his wristband.

"No!" Monica and Simon helped Ten stand against a corridor wall, and Monica raced inside to Jacob. "No, no. Not Faye." She pushed Jacob's fingers from the wristband, revealing a blank screen. Simon shuffled up beside her and touched Jacob's neck. "He's still alive, but his heartbeat isn't very strong." He dropped the first-aid satchel in front of Monica. "It looks like we'll have to copy someone's chip to his to revive him."

She grabbed the bag. Simon was right. Cloning might be their only chance to save the slaves. If Jacob refused to shut down the computers, they could threaten to put the viral-execution program back onto his chip.

The computer fans hummed louder, as if urging her to hurry. She pulled out Fahltrid's tablet, then Amelia's. "Whose chip should we use? Yours?"

"I don't see why not," Simon said. "The coding is working fine for me, so—"

"Wait!" Ten stumbled into the room, her hand pressed to the back of her head. "We can't use Simon's. He has Dedrick's number. We don't want Jacob to have that one. It's too powerful."

"Good thinking, Ten." Simon motioned for the computer.

Monica handed him Fahltrid's computer, her hands shaking. "Dedrick's chip isn't powerful anymore. Jacob told me that he made Dedrick a Seen, so maybe making Jacob a Seen would be appropriate."

"No." Ten knelt and laid a hand on Monica's shoulder, steadying herself as she reached the floor. "Mine would be more appropriate. I'm his daughter. He should become a merchant, like me."

"Good idea." Monica began inputting commands to Amelia's computer, telling it to talk to Fahltrid's tablet so they could clone the chips.

Ten turned Jacob's head to the side, exposing his neck. His clean-cut hairstyle revealed the fingernail-sized puckered scar at the base of his skull. "All this time I was sure he was dead, especially since their older brother who lives here couldn't locate him."

Simon furrowed his brow. "I wonder why Fahltrid didn't mention recognizing his brother before. But we can't dwell on that now. Your chip will do as well as any. It's still hidden from the city's computers, but I should be able to see it on a tablet computer since we have the number." He held one end of Fahltrid's tablet up to Jacob's scar. "Now hold still, Jacob. Or should we call you Drehl?"

When the computer beeped, Simon nodded to Monica. "Why are Nobles all of a sudden changing their names and statuses?

I hope it's a habit that doesn't continue. Such behavior incites confusion, even chaos."

"Maybe after today we won't have to worry about it." Monica held the computer up to Ten. "Ready?"

"Ready as I'll ever be." Ten pulled her tangled blonde hair away from her neck, revealing her chip insertion scar—a red mark about half the size of Jacob's.

Monica pressed Amelia's computer against Ten's neck and nodded to Simon. "Run it."

Simon readied his thumbs over the tablet screen. "You'll feel a pinch, Ten, similar to the one we felt in the hallway when Jacob—Drehl—was resetting the computers. He'll feel it too, but since he's unconscious, I doubt he'll care."

Laying a hand to the wound on her head, Ten nodded. "Do it."

Simon entered a command into the tablet and kept it firmly pressed against Jacob's neck. "This should take only a moment to process."

Ten flinched.

Wincing, Monica made sure to keep her own computer steady.

The computers both beeped, and Ten let out a long sigh. "It's done?"

"It should be." Simon drew the tablet away from Jacob's neck and tucked it back into Aric's bag. "Jacob should wake up in a few minutes and be able to assist us." He put his hands on his knees and slowly rose to his feet. "Where are Aric and Fahltrid? They should be here by now, even with Aric slowing Fahltrid down."

Rubbing the back of her neck, Ten climbed to her feet. "That did pinch." She shuffled over to the console and ran a hand along the side of the glossy screen.

Monica glared at Jacob's unconscious form. How could someone put his daughter through this just to gain power? At least her own parents were trying to save people when they cast her into the world of wall slaves.

Stumbling steps sounded nearby. Monica whirled around. Had Jareasa recovered? Or maybe the security guard Simon knocked out?

Fahltrid appeared in the doorway, supporting Aric on one shoulder. "Were you in time?"

Monica nodded. "I think so."

Fahltrid helped Aric, still semiconscious, sit against the wall. A frown growing, Fahltrid walked to Ten's side. He took her by the shoulder and rubbed a thumb next to the knotted bruise on the side of her head. "What happened? Are you all right?"

"I'm fine." Ten pushed his hand away. "It's just a bump on the head."

"Good." Fahltrid turned to the main computer console "We need to get to work. Drehl's program is probably completely installed now, but we can still try to stop it."

Monica tugged on Fahltrid's sleeve. "Jacob said he was trying to keep his program from finishing. We had the aging program hanging over his head, so the program to stop the takeover could still be salvageable."

Toeing Jacob's leg, Fahltrid shook his head. "Not likely. Drehl is very thorough."

The computer made a beeping noise, and something rumbled nearby. Jacob's fingers twitched.

Fahltrid grunted something unintelligible and began typing on the main computer console. "The wall he built is impenetrable. I can't undo it, not without him."

"He was supposed to be working on undoing it," Monica said. "My mother was watching over his shoulder. Should I try to find her?"

"No time. I'll see if I can persuade him." Fahltrid knelt by Jacob. "Well, brother. It's been a while. Now you need to wake up and reap the consequences of your actions." He shook Jacob's shoulder. "And to think I've spent my life believing I was continuing your work."

Viral Execution

As Fahltrid continued to shake Jacob, Monica hugged herself. It must be awful for Fahltrid, knowing now that his brother had been alive all this time, working against him, keeping the slaves trapped and betraying his original beliefs.

Groaning, Jacob opened his eyes. His gaze locked with Fahltrid's, and he groaned again before closing his eyes once more.

"Wake up!" Fahltrid smacked Jacob's cheek.

"Captain." Ten reached toward Fahltrid but drew back without touching him.

"Silf des …" Jacob's words came out slurred and incomprehensible.

Fahltrid hoisted Jacob to his feet and slapped his cheek again, "Snap out of it! We need you to fix this mess you've created."

"There will be no fixing it, Fahltrid." Jacob's eyes opened fully.

Fahltrid flexed his free hand into a fist. "I think you'll find there will be, Drehl." He glanced at Ten as she stood trembling. "Don't make me hurt you in front of your daughter."

Monica held Ten's shaking hand. She clasped Monica's in return.

Jacob whispered a word, but the computer fans drowned it out.

Monica squinted at the console where the red light still flashed. Were the fans running more labored now? They sounded different than before.

"Speak up, man!" Simon waved a bony finger at Jacob. "Your scheme has unraveled."

"Enough." Fahltrid picked Jacob up by his collar and slammed him against the computer, bending the metal panel. The computer buzzed angrily, and the strobe light flashed in quicker rhythm. "Speak now, brother. How do I correct this mess you've created?"

Jacob smirked. "Like you've always been trying to correct my messes? You and Father always cleaning up after me. I had no interest in marrying Katrina or being a merchant."

Fahltrid slammed Jacob against the computer again. "This is no time to dig up old bones!"

Monica touched Simon's elbow. "Guards might be coming. Maybe we should get my mother."

"She's right." Simon tapped Fahltrid's shoulder. "If you are unable to gain his assistance soon, we must leave."

Fahltrid's grip on Jacob tightened. "You're stalling, aren't you, Drehl?"

"Ah! So you do recognize me." Jacob gasped out the words. "You didn't seem to recognize me in the holding cell, so—"

Fahltrid pushed Jacob harder against the computer. "Cut the stalling! Tell me what the computer is doing!"

Jacob's gaze slid to the control panel. "It's too late now. The sequence is initiated, and no amount of programming will stop it."

Fahltrid gritted his teeth. "What sequence?"

"I wrote a Cantral-issued termination order. The dome should be closing within the next half hour." He brushed Fahltrid's hand away. "So it doesn't matter what you do to me. We'll all be dead soon."

Monica gasped. "But the Cantral computers are destroyed!"

"Yes, silly girl, I know." Jacob sighed. "That's why I had to make the computer believe the command was coming from Cantral. I thought I was going to die, so it didn't matter to me." He laid a hand over his heart. "You spared me, but a termination order cannot be overturned without special consent codes sent from Cantral itself. Those cannot be faked. Even trying at this point would only release the gas immediately."

"Drehl!" Fahltrid slammed his fist against the wall. "I always knew you were rash, but this?" He whirled around, his hands still clenched into tight balls.

"Well, I must say that this is a stunning turn of events." Simon stared wide-eyed. "Any suggestions, Monica? You seem to always be getting us out of these types of situations."

Viral Execution

Her heart thumping wildly, Monica bit her lip hard. What should they do? They could escape, since their chips were disguised from the computers, but could they abandon Penniak to Jacob's sentence? She tugged on a lock of her hair, panic rising in her throat. "I just don't know!"

CHAPTER THIRTY-NINE

"What do you mean you don't know?" Simon glared at Monica. "This is no time to run out of ideas."

Monica backed away and bumped into Ten. He couldn't expect her to always have all the answers. "I just don't know what to do. Everything I've tried, everything I've suggested has failed." Her words caught in her throat, threatening to choke her. "This is my fault. I wasn't fast enough."

"No, it isn't you fault." Simon jabbed her shoulder with a finger. "Jacob—Drehl did this! But I suggest you start thinking of something to stop him. You *can* do this. You've proven your resourcefulness too many times before to deny it now."

Jacob growled something too low to hear. Fahltrid shot him a disgusted look.

Monica glanced from Aric's motionless form to Ten, to Simon, and to Fahltrid. They all counted on her, but what could she do? She closed her eyes and replayed the recent events in her mind, everything from hacking into the computers, to seeing her mother in the main computer room, to getting knocked out with Simon, to sneaking through tunnels with Aric and Ten, and visiting Shal and Chrom's shop.

A shudder ran through her body. Shal and Chrom's shop. Chrom's whining about them not using his products. Monica nodded to Aric. "Thanks for the Antrelix." The memory drug had certainly served its purpose.

"What are you muttering about?" Simon gestured to the computer console. "We're running out of time."

Jacob slid to the floor, his face white again. "Why the rush to die? Like I told you, anything entered into the system now will only bring the gas sooner."

Shooting Jacob a glare, Monica shook her head. "I'm not talking about reprogramming. I have another idea." She rubbed her arm where Jareasa's too-big wristband clung. "We'll get Chrom to blow the computers up. Maybe we can't get everyone out in time, but we have to try. They'll die anyway if we sit here and do nothing."

Simon squinted with one eye. "Very good idea, Miss. I should have thought of that myself. We'll blow the computers up. Or make the palace implode. That would be less messy." He whirled around and pointed his finger at Ten. "So this Chrom fellow has explosives, does he? I assume he would be willing to sell them to us, considering the alternatives, perhaps even donate them. And do you think he has enough to cover the strategic points?"

"He probably has enough." Fahltrid laid a hand on Ten's head. "We'll try to convince him. Even if he doesn't listen, Shal will. She knows the inner workings of the system. She'll believe us."

Ten's whole body tensed. "Should I run to the shop, then? We don't have much time."

"Quite right, little time indeed." Simon pointed at Monica. "Both of you. Shoo! You know where the shop is."

Monica blinked at him. What about her mother? Was she still in the holding cell or had she escaped?

Fahltrid tousled Ten's hair, then nudged her toward the door. "Run ahead and warn Shal and Chrom. I'll be right behind you to talk to them."

Ten nodded and darted out the door.

"Of course, of course. And I"—Simon picked up the first-aid satchel and withdrew the gun—"will stay with these two, though I don't think Jacob's in any condition to retaliate."

"I'm sure you're a capable guard." Fahltrid yanked his belt off and crouched by Jacob. "But I'm still going to tie him." He made short work of binding Jacob's hands behind his back. Jacob sat motionless, his face stony.

Monica shuffled in place. "Then if you don't need me, I should go and—"

"Check on your mother." Fahltrid straightened and provided a short explanation of where the holding cells were, then waved her toward the exit.

Monica nodded. "Thank you."

"You might want these." Simon withdrew the two computers from Aric's bag. "You never know when you'll need to clone a chip. Seems like it's happening all the time nowadays."

"Thanks, Simon." Ignoring the pain in her side, she tucked the computers under her arm and broke into a run. She raced from the room, pumping her legs as fast as she could. After thundering down a flight of stairs, she headed through a corridor, past the two rooms where Jareasa and Jacob had held them captive, and finally down another flight of stairs.

A Seen guard relaxed in a folding chair next to an iron door. She charged past him, slid the bolt on the door, and slipped through before the guard could even react.

As her eyes adjusted to the light, she glanced around, taking everything in as quickly as possible. The guard wouldn't sit outside long. A row of small rooms, partitioned by steel bars, lined one side of the hall. Almost all of the rooms stood empty, with only a buzzing light in the ceiling to lighten the dark corners. The room on the end contained a motionless body dressed in Seen uniform.

"Monica!" Rose's voice echoed through the stone hallway.

"Mother?" Monica rotated slowly, searching for the source of the call.

Rose and two other forms huddled at one end of the corridor, outside of the bars. Rose stood and beckoned. "You're safe! How did you get away?"

Viral Execution

Monica raced over. As she neared, the other two forms grew clear—Dedrick, sitting up and cradling a motionless little girl in his lap. Faye!

Monica reached her mother's side and took the computers out from under her arm. "Are you all right?"

Rose nodded. "We're all fine. Faye's just sleeping." She motioned to Dedrick as he rose, still holding Faye in a tight clasp.

Dedrick nodded to Monica. "So you're Brenna's supposedly dead daughter." A small smile twitched at the corner of his mouth. "I can't say I appreciate you knocking me unconscious, but if we ever get out of this mess, you need not worry about punishment. Brenna explained everything."

"Thank you, sir." Monica stared at him. Faye rested easily in his well-muscled arms, and he looked down at his daughter with kind, worried eyes. So this was the ruler of Penniak. Rose said he wouldn't listen to her about her plans to free the slaves. Could he really be kind to her yet cruel to others?

Monica glanced at Rose. Her features seemed unreadable. "I'm surprised the guard didn't stop me," Monica said.

Dedrick adjusted his hold on Faye. "Fortunately for us, that Seen guard is on our side. Jareasa's threats didn't carry very far."

Rose embraced Monica. "I'm so glad you're all right."

Monica pushed away. "We won't be for long. Jacob put in a termination order for the whole city. The dome is going to close in less than half an hour."

"What?" Dedrick growled. "I purposefully cut us off from Cantral for that reason. How could he do that?" He turned to Rose, his brow furrowed. "You told me she was going to disable the computers."

Monica held up the computers as if they would shield her from Dedrick's anger. "He faked a signal from Cantral. I don't know how he did it, but Fahltrid said there's no way to stop it."

"Fahltrid?" Rose laid her hands on Monica's shoulders. "Ten mentioned him. Who is he?"

Biting her lip, Monica met Rose's gaze. "He's an ex-Noble merchantman. He rescues field slaves, but he's an expert programmer. Jacob is his brother. His name is really Drehl." She pressed a hand to her forehead. It was all so confusing! "So we're going to blow up the palace."

Rose pulled back, her brow rising. "Blow up the palace?" She shook her head slowly. "We can't get everyone out in time, and with us locked out of the system, we can't get the Seen or Slinks out at all. They're confined to the palace by their chips."

"I—I forgot about that." Monica winced. How could she have forgotten? "Isn't there some sort of program we could write and insert into the computers to widen their boundaries? There has to be something!"

Dedrick stared down at Faye and brushed a lock of hair from her face. "I might be able to write something. There are reassignment protocols. If I reassign all the Seen and Slink to other cities, transports would be called to take them away. But doing so might speed the release of the gas." He met Rose's gaze once more. "And with the chip cloning, we no longer have the authority to initiate it. You'll have to find someone else."

Rose sighed. "We'll have to find another programmer." She looked off to the side, as if trying to remember something. "Do you know of one who would agree?"

"No one comes to mind."

Monica closed her eyes. What about Aric? No. He probably didn't have jurisdiction here. Maybe—? She opened her eyes. "Jareasa could do it."

"Jareasa?" Rose's brow lifted. "She knows she would die otherwise. Maybe she could be persuaded."

"That's not what I mean. We knocked her out near a slave passage." Monica held up a hand. "But we could clone her chip and put her number on Dedrick's or your chip. You could insert the program as her."

"More chip cloning?" Dedrick shook his head. "Brenna, that's one of your tales I still have a hard time believing."

"It is possible, despite what most people think." Rose pressed a finger to the back of her neck. "The chips are far more vulnerable than we first believed."

"In any case, we have less than half an hour." Dedrick shifted Faye in his arms. "We'd better get moving."

Rose whispered something in the nasally language Monica had heard earlier.

Nodding, Dedrick murmured something back in the same language.

Monica squared her shoulders and strode to the door with Dedrick and Rose following. She resisted the urge to glance back. Faye and Rose were part of her family, but she still felt like an outsider.

She turned the doorknob. Why shouldn't she feel that way? She had known them for only a few hours. And to Faye, she was just a Seen assistant, no more important than any other.

Breathing out a deep sigh, Monica pushed the door open and walked through. The Seen guard still sat relaxed in his chair by the door. As Monica passed, he nodded to her, but as Dedrick and Rose walked by, he shot to his feet, folded his hands behind his back, and gave a short bow.

Dedrick stopped beside the guard. "Elliot, go warn the other Seen to prepare for transfer. The city is about to be terminated. We're going to have everyone transferred to another city-state. Gather them at the station as fast as you can."

Elliot's eyes widened. "Yes sir. Right away, sir."

Dedrick started walking again but stopped once more. "And see if you can awaken Felix. He's unconscious in the last cell. If not, take him with you."

"I will." Elliot ran down the hall ahead of them.

"Dedrick," Rose whispered, "the people might panic."

"A risk we'll have to take." Dedrick led the way down the hall, now accelerating to a determined march. "Their chips will keep them from getting into too much trouble."

Monica broke into a slow jog. "We have to hurry and find Jareasa. The security team might have moved her to the infirmary."

"That would be protocol." Dedrick patted Faye's back with his free hand. Monica followed Dedrick's long, sure strides, her heart thumping. The slaves and Nobles all had to be moved from the palace in less than half an hour, or they would all die, with or without an explosion.

CHAPTER FORTY

Now standing on the cold tile floor outside the infirmary, Monica rocked back and forth on the balls of her feet. As a Seen, the doctors wouldn't allow her to enter, and because of their hurry, Rose thought it wise to avoid a debate. She and Dedrick could clone Jareasa's chip without help.

Soft voices sounded on the other side of the thick oak door. Monica resisted the urge to press her ear to the wood. Rose knew how the cloning program worked. She knew about it before Monica was even born—a story Rose still needed to reveal in its entirety.

The door opened, and Monica snapped to attention. Rose walked out leading Faye by the hand. Dedrick brought up the rear and closed the door behind them. "It's done." He handed the two computers back to Monica.

Dedrick laid a hand on Faye's head, his expression tense. "Brenna, take her into the Noble sector, away from the palace. I want you both to be safe."

Rose opened her mouth as if to argue but closed it again.

"Brenna." His shoulders trembling, Dedrick gave her a quick kiss, then said something in the other language.

Rose looked down. "Dedrick, there's so much to say."

"Go. There will be time to explain later." He stroked her cheek. "I trust you. Keep our daughter safe."

"I will." Rose inhaled a tremulous breath. "Dedrick, please keep my daughter safe."

He nodded. "For your sake."

Rose gave Monica a swift embrace. "God be with you both. I'll be praying for you." She turned and walked away, leading Faye by the hand.

Monica's shoulders tingled where her mother's arms had been. Would that be the last time she felt them? She firmed her jaw. No. They would succeed. There were too many people counting on them.

When Rose and Faye disappeared around a corner, Dedrick jogged down the hall in the opposite direction. "Let's go!"

Monica scurried after him. After negotiating a flight of stairs and two turns to the right, they entered the passage leading to the computer room. The door stood open, light pouring out from inside and voices murmuring within.

Monica walked into the room and glanced around. Fahltrid and Simon stood near the computer console, discussing something in harsh tones. Aric now lay on the tile floor on his back. Ten mopped his pale face with a damp rag while Jacob reclined by the computer, his eyes half closed and a cocky smile on his face. But how could Ten be here? Hadn't she run out to warn Shal and Chrom?

Dedrick surveyed the scene as well. "Tell me everything you know. Immediately."

Simon flinched and glared at Monica. "Why did you bring him here? Can't you see we're in the middle of a crisis?"

"I've come to help." Dedrick strode forward. "And I won't take any flak from a Seen—especially when my family is in danger."

"Gangway!" someone shouted.

Monica whirled around. Chrom charged into the room, his arms loaded with beige bricks labeled with black letters. He dumped the bricks on the floor.

Simon jumped back. "You can't throw explosives around like that! They might go off."

Chrom huffed. "Isn't that the point?"

Viral Execution

Shal strolled in, a tattered bag with protruding wires slung over her shoulder. "Don't worry, Seen. That's C4, as some call it. It can't go off without a detonator, and I have those."

"Thank you for coming, Shal." Fahltrid smiled and nodded. "If we survive this, you'll have your way after all."

Her eyebrows rising, she stepped toward him. "Fahl, I—"

"And I get no thanks?" Chrom wiped a hand on his greasy shirt and extended it to Dedrick. "Chrom, at your service."

Dedrick waved the hand away. "How are you two even here? You're not Nobles."

"According to the computers, no." Shal flashed Dedrick her brilliant smile. "But we're able to be here thanks to Fahltrid's disguising our chips. It won't be any of your concern in a moment."

Dedrick turned to the computer console. "I need to get to work."

"Quite rude, that one." Chrom picked up a beige block and tossed it to Ten, who caught it one-handed. "Where do you want these placed?"

"Ten and I will show you," Fahltrid said. His brow downturned, he looked at Dedrick. "Monica, why is he here?"

"He's here to order the slaves and Seen reassigned to different city-states. If he doesn't, we can't evacuate them. Their chips won't allow it."

"That problem"—Simon waved a finger at them—"is precisely what we were discussing when you came in. Reassigning them would be a simple way to evacuate the slaves." He patted Dedrick's shoulder. "Good idea. I should have thought of it myself."

Dedrick ignored him and continued typing.

Shal withdrew some wires and black knobs with metal ends from her bag and handed a few to Fahltrid. "If we're going to cover the whole palace, we need to move quickly."

"Right." Fahltrid picked up a few blocks of C4 and stowed them in the first-aid satchel along with the wires. "Monica? Are you assisting us with the explosives or do you have other plans?"

"I can help," she said, "but how are you getting the Nobles out of the palace?"

Chrom waved a brick of explosives. "I say we leave them in here. They'd die without our help, and they've killed enough of us."

"No!" Monica gaped at him. "That would make us murderers!"

Dedrick glared at them from the computer console. "The fire alarms will signal an evacuation. Just pull every one you come to. Everyone should know what to do."

Monica nodded. "Thank you, Dedrick." He kept his focus on his work.

"Perfect." Fahltrid drew Ten to his side. "That leaves us just placing the charges and pulling alarms. No one to herd. The slaves can find their way to the transports."

"Still." Simon tapped his chin. "Someone should direct them to make sure they don't overcrowd or panic. It's not as though a mass evacuation by transport has been done before, not that I've read about, anyway." He raised a wrinkled hand. "I volunteer. I'm good at directing, if I do say so myself."

"Thank you, Simon," Fahltrid said.

"Just don't forget to come fetch me before you set those things off. I've died enough today." Simon shuffled out of the room.

Ten handed some of the bricks to Fahltrid. "How do we know which walls to place these at?"

Dedrick beckoned to them. "Give me a tablet. I can transfer blueprints and mark strategic points."

Monica handed him Fahltrid's computer.

Shal squinted at him. "You know about architecture?"

"No." Dedrick plugged the tablet into the console and began tapping on the screen. "I just know all the vulnerable points of the computer system." He handed the tablet to Fahltrid. "Now hurry! We're running out of time."

Viral Execution

Fahltrid tucked the computer under his arm. "You must care for your family very much—to be helping us—knowing we might fail."

"I do, and my family is already safe. I have other reasons." Dedrick's jaw tensed. "Now I need to get back to work to make sure the slaves get out so you can blow up the palace as planned."

"Very well." Fahltrid handed the map to Shal and looked over her shoulder as she scrolled across it.

Standing on tiptoes, Monica barely made out the red dots on the screen, each marking a wall with a vulnerable computer component.

Chrom laid some explosive bricks into her hands. "Here you go. I told you you'd have use for my product someday."

Monica fumbled with the C4, cradling five at once. "Hey!"

Fahltrid handed Ten the tablet. "You and Monica take some charges and cover this upper floor. Shal and I will take the two lower floors. Once we start pulling the alarms, it could get hairy down there."

"What about me?" Chrom folded his arms over his chest. "I'm not sending you and my sister off without me."

Fahltrid picked up a stack of bricks and shoved them into Chrom's hands. "You're taking the basement and kitchens. You're good at sneaking around."

His shoulders relaxing, Chrom nodded. "Right you are."

Shal dug into her bag and drew out two handfuls of wires before passing the bag to Ten. "There's enough detonators in there for this level. More, even." She dropped a handful of wires into Chrom's arms. "Don't blow yourself up."

Nodding, Ten picked up some bricks. "Let's go, Monica."

"Wait." Monica steadied her pile of explosives and took the tablet from Ten. "Shal and Fahltrid should take the tablet. I can memorize where the charges go." She studied the map for a moment, ingraining each marked corridor in her mind before handing the tablet back to Shal.

Shal raised an eyebrow. "You're sure you'll remember?"

"Yes. I've got a good memory." Monica turned and followed Ten out the door.

As they hurried down the hall, Monica kept the map points in mind while trying to balance the load. The explosives felt oddly sticky, similar to the putty the slaves used to repair cracks in the walls. Dropping a brick hadn't made it blow up before, but it didn't seem wise to handle it casually, no matter what Chrom said.

CHAPTER FORTY-ONE

"Here's the first spot." Monica pointed at a blank space on the stone wall. A tapestry hung to one side, and a statue stood to the other. A loud wail filled the hall, joined by another.

Ten laid her bricks of C4 on the ground. "The captain must be pulling fire alarms." She ripped one of the bricks in half and plastered it to the bare wall, smoothing the edges against the stone like putty. "If you see one, go ahead and pull it."

"Right."

Ten pressed two of the metal ends of a detonator into the explosive block. She double-checked the black knob attached to the two wires, then let it dangle from the C4. "Finished."

Monica gestured down the hall. "This way."

As they ran as fast as their loads allowed, Monica looked at Ten. "How do you know so much about the explosives?"

"Chrom, Shal, and the captain used to be good friends. Chrom taught me a long time ago."

The sirens continued their piercing calls, growing distant then loud again as Monica and Ten passed by stairs leading to the lower floor. Shouts and thundering footsteps echoed below. At least the Nobles were hearing the alarm.

As they rounded a corner, a red box on the wall came into view—a fire alarm. Monica shuffled her blocks of C4 into one arm and yanked the box's lever down. More wailing filled the hall, ringing through her ears, making her want to slap her hands over them, but the explosives made it impossible. "The next place is straight ahead!"

Monica ran to the spot and examined the wall—another blank area, a tapestry to the left, but no statue on the right. She pushed one of the blocks against the wall and set the wires as Ten had. "Done."

During the trek that followed, they pulled four more alarms and set three more blocks, each on a blank wall with a tapestry to the left. Ten carried five chargers and two more blocks, while Monica carried one of each. "Almost finished."

Ten grinned. "We might just make it in time."

A rumbling shook the room. Monica tightened her grip on the blocks, leaving finger marks in the putty. "The dome?"

As the rumbles increased, Ten's eyes widened. "I have no idea."

The floor shook beneath Monica's feet. Screams echoed down the hall. It had to be the dome. What else could it be?

"Monica." Ten's voice quaked. "We should split up."

"Okay." Monica inhaled deeply. "Keep going down this corridor and turn right. I'll go left. There are just the two points left. Look for the tapestry, like the others."

"Right. The tapestry." Ten headed down a hall, and Monica ran down the other trying to ignore the increasing rumblings. She leaped into a sprint and focused on the tapestry ahead. After skidding to a halt, she gasped, trying to catch her breath.

As she pressed the C4 against the wall, smoothing it flat, her fingers trembled. The tremors increased. She poked the metal ends of the wires into the putty, but they fell loose.

The sirens pounded relentlessly. The deadly mist would start soon.

"No!" She grabbed the wires again and jabbed them in farther.

"Monica!" Ten darted toward her from around a corner. "We have to go!"

Viral Execution

A hissing noise filled the air, barely audible under the fire alarm's oppressive wail. Monica dropped her remaining block of C4. "It's the gas!"

Ten sucked in a deep breath and stopped in her tracks.

Monica grabbed Ten's hand and jerked her forward. "Try not to breathe!"

A fine white mist issued from cracks in the wall and from the ceiling.

Monica tugged her along. "Run!" Panic rose in Monica's chest, but she forced herself to keep going. Death was the only alternative.

"Ten!" The shout reverberated across the halls, echoing over the siren. "Ten!"

Fahltrid and Shal appeared at the top of a staircase. Fahltrid threw the first-aid bag to the side and dashed forward. "Ten!" He pulled her out of Monica's grasp. "No more time. We can't wait for anyone else to escape. The charges must be blown or everyone will die."

"Are Simon and Aric out?" Monica laid a hand over her mouth. She had to calm her heart, or she would breathe in too much of this gas!

"I don't know, but I have to get my brother." Fahltrid pushed Ten into Shal's arms. "Shal, get her out safely." He hugged Shal tightly, pressing Ten between them before turning and sprinting down the hall toward the computer room.

"Captain!" Ten screamed and lunged for him, but Shal grabbed her arm and held on.

"Ten." Shal's voice quivered. "We have to go."

As Shal half-carried and half-dragged Ten down the stairs, her screams sounded even over the blaring siren. Monica jogged after them. She fought back cries of her own as they entered the main floor. Aric. Had he gotten out? How could he? He was still unconscious.

"Go on without me!" She turned and darted up the stairs.

"Monica, no!" Shal called.

"I have to save Aric!" Monica sprinted up the stairs two at a time and careened into the hall.

Fahltrid's form appeared ahead in the haze. She focused on him, taking the turns he did until he disappeared into the computer room.

As she followed, she gasped for breath. Black spots flashed. How could she make it out with Aric? There wasn't enough time!

When she burst into the room, Aric lay on the floor, seemingly unconscious. Jacob rested nearby, his hands still tied.

Fahltrid grabbed Jacob under the arms and heaved him onto his shoulder. "You don't deserve this, Drehl, but I promised your daughter."

Monica stumbled toward Aric, but everything grew fuzzy. She teetered in place. Why couldn't she think?

Dedrick emerged from the fog carrying a metal bottle in one hand, a mask pressed to his face with the other. "Monica." He removed the mask from his face and pressed it to hers. "Breathe, child."

She inhaled a stream of pungent air and almost choked. As her vision cleared, she pressed the mask to her face and took in two more deep breaths before pushing it back to Dedrick.

"No, you keep it." He held it to her face again.

"I have to help Aric!" Her words sounded muffled through the plastic mask.

"I will help him." Dedrick hooked Aric under the arms.

Fahltrid strode over, Jacob dangling from one shoulder. He waved Dedrick away. "I'll carry him. You get Monica out of here."

Monica removed her mask for a second. "You can't carry them both! Let me help!"

She tried to stand, but Dedrick forced her to sit again, then heaved Aric to his feet. "I won't let this man carry them alone."

"I'm a seaman, Dedrick. Don't doubt my strength." Fahltrid lifted Aric onto his other shoulder. "Now take Monica and get out of here before you make your wife a widow."

Dedrick nodded, his face veiled by the haze. He took the oxygen from Monica and strapped the mask in place over Fahltrid's mouth. "You'll need this more than we will." Dedrick scooped Monica into his arms.

She craned her neck to see over Dedrick's shoulder. Fahltrid stumbled along behind them, his shoulders bowed under the weight of two grown men.

As Dedrick carried her down the stairs, his breathing grew labored. The air around them thickened with haze, making Fahltrid disappear.

Monica tightened her fingers into a fist. He had to get out with them. He just had to.

Soon, Dedrick burst through the front doors of the palace and onto a cobblestone drive. An arching shadow covered the green lawn and front gate in darkness. The poisonous vapor floated in the air in clouds, though not as thickly as inside the palace. Crowds of people stood outside the gate, but no one seemed willing to enter the courtyard. Screams and shouts echoed from the streets, hidden by the stone wall surrounding the palace.

"Do you see Brenna anywhere?" Dedrick asked, coughing.

Monica slid down from Dedrick's arms and looked in every direction. "She must be away from the courtyard, somewhere in the crowd." She ran down the drive and through the open gate.

People jostled her this way and that. She pressed herself against the stone wall to get past them. Dedrick appeared at her side. "If they don't pull the charge soon," he said, "the dome will be closed, and it will be too late."

Monica looked up. The dome rose overhead, the metal sheets clanking and sliding into place like scales on a snake. Only a palace-sized hole revealed the bright sky overhead. Gas escaped through it, but not for long. Once the dome closed, the gas would be trapped inside.

Rose and Faye pushed their way to the front of the crowd, Ten and Shal following at their heels.

"Dedrick! Monica!" Rose rushed forward into Dedrick's embrace.

One arm hugging her, he led her farther away from the gate. "With the amount of explosives they set, we need to find cover." He scooped Faye up with his free arm. "Were you brave for your mother?"

Faye smiled. "Yes. When can we go back inside?"

Dedrick's reply was drowned out in the clanking of the dome.

Monica edged toward Shal and Ten. The sky grew darker with each passing second. Shal gripped Ten's arm with one hand and a small black box with another.

The fire alarm sirens fell silent. The crowd's tumult died down as well.

"The captain's not out yet." Tears streamed down Ten's cheeks.

"Shal," Monica whispered. "What are you going to do?"

Shal clutched the black box and gazed at the sky. "I need to detonate."

"The captain's not out yet." Ten repeated the words in a whisper.

"If we don't ..." Monica murmured, "then he'll die anyway. We all will."

Tears welled in Shal's eyes. "She's right, Ten."

Ten covered her face with her hands. "I know."

Monica hugged her, fighting her own tears. It wasn't just Fahltrid. Aric and Jacob were still inside as well. She closed her eyes. Maybe Simon, too. Had he gotten out of the transport station safely?

"Okay." Shal blew out a long breath, then coughed. "I have to do it."

Viral Execution

Monica opened her eyes and faced the palace. Soon it would be a pile of rubble and broken bodies.

Chrom appeared out of the crowd. "Shal? You have the detonator?"

She nodded, her thumb poised over a red button in the box's center. "I don't know if I can do it."

Monica clasped her hands together. "Come on, Fahltrid!"

The shadow cast by the closing dome expanded to the palace gate.

"You have to, Shal." Chrom turned to the crowd. "Everyone go for cover! The palace is about to explode. Get out of here!"

The crowd started to disperse, but a few Nobles stayed behind.

"Do it, Shal!" Chrom coughed into his arm. "Now!"

Her thumb trembled over the button. "I can't, Chrom. Not with Fahltrid still inside!"

Monica clenched her fists until her fingers hurt. As much as she hated it, Chrom was right. "Shal!" She kept her gaze trained on the building, but no figure appeared out of the mist. "We don't have a choice."

Shal shook her head, tears pouring from her eyes. "I know, but I can't."

"God forgive me." Chrom snatched the detonator and punched the red button.

CHAPTER FORTY-TWO

The moment Chrom's finger lifted from the detonator button, Monica relaxed her fists. Besides the murmuring of the lingering Nobles and the clanking from the rising dome, everything quieted again. She held her breath. Where was the explosion?

Ten slumped her shoulders and leaned against Shal. "Where is he?"

Dedrick walked up beside them. "What's going on? You should have blown it by now! Children and the elderly are dying!"

Chrom popped open the detonator box, revealing wires and a computer chip inside. "Ah, loose circuit." Bowing his head, he jiggled something inside with a finger. "That should do it. Let's try this again." Chrom raised a finger over the button.

A figure bowing low under a burden appeared in the mist, staggering from the palace.

"Captain!" Ten screamed.

Chrom's finger came down on the button again. A plume of orange fire rocketed toward Fahltrid's hazy figure. Stones shot into the air, and a shock wave pulsed through the ground, knocking him to his knees.

The wave punched past the palace wall and hit Monica in the face. She raised her hands to her eyes. Grit and heat assaulted her skin.

Viral Execution

Faye cried out and buried her face against Rose's chest. Dedrick pulled Monica and shielded them all with his body.

The heat intensified, pressing against them. Faye wailed. The hair on Monica's arms stood on end.

Another shock wave rolled across them, followed by another and another.

During a lull, Chrom called over the roar of the fire. "That should be all of the charges!"

Pebbles and rocks rained, and ash floated in the air, thick enough to hide the poisonous mist. The groaning of the dome stopped, and the heat dissipated.

Dedrick released Monica and Rose. "It's over."

Rose let Faye slide to the ground. "Are you all right, Dedrick?"

"I think so." Dedrick gritted his teeth. "Some burns and bruises."

Monica laid a hand on her chest. Her breathing came easier with each passing second. The ash and mist swirled up in a funnel through the dome opening and floated high in the sky.

Ten and Shal huddled low near the stone wall, Chrom standing over them. Monica rushed to their side. "Are you okay?"

Shal nodded and climbed to her feet before helping Ten up. "Are you?"

Monica glanced back at Dedrick. Rose spoke with him in hushed tones. Black marks and pin-sized holes covered the back of Dedrick's shirt, but he looked fine other than that. "I think so. Thanks to Dedrick."

Chrom tossed the detonator on the ground and crushed it with his heel. "I'm sorry about Fahltrid, Shal."

"He might have survived." Shal took Ten's hand and ran into the rubble-littered courtyard.

"Shal, it's too dangerous!" Chrom jogged after her.

Someone laid a hand on Monica's shoulder. She flinched and whirled around.

Simon stood behind her, grinning from ear to ear. "There you are. I was afraid you were lost in the explosion. Chrom helped me get out in time. I insisted on searching for you, but Chrom overpowered me. I had no choice."

"Simon." The word caught in her throat. "I'm glad you're okay, but please—Fahltrid—he …"

Simon looked toward the courtyard. "Oh, dear."

Monica shuffled past the gate and into the courtyard. As she walked, a hot breeze rushed by.

Chrom, Shal, and Ten bent over a man's figure. Soot and dust blackened his clothes and hair. His torn and burned shirt revealed raw red wounds.

Sinking to her knees, Shal rolled him over, revealing Fahltrid's face and two bodies lying on their backs beneath him—Jacob and Aric. A mask covered Jacob's mouth and nose, a plastic tube running from it to a metal bottle stuffed behind his belt.

Ten patted Fahltrid's cheek, tears streaming down her own. "Captain. Captain, wake up."

His eyes remained closed, his face peaceful, as if he were really just sleeping.

Aric moaned and started to sit up but fell to the ground again. Jacob stirred as well, but Fahltrid remained motionless. "Fahltrid?" Shal ran a hand through his hair. Bits of the brittle locks broke off in her fingers. "Fahltrid, why did you have to go back? Why?"

Aric's eyes blinked open, and Monica helped him sit up. He held his injured arm to his chest. "What's going on?"

"Shhh." Monica pressed a finger to her lips. Fahltrid couldn't really be dead, could he? Had he given his life for Aric and Jacob? Who would take care of Ten? And what would happen to the *Katrina* and her crew?

Ten bit her fist and let out a quiet sob.

Crouching beside them, Chrom patted Shal's shoulder. "I'm sorry, Shal, but I think he's gone."

Viral Execution

Aric scooted forward across the singed grass. "I'm a doctor. Allow me to check."

Monica stood next to Jacob's prone body as Aric felt for a pulse at Fahltrid's neck. His face pale, Aric rose, then stumbled, but Chrom caught him.

Ten's jaw quivered. "Aric? Is he ..."

"I'm sorry, Ten." Aric shook his head, leaning on Chrom for support. "The good captain is no longer with us. Even if he had survived the blast, the gas would have killed him. The mask saved Jacob, and since I was barely conscious, I assume I didn't breathe in much of the gas."

"No!" Ten laid her head on Fahltrid's chest, wailing, "Captain! Captain! Why did you do it?"

Shal rubbed Ten's back. "I'm so sorry, Ten." A lump grew in Monica's throat as she fought back tears.

Aric shifted over to Jacob, crouched at his side, and checked his pulse. "He's alive and breathing well." He compressed Jacob's arms and legs. "No sign of broken bones. I'll examine him more thoroughly later." He rose and hobbled toward the courtyard exit. "So much pain. So much suffering."

Smoke billowed from the rubble, but the sky seemed to grow lighter despite the smog. The dome started its slow descent, clanking softly as each piece slid back together, foot by foot.

Monica kicked at the blackened grass and gazed at the remnant flames flickering in the burning palace. Fahltrid. Dear Fahltrid. If anyone had to die here, why him? Why the man who had done so much to rescue tormented slaves? The man who had now given his life for the cause. A true hero.

She clenched a fist. He would be the computers' final victim. With the fall of Penniak's palace, there were no more command computers. No one could send a termination signal to any other cities. There were still systems out there, along with oppressed Seen and wall slaves, but with the fall of three central city-states, the others would slowly crumble, slowly lose power.

She shuffled after Aric. He would help make sure even the smallest system was gone. He had proven that. Ten might join the fight, too, though it could take some time for her to recover from Fahltrid's death.

Monica looked up and came face-to-face with Rose. No ... not Rose. That could no longer be her name. "Mother."

She wrapped Monica in a tight hug. "Oh, Monica, I'm so sorry. Fahltrid was a great man."

"He was." Monica relished the comfort, comfort she had longed for for years. All her time alone as a wall slave, jumping from one identity to another, starving in between, hungering for someone to love her, someone to care, and now, just as her assignments were over, that someone had come.

She closed her eyes. But poor Ten's troubles had just begun. Monica pushed away gently. "Thank you ... Mother."

Smiling, Mother cupped Monica's cheek with a hand. "For what?"

"For everything." She nodded at Dedrick who stood nearby holding Faye. "For giving up your luxuries and helping, knowing it could cost you everything. For loving me, even though you don't really know me."

"Oh, Monica." Mother kissed her forehead. "I can only show the love that has been shown me." She withdrew a book from her pocket, a book with a worn yellow binding. "Love first shown me by my Heavenly Father and then reflected to me by your earthly father. Two people I long to tell you about. I've prayed for you every day since I was forced to leave Cillineese." Holding her diary tightly, she whispered, "I never expected our meeting to be quite like it has been, but I'm thankful that it occurred at all."

Dedrick cleared his throat and walked over, again carrying Faye in his arms. "I would be grateful for an introduction. It was rather rushed before."

"Yes, it was. So much has happened." Monica looked over her shoulder to where Shal and Ten sat huddled close to Fahltrid's body. They needed time to be alone to mourn. Chrom sat under a nearby tree where he had carried Jacob, probably to give Shal and Ten some space. Aric and Simon sat beside the stone wall, talking in low tones.

Monica turned back to Dedrick. "Well, sir, I'm Monica." She extended a scarred hand. "Or Sierra, if my mother prefers."

Mother smiled. "I think you're quite capable of choosing for yourself."

Dedrick inclined his head and shook her hand with a gentle grasp. "It's good to meet you ..."

Inhaling the now-fresh air, Monica said, "Sierra. My father gave me the name Monica because I had a job to do, but it's finished now, and I can rejoin my family just as they named me."

"Then it's good to meet you, Sierra." Dedrick smiled and released her hand. "So you are Brenna and Joel's daughter. I'm curious as to how you escaped the Cillineese termination. I know how Brenna did. She married me." He let Faye slide down from his arms.

"I ... I don't have a chip." Sierra felt the back of her neck with her fingertips. She explained as quickly as possible the situation surrounding her rescue. Dedrick remained silent the entire time, nodding once in a while.

When Sierra finished, Faye piped up, squinting in the brightening light. "So you're my sister?"

Sierra looked to Mother who gave a slight nod. "I guess I am, Faye. Do you mind?"

Wrinkling her nose, Faye stared at her for a second. "But you're a Seen. Does that mean I'm a Seen, too?"

"No, Faye." Mother ruffled her hair. "There are no more Seen, Slinks, or Nobles now. Sierra is just Sierra—my daughter, your sister."

"And Alex's?" Faye frowned at Sierra, as if still considering this new relationship.

Mother inhaled sharply. "And Alex's." She turned to Dedrick. "Honey—"

"We'll find him, Brenna. It's likely the other city-states haven't been affected much. At least not yet." Dedrick smiled. "He's in Troussell. It's close enough to walk to if need be."

"You'll like Alex." Faye hopped on the balls of her feet. "He's funny."

"I'm sure I will." Sierra grinned at her sister's antics.

A distant roar drifted up the street toward them. Sierra tensed her muscles. What now?

Dedrick laid his hands on Faye's shoulders. "Is that—?"

"Cheering." Mother laughed, her eyes twinkling. "Dedrick, they're happy to be alive, happy to be free." She clasped her hands to her chest. "I never dreamed I'd live to hear that sound."

Aric hobbled over, supported by Simon, who muttered, "Look who's helping whom now, eh, Aric?"

Aric nodded and maneuvered to Sierra's side. "I think we should head to the *Katrina* as soon as possible. It's unfortunate but inevitable that there will be danger in the streets once everyone calms down and figures out what's going on. We saw it happen in Cillineese and Central. Many will hunger for revenge."

"And who are you?" Dedrick raised an eyebrow. "I saw you unconscious in the control room, but no one told me who you are."

Aric extended his uninjured hand. "Aric, Rian's son. Brenna's nephew, actually. And I was heir to the north wing of Central until Monica decided to change things."

Dedrick shook Aric's hand. "Brenna, you have relatives popping up all over the place. Are there any more I should know about?"

"Well, that security agent who worked with Jacob for a while was my brother." Mother smirked. "Half brother, which is another topic I have to disclose to both you and Sierra."

Simon waved his hand in an authoritative gesture. "Another time, Madam Rose, another time. We must get to the ship while we can. How we're going to transport a body, a cripple, and a half-conscious man, I don't know. But when there's a me, there's a way."

"First of all," Aric said, "I am not a cripple. Just my arm is injured. I can walk by myself."

"Then walk, man!" Simon shooed him a few feet down the road. "Chrom can carry Fahltrid." He pointed at Dedrick. "And you can carry Jacob."

"Simon." Mother's words carried a warning tone. "I don't think—"

"It's all right, Brenna. I'll carry him." Shaking his head, Dedrick let out a short laugh. "Though you are going to have to explain all of this to me sometime. Madam Rose?"

"I'll try," Mother said. "But it's a long story."

Dedrick walked to where Chrom sat under the blackened tree next to Jacob. Dedrick picked Jacob up, the mask no longer on his face, and Chrom helped position him over Dedrick's shoulders.

"Now to get Fahltrid," Chrom said. "I hope Ten will eventually forgive me."

Sierra crossed her arms. Dedrick seemed to be taking this very well. Either he was hiding his emotions with ease, or he cared more about his family than his power. She shook her head. He had held hundreds of thousands of lives in his hands. How could he just let that go?

Dedrick stooped under Jacob's weight and made his way back to their side. "Shall we go find this *Katrina* of yours, Sierra?"

Sierra looked over her shoulder at the courtyard. Ten and Shal stood now, walking toward them. Ten's head stayed bowed, and Shal guided her with a hand. Chrom lingered behind a moment and picked up Fahltrid's body.

Nodding, Sierra sighed. "Yes, let's go."

CHAPTER FORTY-THREE

Sierra, her family, and the others walked through the crowded city streets. Ten, Shal, and Chrom brought up the rear, Chrom carrying Fahltrid with care, as if he were only sleeping. Ash and smoke floated all around, falling in people's hair and stirring the nervous crowd. Only moments ago, the cheers had ebbed. The reality of grief was now sinking in, especially for the less fortunate souls.

People darted left and right, goods cradled in their arms. A woman sat in the doorway of one of the rundown houses, an unmoving child clutched to her chest as she rocked back and forth, moaning.

Sierra walked beside Mother as she carried Faye so the little girl wouldn't be swept away in the pressing crowd. The loud clanking of the dome descending from overhead drowned out the few remaining cheers and mounting wails, but it couldn't hide them all. Once again, there had been too many deaths. The old and very young couldn't take the gas, and they and their families had suffered for it.

Turning away from the scene, Sierra led her group toward where the Katrina was moored. After several moments, they arrived at the dock. The ship floated a few yards away, the gangplank raised and the crew leaning on the rail, watching the goings-on in the street.

Viral Execution

Sierra waved to Fern, who stood nearby where the gangplank was stored.

Fern waved back. "We were getting worried!"

Yerith and the other sailors nodded. Two of the men lowered the gangplank, and Fern motioned for everyone to board. "Quick, before anyone else tries to get on."

They trooped up the gangplank, Dedrick in the lead, Jacob still dangling over his shoulder.

Holding his injured arm close to his chest, Aric followed.

Yerith grinned at him. "Good to see you back on your feet, Aric."

Aric smiled wanly. "Many thanks for your care when I wasn't, Yerith."

Fern raised a hand to her mouth and pointed. "Is … is that the captain?"

Chrom mounted the gangplank and edged past Sierra and Mother. He started to lay Fahltrid's body on the deck, but Yerith stopped him. "Wait. Put him in his cabin."

Chrom followed Yerith to one end of the ship. They disappeared into the cabin and closed the door behind them.

When Shal, Ten, and Simon climbed aboard, Fern and another sailor pulled the gangplank up. After laying Jacob on the deck near the main mast, Dedrick wiped his hands on his pants and strode to Mother's side.

Sierra looked at Ten. "Ten? What do you want to do?"

Leaning against Shal's arm, Ten gazed into the distance. "The captain always wanted to be buried at sea."

Shal laid a hand on Ten's head. "I'm sorry, Ten, but sea burials have been illegal for some time. The only lawful way to … to …" She choked up and shook her head.

"All bodies must be cremated." Dedrick stood behind Mother and Faye, a protective arm around his daughter's shoulder. "But considering the circumstances …"

"A sea burial it is!" Simon piped up, slapping Dedrick's back. "Any captain of Fahltrid's caliber deserves such an honor."

A flicker of a smile appeared on Ten's lips. "I … I would like that … very much."

Chrom and Yerith reemerged from the captain's quarters, Yerith holding his cap in his hands. He approached Ten with his eyes downcast. Extending a clutched fist to Ten, he muttered. "The captain would want you to have this." He dropped something into her hand and turned away.

She grasped the object and held it close to her chest. "Thank you, Yerith."

"Well?" Simon raised an eyebrow. "What is it?"

She opened her palm to reveal a thin chain with an attached key—the key to Fahltrid's desk, which had held the crew's papers. "We don't need to worry about being discovered anymore." She hung the necklace around her neck and smiled at Sierra. "Our job is done."

Sierra met her gaze and smiled back. It *was* done. The field slaves would go free along with everyone else. Fahltrid had no more cause to worry that a Noble would find out about his illegal crew. None of that mattered now.

She turned her gaze upward. Ash still floated from the sky—remnants of the palace casting a final shadow over the people. The dome crept farther down until it remained only a few feet above the land. As soon as it sank low enough in the water to pass over, they would set sail, and Fahltrid would have the memorial service he deserved.

"Are you sure you're ready for this?" Sierra whispered.

Ten stood beside her, gazing over the railing. "I'm sure."

"We could wait until morning." Sierra stared at the water rushing past under them, dark black in the dimness of the night. A full moon lit the way at the front of the ship. The sails snapped overhead in the gusting breeze that had carried the *Katrina* out of sight of the city and its curtain of ash that afternoon. Evening had come before they reached open water. Mother and Faye rested in the supply room below, worn out from the ordeal in the city.

"No, it's better to do it now." Ten turned from the railing and stared toward the captain's quarters where Chrom, Yerith, and Shal had retreated to prepare Fahltrid for burial. "The sooner he's laid to rest, the sooner we'll come to grips with it."

Sierra nodded. Did Ten really believe that? Fahltrid was like a father to her. How could she ever come to grips with it? His death was an ache that would probably stay with her for the rest of her life.

Sierra's gaze drifted to where Jacob sat on a barrel near the mast, illumined by one of the many hanging lanterns. He cradled his head in his hands. He would only add to Ten's ache—a constant reminder that he took away Fahltrid but could never fill his place. He didn't even *want* to fill his place.

"I wish he had died instead," Ten murmured as she glared at Jacob.

Sierra stared at Ten. "What?"

"I wish the Captain had left him behind and gotten out in time." Tears welled in Ten's eyes. "Why couldn't he at least have kept the mask on? Why did he have to give it to Jacob?"

"Oh, Wheaten," Shal said as she walked from the captain's cabin. "Fahltrid wanted to give you a gift. He wanted you to know your father. That's been his entire purpose since he found you and rescued you from the fields."

Ten whirled around and gazed at the sea. "How could you know that?"

"Because he told me." Shal leaned against the rail at Ten's side.

Sierra backed up a few steps. They probably didn't want her to intrude.

"Why would he tell you?" Ten folded her arms along the rail and rested her chin on them.

Shal smiled. "Because I asked him to marry me."

Ten frowned. "I thought he asked you, but I figured you turned him down. I thought that's why we hadn't been to Penniak in so long. He was avoiding you."

"No, not at all." Shal shrugged. "He never asked me, and I was tired of waiting. It's not traditional, but I finally got the courage to ask, and he said yes. We were engaged, but …"

Ten reeled back. "Because the captain would never leave the sea."

Sierra sidled back another step. Shal and Fahltrid? In the palace, he had said he trusted her …

Shal nodded. "I would have been happy to join him, but he said he couldn't let me do that. If I went to sea, I would become a full-status merchant and lose all privileges having a Noble father provides." Her shoulders slumped. "And if we were to have children, they would lose hope of having those privileges as well."

"Oh." Ten's eyes glimmered with tears. "I see."

Shal smiled. "And Fahltrid said he wouldn't give up the search, even though he loved me. He couldn't stop sailing. Not until he found his little Wheaten's father. He told me he couldn't rest until he did, and we would marry as soon as he found Drehl, dead or alive. I settled for the longest engagement in history."

Her shoulders shaking, Ten covered her face.

Shal hugged her close and looked over to where Jacob sat. "Don't think I wasn't upset about Fahltrid's decision to go back for Jacob. I was—am, but he did it for you. He loved you enough to sacrifice his entire life for you. Don't throw that away by hating the man he sacrificed everything to find."

Folding her arms over her chest, Sierra backed away farther. They both needed time to grieve for Fahltrid. He had given them all so much. Had he realized what he was signing up for when he agreed to take three Cantral refugees to Penniak? He couldn't have known he wouldn't survive the journey.

She headed for the stairway leading down to the supply room. As she approached, Mother and Faye mounted the steps below.

Faye rubbed her eyes and yawned. "Where are we?"

"Still on the ship *Katrina*." Sierra smiled at her sister's rumpled hair and dress. How nice it must be to sleep in ignorance, just as she herself had done as a child until her father was killed by the Cillineese termination.

Sierra took her mother's hand. The same would not happen to Faye. She would have a real childhood if they had anything to do about it.

Mother gave her hand a reassuring squeeze. "Is it time for Fahltrid's funeral? Or are they waiting until morning?"

"It's almost time," Shal said as she walked over, leaving Ten staring out at sea. "Ten doesn't want to wait." She cast a quick glance at the cabin door. "Chrom and Yerith will bring him out soon."

"It will be a great blessing to honor such a hero," Mother said. "I hope many others will emulate his strength, courage, and love."

"Thank you." Extending a hand to Mother, Shal smiled. "I'm Shal, by the way. We weren't properly introduced. I recognize you, though. Head programmers' faces are generally known around the public. It helps that my father knows you, too."

Shaking Shal's hand, Mother smiled and inclined her head in a half nod. "Shal, I'm Brenna. Monic—I mean—Sierra and Faye's mother."

The door to Fahltrid's cabin opened. Chrom and Yerith walked out carrying a man-sized, cloth-wrapped bundle between them.

When they laid it on the deck near the railing, Chrom straightened and beckoned to Shal.

Shal nodded. "They're ready. Would you gather everyone please, Monica?"

"Of course." Sierra trotted below deck and told each crew member the news. She located Dedrick and Simon in the bunk room, conversing in low voices. "Simon? Dedrick?"

Simon slid from his seat in a hammock. "It's time?"

Sierra nodded. This was going to be difficult. The whole crew owed Fahltrid their lives. If they had stayed in the fields, they would be dead.

She followed Dedrick and Simon back up the stairs. Three crewmen stood nearby, holding their head kerchiefs or caps at their waists along with green glowing lanterns to help light the deck. Fern kept her hands clasped behind her back, her head bowed in classic Seen form, her lantern near her feet. Jacob still sat on a barrel by the mast, his face once again hidden by his hands.

Inhaling deeply, Sierra joined the lineup between Faye and Mother. Dedrick hooked Mother's arm under his and stood silently. Chrom knelt by the cloth bundle and pulled back a piece of the linen, revealing Fahltrid's face. The captain's closed eyes and somber expression looked peaceful despite his skin's pallor.

Stepping forward, Yerith motioned to Fahltrid. "I've never been to a formal funeral, and I don't know anything about what they do at them, but—"

"I offer my assistance." Dedrick strode from the line and stood near Fahltrid's body.

Yerith nodded, his shoulders relaxing. "By all means."

"Does anyone have any last good-byes?" Dedrick folded his hands at his waist. "Feel free to approach."

No one moved for a moment.

Sierra clung to Mother's and Faye's hands. It wasn't their place to speak. Even though she had known Fahltrid for a while now, it was better to give priority to those who were closest to him.

Ten knelt by the body, tears streaming down her cheeks. "Thank you for everything … Uncle. Shal helped me understand why you did it. I—I'll try to forgive Drehl. I know that's what you would want." She wiped her eyes, rose to her feet, and backed away before pushing Shal forward.

Redness tinted Shal's cheeks as she folded her hands in front, her head bowed. "I'm … really not used to public displays of emotion, but neither was Fahltrid." She switched to a different language, speaking in soft tones before stooping and kissing his forehead. Tears dripped down her cheeks and landed in Fahltrid's hair.

Chrom helped her rise and pulled her away from the body. She laid her head on his shoulder, crying silently.

Fern murmured something indiscernible but stayed where she was.

"Well." Yerith cleared his throat. "Captain Fahltrid saved many lives, and I owe him a lot." He nodded to Ten. "Wheaten, if you want to keep this ship sailing, I'll keep sailing along with you, for as long as you want. I owe it to you and Fahltrid."

Each of the crew members nodded, and a few murmured, "Yes."

Ten sniffled and smiled. "Thanks, everyone."

Dedrick crouched and re-covered Fahltrid's face with the cloth. "It's often customary for someone, often a trusted friend, to give a eulogy, but—"

"The captain didn't like much ceremony." Ten pushed her hair out of her face, revealing her bright blue eyes, red-rimmed from crying. "He'd be happy with what's already been said."

Chrom released himself from Shal's embrace and stood beside Fahltrid's body. Yerith joined him, and they lifted Fahltrid together and moved toward the ship's railing.

"Good sailing, Captain." Chrom nodded to Yerith, and they let Fahltrid's body slide into the waves and disappear under the dark water.

CHAPTER FORTY-FOUR

After Fahltrid's burial, Sierra leaned over the *Katrina's* railing. Again, water rushed beneath the prow, though difficult to see even in the moon's light. She fingered the glass vial holding Amelia's chip that hung around her neck. It had felt wrong not to wear it while in the city, so she put it back on soon after they boarded. Ten and the crew had returned to the business of running the ship, and Simon had gone below to sleep for a while, complaining of chest pain.

A chill crept up Sierra's arms. She rubbed her skin, bringing a little warmth. Simon might never recover from his ordeal with the gas. No computer program could alter lung damage, especially in someone his age.

She turned and looked over the ship's deck to where the stairs led to the bunk rooms. At least Aric was with him. Even injured, he was a good doctor and could take care of both himself and Simon.

Mother mounted the steps coming from the supply room where the women of the ship slept. She and Sierra locked gazes. Smiling, she strode to the railing. "Are you doing all right?"

Sierra sighed. "So many people died, Mother. We waited too long. And Ten lost the only father she had, just to be replaced by one who doesn't even want her."

Mother wrapped Sierra in a one-armed hug. "It is a bitter victory, but consider the people you've saved. Everyone would have died without your efforts, without Fahltrid's efforts. He didn't just save Jacob. He saved Aric, too, and he helped you with the explosives."

"How did you know about that?" Sierra gulped down a sob. It was true, just hard to accept.

"Dedrick told me everything that went on while Faye and I were outside." Mother rested her hands on the railing. "He's down in the supply room now, talking to Faye and putting her to bed. She's a little upset that we won't be going home again. Ten and the others have agreed to sail to Troussell to find Alex. Then we'll be going on to Central, if that's what you want."

"It doesn't matter to me." Sierra shrugged. With no ties other than to the people on this ship, why would it matter? She could go wherever they went, wherever they cared to sail. "Do you want to go to Central?"

Mother gazed at her for a moment, as if trying to read her thoughts. "Yes, I would, Central the continent anyway. The actual city, I don't know. I would like to see my sister again. It's been twelve years since she helped me escape, and I haven't seen her since."

Rubbing a hand along the weather-worn railing, Sierra nodded. That was a relationship Mother still hadn't explained, despite Simon's prodding. "Veronica."

"Yes, Veronica." Mother's eyes brightened, and her face lost its worried look. "Did you say you met her? Is she well?"

"She seemed fine, but I didn't see her long. She was taking Regina home to New Kale from Cantral." Sierra avoided her mother's gaze. It would be so nice to tell her mother more about her sister, to share some pleasant news, but there really wasn't anything to tell. "You still haven't explained, Mother, about your relationship to Veronica, and why you say you're a Seen."

Mother bowed her head, her look of joy vanishing in a split second. "Not even Dedrick knows about that, I'm ashamed to say.

I don't believe in deceit, but what could I do? If I revealed my past, I couldn't help the people of Penniak, and lives would be lost."

"I understand. Do …" Sierra looked over her shoulder toward the steps leading below. "Do you want me to go get him so you can tell him now?"

"No." Mother laid a hand on Sierra's arm. "Dedrick's been amazingly understanding so far. He hasn't said a word against me, despite what I know he believes about the computer system being the right way to govern the people. Let me tell him in my own time. It would be best to let him know when he and I are alone." She released Sierra's arm. "Besides, I don't think I can handle telling more than one person right now. I've kept quiet about it for more than eighteen years."

Pursing her lips, Sierra nodded. If she said anything now, Mother might find an excuse to keep her silence even longer.

Mother hunched her shoulders. "I'm Veronica and Fox's half sister. My mother was a Seen. My father was … well." She sighed and pushed a lock of hair behind her ear. "Unfaithful to Veronica's mother. He was a wicked man, one whom we all avoided as much as possible. When his wife, Nyla, found out about me, she had my mother transferred to another city-state when I was just two, for my mother's sake as well as Nyla's, but Nyla kept me behind in Cantral. I never saw my mother again after that. I don't even know her name or really remember her at all."

Sierra stifled a gasp. "I've heard of Nobles having half-status children before, but why would she take you from your mother?"

"I don't know." Mother shrugged, but her face told a sadder story. "Perhaps as a reminder to my father of what he did. She was kind to me, though. She assigned me as a play companion to my half sister Brenna. Brenna had a heart condition that required her to have many surgeries, and they didn't help much. I spent countless hours reading aloud to her and thinking of ways to entertain her. We grew very close, closer than Veronica and I were at first. Besides Foxlar's teasing and tormenting, I had an easy life for a Seen."

Sierra furrowed her brow. Her mother had the same name as her half sister?

Mother pressed two fingers to her temples. "This is more than you want to hear, isn't it? You're probably more curious about the cloning program and how I met Joel."

"Not at all." Sierra laid her hands over her heart. "I've dreamt of meeting you and talking about our family for most of my life. You know what it's like to live in the dorms, don't you? There were plenty of sleepless nights spent hoping to learn about my family but knowing it would never happen, that I'd never see them again. Yet you're here. I want to know everything."

"Oh, no, dearest." Mother let her hands fall back to her sides. "Everything is much too painful. The torment I went through as a child at Fox's—my own brother's—hands, the ridicule from other Seen. I can't relive that now, not after all this. Please don't ask me to. At least not yet."

Sierra hooked an arm through Mother's. "I won't, but if it's not too much, could you tell me about the cloning?"

"Yes, I'll try." Mother inhaled a shaky breath. "Brenna was supposed to marry Joel. It was an arranged marriage, for political reasons, and I traveled to Cillineese with her as her Seen helper.

Because of her health, I went with her most places. Joel and I met the first evening we arrived. Brenna wasn't feeling well and sent me to the library to get a book to keep her mind off of things." She smiled and fiddled with her wristband. "Joel was there, working on the cloning program, but I didn't know it at the time. Simon was there, too—though only visiting—and he introduced us. You could say the rest is history."

"But you were a Seen, and you said Brenna ..." Sierra widened her eyes. "You cloned Brenna's chip to yours." She reached under her collar and pulled out the vial holding Amelia's chip. "But didn't you say Joel never figured out how to have two chips signaling at the same time like Amelia did?"

"Your memory is very good." Mother's gaze traveled to Sierra's necklace. "You're right. We couldn't get two chips to emit the same signal at the same time without the computer terminating both." Mother ran a finger along her own neck where her chip was buried beneath her skin. "Brenna gave her life for mine. Her condition was getting progressively worse. A month before the planned date for her wedding, she was not doing well, and ..." Mother wiped away a tear. "Joel, Veronica, and I were at her side when she died. Joel switched her identity to mine as she breathed her last, and I became Brenna. Rose the Seen was recorded as dead, and no one was the wiser. Not many people had ever met Brenna. Since she was ill so often, she kept to herself. Of course, we had to tell Nyla about the switch, but she was happy for me, even in the shadow of Brenna's death. Fortunately for us, Brenna and our brothers were not on speaking terms, so they didn't have to be involved."

"Oh ..." Sierra sighed. All this time, she had often wondered if there were any good Nobles out there. Now almost everywhere she turned, one would surprise her. Brenna, Joel, Aric, and even Dedrick. "That's a lot to take in."

"I know. Maybe I shouldn't have sprung it on you all at once." Mother hugged Sierra again. "Just know that, really, our past doesn't matter much now, not with everything that's happened. And no matter what, I love you and always will." She slipped her little yellow diary from her pocket and handed it to Sierra. "I want you to have this. To keep. I'll translate it for you. There's so much I want to teach you about our family, about the Lord who carried us through these events, even if you didn't realize it."

Sierra held the book close, rubbing a finger over the coarse binding. She realized it more than her mother knew. God had answered so many prayers. "Thank you, Mother."

Viral Execution

Mother patted Sierra's arm and turned toward the deck. "I'm going to check on Faye." She walked away and disappeared down the stairs.

Sierra clutched Amelia's chip in a fist and her mother's diary in the other, rolling her mother's information over in her mind. Brenna Rose was an illegitimate child, a Seen whom others wouldn't accept, a Noble who shouldn't be, and yet she had helped free the world.

Sierra untied her necklace and let the glass vial dangle from the string, swaying it like a pendulum over the open water. It glinted in the light from the full moon. She had so many things to learn still, so many things left to do. When she started this journey, she had been alone, and now …

Holding the diary to her chest, she gripped the vial and threw it into the sea. It disappeared in the waves, joining Fahltrid at the ocean's floor.

Aric walked up beside her, his arm in a sling and a fresh bandage plastered to his shoulder. "So we're going to Troussell, are we? I've never been there before."

She turned to him and smiled. "Shouldn't you be resting after your ordeal?"

He raised an eyebrow. "I thought I was the doctor here."

She nodded. "Yes, we're going to find my brother, then head to Cantral. The mobs should have quieted by the time we get there." She let her smile fall for a second, then lifted it again. "I can't wait to see our mothers reunite. Regina will be pleased to find out we're cousins."

Aric shrugged. "Probably. You never can tell with her."

A cranky voice broke in. "There's no hope of sleep in those rickety hammocks." Simon strode up to the rail. "I endured them on the trip here because I was unconscious half the time." He rubbed an elbow and nodded at them in turn. "So you two, are you ready for another adventure?"

Amanda L. Davis

Touching his injured shoulder, Aric backed away a step, smiling. "You won't get me to go anywhere with you again, Seen."

"Aric …" Sierra forced a warning tone, though she bit back a laugh. "I thought you said you wouldn't call him that."

"She's quite right, you know." Simon wagged a finger at him. "I'm a Noble now. My chip says so."

Aric smiled. "And thanks to Monica, that doesn't matter anymore."

"True, though now the heroine is named Sierra." Simon bowed low. When he raised up, he gazed at her with sparkling eyes. "My dear girl, we are all greatly indebted to you. Without your courage, your sacrificial love, and, if I may use the phrase, your gritty stubbornness, we would all likely be dead. If I have anything to do with it, your name will be recorded in the history books alongside the greatest heroes and heroines of all time. You are deserving of the highest praise."

"Hear, hear!" Aric edged close to Sierra and kissed her on the forehead. "Thank you, Sierra. Thank you for everything."

She pressed her lips together, tears again welling. "And thank you. Both of you. You're both heroes in my book."

Aric turned to Simon and clapped him on the back. "Not too much praise, or this old Noble will get a bigger head than he already has."

"Nonsense. I am as humble as they come." Simon grinned. "But instead of 'Noble' you are free to call me 'Your Majesty.' "

"Oh, Simon!" Sierra playfully punched his arm. "Please don't ever change."

"Why should I?" He leaned on the railing and looked out over the sea. "You can't improve on perfection."

"And who are we to disagree?" Aric joined him at the railing, a smile spreading across his face. "What do you plan to do when you return home, Your Majesty?"

"That depends on how the riots against the Nobles turned out. I suppose when the dust settles, the people will come to their senses and realize who saved them from the Nobles, and I will again be in charge in Cillineese, but I hope not for long. I would find a replacement as soon as possible."

Sierra leaned on the railing next to him. "Why?"

"Despite the reprogramming in my chip, I am too old to be a caretaker for our impulsive citizens. And speaking of caretakers, I still have to see about Gerald and Audrey. I left them in the care of a trustworthy farmer who is probably wondering by now why I haven't checked on them for so long. When it's time to release them, I hope Gerald is grateful that I kept him safe from the wrath of the rioters. I wouldn't want him to try to seize control again."

Sierra grasped Simon's hand. "I'm sure you'll convince him that it's better to behave himself than to die. If you appeal to his love for Audrey, he'll remember that our loved ones are more important than power. "

"Indeed." Simon looked at the hand clasp and smiled. "Our loved ones are the most precious treasures in the world."

Her own smile growing, Sierra inhaled the fresh salty air and gazed at her friends, a pair of her own loved ones. She wasn't alone anymore. No matter what troubles lay ahead—whether finding her brother or making sure the computers stayed dead—she now had help to overcome them. The remaining computers would fall one by one, losing their power and their brutal hold on the people. No one had to be a slave anymore. Everyone was free … forever.

PREQUEL CHAPTER TO PRECISELY TERMINATED

"You want me to run away and leave my husband to die?" Rose clenched her fists, glaring at Veronica, who stood by the large four poster bed folding clothes and laying them into a suitcase. "And hide in the arms of another man?" Heat spread across her face. "Never! I'm not a coward!"

Veronica met her gaze, her expression serene. "Not a coward. Just making the best of a terrible situation." She snapped the suitcase closed. "And I won't let Brenna's sacrifice go to waste. Do you think I haven't mentioned the escape option to Joel already? It's the only way to save you."

Biting back tears, Rose looked away. *A terrible situation* didn't begin to describe the doom awaiting the people of Cillineese—her people. If the trial ended badly, they would all die. Millions of people. "Joel didn't say anything about it to *me*. He can't possibly have agreed to this insane plan!"

"Not agree to a way to save his wife?" Veronica said. "He's already sentenced to death. Why shouldn't he at least try to save you?" She crossed the room and laid a hand on Rose's shoulder. "I wouldn't have suggested it if I could think of any other way, Rose. He probably hasn't mentioned it, because I told him not to, not until I could be sure it would work, and that Dedrick would agree. I wasn't sure he would want to marry a dead traitor's wife."

Rose clasped her sister's hand. Joel might not die—it wasn't decided yet. "The verdict won't be read until tomorrow. Maybe…"

"Rose, I love you, but don't be stupid." Veronica squeezed her shoulder, then walked around the room, probably looking for anything else Rose might want to pack. "He's under house arrest. The evidence is stacked against him. You know Fox will do whatever is necessary to prove his case. I'm doing my best to persuade Rian to lighten the sentence but…" She picked up a framed picture of Rose, Joel, and Sierra from the bedside table. "He can't afford to lose face. He won't budge. Not on this." She lowered her voice to a whisper. "In fact, the only progress I've made is getting him to approve this last minute divorce, and he's only doing it because you're my sister."

"Veronica!" Rose took the photo from her. Divorce Joel? She could never. Just the thought of it turned her stomach, which was already roiling over the turmoil her city faced. "I can't abandon my family."

Veronica gritted her teeth. "And I told Rian I wouldn't speak to him again if he let you die. Don't make me keep that promise. You're coming with me." She looked at her wristband computer screen. "Today."

Choking back tears, Rose shook her head. "And Sierra? I'll need to pack for her. She's not even five, she doesn't have a chip yet. We can stay with you until Joel is cleared." She inhaled shakily. That would work. There wouldn't need to be a divorce. Joel finished his defense today, made his case, and he would be cleared tomorrow when the verdict was read. Foxlar was a good debater, and he would try his best, but Joel would prevail.

"She can't come, Rose." Veronica set the small travel case by the door. "The Council of Eight knows about her. She's Joel's daughter, she doesn't have a chip, and so she can't legally travel. If she showed up in Cantral, there would be trouble." She shook her head. "I've already discussed it with Rian. He couldn't think of a legal way to save her."

Anger bubbled in Rose's chest. "Legal? This is my daughter we're talking about, Veronica. Since when did legal matter to you?" She tapped the back of her neck, feeling the small scar hiding her computer chip. "I am only in this position because legal didn't matter to you."

"But now I have children of my own," Veronica said, "and I need to be more careful than ever. This may be the last time I'll be able to help you. Let's make it count."

Rose took a deep breath and looked at the photo of her family on the nightstand. Her happy, smiling family, soon to be broken and ripped apart. Her daughter was sick so frequently, she needed her mother. "Sierra's old enough to have a chip. We could have one implanted in time for her to travel. She needs me."

Veronica stared at her, her face passive. "And that would lock her into the system with the rest of us, Brenna."

Rose flinched at the name. She was used, to it, everyone called her that, but not Veronica. Never Veronica. But she was right. Could a mother do that to her own daughter? They had put it off for as long as possible, with her pediatrician raising concerns about integration of the system in the brain, plus concerns of their loyalty. He had threatened to report them if they waited much longer, but now she might die without one.

"Brenna!" Joel's deep voice echoed from down the hall.

Veronica raised an eyebrow. "You can talk to him about it now. Apparently the hearings are over."

The door banged open, and Joel strode in, his normally crisp button-down shirt undone at the cuffs and collar. He threw a suit jacket onto the bed, his gaze roaming the room. When it landed on Rose, his shoulders sagged. "Thank God, I didn't miss you."

"That's my cue to go wait outside." Veronica walked to the exit and picked up the suitcase. "Good luck convincing her, Joel." She pulled the door shut behind her.

Rose crossed her arms over her chest. Indignation stirred in her stomach. How could Joel plan all of this without including her? As she gazed at his face –his clenched jaw and the worry lines creasing the skin around his green eyes, the angry thoughts melted away. Rose forced a smile. She had to stay strong for him. Maybe the hearings hadn't gone badly. Maybe he was bringing good news. Maybe.

He crossed the room and pulled her into a strong embrace. He pressed her tightly to his chest, his breathing fast and labored. Rose relaxed into his arms and returned the hug. His shoulders started to shake as he pressed a kiss to the top of her head. "I'm sorry. I'm so, so sorry." His voice cracked. "I tried, Rose. I was doing what was right. I was trying to help my people, and now I've killed them."

A sob tried to break through from Rose's gut, but she fought it down along with the lump forming in her throat. "You tried, my love." She pulled back and met his stricken gaze. "You did everything you could. I watched you write those programs. I helped with the research. We did our best. If the people knew, they would be grateful you tried."

"Grateful to die?" He turned from her gaze. "I moved too quickly. I should have waited to be sure. Wouldn't they rather live as slaves than die because of one Noble's mistake?"

"I wouldn't." She laid a hand on his arm, turning him to face her. "I know many would agree with me. A chance for freedom at the risk of death?" She wiped a tear from his cheek. This man loved his people so much. A Noble who had everything to lose, put it all on the line for them, and no one would know it. He would go down in history as a traitor, hated by those who came in the future to fill this murdered city. "I took that chance five years ago, Joel. I don't regret it." He deserved to have words of comfort at a time like this, if there was any to be had.

"I hope to God you're right." He hung his head, the image of defeat as he sat on the edge of the bed. "I can only hope to get you and Sierra out. It's my one redeeming thought."

Rose sat next to him. What to say? Her earlier anger at her sister had all but disappeared, but the plan never stopped nagging. How could she even think of leaving him? To save her daughter, maybe, but just herself? "Can we appeal the decision? Maybe if I had been there, I could have—"

"And risk Fox seeing you?" He shook his head. "And there will be no appeal." He took her hands in his. "The last hearing was today. The verdict will be tomorrow, but we all know what that will be at this point. I'm under house arrest except when being escorted to Cantral. Once the sentence goes through, we will have a week before the dome closes." His voice cracked as he spoke, "I'll send all the merchants out and make sure all the field workers are assigned to areas outside the dome. I'll see what Seen and wall slaves I can sell off to other city-states, but I don't know who would buy them. They'll be marked as tainted goods, possible betrayers."

"You'll save as many lives as possible." Rose squeezed his hands. Her heart sped up. This was all too real. It was really going to happen. "That's what matters. And I'll stay with you to the end. We'll sneak Sierra out. She's been sickly, but she'll be fine. Faye could take her to Simon. He has contacts, he—"

"No!" Joel jumped to his feet, pulling her up with him. "You will not stay here." Determination flashed in his eyes. "I will see you saved, if it's the last thing I do." He kissed her hands and fingered the ring on her left. "There's no need for you to die for my mistakes. If I can save other Seen, I have to save my favorite."

"Joel, please." She took her hands from his. How could he joke about that now? "If it weren't for my status, Foxlar would never have investigated so thoroughly. You might have gotten away with it if I were really Brenna." She rubbed the back of her neck. The memory of her sister's death was still so fresh, even five years later. "And if I go back to Cantral with Veronica? Foxlar is there now. I can't keep him away from me forever. Better I die here with you than face trial and death there. That would only bring more attention to our family and make it harder to get Sierra out."

Joel covered her hand on the back of her neck with his, drawing her head to his chest. His heartbeat thrummed against her fingers through his soft sweat-dampened shirt. "Give me this dying wish, Rose. Let me know that you have a chance to be safe. Veronica has arranged for the divorce. Rian has already signed the papers. All you need to do is sign as well. They'll unlink our chips, and you'll be a free woman, but it has to be done before the sentencing tomorrow."

She gripped the loose fabric of his shirt, balling her hand into a fist. Anguish flooded in, threatening to tear her apart. Sobs wracked her body, and she pressed her face into his chest, adding her tears to the damp fabric. How could she even consider this? How could she revoke her vows, and worse, Veronica had said she had to remarry this Dedrick in Eursia to ensure her complete safety. Could she do it? Even as Joel's last request, it hurt too much! To abandon her husband and child, sail away across the ocean, and forget this life existed?

Joel hugged her and rocked back and forth as she cried. "I'm sorry, Love." He kissed the top of her head again. "It will give me strength to know you and Sierra are safe. I've already been in contact with Simon. He put me in touch with a resistance group."

The words barely registered, sounding like buzzing in her ears. She swallowed her tears and nodded. "You can get her out another way, then? I trust Simon."

"I do, too. There is a wall slave in Cantral who will help get her out. We will have to wait until the last day, but Faye has agreed to help. We'll probably have to teach Sierra a new name to help her stay hidden."

Rose pushed his arms away. If he could stay strong during this, then so could she. Her training as a Seen had forced her to stay quiet and straight faced even under duress, and as a child she had endured torment at Foxlar's hands in stony silence. These last few years had made her too soft. She was going to have to work on that to survive this ordeal. "I need to see her. Veronica wants me to leave now, but I cannot leave without saying goodbye, Joel. I won't budge on that."

"I expected nothing less." He gave her a quick kiss and led her to the door. "No one cares for our daughter better than you."

She fetched a handkerchief out of her pants pocket and wiped her eyes. When she pulled it away, a smear of makeup marred the white fabric, but no one would care what she looked like right now.

When they entered the hall, Veronica was nowhere in sight, probably off making further preparations somewhere else in the palace. Rose clung to Joel's arm as they walked down the corridor. Even now, so many years later, she still relished holding his hand in public, even though the hall was empty. Such a display of affection was something she had never dared do when they were first married. The Seen training had run too deeply. She would hold this moment forever in her mind. This could be the last time they walked side by side.

Opening the door to Sierra's room, Joel beckoned Rose in. She crossed the dimly lit bedroom, her footsteps making no sound on the pink carpet as she approached the four-poster bed at the center. Her daughter's small form lay curled under the bed quilt, sound asleep for her afternoon nap.

Rose sat on the bed next to her and pulled the covers down. "Sierra. Sierra, sweetie, wake up."

"Momma?" Sierra rolled over and reached her arms up.

Rose scooped Sierra into her lap and rubbed her cheek against her daughter's brown curls. The scent of shampoo and clean sheets wafted to her nose. Would they ever experience this again? She smiled at Joel as he sat next to them and put his arms around both. They would have to cherish this moment for what it was and pray that more would come. "God," she whispered, "Please, bring us back together. Don't let this be in vain."

"Amen to that." Joel kissed her cheek.

"Are you praying?" Sierra sat up straighter and looked around the room. "But it's time to get up, not time for bed." She looked at a spot in the wall where the slave access door was hidden. "Where's Faye?"

"You can pray anytime, honey." Joel patted her back. "Not just at bedtime." He stood up and held his arms out to her, and she jumped into them. "Now it's time to say goodbye to Momma. She has to go on a trip, and we don't know when she'll be back."

"Why?" Sierra clung to his neck, supporting herself with her little arms. "Can I come?"

"No, Angel," Rose whispered. The words almost caught in her throat. If only Sierra could come, but they had to trust Veronica. She had been a life-saver before, and there was no one better at planning and overseeing the smallest of details. "You'll be going on a different adventure next week. Daddy's going to help you get ready for it. You'll have to play pretend for a while, but I know you like that."

She nodded. "And you'll come back?"

Rose bit her lip. "As soon as I can. I will find you."

A knock sounded on the door, and it swung open before they could answer. Veronica stood in the entrance, still carrying Rose's suitcase, her slender form outlined by the hall light. She slammed the door closed and rushed to them, her gaze tracking something on her wristband.

"We have to go." She dropped the suitcase to the floor and dug a small piece of paper out of her pocket. "My contact in Cantral says Fox petitioned the Council of Eight to do some further investigating here before the verdict tomorrow."

"What?" Rose gulped. "But they've already finished the hearing. He can't look for more evidence now."

"He's on his way here this very moment." Brandishing the piece of paper at Joel, Veronica raised an eyebrow. "A messenger just brought this to me, and he was on foot. Fox will be in a shuttle. He could arrive at any moment."

Joel snatched the paper and read it over, still holding Sierra in one arm. He wadded it up and threw it to the ground. "Your brother is a snake, Rose. He's trying to stop your deal from going through." He passed Sierra to her. "He might not have enough evidence yet to prove you're not Brenna, but if he sees you…"

Her heart thumping, Rose took Sierra and hugged her close. Fox would know she wasn't Brenna the moment he saw her. Veronica and Nyla had helped her manage to avoid seeing him all these years, but that time had obviously run out. She squeezed Sierra close and showered her face and head with kisses. "I love you so much, Sierra. You, and your daddy both. More than you'll ever know."

"Momma!" Sierra returned the hug, her arms squeezing tightly around her mother's neck. "Don't go!"

"He's at the shuttles, Rose." Veronica tapped her wristband where an ID tracker ran on the screen. She took Sierra from her. "Sisi, she has to go. It'll be ok."

"But Aunt V, I want to go to." Sierra rubbed her sleep-filled eyes.

Anguish tore through Rose, a shredding that may never heal. She dashed to Joel and kissed him, knowing it may be their last. He returned it, pressing her close. "Remember me next week, my love. Although doom awaits, there is always hope. Always." He pushed her away.

"I will remember you. Next week and forever." She stumbled back, tears streaming down her cheeks. "I love you."

"He's coming, Brenna," Veronica hissed as she picked up the suitcase. "Main landing."

Sierra hugged Rose's legs, but Joel pulled her off, holding her wriggling little body away from her mother. "Momma!" Sierra wailed. "Don't go! Don't go!"

Viral Execution

Knifelike pain cut at Rose's emotions, but she pushed it down. There was no other option. Her husband would keep their baby safe. He would get her out, and Rose would run away, but maybe not as a coward.

Without another word, she and Veronica dashed down the stairs and chose a side corridor to avoid the main entrance. This would be a longer route to the shuttles, but it was necessary to avoid Fox.

When they neared a shuttle, Veronica whispered, "Slow now. Casual. Relaxed facial features."

"I understand." Rose matched her gait. The slower pace felt agonizing, like walking while being chased by a lion that was ready to pounce.

Soon, they entered a waiting shuttle through its open doors and sat next to each other in the sparsely populated car, the last in a train of five. When the doors slid closed, the hiss and thud make Rose flinch.

"That's not relaxed." Veronica set Rose's suitcase on her lap and flipped the latches open. "I brought something you need to take care of immediately." She withdrew a yellow journal from the case and set it and a pen in Rose's hands.

"My diary?"

Veronica nodded and lowered her voice to a bare whisper. "Add a message to Sierra. I'll make sure Simon gets the diary. Maybe someday she'll get to read it."

"That's so thoughtful. Thank you." Rose ran a trembling hand across the diary's cover. "But what can I write besides I love you and miss you?"

"Well ..." Veronica fidgeted and looked straight ahead. "There's something I haven't told you yet."

"What?" Rose gave her a nudge. "Tell me."

Veronica laid a hand over Rose's and looked her in the eye. "Joel and I made more plans you don't know about. We set the wheels in motion for Sierra to be a spy of sorts when she comes of age."

Rose swallowed a shout and answered in a low hiss. "A spy? What are you talking about?"

"She'll be the only chip-less person in the world and invisible to the computers. Maybe by the time she's sixteen or so, she can infiltrate the system, a tiny mouse crawling between the walls, unnoticed until it's too late to stop her from destroying the computers."

Rose felt her mouth drop open, then quickly shut it. "You're serious, aren't you?"

"Completely." Veronica tapped a finger on the diary. "Write to her. Encourage her. I have no idea how much danger Sierra will face, but if she's going to be the hero this trampled, oppressed world is praying for, she'll need to read about her mother's love and hope for her. You can be her counselor, her encourager from afar. You can tell her that God is watching over her every moment, guiding her to the light, even when she feels alone in the darknees."

A tear trickled down Rose's cheek. "I can't believe you did this without telling me. You could've convinced me. I would've realized it was all for the best."

"So you say." Veronica offered a light shrug. "Joel said we should tell you up front, give you a chance to agree to the plan, but since it was my plan, I wouldn't let him. Blame me if you want, but it is what it is. I couldn't allow the slightest chance of failure."

"And you couldn't allow me to a chance to make the right choice."

Veronica gazed a Rose for a long moment before replying. "You're right. I wasn't being fair." She nodded toward the doors. "When we arrive at the station, we can take the next shuttle back. Foxlar will be gone by then, and you can undo the plan. Maybe come up with another one. Sierra is your daughter, so it's your choice. I'll do whatever I can to make it work."

Viral Execution

Rose set a hand on Veronica's cheek. "No, Sister. You did the right thing. My emotions were a roadblock, and you had to dodge them. Now that we're on our way, I can see the truth. I need to give Sierra to the world. She might be their only hope."

Veronica offered a trembling smile. "Thank you for saying that."

Rose drew her hand away. "And there's no turning back now."

"No. We can only go forward. Forward to freedom."

"You're right. No regrets."

Veronica pointed at the diary. "I think you're ready now."

"I am." Rose heaved a deep sigh, set the pen to the blank page, and began writing. *My dear Sierra …*

As she poured her heart out to her beloved daughter, tears blurred her vision. Veronica was right. This poor world needed Sierra, and Sierra would need to hear from her mother, whenever that day in the future might arrive, a day that would prove the love and courage behind this parting of mother and daughter.

The daughter was walking into the darkness, guided by a light she did not yet know. The mother needed to shine that light through her written words—not the words of a fleeing coward but rather those of an abolisher of slavery who was willing to do whatever it might take to bring freedom to the world. In the meantime, she could do some good in Eursia and carry to those people her family's hopes and dreams of freedom. And maybe someday Sierra would bring even more—freedom in reality, both from the computers and from the Nobles who used them to shackle the slaves in tyranny. She could do it. She had to do it. No one else could.

Made in the USA
Monee, IL
10 November 2020

47031299R10201